Simple Deceit

Simple Deceit

Nancy Mehl

ISBN 978-1-62416-265-7

For more information about Nancy Mehl, please access the author's website at the following Internet address: www.nancymehl.com

Cover photography: Chris Reeve/Trevillion Images

Published by Barbour Publishing, Inc., P.O. Box 719, Uhrichsville, OH 44683.

Our mission is to publish and distribute inspirational products offering exceptional value and biblical encouragement to the masses.

Printed in the United States of America.

Dedication:

Sometimes in life, God sends us friends who are so special they can never be replaced. When they leave us, they leave a hole in our lives that stays empty. My friend, Judy Roberts, was such a person. I miss you so much, Judy. But I can still hear your sweet voice saying, "Can you feel my love?" And the answer is, "Yes. Now and forever."

Acknowledgments:

My thanks to the following people who helped me to create *Simple Deceit*. First of all, my thanks to Judith Unruh, Alexanderwohl Church historian in Goessel, Kansas. You are the voice that whispers in my ear while I write.

To Sarah Beck, owner of Beck's Farm in Wichita, who has been so much help to me. The only bump in our road happened when I asked her how someone would go about destroying a fruit orchard. She admits that my question made her a little nervous—LOL!

To Gordon Bassham who answered all my real estate questions.

Thanks again to my friends Penny and Gus Dorado for being willing to help me with my Mennonite research.

Thank you to Alene Ward for her constant encouragement, for editing under extreme pressure, and for creating Sweetie's Christmas quilt. I can hardly wait to see it finished!

I want to acknowledge a few other writers of Amish/Mennonite fiction for their support and encouragement: Cindy Woodsmall, Kim Vogel Sawyer, and Wanda Brunstetter. Thank you for being more than just great authors. You are also wonderful, gracious people.

As always, my thanks to the folks at Barbour. You guys are the best!

To the readers who are willing to take a chance on me. I appreciate you all so much.

As always, to the Mennonite people who have given our country such a rich heritage of faith and taught us to respect the things in life that are really important.

Lastly, and most importantly, to the One who never gives up on me. I will always believe.

One

There are five words guaranteed to strike terror into the heart of any human being. No, it's not "Step up on the scale," although this phrase is certainly a contender. And it's not "Can we just be friends?" which might actually run a close second. Of course, I'm ruling out all scary medical conditions that elicit remarks like "Let's run that test again." I'm talking about day-in, day-out, non-life-threatening situations that we all face but hope every day when we roll out of bed that today won't be *that* day.

Unfortunately, today was *that* day.

"License and registration please, ma'am."

I fumbled through my purse, looking for my driver's license. The setting sun pierced through the windshield like some kind of spotlight on steroids, almost blinding me. My hands shook as I flipped open my Garfield wallet. I flashed a smile at the basset hound–faced man who watched me through narrowed eyes. He was obviously not amused.

"I—I know it's here," I said a little too loudly. A quick thumb through all the cards jammed into the dividers revealed my debit card, an old library card, several business cards belonging to people I couldn't remember, and my only credit card. The credit card had never been used because my father had convinced me that the first time I pulled it out of my wallet, I would end up on the street, overcome by high interest rates and personal degradation. I found a reminder card for a dental appointment I'd completely forgotten, an expired coupon for Starbucks, an expired coupon for a Krispy Kreme doughnut, and a card from a video store that had gone out of business two years earlier. No license.

The officer's breathing became heavier and created steam in the frigid November air. I was reminded of one of those English horror movies where the thicker the fog, the sooner the intended victim bites the dust. The cold seeping into my car through my open window did nothing to dispel the beads of sweat forming along my hairline. Where was that stupid license? Could it have fallen out inside my purse? But why would I have taken it out of my wallet? Another quick look revealed a bank envelope with the cash I'd withdrawn before I left Wichita. I tore it open like an addict looking for drugs. Sure enough, my fingers closed around the small piece of plastic that would surely save me from being hauled to jail.

"Here it is!" I declared with gusto. "I had to show it to the bank when I withdrew cash from my account. I forgot it was still in the—"

"And the registration, ma'am?" The officer's cold expression and stern tone made it clear that finding my license hadn't ignited elation in the man's obviously stony heart. However, this time I was prepared. My father actually checked my glove compartment every time I went home to Fairbury, Nebraska. He was almost paranoid about making sure my registration was where it was supposed to be. Between that and the "credit cards are straight from hell" lectures, I knew where my car registration was at all times. This balanced out the fact that I had almost no credit. Even my car was a gift from my parents. At least the rent on my old apartment had been in my name. My one accomplishment as an adult.

I pulled the registration out of the blue plastic folder in my glove compartment and handed it to the waiting officer. If I'd expected him to congratulate me on this show of responsibility, I would have been disappointed.

"Wait here."

Like I was going to take off and let him chase me? I was pretty sure his patrol car had more power than my Volkswagen Bug, even if it *is* cute and perky.

While he ran my license, no doubt hoping I'd pop up on some Most Wanted list, I tried to figure out what crime I'd just committed. I always drove under the speed limit, even if it meant everyone raced around me, many times blaring their horns like I was breaking the law instead of abiding by it. I hadn't passed anyone in a no passing lane. In fact, I hadn't passed anyone at all for quite some time. I'd stopped at every stop sign and slowed down to a crawl in every small town I'd driven through. Why in heaven's name had he pulled me over?

In my mind I quickly ran over my exit from Wichita. I'd spent the last two and a half months there, working with my boss at Grantham Design to set up a way to freelance for him while training his newest in-house designer. I'd cleaned my apartment and finished out my lease so I wouldn't lose my deposit. All my utilities had been turned off, but I was pretty sure utility companies don't contact the police if you fail to end your business with them correctly.

I glanced at my watch. Almost six o'clock. I'd told Sam I'd be back to Harmony by sunset, but there was no way I'd make it. Being gone so long had been necessary, but I'd missed him and Harmony more than I'd anticipated.

I glanced in my rearview mirror. The officer was heading my way with a flashlight in his hand. What now? Was he going to go through my car? If he thought he'd find drugs or alcohol, he'd be disappointed. About the only exciting substance in my car belonged to my cat, Snicklefritz, who was sleeping peacefully in his carrier. If the officer wanted a real fight on his hands, all he had to do was try to wrestle Snickle's catnip toys away from him.

I know the smile I gave the officer was goofy, but I couldn't help it. I felt goofy even though I had no idea why.

He leaned in and handed me back my license. "Ma'am, do you know your right taillight is out?"

I breathed a sigh of relief. "No. No, I didn't, Officer. It was working when I left Wichita."

His frown deepened. "And how do you know that, ma'am?"

His deep, throaty voice and slow drawl didn't help to dispel my nervousness.

"Well. . .I mean, I guess I don't. It's just that I took my car to Jiffy Jump before I left town, and they checked everything out. N–not that you're mistaken or anything. I mean, I guess it went out after I left. I–I'll get it fixed right away."

His raised eyebrows confirmed what I already knew. I sounded guilty. And slightly insane.

"Just where are you headed, ma'am?"

"I'm going to Harmony. I recently moved there. You see, my family used to live in Harmony, and—"

"You have anything to do with that body they dug up a few months ago?"

"Why, yes. In fact, the body was found on my property. Well, it was my family's property when it was buried there. Then, of course, it went to my uncle, who—"

He snapped his notepad shut so forcefully the sound made me jump. "Ridiculous goings on," he growled, giving me a look obviously designed to frighten me. It worked. "You should have called me the minute you knew someone had been killed. People like you, thinking you can handle things outside the law. You're lucky you weren't charged with aiding and abetting. If I'd had anything to do with it. . ."

Okay. That did it. Maybe it was being stuck in Wichita for so long, or maybe it was simply my desire to get home to Harmony, but this man had jangled my last nerve.

"Excuse me, Officer," I said, sarcasm dripping from my words like warm honey. "We weren't sure the man had actually been murdered until someone admitted to it. And then we called the authorities immediately. If you'll check with your superiors. . ."

His rough laugh silenced the rest of my sentence. He leaned over and put his face up close to mine. Too close for my liking. "The pastor of that crazy

Mennonite church called the sheriff in this county once you all had finished playing detective. Do you know who the sheriff is, little lady?"

I felt myself bristle at his *little lady* comment. "As a matter of fact, I do," I retorted. "His name is Patrick Taylor."

"And have you ever met Sheriff Taylor?" The officer's voice dropped an octave and his frown intensified.

I don't know what made me glance at his badge, which was partially hidden by his jacket, but something inside me knew. It was a sinking feeling followed quickly by a wave of nausea. The name on his badge was Taylor, and for the first time I realized he wasn't with the police. He was with the sheriff's department. "N–no, I never met him in person. After Abel Mueller called him, the FBI took over the case. I dealt with them directly."

A grin spread across the man's face that could only be described as evil.

"Y–you're Sheriff Taylor, aren't you?"

The sheriff spat on the ground and slowly put his notepad in his pocket. "I'm lettin' you off with a warning, little lady, but you'd better have that light fixed right away. If I see you again and it's not workin', even your little Mennonite friends won't be able to save you."

I put my hand over my eyes in an attempt to shield them from the sun and gazed up at him. Was he serious? I remembered something someone had said once about Pat Taylor—that he had a bad attitude toward the residents of Harmony. That he thought they were all a bunch of religious zealots.

"I'm sure I don't know what you mean, Sheriff. I assure you that I can take care of my own problems.

Thank you for the warning. I will make sure the light is fixed as soon as possible."

Sheriff Taylor glowered at me for a few more moments. From what I could see of his expression, my assurances to take care of my taillight hadn't endeared me to the ill-tempered law officer one little bit. "Be sure you do," he said finally. "I'll be keeping my eye on you. That uncle of yours tried to subvert the law." He leaned down until his face was just inches from mine. "Blood ties are strong, Miss Temple. Stronger than you could ever imagine. Don't you forget it."

With that, he turned on his heels and strode back to his patrol car. I sat there with my mouth hanging open. He was already inside his vehicle by the time I could come up with a response to his outrageous statement. But as his odd comment rolled through my mind, I had the strange feeling that Pat Taylor had known who I was from the first moment he pulled me over. I found the idea unsettling.

I waited a couple of minutes, hoping he would leave first, but his cruiser didn't move. Finally I put my car into gear and pulled back out onto the highway. The sheriff's car slid right into line behind mine. I kept my speed low, hoping he would pass me, but he kept a steady distance between us. I had at least thirty miles to go before I reached the turnoff to Harmony. Surely he wasn't going to follow me all that way. I slid my favorite Rich Mullins CD into the player. His music always calms me, and I needed that now. I tried to concentrate on the words and forget that I was being tailed by the sheriff from you-know-where.

As Rich began to sing about another hour in the night and a mile farther down the road, I could feel the tension leaving my body. I was so into the song that I forgot all about my new law enforcement buddy. When I finally checked my rearview mirror again, he was gone.

A few minutes later, I spotted the road to Harmony. The sun had set behind the trees, so I could finally see my way clearly. I looked at the clock on my dashboard. Almost six forty-five. I'd planned to be at Sam's by six thirty for supper. Myrtle Goodrich, his rather persnickety aunt whom everyone called "Sweetie," had to be fuming. It would take another forty-five minutes at least for me to get there. Unfortunately, I couldn't blame everything on my impromptu visit with Sheriff Taylor. I'd left town later than I'd meant to.

I slowed down some and fished my cell phone out of my purse. Once I reached Harmony, it was virtually useless. But maybe I could get Sam while I was still a good distance away. I punched in his telephone number and was gratified to hear ringing.

"Hello!' a voice screeched through my small phone. "Is that you, Gracie Temple? Where in tarnation are you? My meat loaf is gonna dry up and turn to dust if you don't get here pretty soon."

"Sweetie, how did you know it was me? What if you'd just yelled at some innocent person?"

"Pshaw. Ain't no one else missin' right now. You're the only one would be callin' me right at suppertime. No one else in this town, specially someone I'd call a friend, would take a chance on rilin' me up like that."

She was probably right. "I'm sorry, but I'm going to be late. It'll be another hour, maybe a little less, before I get to town. You and Sam go ahead and eat. If there's anything left, you can warm it up when I get there."

Sweetie's voice softened just a little. "Nah, I'll just spoon some juice over it. Me and Sam would rather wait for you, Gracie. Been kind of lonely here without you."

"I missed you, too, Sweetie. Is Sam nearby?"

"Sam!" She yelled so loud I almost dropped the phone.

After some odd crackling noises and a thud, I heard Sam's voice. "Where are you, Grace? I've been sitting on the porch watching for your car, and I'm slowly freezing to death."

I explained my late departure from Wichita and briefly described my meeting with the Morris County sheriff. "I'll tell you more about it when I get there," I said. "I don't like talking on my cell phone while I'm driving."

Sam's warm chuckle drifted through the phone. "You're on the county road leading to Harmony, Grace. Do you see another car anywhere?"

I had to admit that I seemed to be completely alone. "I know, but I just feel uncomfortable when I'm not focused on my driving the way I should be. I guess it's not such a big deal right now, though."

He sighed. "Boy, I've missed you. I can't believe it took so long to get everything tied up in Wichita."

"I know. Between my landlord and Grant, I wondered if I'd ever get out of there. But the lease is settled, and I got my deposit back even though they tried to keep half of it."

"Half? Why?"

"Because Snickle tore up part of the carpet with his claws."

"But Snickle is declawed."

I snorted. "Yeah, that kind of took the wind out

of their argument, and they forked everything over."

Sam laughed. "Glad that's behind us. But what about Grant? What if he fires this second guy? Will he expect you to go back and train a third designer?"

My old boss, Grant Hampton at Grantham Design, was having a tough time replacing me. After spending almost a month in Wichita training his first pick, I'd been persuaded to come back and work with the second. Since I really needed the freelancing work he'd promised me, I was kind of between a rock and a hard place.

"He promised I wouldn't have to teach my job to anyone else. I think we're safe for a while. Four trips to Wichita in the past six months is more than enough."

"I can hardly wait for you to get here, Grace. To be home for good."

Home for good. Those words were music to my ears. "Hey, I'm working on a project that I can't wait to tell you about. Believe it or not, I think it will actually help Harmony."

"That sounds great, but right now all I want to do is put my arms around you and hold on for the rest of our lives."

I couldn't respond for a moment. My heart felt like it had lodged in my throat. "Hey, I'm going to hang up now," I finally croaked out. "I'll see you in a little while."

"I love you, Grace."

"I love you, too, Sam. Bye."

I clicked off the phone and dropped it into my purse. Then I settled back in my seat and clicked the CD to Rich's song about Kansas. As he sang about the prairies calling out God's name and our sunsets resembling a sky set ablaze with fire, I watched the incredible countryside pass by me, perfectly portrayed in his lyrics. I'd always thought of myself as a city girl, but the last few months had shown me that I belonged out here where God's creation outshines anything man can possibly fashion. Gratitude for His awesome power and tender provision overwhelmed me, and a tear slid down my cheek. I whispered a prayer of thanks. "You led me to Harmony, Father. And I found my life there. I'm so thankful. . . ."

I wiped my face with my sleeve and checked the mirror to make sure my mascara hadn't run. I didn't wear much, but I had no intention of seeing Sam for the first time in months looking like a raccoon.

Rich had just started to sing the first song again and Snickle was beginning to let me know he was ready for freedom when I pulled into Harmony. I slowed down because of slick spots on the road that led through the center of town. A recent ice storm had left its mark. Sam had explained to me that while most small towns had the resources to clear their main streets, there were no funds for that kind of thing here. For the most part, residents just waited until the ice melted. The Bruners, who run the local feed store, donate coarse salt that clears off the wooden boardwalks, but there's not much they can do about the streets. Snow can be scooped up with plows, but ice is another matter.

The sun had set, and the old-fashioned streetlights had flickered on, lighting up the wooden boardwalks and all the interesting buildings that sat side by side, no two structures alike. Each business had its own personality—and paint color. Harmony was certainly colorful—literally and figuratively. I loved its quaint style and unique presence.

No one was in sight, although I could see cars parked in front of Mary's Kitchen, the only restaurant in town. I'd heard about small towns that figuratively roll up their sidewalks after dark. Harmony certainly fit the bill. Most of the population consisted of Conservative Mennonite families who spent their evenings at home. Children did not run wild and parents did not carouse. Family time was sacred, and evenings were spent having dinner, doing homework, and reading the Bible before early bedtimes. A good way to live, in my opinion, even though I actually enjoy staying up late. I love the peaceful quiet of the country and like to spend time sitting out on my front porch at night, watching the sky become christened with God's flickering jewels. There would be none of that tonight, though, and perhaps the rest of the winter. I had no intention of having someone find me frozen solid to my wooden rocking chair.

I passed the old cemetery where my uncle Benjamin was buried and had just driven past the huge Bethel Mennonite Church building on the edge of town when I noticed something in my rearview mirror. A figure stood near the front door of the church, holding a large object. I pulled over to get a better look. All the inside lights were off in the church except for the pastor's office. Sure enough, Abel's dark blue car with its black-painted bumpers sat off to the side of the building. The frigid temperature caused me concern. Was it Emily, Abel's wife, trying to get inside? Had she been locked out?

I turned the car around while trying to calm

Snickle and drove back. I pulled into the circular drive in front of the building. My headlights shone on a figure in a dark cloak, her hood hanging over her face. The woman seemed startled to see my car and froze for several seconds while I drove up closer. Just as I opened my car door, she set her package down and backed slowly down the steps. A strange, plaintive wail rose through the quiet Harmony evening. I ran up next to a large basket and pulled back the thick blanket on top. A tiny baby reached out its little fingers toward me.

"Hey," I yelled to the woman who watched me from the driveway. "What are you doing? This—this is a baby!"

With that, she spun around and began to run toward the thick grove of trees that lined the edge of the church's property. Not knowing what else to do, I pounded on the church door as loudly as I could and then took off after her. Unfortunately, the grass was slick with ice that had melted and refrozen. Although it impeded my progress, it also caused the woman her own problems. A few yards before the tree line, I reached out and grabbed her cloak. She spun toward me as I tried to secure her with my other hand. Suddenly pain exploded in my head and everything went black.

TWO

"Gracie, can you hear me?"

I slowly opened my eyes. "Please. Get that light out of my face." My voice sounded far away. "Wow. My head hurts. What happened?"

"You knocked yourself out." I'd recognized the first voice as Abel's, but this was someone else. I squinted through the throbbing and discovered John Keystone leaning over me. He flicked a small flash-light back into my eyes and caused an explosion of pain to shoot through my head.

"Would you stop doing that?" I pleaded. "It isn't helping." I glanced around the room and realized I was in the pastor's office.

"I carried you in here," Abel said gently. "I heard a commotion outside, and when I got to the door, I found. . ."

"A baby?" I finished.

"Yes, a baby." He stepped closer and frowned down at me. "What do you have to do with this, Gracie? Did you see who put this child near the door?"

I struggled to sit up over the protestations of both men. "Hey, I just got hit on the head. It's still attached. I'm all right." I shook my head slowly at Abel so as not to cause myself further agony. "I saw a woman put the basket there, but then she ran away. I was trying to catch her when she clobbered me."

"I don't think she actually hit you," Abel said, handing me a glass of water, which I gratefully took. "I think you slipped on the ice and hit your head on the ground."

I rubbed my offended noggin. "Well, maybe so. I didn't see her slug me, and we both fell when I grabbed her." I looked up at Abel with one eye closed. "I don't suppose you saw her, did you?"

"I'm sorry, Gracie. I didn't. She was gone by the time I reached you. Did you recognize her?"

"No. She was wearing a long dark cloak, you know, like the one Ida wears. She had the hood pulled over her face."

John wiped the side of my face with a warm, wet cloth. There was dirt and dried grass on the fabric when he took it away. "I hope you're not telling us that the baby is Ida's," he said with a grin. "She's in her eighties or nineties, isn't she?"

Abel chuckled.

"Very funny. No, it wasn't Ida." I glanced toward the basket. "How's the baby?"

"She seems fine. I'm grateful you knocked loudly enough for me to hear you. I usually leave by the side door. If she'd been left outside all night. . ."

"I think the mother was trying to get your attention. Did you hear anyone else at the door?"

Abel rubbed his beard. "To be honest, I did hear something, but I thought it was the old pipes acting up again, so I ignored it. But when I heard a loud banging and you yelling, I came downstairs."

I sighed. "That was definitely me. Banging, yelling, and falling on my head."

Abel chuckled. "I missed the falling-on-your-head part. Sorry."

I grabbed John's arm and pulled myself up. "Look, I've got to get home. Snickle needs to get out of his carrier. The last time I looked, he had his legs crossed. Besides, Sam and Sweetie are waiting dinner for me."

"I think you need to rest awhile longer," John said, his handsome face twisted in a frown. His dark eyes showed concern.

"What do you know?" I said teasingly. "You sell meat."

He laughed. "My advice comes not as a butcher but as a doctor."

"You *were* a doctor."

"It wasn't so long ago I can't tell pretty girls to take it easy after they knock themselves silly."

"Do I have a concussion?"

He shook his head. "I don't see any signs of one, but it wouldn't hurt for you to drive into Sunrise tomorrow and see the doctor there."

"How about this," I said, trying to ignore the pounding in my head. "I'll drive to Sam's very slowly. When I get there, I'll take some aspirin. After dinner I'll go home and lie down. If I don't feel better tomorrow, I'll call the doctor in Sunrise and make an appointment. Will that satisfy your doctor/butcher sensibilities?"

"Yes, I suppose that will have to do. But I really don't think you should ever use the words *doctor* and *butcher* together. Puts a bad image in people's minds."

"I see what you mean." I grabbed my coat and

held my hand out to John. "Thank you for checking me out and cleaning me up. I owe you one."

After shaking my hand, he picked up the cloth again and wiped my other cheek. "There. Now you're presentable." He smiled at me. "I'm just glad you're back, Gracie. Harmony missed you."

"Thanks."

I shook my finger at Abel. "If I were you, I'd call Emily. Your wife is a wise woman. And I'm sure she knows how to change a diaper. From the smell of things, that's going to get more and more important as the evening wears on."

He nodded. "She's on her way. She's great with babies."

"Maybe you should call someone else, too. You know, like Child Services."

Abel's mouth tightened. "What if this little girl belongs to someone in our congregation? Perhaps the mother will regret her action and come back." He stared at the now-whimpering baby. "No. Maybe I can find a way to restore this family."

I reached out and patted his arm. "I guess the person who left this child here trusted you to make the right decision. I'm confident you will."

His face relaxed and he smiled at me. "Thank you for the vote of confidence. Have I told you how happy I am you're home?"

I grinned at him. "No, but you've had your hands full."

"Go see Sam. I'll talk with you tomorrow."

John stood up. "I'll walk you downstairs to your car."

I didn't want to admit it, but I felt a little woozy. I appreciated his offer and gladly accepted it. I waved good-bye to Abel, but his attention had turned to the baby, who had started to fuss.

"I know he wants to find the mother," I told John as we walked down the stairs. "But what kind of woman would desert her baby like that? I think it might be better if Child Services was called in. It's possible the woman who gave birth to that baby isn't capable of raising her."

John was quiet for a moment. "Maybe," he said finally. "My mother kept me even though she wasn't married. Her own parents had no faith in her ability to be a responsible parent, but she was a wonderful mother. I knew every day of my life that I was loved. Some kids don't have that. Maybe this little girl's mother is scared, afraid she won't measure up. I hope Abel finds her and she decides to give things a chance. She might surprise herself."

I looked at him and smiled. "Well, that's awfully upbeat and hopeful. Not what I'm used to hearing from you. What happened to the grumpiness and negativity we've all come to love?"

We reached the bottom of the stairs and John stopped. "I don't know," he said quietly. "I guess it's the company I keep. It's turning me into a pussycat."

Maybe it was the bump on my head, but "You're talking about Sarah Ketterling, aren't you?" popped out of my mouth before I could stop it.

John's eyebrows shot up. "How—how do you know about. . .about. . ."

"John, the way you two look at each other, I mean, it doesn't take a genius to see how you feel."

"Who else knows?"

I shrugged. "No one that I know of, except Sam.

We haven't told anyone. We'd never do that."

John's worried expression made me feel the need to reassure him. "Seriously, I don't think anyone else is aware of it. Maybe I'm just overly observant." Actually, it hadn't been that hard to figure out. I'd seen the Old Order Mennonite girl leaving John's store late at night. And every time she walked past him, the longing in his eyes was clear. They'd obviously been successful in keeping it from Gabe, Sarah's father. To say he wouldn't approve was an understatement. In the past few months, he'd started to come out of a rigid shell of protection he'd erected around his daughter and himself. If he found out about John and Sarah. . . Well, it would be a disaster.

"You know, I'm sorry Gabe's wife ran off with some guy, but it's not my fault. And it's not Sarah's. How long will she have to pay for her mother's mistake?"

I patted his arm. "I don't know," I said softly. "But if you and Sarah are to ever have a chance, you'll have to tell Gabe. Hiding the truth never turns out well in situations like this."

He gave me an amused look. "Is this one of those 'The truth will set you free' speeches?"

I laughed. It hurt. "Ouch. And yes, it is."

"You're still taking lessons from Sarah, right?"

I nodded. That hurt, too. "Yes. Wood-block printing. She's very talented. It's a new art form for me, and I'm enjoying it very much. I'm not as good as Sarah, but I'm getting better." John's distracted look made it obvious he wasn't interested in my wood-block printing skills. "Why?"

"Has she ever. . .I don't know. . .said anything about me?"

"For goodness' sakes, John. This isn't high school."

His face turned red. "Never mind. Sorry I asked."

"It's okay. I'm just teasing you. No, she's never said a word. But she wouldn't. I'm sure she's as committed to keeping your secret as you are."

"If she told anyone, it would be you, Gracie. She considers you her best friend."

It was my turn to blush. "I didn't know she felt that way. Wow. That means a lot to me."

"Thanks for getting me to talk about this," he said. "I've never spoken to anyone about Sarah. It feels good to finally get it out." He walked me toward the door. "So how are you feeling right now?" he asked, steering the conversation in another direction.

"Yes, I know. I really am feeling better, but I have an awful headache. The sooner I get to Sam's, the sooner I can gulp down a handful of aspirin."

John started to say something, but I held up my hand to stop him. "Just kidding. I won't do that, I promise. Just a couple. To start."

"How about four to start and two more every four hours until morning?"

"You've got a deal. Am I released?"

John ran his hand through his thick black hair. "I suppose. But do you promise to call me if you're not better when you wake up?"

"Yes, I promise. And thanks, Doc."

He chuckled. "No one's called me that for a long time."

I smiled at him as I buttoned up my coat. "Maybe they should."

He didn't respond, just patted me on the back.

After saying good-bye, I pushed against the big

front door of the church. The cold slapped me in the face, and I gasped involuntarily. Watching for ice, I walked carefully to my car. Jarring my head in another spill was the last thing I needed. I wasn't angry at the runaway mother because of the bump on my head, but I was frustrated and sad that someone was so desperate for help that they'd leave their baby on the steps of a church. My joy at coming home was overshadowed by concern for the abandoned baby and her mother. At least the woman had brought her child to Abel. If anyone could help, it was the Muellers.

Pain shot through my skull as I got into my car. A sharp yowl reminded me that Snickle had surpassed his level of tolerance inside his carrier. I spoke soothingly to him and tried not to think about my headache as I drove through downtown Harmony. A dozen cars and a couple of buggies sat outside the old redbrick building that housed the restaurant. Ruth Wickham of Ruth's Crafts and Creations was just locking up, probably on her way to Mary's Kitchen. She waved enthusiastically when she spotted me. Three other people walking down the wooden sidewalk stopped and waved, too. Cora and Amos Crandall owned Cora's Simple Clothing Shoppe. They sold most of the garments worn by the Mennonite population in Harmony. I waved back at them. Their son, Drew, put his hand up and laughed at me.

Drew has Down syndrome, but his parents' patience and love have done wonders for him. A sweet, gentle young man, he holds a special place in the hearts of everyone in town. Of course, Harmony is like that. As Sam reminds me constantly, it's more a family than a town. Although it might be a really small town by anyone's standards, it was still the most interesting place I'd ever been.

Ruth waited until the Crandalls caught up to her. They were most likely having dinner together before going home. Even though Ruth lives alone, she doesn't have much time to feel lonely with friends like the Crandalls who go out of their way to include her in their lives. I glanced up and down the street, but it seemed that almost everyone else had already gone home.

I drove past shops and businesses owned by people who were no longer strangers, but friends. Besides Ruth's Crafts and Creations and Cora's Simple Clothing Shoppe, there was Menlo's Bakery, Bruner Leather Goods and Feed, Scheidler's Farm Supplies, Nature's Bounty, and Keystone Meats. All the stores belonged to people I had come to know and care about. I noticed that the sign for Hoffman's Candles had been taken down. I wondered where Levi was tonight. He'd been accused of a long-ago murder, but many folks in Harmony hoped someday he'd come back. I was one of them. But for now, someone else occupied his old store.

I thought back to my first introduction to Harmony. Expecting my visit to be uneventful, instead I'd been greeted by a dark family secret that turned my world upside down. God not only brought me through it but had opened up a new life for me. Now I looked forward to some peace and quiet. I'd had enough excitement to last a lifetime. All I wanted was to settle down and see where my relationship with Sam would go. That was stimulation enough for now.

A few minutes later, I turned onto Faith Road.

To the left was Sam's, and to the right was the house where my father had grown up and where my uncle had died. I remembered wondering why an uncle I'd never met had left me his house. All I'd wanted to do was sell it and leave this little town in the dust. Now I couldn't wait to get back to the place I called home.

As I turned toward Sam's, I could see the beautiful red Victorian house aglow with lights. Homecoming lights—for me. In spite of my sore head, my eyes immediately filled with tears of happiness. I bounced down the dirt road until I pulled into the driveway. Sam's old truck sat in the curved driveway, and I parked behind it. After grabbing my purse and Snickle's carrier, I got out of the car and almost ran toward the large wraparound front porch that graced the Queen Anne–style house. Sam wasn't on the porch, but the frigid temperature was explanation enough for that. I thought about knocking on the door, but I was too excited to wait a second longer. I pushed the door open and hurried down the hall toward the kitchen. I almost ran into Sam, who'd stepped out into the hall. He laughed and grabbed me, immediately putting his lips on mine.

"Mmm. . .mumph. . .mucca. . ."

"For cryin' out loud, boy, let the girl speak."

At Sweetie's admonition, Sam finally stopped kissing me. His gray eyes sparkled. "Did you say something?"

I smiled up at him. "Yes. I said, 'I'm so glad to be home!' "

Wrong thing to say. Or the right thing. Depends on how you look at it. "Mmm. . .mumpha. . .moley moo."

This time when he unlocked our faces, I laughed and wrestled out of his arms. "Give me a chance to unwind a bit. I'm tired, hungry, and injured."

Sam frowned at me. "Injured? What are you talking about?"

I took off my coat and handed it to him. "Get me some aspirin and some food, and I'll tell you all about it."

Sweetie shook her finger at Sam. "You go get the aspirin outta the medicine closet, boy," she ordered. "I'll take care of the food part." She guided me toward the dining room. "You park yourself at the table while I serve up this supper that's been waitin' around all night."

A few minutes later, after I'd swallowed four aspirin, we were chowing down on thick slabs of rich meat loaf, creamy mashed potatoes, homemade applesauce, and flaky rolls that almost melted in my mouth. A far cry from the fast food and frozen meals I'd been living on for months. Within minutes, my headache began to subside.

"It's delicious, Sweetie," I said. "I've missed your cooking so much."

"Looks like you ain't been eatin' too good in Wichita. You're skinny as a rail."

"I've lost ten pounds. If you don't mind, I'd rather not put them back on. I've got to exercise self-control if I'm going to live in Harmony. Too much good food. Too many great cooks."

"Wait a minute," Sam said. "You lost that weight while you were by yourself. That doesn't say much for your cooking skills."

"You're right about that," I said, grinning. "The truth is, I'm a terrible cook."

Sam's mouth dropped open in disbelief. "You can't

cook? You never told me that before."

"Does this mean you don't love me anymore?"

Sweetie grunted and adjusted her graying bun. "Gracie girl, this boy has been so poky-faced while you been gone, he didn't even eat much of *my* food. I don't think your cookin' abilities are too important to him." She sighed as she looked at her nephew. "He certainly missed you. I'm glad to see him smilin' again."

Sam brushed a lock of blond hair off his face and stared at me innocently. "I have no idea what she's talking about. Were you gone? I didn't notice. . . ."

I laughed and pointed my fork at him. "You'd better watch it, bub. I can head back to Wichita anytime."

He tossed me a lopsided grin. "No, you can't. No apartment anymore, remember? Seems to me you're stuck here now."

"Speaking of being stuck here, I'm almost afraid to ask. Did you get the problems with my electricity figured out?" Although my Mennonite uncle's house had been wired for electricity, there had been a lot of problems with it. I never knew from one day to the next if it was going to work.

"The furnace is in, the electricity is on, but it's a work in progress, I'm afraid. I'll have to keep tweaking it. When summer comes, we'll have to add a couple of air conditioners."

I breathed a sigh of relief. "I'm more concerned about freezing my toes off than I am about air-conditioning right now. Thanks for taking care of things for me. Sorry to put all this on you, but with having to go back and forth so much. . ."

Sam waved his hand at me. "No apology necessary. It's worth it. I'm just glad you're here."

"Me, too. You have no idea."

A tiny meow and the sensation of something rubbing against my leg reminded me that Snicklefritz was glad to be home, too.

"Snickle will be glad to get settled down in his own house tonight," Sam said. "Just remember what we said about keeping him inside."

I swallowed a bite of mashed potatoes. "That won't be a problem. He's always been an indoor cat. I don't think he has any desire to go outside."

"You might be surprised, Gracie," Sweetie retorted in her low, raspy voice. "Animals is animals, you know."

Sweetie wasn't crazy about cats. Of course, this meant Snickle gravitated to her like white on rice. What is it about cats that makes them hound the people who dislike them the most? Sam and I thought it was kind of funny.

"It's especially important that you keep an eye on him, Grace," Sam said. "Without claws he's a sitting duck for coyotes or other animals."

"I know, I know. You've told me that a hundred times."

"I think you might be exaggerating just a little."

"I had him declawed so he wouldn't tear up my furniture," I retorted. "Guess I should have realized I'd end up someday as Gracie of Sunnybrook Farm."

Sam snorted. "That's ridiculous. You don't have a farm."

"All right, you two," Sweetie said. "Let's quit talkin' about that mangy cat."

As if on cue, Snickle took that moment to jump into her lap. Sweetie shrieked and waved her fork around, which caused a piece of meat loaf to sail up into the air and land on the floor a few feet away. Snickle jumped down and made a beeline for the tasty morsel, scarfing it up before any of us had a chance to react.

Sam burst out laughing. "Hope meat loaf is okay for cats."

Sweetie stood to her feet, her face beet red. She beat one hand against the bib of her overalls. She reminded me of King Kong defending himself against his attackers on top of the Empire State Building. "You hope my meat loaf's okay? That cat did that on purpose. He planned it!" She pointed her fork at Snickle, who gazed at her interestedly while he chewed and swallowed the last juicy morsel of Sweetie's main course. "It's a good thing you're goin' home tonight, cat. If you was around here much longer, I'd. . ."

"You'd what?" Sam asked. "You wouldn't hurt an animal if it set fire to your hair. I couldn't even get you to put out traps for the mice and rabbits that chew our irrigation lines. You talk big, but you have no intention of hurting that cat."

Sweetie gave her nephew a fierce frown. "Them mice weren't flippin' my meat loaf in the air, neither."

Snickle chose that exact second to rub up against Sweetie's leg. Her complexion deepened, and I began to worry she was having a stroke. After glaring at my poor cat, she seemed to surrender and plopped back down in her chair. "Now just what caused that bump on your head, Gracie? That cranky old Pat Taylor better not have anything to do with it. You need to start fillin' us in on the details, girlie."

Since the baby was the more important story,

I decided to get my meeting with the sheriff out of the way first. I quickly recounted my run-in with the fussy lawman, first assuring them that he had nothing to do with my injury. "He let me off with a warning, but I got the feeling he would have rather executed me on the spot." I pointed my finger at Sam. "You're the one who told me he hates everyone in Harmony. I guess you're right. He was especially upset about Jacob Glick's body. Seems he thinks we should have called him in sooner."

Sam shook his head. "That would have been a disaster. Frankly, if there'd been a way to keep him out of it altogether, I would have been happier about it. That man makes me uncomfortable. He used to come to town and park himself in the diner. Then he'd watch everyone, like a snake looking for its next meal. Even came around here a few times, poking his nose in our business, like he wanted to make sure we were doing everything by the book. Some of his questions were weird, though. Personal stuff." He speared another piece of meat loaf and held it up in front of him. "I was very relieved when he stopped hanging around so much."

"You must not be the only one who thinks that," I said. "I heard folks in Harmony try to solve their problems without bothering him. I certainly understand how they feel. I know it sounds crazy, but it was almost like he knew me. And when he said he was going to keep an eye on me. . . Well, it seemed, I don't know, like a threat."

"I don't like the way that sounds," Sam said after swallowing the food in his mouth. "I just don't trust the guy. And you're right about people here trying to keep him out of their business. Of course, there have been a handful of times when there wasn't much choice. He'd either come or send a deputy, but it was clear he wasn't happy about it."

Sweetie, already stirred up by Snickle's antics, exploded. "That man's a sharp-tongued, nasty-minded, side-winding snake in the grass who—"

"So something really interesting happened when I got into town," I said quickly, hoping to pull Sweetie's attention away from her newest source of contention, Sheriff Pat Taylor. As I told them about the abandoned baby and my subsequent fall, Sam's mouth dropped open.

"Grace, are you sure you're okay? I can drive you to the emergency clinic in Sunrise. You should probably get X-rays."

I grinned at him. "Are you trying to tell me I should have my head examined?"

"It's not funny. Head injuries can be serious."

"Thanks, Sam, but Abel called John, and he came over and checked me out. I'm fine. Just a headache and it's already better. Between the aspirin and the good food, I'm recovering nicely, thank you."

"John Keystone is not a real doctor," Sweetie sputtered. "For cryin' out loud. He sells meat. You're not a side of beef."

"But he *was* a doctor," I said gently. "He examined me thoroughly. No sign of a concussion. Just a nice bump on the head. Really, I'm fine."

"What about the baby?" Sam asked. "Is it okay?"

"She seemed fine. She needed to have her diaper changed, but other than that, she looked healthy and well fed."

Thankfully Sweetie's attention turned from my welfare to the baby's. "Oh my goodness gracious," she said in a tight voice. "And no one knows who the mother might be?"

"No. Abel's wondering if it could be someone in his church. He wants to keep the baby for a while to see if the family comes to get it." I shrugged. "I told him he should contact Child Services if he doesn't find the mother soon. I wouldn't want to see him get in any trouble."

I noticed that Sam had little to say about the abandoned baby. He seemed to be concentrating on his food.

"It's wrong to leave your child behind and take off," Sweetie said. "Seems to me that mother ain't much of a mother."

"We don't really know what's going on," I said. "Hopefully Abel and Emily will find the right solution."

Sam finally broke his silence. "One thing I know. Abel Mueller will do everything in his power to make things come out right."

I nodded my agreement.

"Changing the subject," he said, "you mentioned something on the phone about some project that would help Harmony. What's that about?"

"It's a developer. A new client of Grant's. He's thinking about building a retirement community down the road a few miles from here. He's in negotiations to buy land he needs from some farmer. He believes Harmony adds charm to the area and his residents will find the town an appealing attraction."

Sweetie slapped her hand on the table. "We don't

need to be overrun by no fancified, rich retired folks who have nothin' better to do than to come down here and gawk at us. Retirement community. What a daft idea."

I cleared my throat. If Sweetie couldn't find anything to be upset about, she'd turn something as innocuous as a small retirement village into the invasion of the Huns. "There will only be sixty homes in the development. I hardly think a hundred people over fifty-five constitutes being 'overrun.' "

She scowled at me. "We like Harmony the way it is. Don't need no hoity-toity strangers changin' things. Besides, we only have around five hundred folks livin' here now. Another hundred? My lands, girl! That's a huge amount for this little town to support."

Sam held his hand up. "You know, this explains some of the rumors I've been hearing. Seems that your developer friend has already visited several people in town. Convinced them that his project will change their lives—bring more business in. Between the folks who actually live in the community and their friends and family members, several of our business owners are seeing dollar signs, especially during the holidays. I hope it's true. Ruth could use the business, and so could Gabriel and Sarah. You know they're working hard to get Levi's candle shop off the ground."

I put my fork down and frowned at him. "I knew Eric was in town, but Grant said he was just here to spread the word about a town meeting tomorrow night. I figured he'd save all the details until then."

Sam shrugged. "When a stranger comes to Harmony and starts asking residents to attend a meeting, there are going to be questions. I doubt he had much choice."

"You're probably right. Still, I wish he'd waited for me to get back. I could have helped him."

"I believe he's been here almost two weeks now," Sam said. "But only during the day, I guess. I doubt he's driving back and forth from Wichita. He's probably staying in Council Grove. No other hotels nearby."

"So what exactly do *you* have to do with all this foolishness?" Sweetie asked me, still eyeing Snickle, who had curled up next to her feet.

"I'm going to be working on this project with Eric. You know, helping to get things set up. Designing the brochures and promotional material for the community. It's my first freelance job for Grant, and I'll be making pretty good money. If this project works out well, Eric promised Grant even more business down the road. That means more work for me." I grinned at Sam. "Makes it possible for me to pay for all that fancy electricity that's powering my house. Also means I might actually have food through the winter."

"Like we would let you starve." Sweetie sniffed. "You don't need no hoity-toity developer to take care of you. You got us."

I smiled at the woman who had become like a second mother to me. When I'd first come to Harmony, I'd seen her as a nuisance—someone to avoid like the plague. Now she was one of the most important people in my life. "Thank you, Sweetie. I know that." I reached over and covered her hand with mine. "I feel the same way about you."

She scowled at me and moved her hand away, but not before giving my fingers a little squeeze. "Land's sakes. No need to get all sloppy about it."

"Okay, but thanks anyway."

She cleared her throat and grabbed another roll. Sweetie didn't express her feelings very often, but when she did, it didn't last long.

"Hope this big-time developer's not plannin' on breakin' ground now. Bad weather will be comin' down on us soon enough. Not a good time for buildin' anything."

"No, he intends to get started in the spring. He wants to get the planning out of the way—and get the community behind the idea."

"So tell me about this Eric," Sam said. "I still haven't met him. Haven't been to town much, and every time I do manage to get there, he seems to be gone. How old is he? Should I be jealous?"

"Eric Beck's around thirty years old, wealthy, and quite handsome." I laughed at the stricken look on his face. "And no, you shouldn't be jealous. Of anyone. Ever. I've discovered I have a thing for farm boys with gray eyes and long blond hair, and Eric is definitely a city guy. All the way."

"Sounds like a slick showman with a tricky streak," Sweetie said sharply.

I sighed. "Well, he isn't. He's a very nice man who truly believes his retirement village will be a blessing for everyone." I shot her a disapproving look. "You might want to reserve judgment until you actually meet him."

Aware that she'd been chastised, she murmured something under her breath and reached for the jelly. Hopefully the storm was over for a while.

I turned toward Sam and rolled my eyes. He

shrugged. We were both used to his aunt's outspokenness, but sometimes she went too far.

"Do you know whose land he's looking to buy?" Sam asked.

"A Rand McAllister. I don't know him."

"Rand McAllister?" Sweetie squawked. "Why, that land of his ain't worth nothin'. Rand is as lazy as the day is long. Spends his time drinkin' in the shed behind his house if you want my opinion. And the way he treats his poor wife and child. . ."

"Sweetie, that's enough."

Since Sam rarely raised his voice, especially to his aunt, Sweetie's jaw dropped and she stared openmouthed at her nephew.

"I'm sorry," he said, his eyebrows knit together in displeasure, "but you've had something bad to say about every single person who's been mentioned at this table tonight. Two weeks ago after church, you asked me to tell you if you were being too critical, remember? Well, I'm doing that now."

Sweetie studied the tablecloth for a moment. Then she nodded. "You're right, Sam. I'm sorry."

Hearing that Sweetie wanted to change her disparaging comments toward others was my first shock. The second was hearing her apologize.

Sam smiled at her and winked at me, but his joy was short-lived.

"But Rand really is a snake in the grass," Sweetie said in a low voice. "Have you seen the way he treats his family?"

The smile slid from Sam's face. He started to say something but apparently changed his mind. Finally, he let out a deep sigh. "Look, let's not roast anyone else over the coals tonight. But the truth is, Rand really is hard to like." He looked at me quizzically. "You've met his daughter, Jessica, right?"

"I hadn't realized he was her father. Yes, I've met her. I must say she doesn't seem like a very happy girl. She's good friends with Hannah Mueller."

Sweetie geared herself up to say something else, but a quick look from Sam made her clamp her jaw shut. Time to steer the conversation in yet another direction. I was beginning to feel like a cop directing traffic.

"You mentioned Gabe and Sarah. How are they doing? When I was here last, things were moving pretty slow."

"They've been busy," Sam said. "Sarah is selling her stationery in the new shop as well as at Ruth's. Gabe is getting the hang of candle making. It was touch and go there for a while, but he seems to be doing okay now."

Sweetie snorted. "Don't know what some of them scents was, but boy, they stank to high heaven."

Sam laughed. "Yeah, I think Gabe got a little carried away with new kinds of candles. His creativity left a lot to be desired. He might enjoy the smell of hay, but somehow it doesn't translate well in a candle. Smelled like. . .like. . ."

"Don't need to finish that sentence, boy," Sweetie said with a grin. "I think Gracie gets the idea."

I took a sip of coffee and leaned back in my chair. Sweetie's great dinner and the long ride home had made me really sleepy. I was ready to go home and climb into bed. I'd sold most of my furniture during a previous trip to Wichita and spent the last two and a half months in a sleeping bag on the floor of my apartment. Snuggling under the quilts on a nice, soft bed sounded like heaven.

"Did they finally come up with a name for their store?" I asked.

Sweetie smirked. "Yep, they sure did. Ketterlings' Candles and Notions. Lots of imagination, huh?"

"I like it. It's simple but appealing."

"Sweetie's suggestion was Wick It Ways," Sam said with a chuckle. "Great name for a business owned by an Old Order Mennonite family, huh?"

"Gabe Ketterling has a sense of humor, you know," his aunt said, bristling.

"Yeah. You should have seen the look on his face when Sweetie suggested it." Sam guffawed. "You'd think someone had painted racing stripes on his buggy. Funniest thing I ever saw."

Sweetie stood to her feet and started gathering the dishes. "You're gettin' a little big for those britches of yours, ain't ya, boy? How 'bout I skip cuttin' you a piece of my coconut cream pie?"

Sam's eyes widened. "Never mind. I take it all back."

"I thought you might." Sweetie looked my way. "How about a piece for you, Gracie girl?"

"I'll take a rain check," I said, stifling a yawn. "I don't think I can keep my eyes open much longer. Think I'll head home."

"Your eyes been tryin' to close all night," she said. "You go on home and sleep till you feel rested up. There'll be time for pie tomorrow."

"I'll walk you to the door," Sam said. "The heat's on over there, and we put some food in your fridge."

"You're too good to me."

He grinned. "That's probably true."

"Don't you forgit that blame cat of yours," Sweetie interjected. "I don't want that varmint gettin' into my kitchen." She glared down at poor Snickle, who patted her sneaker with his fluffy paw.

I went over and scooped him up. Then I planted a kiss on Sweetie's cheek. "I happen to know that your bark is worse than your bite. If Sam and I weren't in the room, you'd be cuddling with this darling little kitty."

Sweetie's mouth opened and closed like a fish gasping its last breath, but no words came out.

I slid Snickle into his carrier and followed Sam to the front door, leaving his aunt still trying to find the words to defend herself. When we stepped out onto the porch, we were greeted with barks of joy from Sam's small dog, Buddy. Part Jack Russell and part rat terrier, he wore a constant smile and acted as if every moment of his existence was nothing but pure joy. I set the carrier down and knelt next to the excited little animal.

"I missed you so much, Buddy." He licked my face and nuzzled up against me. A plaintive meow from Snickle redirected Buddy's attention. My cat, who'd hissed at every dog he'd ever seen, had fallen in love with Buddy. Anytime they were together, they played like two siblings.

"You and Snickle can get together soon," I said, scratching the small dog's head.

Sam took the carrier and loaded it into the backseat of my car. "Goodness," he said, gazing at the interior. "This thing needs a good cleaning."

The floor of the backseat was full of cat toys, snacks, water bottles, and maps. "You try driving back and forth from Harmony to Wichita every couple of months. I started leaving things in the car I'd need for the next trip."

Sam grabbed me and pulled me into his arms. "Throw it all away, Grace. No more trips. No more being apart."

He kissed me soundly.

"Now this I could get used to."

He laughed. "You'd better. It'll be happening a lot."

With his promise ringing in my head, I started to get into my car. Suddenly the face of Pat Taylor popped up in front of me. I stopped and called out to Sam. "Will you take a look at my taillight? I should probably get it fixed right away. I certainly don't want Sheriff Taylor tracking me down. I think he plans to throw me into the slammer the next time any part of my car malfunctions."

Sam walked around to the back of the car. "It's not broken," he called out. "Start your engine and turn on your lights."

I slid behind the wheel and put my key into the ignition. After the engine turned over, I clicked my lights on. Then I stuck my head out the door. "What's going on?" I yelled back to Sam.

"Step on the brake," he hollered.

I put my foot on and off the brake several times.

"Okay, that's enough." He came around the side of the car and leaned into my window. "It's working now," he said with a frown. "Maybe there's a short in it somewhere. I'll look at it again sometime in the next few days."

"Thanks. And thanks for putting honest-to-goodness heat in my house. Man, I'm freezing. Sure glad I don't have to warm the house up with that old cast-iron stove of my uncle's. It would take forever."

Sam kissed me on the nose. "As long as everything's working, you should be fine. Why don't you call me in the morning when you get up? I don't want to wake you."

"Sounds great. I feel like I could sleep for at least a week."

He kissed me once more before I drove out onto the dirt road that led to my house. My house. I still wasn't used to it. Funny how putting your future in God's hands can take you down paths you couldn't have found on your own. I'd never aspired to live in any small town—especially one like Harmony, Kansas. Founded by German Mennonites in the 1800s, it was an enigma—a town that shouldn't exist in today's modern world. But it does. Strolling down its streets is like being inside a Norman Rockwell painting. Every time I come home to Harmony, it's as if I've crossed the border into a place of safety—a place where evil can't come. Or at least, where it can't stay. Evil has visited this town—but it hasn't made its home here. Harmony has a way of finding it and rooting it out. I firmly believe the prayers and faith of the unique people who live here have made this a very, very special spot.

As my house came into sight, I thought about my neighbor Ida Turnbauer. Ida lives about a quarter of a mile down the road from me. I wanted to stop by and say hello, but it was late and she usually turned in early. I'd call her in the morning. I laughed remembering how funny she was when she first got a phone. Raised Old Order Mennonite, she'd never used one until a few months ago. At first she couldn't get the hang of it and kept hanging up on people when they called.

I turned into my dirt driveway and pulled up next to the house. Sam had installed lights in the yard and on the porch. Being out in the country and not having streetlamps means it gets incredibly dark on nights when there's no moon or it's hidden behind thick clouds.

My once stark-white house had been painted a pale yellow. Cream-colored shutters adorned the front windows. The white wooden rocking chair my uncle made sat on the porch, waiting for spring.

I'd started to turn off my car lights when I thought again about my taillight. Odd. I felt certain it was working when I left Wichita, and Sam hadn't found anything wrong. Maybe there really was a short in the electrical system. Still, for some reason my run-in with Sheriff Taylor made me feel uncomfortable. Did he really stop me because of my taillight, or was it something else?

With a sigh, I scolded myself for being ridiculous and turned off the engine. Then I grabbed Snickle and one of my bags from the backseat and headed toward the house, grateful for the lights and warmth that awaited me. I put my bag and the pet carrier down on the front porch, found my key, and opened the door. As soon as we stepped inside, Snickle began meowing. He knew he was home and wanted out. I opened the door of the carrier, and he took off for the kitchen as I followed behind him. A can of cat food and a bowl of water would go a long way toward calming my travel-wearied feline.

I'd just reached for the light switch when something outside the kitchen window caught my attention. A light moving in the darkness. I crept cautiously up to the glass and pulled the curtain all the way to the side. Someone with a flashlight was skulking around in the trees behind my house.

Three

"I can't find anything, Grace. I've gone over the whole area—from your back door to the lake."

"Well, someone most certainly was out there. It's almost ten o'clock. Why would anyone be prowling around in the dark like that?"

Sam sighed and sat down at the kitchen table. We both watched the row of trees that lined the back of my property. Nothing stirred.

"Maybe it was the reflection of the kitchen light on the glass," he said helpfully. "It could easily look like a flashlight."

I crossed my arms and scowled at him. "Well, that might be a possibility, except that the kitchen light wasn't on." He opened his mouth to speak, but I held up my hand to stop him before he headed a direction he shouldn't go. "And no, there wasn't any light on in the living room that could have shone on the window. I already checked that out."

He shook his head and didn't respond.

"You don't believe me, do you?" I hated the petulant tone in my voice, but Sam's attitude left me feeling slightly defensive. I'd looked forward to finally coming home, but having a run-in with Morris County's sheriff and discovering an abandoned baby had already left me shaken. Seeing someone lurking in the dark behind my house was the cherry on top of an already disturbing sundae.

"Of course I believe you, Grace," Sam said in clipped tones. "I was just trying to offer alternative explanations to what you saw. If you tell me someone was out there, then that's good enough for me. I just can't figure out who would be hanging around outside in twenty-degree weather. Sometimes kids like to run around near the lake, and since Jacob's body was dug up last spring, quite a few people have come by to get a glimpse of the spot. But that's during the day, not at night when you can't see your hand in front of your face. And as far as this being kids, you know what Harmony's like. I'm sure by this time of night everyone's children are accounted for and in bed. No one has a reason to be out there for any. . .any. . ."

"Disreputable reason?"

Sam ducked his head for a moment. I suspected it was to hide a grin, but I didn't find the situation the least bit funny. His inability to take me seriously made me angry. When he looked up, his expression was composed. "Yes, disreputable reason. What would anyone want behind your house this late and in these temperatures?"

"I have no idea, but I know what I saw. Tomorrow when it's light, I'm going to look around."

Sam stood up. "I searched all through there once, Grace. But if you feel it's important to go over the area again, why don't you call me first and we'll do it together?"

I frowned at him. "You don't think there's anything

to this, so I'll check it out myself, thank you."

Sam came over and wrapped his arms around me, nuzzling my neck. Goose bumps crawled down from my scalp and broke out all over my body.

"Okay, maybe I'll wait for you after all," I said, my voice husky.

He lifted my face with his hand and looked in my eyes. His stormy eyes seemed to peer into my soul. His gentle kiss gave me double goose bumps. If he didn't leave soon, I was going to be one big, strange-looking lump.

"If I don't get out of here, people will think there's a disreputable reason for my visit," he said when he finished kissing me.

"You–you'd better take off." I gently pushed him away. "We'll take this up again tomorrow."

"The person with the flashlight or the kissing?"

I smiled up at him. "Both." I reached out and took his hand. "Sam, I'm sorry I've been so snarky. I'm just ready for my life to be peaceful—without all the drama of the past several months. Then I come home and find someone creeping around outside. Forgive me."

He let go of my hand and grabbed his coat from the back of the kitchen chair. "Don't worry about it. I understand, and believe me, I'd feel exactly the same way." He studied me for a moment. "You know you can come back to my house if you'd feel safer."

I'd taken up residence in his home for a while when it appeared someone in Harmony meant to harm me. Sweetie's impeccable restoration to the home's original Victorian glory had produced an incredible interior as well as an eye-catching exterior. You'd never know she had the talent to design and furnish a house by just looking at her. She's eternally dressed in old, ratty overalls from her homeless haute couture collection. I almost said yes to Sam's proposal just so I could snuggle into my favorite bedroom. Decorated with purples and reds, it's one of the most beautiful rooms I've ever seen. I'd loved every moment I'd spent in it. But I finally had my own house, and I had no intention of allowing anyone to chase me out.

"Thanks, but I'll stay here," I said with as much conviction as I could muster. "I'm sure I'll be fine. And now that I actually have a phone, I can call you if I need help."

He chuckled. "Remember when we had to use walkie-talkies to communicate with each other? Seems like a lifetime ago."

I shook my head. "To you maybe, but not to me. I still thank God every time I walk past that beautiful telephone."

"Well, I'd better get back before Sweetie comes looking for me. You call me if you see anything else, Grace. Do you want me to take one more quick look before I go?"

"Oh, would you? I'd feel so much better."

He smiled. "Sure. If I see any cause for concern, I'll come back to the house. If not, I'll just head on home, okay? And we'll still take another look in the morning when it's light if that will make you feel better."

I grabbed his arm. "Yes, it would. Thank you, Sam. I want to enjoy this house without feeling like someone's out to get me. There's been enough of that."

He nodded slowly, his expression grave. "I'm sorry. I should have been more understanding." He started toward the front door but turned back before putting his hand on the knob. "I know you're tired and want to sleep late and putter around in the morning, but why don't we go to lunch at the café? Mary's been asking about you, and I know there are other people who would like to say hello."

"I'd love to. Mary sent me the sweetest note before I left Wichita. Believe it or not, I think your ex-girlfriend and I are going to be great friends."

He brushed a lock of hair out of his eyes. "I'm glad. She's been pretty nice to me lately. It didn't happen overnight, but I don't get a knot in my stomach anymore when I see her."

I laughed. "That's a huge improvement over a few months ago. Why don't you come by around noon, and we'll drive into town together? I'll probably run over and visit with Ida first, so if I'm not home when you get here, check for me over there."

After assuring me he would, he left. I went back to the kitchen and sat in the dark, gazing out the window. True to his word, he headed out toward the trees once again with his flashlight. The moon was only a sliver tonight and clouds passed quickly in front of it, plunging us into inky blackness. The beam from Sam's light bounced around for several minutes, disappearing for a while when he stepped past the tree line. Finally, he reappeared and strode quickly toward the front of the house. I heard the engine of his old truck start up and listened as he drove away. Obviously he hadn't found anything this time either. I felt a little guilty for making him look twice, but his thorough searches comforted me. Whoever had been out there was obviously gone. I'd probably never know the identity of my late-night visitor, but it was a mystery I felt no strong desire to uncover—as long as it never happened again. The light had been suspiciously close to the place where Jacob Glick was once buried, but I had to agree with Sam. It didn't make sense to think someone had been out there in the dark and the cold trying to find a grave that had been empty for months.

I fixed myself a cup of hot tea and sat at the table for another thirty minutes until I decided to turn in.

Before leaving the kitchen, I set Snickle up with food, water, and a new litter box. He seemed happy to be home and purred as he christened his box. Then I grabbed my suitcase and headed upstairs to my bedroom. It had originally been my grandparents' room, and although I'd kept the original furniture, I'd added some of my own touches to make the space belong to me. Buttercream wall paint created a warm glow. A large overstuffed chair with a matching footstool sat in the corner where the old potbellied stove had once been. I'd found the chair at a church rummage sale. The lovely dark green patterned upholstery had called to me. A friend helped me to move it to my apartment, where it had never really looked right. But it fit perfectly here. Funny how things turn out. The chair was like an omen for change, although I hadn't recognized it at the time.

The faded quilt that had originally been on the bed had been bundled up and placed in a trunk in the basement for safekeeping. I'd covered the bed with the quilt Mama Essie, my grandmother, had made just for me. I'd always been afraid to use it—afraid it would be damaged—but it belonged here. On this bed. In this room. Mama Essie would be pleased to know I'd finally taken it out of mothballs.

I stared at the large picture on the wall. A portrait of an Old Order Mennonite family in their simple garb—the men and boys in wide-brimmed black hats. Although Old Order Mennonites were discouraged from having their pictures taken, Papa Joe, my grandfather, had bucked tradition for this one photograph. I smiled at Mama Essie, young and beautiful, and Papa Joe, strong and manly with a twinkle in his eye. My father and my uncle, both young boys, gazed stoically at the camera. This was the only early family picture I had and the only photograph of my uncle, Benjamin Temple. My red hair and freckles had come from him. As had my dimples.

I unpacked my clothes under the soft, golden glow of a single lamp on the dresser. All the light in the house came from a few well-placed lamps. Sam had said that later on he could wire the house with ceiling lights, but for now, this would have to get me by. After living without electricity, I felt like every outlet in the wall was a blessing.

I reached down and flipped on the electric heater. The downstairs had heat in the living room and in the kitchen. But the bathroom still needed to be set up with an air duct and a vent. The upstairs would be last to receive attention. At least we were on the right track. To be honest, I kind of liked the warm luminescence of the heater in the room. I'd considered leaving the old potbellied stove until the central heating system was completed, but Sam showed me where the metal had rusted through. Besides, it took up so much space that once it was gone, the bedroom seemed much larger.

After preparing for bed, I checked all the doors and windows before retiring for the night. Everything was locked tight, and there were no more odd lights outside that I could see. I fell asleep with Snickle curled up next to me.

When I woke up the next morning, it was almost ten o'clock. I took a quick bath, got dressed, and headed over to Ida's house.

As I pulled up next to the plain white house, Ida's old horse, Zebediah, trotted up to the fence near my car. I got out and went over to pet him. Zeb nuzzled my face with his soft muzzle.

"Hey Zeb," I said quietly, "I missed you. How are you?"

He shook his head up and down. Then he whinnied softly.

"Good." I stroked his face a few more times before heading toward the house. I'd just reached up to knock on the door when it swung open. Ida stood there with a big smile on her face.

"*Ach*, my Gracie is home!"

I leaned into an exuberant hug. I hadn't realized how much I'd missed the elderly woman until I had my arms around her. She'd been friends with my grandparents and had known my father when he was a boy. She'd also been close to my uncle most of his life. And now she'd become my dear, treasured friend.

"It is so cold out here," Ida said. "Come inside where we can warm up."

Stepping inside Ida's house is like walking back in time. Wooden floors with handmade rag rugs and old furniture polished to a high sheen decorate the living room. Light and heat come from the fireplace, which was crackling and blazing, sending warmth throughout the room. Additional light comes from oil lamps scattered around the house. An old hurricane-style lamp flickered from a wooden table near the couch. The day had dawned dark and overcast. The light from the fireplace and the lamp pushed against the gloom and gave the room a comfortable ambience.

Ida lives without electricity as her choice—a throwback to the Old Order way in which she was raised. Although she has no belief that electricity in and of itself is evil, she prefers to live in the quiet—without the noise and interruptions that can spring from modern technology. I have to admit that Ida's simple life holds great appeal to me.

"So you are here to stay, *ja*?" she asked. Traces of a German accent added a guttural tone to her voice. She pointed me toward her couch.

"That's the plan. I've surrendered my apartment and have a promise from my boss that he won't call me back to Wichita again."

"I think that man asked too much of you," she huffed as she sat down next to me, smoothing out her dark blue dress and black pinafore. "But you were so good to help him anyway."

I smiled. "I don't know how good I was. I needed the money."

Ida reached for a ceramic teapot that sat on the coffee table in front of us. She poured hot tea into a lovely china cup decorated with small red roses and handed it to me. "I heard you were supposed to be back last night, and I so hoped you would stop by today. I kept an extra cup on the table just in case." Her sweet smile warmed me even more than the tea possibly could, although I was grateful for it. It promised to be a frigid day. A brisk winter wind had chilled me inside and out.

"I should have called to let you know I was coming. To be honest, I completely forgot about your new phone."

The old woman laughed. "You are not the only one. Every time it rings I almost jump out of my skin. I cannot get used to that loud noise."

"Maybe you have the ringer set too high."

She wrinkled her nose. "Ach, I did not know it could be adjusted."

I got up and walked over to the black phone that sat on a small table between the living room and the dining room. The instrument had a large keypad so that the numbers were easy to read. I picked it up and checked the side. Sure enough, the ringer had been turned up all the way. Not sure how good Ida's hearing might be, I reset the tone level to medium.

"Try this," I said, putting the instrument back on the table. "It won't be as loud. There's an even softer setting, but you don't want the ringer to be so quiet you can't hear it if you're in the next room. Of course, if this is still too loud, we can certainly try it."

She clapped her hands together. "Thank you, Gracie. I know I made the right decision to have a phone, but when it jangles, I begin to regret allowing it inside my peaceful home."

As I sat down next to her, I gently reminded my friend about a couple of situations that might have caused less stress on her and others if she'd had a phone. She nodded as I talked.

"Ja, ja. I know you are right. Thank you for

bringing these things to my remembrance." She reached over and grasped my hands in hers. "Now tell me everything that has happened to you since we have been apart."

I briefly described my time in Wichita and finished up by telling her about the baby left on the church's doorstep.

Ida's already pale complexion turned even whiter. "Ach, no. A baby? Some poor unfortunate mother left her baby alone in the cold? What could she have been thinking?"

"Well, Abel's car was outside and his office light was on. She knocked on the door, so I'm pretty sure she believed the baby would be taken care of right away." I shook my head. "It really is a tragedy. A child should be with its mother."

"That's the truth," Ida said. She adjusted her prayer cap, tucking in one long gray braid that threatened to come free of its pins. "But it sounds as if more needs to be done than to just deliver the child back to her. She must need help. Someone to guide her. If she does not get the support she needs, perhaps she will remain unprepared to deal with her situation."

"You're right," I agreed. "I'm sure Abel and Emily would be willing to provide some counseling. If anyone can help her, they can."

Ida nodded, took a long sip of her tea, put the cup down, and scooted up closer to me. "Gracie, I have heard that a man is in town who wants to build some kind of new development here. Mary told me that you know something about this, ja?"

"Yes, it's a small retirement community. It will be a couple of miles from town, but I believe the people who live there will visit Harmony and bring some much-needed revenue to our businesses." I smiled at her. "It's a win-win situation."

She frowned and gazed into my eyes for several moments without saying anything. "Win-win situation?" she repeated hesitantly. "And what does this mean?"

From time to time, Ida and I have a slight communication problem. Talking to a person who never watches television or reads large newspapers means that many phrases and concepts are foreign. Obviously "win-win" was one of them.

"It means that there is no downside to the situation," I assured her. "This project should be positive for everyone."

She looked down as if studying her black leather shoes. "Ach, I wonder."

I reached over and touched her arm. "What is it about this that concerns you, Ida?"

"I—I do not know. I cannot explain it. It is a feeling. A stirring inside my spirit that tells me something is wrong."

"Please don't worry about it," I said, trying to reassure her. "If there was any chance the project would hurt Harmony, I wouldn't allow it to happen. I hope you believe that."

She grabbed my hand. "Ach, dear one. I trust you completely. It has nothing to do with you. Perhaps it is just my upbringing. My parents were very suspicious of English ways. They fought hard to keep them from contaminating our community. The idea of bringing strangers into Harmony concerns me. But I am most probably overreacting." She squeezed my hand. "You know about the prayer that went out many years ago by the women of this town—believing that Harmony would be a special place of peace and blessing? I would hate to see anything war against the wonderful miracle God has granted to us. I do not know much about the outside world, but I have been told that there are not many locations left that are like our Harmony." She gazed at me with tear-filled eyes. "You will protect us, ja? Make certain nothing ever comes here that does not belong?"

"I promise you, Ida. I'll do everything I can to protect this town. It's my home now, too, you know."

She smiled at me and nodded her head. "Ja, I do know. And how happy that makes me. I almost feel as if my Essie has returned to me. She was my very best friend in the whole world. Now her beautiful granddaughter has taken that place."

Ida had lost her close friendship with my grandmother when she'd moved to Nebraska to be near me when I was a child. It had fallen on me to tell Ida that Mama Essie had passed away several years ago. That news had caused the old woman pain. I was pleased to know that my presence would help to return some joy. Ida had become very important to me as well. She had begun to fill the empty place my grandmother's death had left in my heart.

We talked about other things that had happened in the community while I'd been gone, although Ida's uneasiness about the new retirement facility kept nagging at me. I'd hoped everyone would see what a blessing the development would be for Harmony.

It was almost noon by the time Sam's old truck rattled up the driveway.

"Oh dear," Ida said. "You must go so soon?"

"We're going into town for lunch. Why don't you come with us?"

She shook her head. "Ach, no. I am afraid the cold does not like my old bones. I believe I will stay here in front of the fire. Besides, you two young people do not need an old woman tagging along with you."

I started to protest, but she shook her head and smiled at me. "Bless you, dear. I know your invitation is sincere, and I appreciate it. Another time, ja?"

I reached over to hug her. "Another time, ja," I repeated softly.

Sam knocked on the door and then pushed it open so Ida wouldn't have to get up and let him in.

"A couple of fine-looking women," he said, grinning at us. "I'm here to take at least one of you to lunch. Both of you if you'll let me."

"Ach, you two young people," Ida said, waving her hand at him. "You are too good to me. When a warmer day comes, we will all go to town together. But that day is not today."

"Ida already turned me down," I told Sam. "I guess we're on our own."

"Oh well. Guess you'll have to do," he said, smiling at me. "Are you ready?"

I hugged Ida one more time and then grabbed my coat.

"Gracie," Ida said before I made it out the door, "will you please let me know if Abel finds that baby's mother? I will be praying hard for her and her child."

"I will, I promise. Hopefully it will be soon." I waved good-bye and followed Sam to the truck. We decided to leave my car at Ida's for now and pick it up after lunch. Leaving the warmth of the old woman's house for the bone-chilling air outside hit me like a slap in the face.

"I swear it's colder now than when I left the house," I grumbled as I climbed into the truck. "I hope the heater in this thing is in operating order." I knew the air-conditioning was useless. I could only hope the heat was a different matter. Sam started the engine, and a blast of hot air spat out of the vents on the dashboard.

"Wow," I said happily, "at least something in this old heap actually works."

Sam grunted. "Hey, everything works. I have no idea what you're talking about."

"What about the air-conditioning? I sweat so much this past summer I thought I'd drown us both."

"The air-conditioning works fine," he said as he pulled out onto the street. "It's called a window. I can't help it if you didn't want to roll them down because you'd mess up your hair."

As we bumped down the road, I was reminded of something else the old truck was missing. Shock absorbers.

"Before you say anything else derogatory about this fine vehicle, it might please you to know that I'm thinking about buying another truck—for backup."

I laughed. "Backup? I thought this incredible specimen of automotive excellence was perfect. Why would you need backup?"

"Well, to be honest, it broke down while you were gone. We almost couldn't get it going again." He stroked the steering wheel like it was a beloved pet. "What if Ida needed help or we had an emergency?"

"Well, there's my car."

He burst out laughing. "I'm afraid your little bitty Slug Bug couldn't haul much fruit or farm equipment." He shook his head. "Thanks for the offer, but I think I'll have to pass."

I frowned at him. "You didn't say you needed to haul anything in it."

"Well, you may not have noticed, but I grow fruit. Lots of fruit. Of course I need something I can use on the farm."

"Okay. I get it. And by the way, what in the world is a Slug Bug?"

He turned to stare at me. "You mean you don't know about the game?"

"Obviously not. What are you talking about?"

"When you're out on the road and someone in the car sees a Volkswagen Beetle, they're supposed to slug another passenger and call out, 'Slug Bug!' "

"Oh, lovely," I said in a sarcastic tone. "So you plan to start hitting me whenever you see my car?"

"No." His mouth tightened slightly. "My mom and I used to play it. We didn't hit each other hard. It was just a game to pass the time. We traveled a lot."

Sam didn't talk much about his mother, so I was surprised to hear him mention her. She'd died when he was a boy. That was why he'd come to live with his aunt.

"Sounds very entertaining if not a little painful. Your mom must have been a lot of fun."

His mouth relaxed and he smiled. "Like I said, we didn't hit each other hard. More like a tap. And yes, she was fun. In fact, sometimes you remind me of her."

"Thank you, Sam. That means a lot to me."

We were quiet the rest of the way to town. I hoped someday he'd reveal more about his mom. I knew so little. Just that she'd died in a car wreck and that she'd never been married. I blew air out slowly between pursed lips. What was it about men that made it so hard to get to really know them? Put two women together and within fifteen minutes they'll be privy to each other's entire life story. But men. . . It takes a lot of trust and effort to get them to open up.

By the time we pulled up in front of Mary's Kitchen, I felt warm and toasty. I could only hope the café wasn't cold. When we entered the quaint seventies-style restaurant with its polished wooden floors and cerulean blue walls, I was thrilled to find that I could take my coat off and still be comfortable.

"Gracie!" someone yelled out. I turned to see Eric Beck waving at me from a table in the corner of the room. He sat across from a thin, rather rat-faced man who glared at me like I'd come into the diner just to annoy him.

I pulled on Sam's arm and guided him over to where Eric sat. In his expensive suit he looked out of place at the old table with its yellow laminated top and stainless steel legs.

"I heard you were in town," I said, smiling. "Sounds like your plans are public knowledge now."

His warm laugh highlighted the kindness in his face. Eric's dark, wavy hair brought out his light blue eyes and perfect white teeth. "Yes, I'm afraid the cat's out of the bag. I discovered that Harmony residents aren't a shy bunch. Nor are they willing to let a stranger keep any secrets."

I nodded. "I could have told you that." I patted Sam's shoulder. "Eric, this is Sam Goodrich. I guess you two haven't met yet."

Eric held out his hand and Sam shook it. "No," he said. "As a matter of fact, I don't think I have. You must not come to town much."

"Haven't lately," Sam replied. "Been kind of busy at my place. Nice to meet you."

"You, too, Sam. I suppose you both know Rand McAllister."

He motioned toward the other man sitting at the table, who glowered at us but didn't say anything.

"Yes," Sam said, ignoring Rand's obvious distaste for our presence. "Nice to see you again, Rand."

Sam's greeting was acknowledged with a grunt.

I ignored the ill-mannered man and directed my attention to Eric. "So is the town meeting still on for tonight?"

He nodded. "Yes. Six o'clock in the empty building next to the hardware store. I'm renting it as a kind of base of operation while I'm here. The church down the street is loaning us some chairs, so we should have plenty of room for everyone who wants to come. I'm just trying to hash out the final details with Rand. Hopefully we'll have everything settled before the meeting."

There was a slight hesitation in Eric's voice that caused me to glance at Rand. As far as I knew, the deal had been agreed upon weeks ago. What still needed to be "settled"? The look I got back was toxic. I pulled once again on Sam's arm.

"Excuse us, Eric," I said, ignoring Rand, who'd fastened his beady eyes on me. "I'm starving. If we don't eat soon, I might pass out right here. We'll see you tonight. If you need any help. . ."

"Thanks, Gracie," he said. "But I'm set. I used the flyers you made to announce the meeting, and I think the whole town knows about it. We should have a great turnout."

I told him good-bye, not even bothering to acknowledge Rand. I was beginning to think Sweetie had described the man pretty accurately. I said the same to Sam when we sat down. We were well enough away from Eric and his unpleasant luncheon companion that I was confident we couldn't be overheard.

"I agree he's not a very nice person," Sam said. "I have no idea why he acts that way, but he's been contrary from the first day he arrived. I think someone in his family left him some land, and he felt he had to move his family here. He's not a farmer, even though he makes a halfhearted attempt to grow wheat. Almost every year some of the other farmers have to help him harvest it. Rand always has some kind of injury, you know. Something that keeps him from doing his own work."

"Why do people help him if they know he's just lazy?"

"Because he has a wife and daughter. You know how people are around here, always looking out for each other. His wife and daughter go through enough just living with the man. No one wants to see them go hungry."

The front door of the restaurant slammed shut loudly, and I turned to see Sheriff Pat Taylor saunter into the room. His gaze swung around until it rested on me. My stomach knotted. He watched me for several seconds. Then he ambled over to an empty table and sat down.

"Sheriff Taylor is here," I whispered to Sam. He started to turn his head to look. "Don't look," I hissed. "I don't want him to think I care one way or the other."

"No, we wouldn't want him to think he has any effect on you." Sam's exaggerated tone made me feel a little silly.

"He has every right to be here, I know that. It's just that. . .I don't know. . .I feel like I'm under surveillance."

Sam raised his right eyebrow. "So you think the sheriff of Morris County drove all the way to Harmony for lunch because he's interested in *you*?"

I started to say something when Sam shook his head. "I will admit it's a little strange. He hasn't been around here for months. Now suddenly he stops you on the highway then shows up in town the next day."

"Well, now I *am* worried. I thought you were going to tell me I'm imagining things."

"I'd love to, but to be honest, that guy makes me nervous. There's something. . .not right about him."

Before I could respond, a woman's voice rang out, interrupting our conversation.

"Well, there you are!" I looked up to see Mary Whittenbauer standing next to our booth, holding two glasses of water. "I've been wondering when you'd stop in." Her wide smile quelled any fear that there was still some animosity between us.

Mary had once considered herself to be engaged to Sam, even though Sam wasn't certain just how their "engagement" happened. Her negative reaction to me when I first came to Harmony only deepened as Sam and I became closer. However, a few months ago, Sam and Mary had finally talked honestly to each other. It had become clear to both of them that their relationship had no future. From that point on, Mary and I had started to mend our broken fences. The letter she sent to me in Wichita expressed her heartfelt desire to be friends. Although I'd forged a relationship with Sarah Ketterling, I really wanted a friend who was a little more like me. Someone I could talk to about everything. There were things I hesitated to bring up to Sarah because of her Old Order lifestyle.

"Got in last night," I said, smiling back at her. "A little later than I'd planned."

"I'm so glad you're back." Mary's sweet, heart-shaped face lit up. "I know just how to celebrate. Lunch is on me. Anything on the menu. The both of you."

Sam and I thanked her profusely and placed our order.

"Boy," Sam said after she left, "she sure has done a one-eighty." He sighed with relief. "Must be God."

"She's probably come to her senses and figured out she missed a bullet when she dumped you."

Sam raised an eyebrow. "Dumped me? She didn't dump me; I—"

"Save it, Romeo." I grinned at him. "Men and their egos."

He chuckled while I glanced toward the sheriff. Although he seemed to be perusing the menu, his eyes kept darting my way. I started to say something about it to Sam when the sound of a chair hitting the floor, followed by a string of shouted obscenities, got my attention. I turned around to see Rand standing over Eric like he was getting ready to hit him. The chair he'd been sitting in lay on its side.

"You'd better come up with what I asked you for, or you ain't gettin' nothin' from me," he snarled. "And don't you come 'round my place again, botherin' me with your highfalutin ways. You hear me, boy?"

Sam got up and walked slowly toward the table where Eric still sat. "That's enough, Rand," he said in a calm voice. "I think you need to leave. Maybe you and Eric should take this up again after you've settled down some."

I glanced over at Pat Taylor, who watched the confrontation with an amused look on his face. Why wasn't he intervening? Why allow Sam to put himself in the middle of this tense situation?

Rand took a step toward Sam, his hand knotted in a tight fist. "Don't you poke your nose in my affairs, Sam Goody-goody-rich. Everyone knows you ain't nothin' special. You ain't even got a real daddy."

I could see Sam's shoulders tense through his shirt, but he held his temper. Mary came out from behind the counter and advanced toward the two men. As if he sensed her, Sam held his hand up. She stopped where she was.

"I'm asking you nicely to leave," Sam said again, his voice steady. "If you refuse, we can take this a step further."

I guess the sheriff had finally had enough, because he hauled himself out of his chair and stood between the enraged man and Sam. "I believe this man invited you to vacate the premises," he said to Rand. "Isn't that correct?"

I couldn't see his face, but whatever Rand saw in

the sheriff's expression made him take a step back. After glaring at him for several seconds, Rand finally grabbed his coat and scurried toward the door. It slammed loudly behind him.

I hurried over and stood next to Sam. His face was tight with anger. I was shocked to see the fury in Pat Taylor's expression. No wonder Rand had run out the door. I put my hand on Sam's arm.

Eric stood up and shook Sam's hand and thanked him profusely, his relief evident. He turned toward the sheriff and stuck out his hand, but Sheriff Taylor abruptly turned on his heel and walked back to his table, completely ignoring all of us. Eric watched him for a moment then shrugged.

"I have no idea what got into Rand," he said to Sam. "We were talking about closing our deal, and he suddenly doubled the price we'd agreed on." His wide eyes shifted back and forth between Sam and me. Then he ran a hand through his hair and stared at the door Rand had slammed shut when he left. Eric was obviously shaken by the strange little man's outburst. "We've already offered him much more than it's worth. It's a fair deal. Honestly."

Several people had left their tables and were watching us with interest. Dan and Dale Scheidler, two brothers who owned the farm implements store, stood peering over the top of their booth. A family I didn't know had also turned around to observe the proceedings.

Mary stepped up to the table then turned to look at her surprised customers. "You folks go on back to your food. There's nothing more to see."

Harold Price, an elderly man who ate most of his

meals in the diner, called out from a table where he sat alone. "Another satisfied customer, Mary?"

His comment broke the tension and several people laughed, including Mary. "I guess that's it, Harold. Funny thing is, he ordered the same thing you're eatin'."

Laughter broke out once again, and all the diners went back to minding their own business. Sheriff Taylor seemed content to drink his coffee and ignore everyone.

"What happened here?" Mary asked Sam quietly. "I don't allow fighting in my restaurant."

"It was Rand," he said, trying to keep his voice down. "Seems he tried to improve his deal with Eric."

Mary grimaced. "He's not gonna blow this deal for the whole town, is he? Truth is, I would love to get some new customers. We get by here, but sometimes it's just by the skin of our teeth. Bringing in some of these well-to-do retirees and their families could really help. I might actually be able to buy some new equipment. My grill is on its last legs, and the refrigerator is making noises no appliance should ever make."

Eric sighed. His encounter with Rand seemed to have shaken him up. His usual ruddy complexion had paled somewhat. "I think it's a last-minute attempt to blackmail me. I'll just have to let him know it won't work."

"Maybe you'd better wait awhile," Sam said. "Don't confront him now. Let him cool down. I don't trust him."

"Thanks, you're probably right. I'm going to finish this delicious cheeseburger and these fabulous fries before I go looking for him." He slapped Sam on the back. "Thanks again for coming to my rescue. Guess I just froze. His reaction completely took me by surprise. He's been real easy to work with up until today."

Mary chuckled. "Rand McAllister? Easy to work with? He must have a twin, then. That man never has a kind word for anyone." She smiled at Eric. "He was nice to you because you offered him money. Now he's figured out he might be able to milk you for a little more."

Eric sat down slowly. "Well, he can't. I have investors, but between this and another project we're involved in, the group is spread pretty thin. To be honest, if Rand acts up too much, I'm afraid they'll walk away."

"I sure hope that doesn't happen," Mary said. "People in this town are really counting on this boost to our economy. Lots of small towns dry up and blow away without the kind of help you're offering. Not only will your retirees want to shop and buy here, but what better place to send the grandkids for some swimming or fishing?"

Eric bobbed his head toward the table where the sheriff sat. "What's his deal? I appreciate his help, but he acts like I did something to offend him."

"It's not just you," Sam said. "It's everyone. To be honest, I'm surprised he bothered to get involved at all." He noticed Eric's puzzled expression. "He has a problem with Harmony. Thinks it's full of religious nuts."

"That's too bad."

"Eric, you're still planning to hold the meeting tonight, aren't you?" I asked.

"Yes." He shrugged. "I'll get it straightened out by tonight. Like I said, when Rand figures out I won't give in to his demands, he'll cave. If that doesn't work, I know someone I can call. He'll pony up a little more. It's not what Rand asked for, but maybe if he feels he got one over on me, he'll sign the contract. He'd be stupid not to, since he stands to make a lot of money free and clear."

I patted him on the shoulder. "I hope he does, Eric. If you need anything, please let us know. Sam and I will do whatever we can to help."

He reached up and grabbed my hand. "Thanks, Gracie," he said earnestly. "I really appreciate it."

I let go of his hand and headed back toward our booth. Sam said something else to Eric that I couldn't hear and then followed after me.

"Wow," I said when he slid into the other side. "Rand put on quite a show. You don't think he's really dangerous, do you?"

"I honestly don't know. I haven't spent enough time around him to have much of an opinion. I sincerely hope not, but that temper of his. . ."

"Should we be worried?"

"I told Eric I'd go with him to see Rand if he wanted me to. He thinks it will be okay, but he promised that if he felt uncomfortable about it, he'd call me."

I smiled at him. "That was very nice of you. You know, you really can be a rather pleasant fellow."

"Well, thank you, ma'am," he drawled.

Mary suddenly appeared next to us, carrying two large platters, which she plopped down in front of us, a big grin on her face.

"I'm pretty sure I know what a chicken salad

sandwich looks like," I said. "And this isn't it. It looks more like steak to me."

She chuckled. "Look, you guys, I appreciate that you both ordered something cheap after I told you lunch was on me, but I really wanted to fix you a nice meal. I know you both love my rib eyes, so I took it upon myself to change your orders." She whirled around on her heels. "I've got two large Caesar salads along with some buttery garlic bread in the kitchen. I'll be right back."

Two huge sizzling steaks sat in front of us, covered with mounds of sautéed mushrooms. On the edge of each plate, stuck into whatever room was left, was a gigantic baked potato slathered in butter, sour cream, and chives.

"Wow!" Sam said, his face glowing with the promise of enough food to feed a family of four. "That was such a nice thing for Mary to do." He gave me a silly, sloppy, sideways smile. I recognized it. Sam had slipped into meat utopia, a place where men live in ecstasy and women live in fear of never fitting into their jeans again.

"I appreciate the sentiment," I whispered, "but I'm not looking to welcome back that ten pounds I lost."

"Whatever you can't finish. . ."

I waved my fork at him. "No way. I don't want to have to roll you out of here."

Sam laughed and then prayed over our food. With a big smile, he speared his steak with his fork and cut off a big chunk with his knife. After stuffing it into his mouth, he closed his eyes and let out a long, slow breath.

"You look ridiculous," I told him in a tone that should have brought conviction. However, my first bite completely explained his reaction. Mary's cook, Hector, sure knew how to grill a steak. I'd taken my third bite by the time Mary returned with our salads and hot garlic bread.

"Now you two enjoy yourselves," she said, covering every open surface left on our tabletop with food. "And for dessert—"

"Whoa." I shook my head. "I doubt I can get all this down. As generous as your offer is, nothing with sugar or chocolate will pass through these lips today."

"What kind of dessert?" Sam asked, happily smacking his mouth.

I started to chastise him when I noticed that Eric was heading for the door.

"Hey," I said softly, "he's leaving. Should you ask him again if he wants you to tag along when he talks to Rand?"

Sam quickly wiped his face with his napkin and hurried over to catch Eric right before he pushed the front door open. Mary and I stared at them, but we couldn't really make out what they were saying. The radio was playing the Marty Robbins song "El Paso." All I could hear was something about "a handsome young stranger lying dead on the floor." A chill ran through my body.

"Does Sam really think Rand might hurt Eric?" Mary asked.

"I don't know. Most people don't really know Rand, and they're not sure just what he's capable of."

Mary nodded. "He's eaten here quite a bit. Sometimes with his family. Sometimes alone. I can't get him to talk. I gave up a long time ago. I just take his order and bring him his food." She leaned over close to me. "He doesn't tip," she said softly, shaking her head.

"Why is it I don't find that the least bit surprising?"

Harold's loud voice interrupted Mary's response. "Hey Mary. Could I get another cup of coffee sometime in this century?"

"Just keep your shirt on, Harold," she shot back. "I have some real customers here."

The elderly man laughed loudly.

"Better get going," Mary said with a smile. "Hey, after you've gotten settled in, why don't we get together for dinner?" She waved her hand in a semicircle. "I'll close early and we'll have the whole place to ourselves. I'm a pretty good cook. While we eat, we can visit and get to know each other a little better."

I smiled warmly at her. "I would love that, Mary."

"You can call me in a couple of days and let me know what night would work for you." The coffeeless Harold loudly cleared his throat. "Knock it off, Harold," Mary hollered. "Or I'll pour that coffee in a place you won't appreciate."

Her comment brought another guffaw from Harold. She winked at me and took off toward the kitchen. She'd just disappeared through the swinging door when Sam reappeared at the table.

"He says he'll be fine, but I gave him my number and told him to call me anytime I can help." He scooted back into the booth and picked up his fork again.

"I hope he's right. There's something about Rand that bothers me. His daughter doesn't look well cared for. And she always seems a little. . .I don't know, frightened. I hope he's not abusing her."

Sam stopped cutting his steak and frowned at me. "Believe me, Gracie, if something like that was going on, someone here would have noticed it. Jessica and Thelma attend Abel's church. And Jessica goes to school in Sunrise. If there were bruises or anything. . ."

"If they're where they can be seen." I noticed Sam's startled look. "I had a friend in school once whose dad beat her. No one knew about it until one day in gym class. When she undressed for the showers. . . Well, it was obvious something was horribly wrong. The gym teacher immediately notified the principal, and he called in the authorities."

"That must have been awful for that girl."

I nodded. "It was. But things turned out for the best. After it was discovered that her mother knew about the beatings and did nothing to help, Caroline was put into foster care. She got placed with a wonderful family who loved her and eventually adopted her. She went to college and married a super Christian man. They just had a baby."

"You stay in touch with her?"

"Yes. We call each other several times a year. She lives in Michigan."

"That's great, but I really don't think Jessica's being abused."

"You know some abuse isn't physical, right?" I said.

Sam chewed another bite of steak but didn't say anything. He seemed focused on his food.

"I mean, someone like Rand could easily be verbally abusing his wife and daughter. That would explain Jessica's demeanor. The only time I've seen her smile is when she's around Hannah Mueller and their friend Leah."

He nodded at me but appeared to be thinking more about his steak than about what I was saying.

"Sam, did you hear me? Maybe Rand is. . ."

The front door of the restaurant blew open. I'd been watching the skies darken and could tell the wind was picking up by the amount of dust swirling around in the street. Abel Mueller struggled to close the door with one hand while holding on to his hat with the other. Harold jumped up to help him. Together they pushed the door shut.

I started to call out a greeting when I noticed Abel's expression. In the seven months I'd known him, I'd never seen him look so upset. He glanced quickly around the room until his gaze settled on me. The way he looked at me sent a shiver down my spine. By now, Sam had also noticed Abel. He looked back and forth between us a couple of times. Finally, he waved Abel over to our booth. After hesitating a moment, the Mennonite pastor walked slowly toward us.

"Hey Abel," Sam said when the big man came up next to us, "what's going on? You look like you've seen a ghost."

"Is everyone all right?" I couldn't control the way my voice trembled. "I just saw Ida. . ."

"No. No, Gracie. I'm sorry. As far as I know, everyone's fine." He took off his wide-brimmed black hat and held it in front of him. His eyebrows knit together in a frown. "I—I know this is going to sound odd, but I need to talk to you." He glanced quickly at Sam. "Alone. I don't mean to alarm you, but it's very important."

For the life of me, I couldn't begin to figure out what Abel would need to say to me that Sam couldn't hear, but I could tell the kind pastor was truly upset.

"Why don't you stay here and finish your lunch," I said to Sam, who seemed as surprised as I was by Abel's strange request. "Abel and I can move to another table." I looked up at him to see if he agreed. He nodded silently, still grim-faced.

I pointed toward an empty table that sat all the way across the room. "Is that okay?"

Once again Abel nodded. I followed him, trying to avoid the prying eyes of customers who wondered why the pastor of Bethel Mennonite Church would call me aside for a private meeting. Even Harold looked interested. Abel and I sat down, and I scooted my chair around so that my back faced the rest of the room.

Abel suddenly scanned the room as if he hadn't noticed we were being watched. "Oh my," he said. "I didn't realize. . . Maybe we should go to my office where it's more private." He nodded for several seconds. "Yes. That would be better, Gracie. I should have thought of it sooner. It's just that. . . It's just that I was so shocked. . ."

"Abel, you're scaring me," I said, trying to keep my voice soft but firm. "I don't want to go to your office. Please just tell me what you came to say. You said everyone is okay. No one is ill? No one is dead?"

He laid his hat on the table and studied it. Finally he cleared his throat. "This has nothing to do with anything like that, Gracie." He reached into his pocket and took out a folded envelope, which he handed to me. "I found this stuck in the door at the back of the church about thirty minutes ago when I arrived to prepare my Sunday sermon. I felt the right thing to do was to bring it to you. I saw Sam's truck in front of the restaurant and hoped you were here with him."

Frowning, I reached over and picked up the envelope. *Pastor Mueller* was written in block letters on the outside. Inside was a folded piece of notebook paper. I opened it up and read it.

Dear Pastor Mueller,

The baby left at the church belongs to Gracie Temple. I saw her put it there.

A Very Concerned Citizen

Four

I had no idea that emotional shock can hit you just like a physical punch in the gut. I couldn't speak. Couldn't seem to catch my breath. Who in the world could do something like this? I'd come home to Harmony—my place of safety. A place where I was loved. A place where I belonged. And now this?

"You know it's untrue, don't you, Abel?" I finally croaked out. "You know the baby's not mine?"

Abel looked past me, unwilling to meet my gaze. "Gracie, I'm a pastor. I may not be *your* pastor, but I still have a pastor's heart toward you." He finally looked into my eyes. "If you tell me this isn't true, I will believe you."

"It isn't true, Abel. I've never had a baby. And if I did, I wouldn't abandon it. Ever. How could you. . ." I didn't finish my sentence because in a flash of clarity I knew the answer. I was outside the church when the baby was found. Abel hadn't seen anyone else there. I'd been gone for almost three months, and I'd come back to town thinner than when I'd left. I put my hand over my mouth to hold back an inappropriate desire to giggle. If a deserted baby weren't involved, this would actually be rather funny. But the look on Abel's face dispelled any urge to laugh.

"Then that's that," he said. He picked up the letter and put it back into the envelope. "I intend to get rid of this. We won't talk about it again."

I reached over and put my hand over his. "Abel, I swear to you as your Christian sister that there isn't a shred of truth to this. Someone is playing a really cruel joke, and I intend to find out who it is. Maybe you should keep the letter for now. It might lead us to whoever wrote it."

He pushed it back over to my side of the table. "You keep it. I don't want it."

"Thank you. If I discover the truth behind this lie, I'll let you know. Will you do the same for me?"

"Yes, of course." He smoothed his unruly salt-and-pepper hair with his hand before placing his hat back on his head. "I'm sorry if this caused you pain. That was not my intention. I felt I had to show it to you. To keep it from you, or to talk to someone else about it before I spoke with you, made me feel. . .uncomfortable."

I smiled at him, although it took effort. "That's because in many ways you really are my pastor, even if I don't go to your church. And besides that, you're my dear friend. I know you love me."

"Yes," he said gently, his dark, compassionate eyes locked on mine. "Yes, I do." With that, the gentle giant of a man got up and left the restaurant. I stayed where I was, trying to figure out what to do next. Life really is full of surprises, and some of them aren't pleasant. Who in the world could be behind this? A small flame of anger began to burn inside me. Starting a rumor like this without proof was irresponsible, even though so much circumstantial evidence pointed to me. I glanced over at Sam, who looked at me oddly. I folded the letter up, stuck it in my jeans pocket, and went back to our table. I looked around the room to see if people were still watching, but everyone seemed occupied with their own business. I guess they'd all moved on.

"What was that about?" he asked as soon as I slid into my side of the booth.

"I—I really don't want to talk about it right now. Let's wait until we can go somewhere more private."

Sam put his fork down and stared at me. "Is everything okay?"

I shook my head. "No. No, it's not. Someone has made an accusation about me that isn't true. I'll tell you about it later. Right now, let's finish this wonderful meal."

Sam didn't pursue it, but I could tell he was curious. I tried to eat the rest of my lunch, but my steak was cold and everything else seemed tasteless. After a few more bites, I gave up.

Sam finished most of his food but left a few bites of steak and about half of his potato on the plate. We waited for Mary to come back by so we could thank her for the meal.

"Why, Sam Goodrich," she said when she saw his leftovers. "You always lick your plate clean and ask for more. And Gracie, didn't you like the steak? Was there something wrong with it?"

"Oh no, Mary," I said, trying to sound reassuring. "It was fabulous. I just couldn't finish it. Besides, I'm trying to watch my weight."

She reached over and patted my shoulder. "I can

tell you've lost quite a bit. You stick to your guns, Gracie. Losing weight is tough, I know. If I didn't run around this place all day long, I'd weigh a ton." She turned her attention to Sam. "What's your excuse?"

Sam grinned and patted his stomach. "Maybe I'm watching my weight, too. Did that occur to you?"

Mary threw her head back and laughed. "Absolutely not. I've never seen anyone who can pack it away like you and still stay lean." She shook her finger at him. "If you ever retire, you'd better watch out. You'll be as big as Harold over there."

"I can hear you, you know," Harold said.

"I know," Mary shot back. "That's why I said it."

"How's he doing?" Sam asked quietly as Harold chuckled.

"Better," Mary said in a soft voice. She swung her gaze to me. "Harold lost his wife early in the year. He started hanging out here almost every day. I think facing a quiet house is too much for him. He likes our noise."

"It's nice of you to care so much about him."

Sam started to say something, but I waved his comment away. "I know, I know. Harmony is just one big family." The edge of irritation in my voice caught Sam and Mary's attention, and they both looked at me strangely. "Sorry." I sighed. "This hasn't been a great day."

"You just got back," Mary said. "You're not allowed to have a bad day yet."

"You'd think so, wouldn't you?" I did my best to smile at her even though I didn't really feel much like smiling. "It's not your fault. You're one of the bright spots. Thank you again for the wonderful lunch."

"You're very welcome. Let me wrap that steak up for you. It will make a great sandwich tomorrow."

I thanked her again before she sailed toward the kitchen.

"Where do you want to talk?" Sam asked.

"I don't care. My house or yours."

"Let's make it mine," he said. "I have something I want to show you. It was too dark for you to see it last night."

"Okay." I watched the kitchen door, hoping Mary wouldn't take too long. I was ready to leave the restaurant behind. Mary's plan to present us with a pleasant meal had been ruined by Rand McAllister and that awful letter. While I waited, I examined the pictures lining the walls of the restaurant. Old photographs of former and present Harmony residents. Pictures of the town down through the years. Not many depictions of its German Mennonite roots, but their influence was still strongly felt. I realized that the photograph of Jacob Glick was gone. Good. Emily and Abel Mueller didn't need to see it, and neither did I. The man had caused enough sorrow. Having to look at him was too much to ask of anyone who'd been affected by his evil. I noticed that more of Hannah Mueller's paintings were hanging on the walls. Since we'd started painting together, her technique had improved. Her work had taken on a professional quality far beyond her young years. She had the talent to go far, but living in Harmony certainly put limits on her ability to make an impact beyond the town's borders.

I gazed out a nearby window. The Open sign was in the window of Keystone Meats. John had originally come here to find out who his father was. No son wanted to discover the things John had. Jacob Glick's legacy was best forgotten by everyone, including his biological son, John. Some folks thought he would take off after realizing his father was a scoundrel, but he stayed. I knew part of the reason was his fondness for Harmony, but what drew him more were his feelings for Sarah. Many folks in Harmony hoped he'd pick up his practice again. Since the nearest doctor was in Sunrise, about ten miles away, the idea of having a doctor here was certainly appealing. Next to John, the closest medical professional we had was old Widow Stegson. Clara lived alone on a run-down farm outside of town. Some of the kids called her "the witch." Her storehouse of herbs and medicinal concoctions was widely known to make people sick rather than cure them.

I wanted to run over to Ruth's shop and say hi, but that would have to wait. I had to tell Sam about the note before he heard it from someone else. I knew Abel would never discuss it, but whoever wrote the note could easily spread the story.

"Here you go." Mary's voice cut through my thoughts. She handed me something wrapped in tin foil. I reached out and took it. Then I slid it into my purse.

"Thanks again. And you're right. This will make a great sandwich. I really appreciate your generosity."

"Don't be silly," she replied. "It wasn't much. I just wanted you to know I'm glad you're back. You call me in the next couple of days, and we'll get that dinner set up, okay?"

I put my hand out. She took it. "Deal."

We left the restaurant and headed back to Ida's to

pick up my car. Sam kept glancing my way during the drive, but I ignored him. For some reason telling him about the letter made me nervous. I tried to reassure myself that he would probably think the whole thing was ridiculous and laugh it off. So why were frantic little butterflies flitting around inside me? Abel's reaction had left me shaken. He'd seemed relieved when I denied the accusation. Had he actually believed it might be true?

We stopped at Ida's to get my car. Sam followed me to my house, where I dropped it off and then got back into his truck. I didn't say much on the way to Sam's. My mind was filled with a faint but distinct dread.

"Before we get to the house," Sam said, interrupting my thoughts, "here's what I wanted to show you." He slowed the truck down and pointed at some land on the north side of his property. The previously undeveloped plot was now cleared. "We'll plant our first pumpkins after the spring rains. By September we'll have lots of big orange pumpkins sitting out there."

"Oh Sam. How wonderful. I know this is something you and Sweetie have wanted to do for a long time. Good for you."

He nodded, a look of satisfaction on his face. "It will be a lot of work, but I already have several stores in Council Grove expressing interest."

I reached over and hugged him. "I'm so excited. Maybe I can help out some. I'd love to be more involved in what you do."

"I'd like that, too," he said, kissing the top of my head as I rested it against his shoulder. "We'd better get going." He put the truck into gear and drove up to the house. "Sweetie's not here," he said as he pulled into the driveway. "She took some food over to Alma Ledbetter's house. Alma's recovering from knee surgery and can't get around very well."

I was grateful Sweetie was gone. It would make it easier to talk to him. We went inside, and I followed him into the kitchen.

"I'll make some coffee to warm us up." Sam took my jacket and laid it over the back of one of the kitchen chairs. "Have a seat."

I scooted into one of the wooden chairs that sat around the large oak table. While the rest of the house maintained an authentic Victorian charm, the kitchen was more updated. Gleaming stainless steel appliances, parquet floors, and shiny pots and pans that hung from hooks over the butcher-block kitchen island made it clear that this kitchen belonged to someone who knew a thing or two about cooking. Sweetie shone in this room. She loved to cook, and those who knew her loved to eat her food.

Sam finished filling the coffeemaker with water and pressed the button to begin brewing. Within seconds, the smell of freshly made coffee began to fill the room. He came over and sat down across from me at the table.

"Okay, so what's going on?"

"Abel found this note stuck in the door of the church this morning." I took the crumpled envelope out of my pocket and shoved it toward him.

Sam smoothed it out and withdrew the notepaper inside. As he read it, the color drained from his face. "I—I don't understand."

"I don't either. It doesn't make any sense. Why would anyone make up a cruel lie like this? What would they have to gain?"

His focus stayed on the note, and he didn't look at me. "I have no idea. Why would someone suspect it was true?"

"I've been gone for almost three months. I came back to town thinner than when I left. And I'm the one who first found the baby. I guess one of Harmony's more pious citizens decided to add up all those coincidences and come to the erroneous conclusion that I had to be that poor child's mother."

Sam finally raised his head. The look on his face chilled me. I reached over to take his hand.

"Sam. Please don't make me deny this charge. Surely you know me better than this. If you don't. . ."

He pulled his hand away, folded the note, and jammed it back into the envelope. "If I don't know you better than what?" he said, his tone sharp. "Is that some kind of threat?"

"A threat?" I said incredulously. "What are you talking about?"

"Look, Grace, I've got some work to do in the orchards. I'll drive you home first."

"Why are you acting like this? Of course that baby's not mine. I think you'd have noticed if I was pregnant, even if I've been gone for a while. Besides, you know me. If I'd been pregnant, I would have told you. And I would never, ever abandon my baby. Never."

His face flushed a deep red. "I really don't want to argue about this right now. Please. We'll talk later. I—I just can't do it now. I mean it."

I grabbed my purse from the table and my jacket

from the nearby chair. "Fine. Take me home, please."

Rage and hurt coursed through me. I could feel angry tears forming in my eyes. How could Sam believe this? It was ludicrous. Suddenly I felt as if I didn't really know him. Maybe I never had. If this was all it took to cause a division between us, how could we ever hope to sustain a real relationship?

I hurried out the door to the truck, unable to hold back my emotions. As I fled down the stairs, I ran right smack into Sweetie.

"For cryin' out loud, girlie," she screeched. "Watch where you're goin'. You almost knocked me into the middle of next week. Why are you. . ." I pushed past her, mumbling an apology. She turned around and watched me get in the truck. As I slid into the passenger seat, I saw her grab Sam before he could get past her. He tried to wrestle away, but she hung on like her life depended on it. Aunt and nephew exchanged a few words; then she let go of him and he got into the truck. As we pulled out of the driveway, I looked back at Sweetie. She hadn't moved, just stared at us as we drove away.

Sam was silent until he pulled up into my driveway. "Look," he said quietly after turning off his engine, "I'm sorry." He reached over and wiped away the tears on my cheeks. "I'm not upset at you, and of course I believe the baby isn't yours. I know we have to talk this out, and we will. I just need you to be patient with me for a little while."

"But I don't understand. What's wrong? Why did this upset you so much?"

He shook his head and gazed out the window. "I'll explain it to you, Grace, I promise. I just need a little time to get my thoughts together. I'm as shocked as you are at my reaction." He turned to look at me, his eyes full of concern. "Give me some space, okay? Just a couple of days. When I'm ready to talk, I'll tell you everything. Hopefully I'll be able to explain myself. Can you do that for me?"

I sniffed, wiped my face with my coat sleeve, and nodded. I really didn't trust myself to say anything at this point. Selfishly, I felt slighted because this attack was on *me*, not Sam. I'd expected his support, and now here I was trying to console him.

I quickly kissed him and got out of the truck, not even looking back as I ran into the house. A few seconds after I closed the door behind me, I heard his truck start up and rumble out of the driveway. It occurred to me that we were supposed to check out the woods once more to see if we could find signs of my late-night intruder. It would have to wait. At that moment, I didn't care much. Last night seemed like it had happened weeks ago.

I went to the kitchen, dropped my purse on the table, and looked out the window. Everything was quiet. No signs of life except for a couple of squirrels chasing each other up and down the trees. I marveled at their agility. How could they run and jump so high and so fast and not fall?

I heard a long, drawn-out meow from behind me. Snickle stood in the middle of the kitchen stretching his body. Must have just awakened from a nap.

"Hard life there, bud," I said. "Wanna trade?"

He answered me by flicking his tail and running out of the room.

"Good answer."

I checked the clock. The town meeting was scheduled for six. It was a little past three. Plenty of time for a nap, although I was probably way too upset to sleep. First I washed some dishes that had been sitting in my sink, soaking. When I had enough power in the house, my next purchase would be a dishwasher. Washing dishes by hand was for the birds.

I'd finished the dishes and was on my way upstairs, trying once again to sort out Sam's strange reaction to that awful note, when I heard loud knocking. I gazed down at the door like I could see who was on the other side. I didn't get many visitors. In fact, I never had visitors. The only person who ever came over was Sam. Maybe he'd come back to talk. I rushed down the stairs, hoping it was him. When I swung it open, I found Sweetie standing there. She looked flustered.

"Hi there, Gracie girl." She wiped her hands nervously on the front of her coat even though they looked perfectly clean. "I need to talk to you. Can I come in?"

"Oh sure. Sorry. I thought you were someone else." I opened the door wider so she could get past me. She made a beeline toward the couch. I sat across from her in the rocking chair.

"The place looks great," she said, giving the room the once-over. "Still looks the way Benny had it, but I can see your touches, too. I like that you kept some of Benny here."

"Me, too. Maybe someday I'll do more decorating, but it didn't seem right to change everything right away."

Sweetie nodded and nervously cleared her throat. "Listen, Gracie, I want to talk to you about Sam.

About why he acted like he did today."

"He told you what happened?" I could hear the sharp edge in my voice, but the idea he'd talked to his aunt before we'd really had a chance to talk upset me.

She shook her head slowly. "Now don't go gettin' your knickers in a knot. I could tell he was upset when he came home. I forced it outta him." She slid off her winter coat and put it on the couch next to her. "Glad to see you got some heat in here. Feelin' a mite warm. Hope you don't mind if I shed this thing for a few minutes."

"Of course not."

Sweetie kept looking at me and then glancing away. I'd never seen the woman so uncomfortable.

"Sweetie, why are you here?" I asked finally. "What is it you want to say?"

She cleared her throat a couple more times. "I want you to know somethin', Gracie. I—I need to tell you. . ." She stopped and stared at the floor. Suddenly her head shot up. "This is stupid. For cryin' out loud, I can't figger out what's wrong with me." She cleared her throat a fourth time, making me wonder if she was coming down with something. "Gracie Temple, I love you. I love you like you was my own daughter. I ain't used to tellin' anyone that 'cept Sam, so it's a little hard for me. I know it shouldn't be, but it is."

My irritation for the woman melted away. "I love you, too, Sweetie. You know that, right?"

"Yeah, I guess I do. That's one of the reasons you mean so much to me. Most folks don't cotton to me at all. They think I'm some kinda hillbilly, redneck numbskull. But you have a way of lookin' past the way I act on the outside and seein' the real me on the inside. That's one of the reasons I care about you so much. And it's one of the reasons I'm so grateful you love Sam." She grunted. "When he was runnin' around with Mary, I was plumb worried. Now understand, Mary and me is friends. I like her. But she weren't right for Sam. I knowed that as well as I knowed my own name."

"Thankfully Sam and Mary figured that out themselves."

"Yep. Better it were them than if someone else had tried to tell them. I figger it would have been me eventually, but it never came to that, thank the Lord."

"You didn't come here to talk about Mary and Sam, did you?"

"Nope." She rubbed her hands together like she was cold. "I know you can tell this is hard for me to say. I know lyin' is a sin, but I been makin' Sam lie 'bout somethin' ever since he was a boy. Now he's payin' the price for it. Actually, you both are. I gotta make this right."

"I don't understand. What are you talking about?" A cold thread of fear wound around my insides. I'd always valued Sam's honesty, and I hated deception.

Sweetie took a deep breath and locked her eyes with mine. "It's Sam's mama. She didn't die in no car wreck. She's alive. When he was a little boy, she just went off and left him, Gracie. Dumped him off in front of a church—just like that poor little baby you found last night."

FIVE

At first, I couldn't seem to find a response to Sweetie's shocking statement. Finally I managed to say, "Why did you lie? Why did Sam lie—to me?"

She cleared her throat again. I knew she did it out of nervousness, but it was beginning to get on my nerves. "One day Bernie told Sam they was goin' out to eat and then to the movies. She never had much money, so Sam was pretty excited. Kept him outta school even. Sure enough she took him to a burger joint for lunch and then to a movie. After that she drove over to the church where Sam had been goin' with a neighbor boy. She told him to wait there for her while she ran a quick errand." Sweetie wiped away a tear. "That's the last time he saw his mama. A couple hours later she called the church and told them to call me. That's how he came to stay in Harmony."

My mind went back to the conversation we'd had about the abandoned baby the night before. Sam had been strangely silent and changed the subject without much discussion. Suddenly his reaction made sense.

"I know tellin' a fib is a sin, Gracie, but how could I let that little boy tell folks the truth?" She shook her head. "I told him to tell everyone his mama died in a car crash to save him from embarrassment. Maybe it was right, maybe it was wrong. But now it's caused this problem between you, and it just ain't right. Sam reacted so bad to that note because it reminded him of what happened to him so long ago. I think he sees some of his mama in you—the good parts. But this thing with the baby. . . Well, it just hit too close to home. Stirred up some kinda feelin's he ain't dealt with yet." She wrung her hands together. "You just gotta wait it out, Gracie. I know he'll come around. If you wanna be mad at someone, be mad at me. I'm the one who caused this unholy mess."

Frankly, at that moment I was somewhat angry with both of them. But the picture in my mind of Sam waiting for his mother, wondering where she was, overcame my bruised feelings and evoked deep compassion. "Sam did tell me once that I reminded him of his mother."

She nodded. "I thought so. You see, there was lots of good things about my sister, Bernie. She was so pretty, and when she laughed, it sounded like sunshine. She loved animals, and she had a good heart. Saw things really deep, you know? Had a way of findin' the good in folks—same way you do."

"Her name was Bernie?"

She nodded. "Bernice. We called her Bernie ever since she was small. She just weren't no Bernice. Just like I weren't no Myrtle."

I frowned at her. "You make her sound like a good person. But she left her son. That's certainly not a good thing to do."

"I know that. This may sound silly to you, but I believe she left Sam at that church because she loved him. She was hooked on drugs back then, and she didn't think she could take good care of the boy. She thought I'd make a better mama than her." Sweetie covered her face with her hands for a moment. When she brought them down, I could see her anguish. "I hope she was right. I been tryin' my best all these years. I sure love that boy like he was my own."

"So what you're saying is that when I showed him that note, he thought maybe I actually *had* left my baby—just like his mother left him?"

Sweetie held up her hands in surrender. "I know it sounds nuts, Gracie, but yeah. I think that's exactly what happened. That boy loves you so much it almost hurts. But this situation made him think of his mama. I think he's afraid you're gonna hurt him like she did." She eyed me carefully. "I know Sam seems all growed up and well-balanced, but he ain't never healed from the pain his mama caused by leavin'. All these years, I been hopin' he'd get over it. But I can see now that he's still hidin' his hurt inside." She ran her weathered hand over her face. "This is all my fault. Not lettin' him deal with the truth. Now I mighta cost him the best thing that's ever happened to him in his whole life. You, Gracie girl."

"It's not your fault," I said, shaking my head. "But I wish Sam would have told me the truth. It makes me feel like he doesn't trust me. Surely he doesn't think something like that would change the way I feel about him."

Sweetie stood up and walked to the window, where she looked out toward the dark clouds that hung over Harmony. "Gonna start snowin' soon." Her voice sounded far away, even though she only stood a few feet from me. As if on cue, big fat snowflakes began drifting past the windows. After a few seconds, she whirled around to face me. "No matter who did wrong, you have to decide if you can work through it. Is Sam worth enough to you to put out the effort it will take to ride out this storm?" She crossed her arms and studied me. "I ain't tellin' you it will be over tomorrow. Sometimes storms blow through with big winds and lots of fury—then suddenly they're gone." She waved her hand toward the thickening snow. "And sometimes they park themselves right over you and take their sweet time movin' along. You gotta have your feet planted firm, Gracie, so the storm don't knock you over." She walked back to the couch and picked up her old coat. "It's like that story about the man who built his house on the rock and the man who built his house on the sand." She shook her head and laughed. "I realized a long time ago that both those men had the same storms. Life ain't always gonna be as smooth as a baby's clean behind. Sometimes there's gonna be somethin' nasty that's gotta be dealt with. I used to blame God for what happened to my mama and daddy. And what happened to my sister. But down through the years I figgered somethin' out. I was lookin' in the wrong place. It ain't God sendin' the storm. It's God who gives us the rock."

I couldn't hold back a smile. "You're a pretty smart woman, Sweetie Goodrich. There are a lot of religious experts who haven't figured that out."

She snorted. "I quit puttin' much stock in them experts a long time ago. Only PhD in religion comes from the Holy Ghost, and He ain't much interested in what kinda title you got after your name. Shoot, them rotten ole Pharisees thought they were experts, too. I think God's more interested in open hearts willin' to listen to His voice." She peered closely at me, her expression grave. "Now I just got one question for you."

"You want to know if I'm willing to stand on the rock and see this through?"

"That's it, Gracie girl. Do you love Sam enough to ride out this storm?"

I got up and went over to where she stood. Then I wrapped my arms around her. "Yes," I whispered. "I'll stand on that rock as long as it takes. We'll make it through this storm—as long as that's what Sam wants."

She squeezed me hard and then shook herself loose. After sliding on her coat, she walked to the door but turned around to gaze at me once more before stepping outside. There were tears in her eyes. "Don't you worry about that, okay? That boy loves you so much he don't know his up from his down. When he's ready to talk, he'll come to you. Trust me. I been around him a long time now. He has to deal with stuff in his own way."

"Okay. I won't push."

She nodded and walked out the door. I was left standing alone in my house, wondering if I'd just promised Sweetie something I couldn't do. Did I really love Sam enough to weather this storm? I'd had such high hopes for us—for my life in Harmony. But things weren't turning out the way I'd expected. Had I missed God?

I puttered around the house for a while, too tense to settle down for a nap. Originally, I'd planned to go to the meeting tonight with Sam, but since he said he needed some time to himself, I had to assume I was going alone. Although I hated to drive my little car in the snow, at least the meeting wasn't far and if I had any trouble, I'd be easily found.

I wasn't in the mood to cook anything for dinner, so I made a quick sandwich with the leftover steak from lunch. I'd just taken my first bite when the phone rang. I quickly swallowed and reluctantly left my makeshift dinner on the kitchen table while I hurried into the living room. As soon as I picked up the receiver, I knew who it was.

"Hello? Gracie, are you there?" Ida's plaintive voice reached me before I had the chance to say "Hello" myself. I'd tried a couple of times to encourage her to wait until the person she was calling answered before she said anything. Obviously we still had some work to do.

"I know," she'd responded with a chuckle. "I just get so nervous I forget."

"I'm here, Ida," I said.

"Oh Gracie, honey, it is snowing so hard I would hate to take Zebediah out tonight. Can you give me a ride to the town meeting in your automobile?"

"I'd love to. I'll pick you up about twenty till six. Is that okay?"

"Oh yes. Thank you so much. Umm. . .so we will hang up the phone now, ja?"

"Yes, that's fine. See you later." The silence that followed led me to believe that she was waiting for me to end our call. Ida would never be rude. The idea of hanging up on me probably horrified her. I gently put the receiver down.

At five fifteen I went outside and started my car

after knocking off the snow that covered it. I wanted the interior to be warm for Ida. In Wichita, the police frowned on allowing cars to run unattended. They quickly became targets for car thieves. Here in Harmony, I could start my car in the middle of Main Street and leave it running and unlocked, and the only person who would touch it might be someone who felt the need to move it out of the way for other drivers. The kind of security the small town offered was wonderful but hard to get used to.

I went back inside and waited until twenty-five till six. Then I drove over to Ida's. I was surprised by her request to ride into town with me. Most of the time, our Old Order Mennonite citizens avoid town meetings and elections. Their belief about keeping themselves separate when it comes to worldly systems of government means they don't take social security payments or accept Medicare. Medical problems are usually taken care of by the community through homespun remedies. However, doctors are certainly consulted when necessary. Because of a lack of health insurance, larger bills are taken care of either by the local community church or through the district's overseeing body. Sam told me once that since he'd come to live in Harmony, he'd noticed that those who lived by the Old Order or Conservative Mennonite teachings seemed to be healthier than most. I'd wondered if the lack of smoking, drinking, and junk food contributed. Sam had laughed and said most of Harmony's Mennonite community would agree with my assessment—after adding one other reason. The most important one. Prayer.

Getting close to Ida's was somewhat complicated.

The snow had piled up and my little car skidded and slid all the way up to the house. Zebediah was nowhere to be seen. I felt confident he was huddled inside his stable, out of the unpleasant weather. As I clomped through the deepening snow, gusts blew ice particles into my face. I struggled to reach Ida's front door. Right before I reached out to knock, it swung open.

"Ach, child," Ida cried. "I would not have asked you to drive me to the meeting if I had known the weather would turn so awful."

I stumbled inside, and Ida closed the door behind me. "It's not really as bad as it looks," I assured her. "There's only a couple of inches on the ground. It's the wind. It's really picked up in the last thirty minutes." I looked down to see the snow from my boots melting onto the homemade rug near Ida's door. "I'm afraid I'm making a mess."

"Do not worry," the old woman huffed. "That rug is only made of old rags. You are worth much more to me than it is."

As she reached for her long, heavy black cape, I said, "Are you sure you want to go out in this?"

"Ja," she replied. "Usually I do not go to town meetings. They seem to be about things that do not concern me. But this time. . ." Her voice trailed off as she tied the cloak under her chin. She pulled the hood up and peered out at me. "I told you that I have a bad feeling about this new building project. Please understand that this is not about the people who will come. I am sure they will be an asset to our community. But there is something else. Something that disrupts my peace. I have learned over many years to listen when that happens. I want to hear this plan for myself. Perhaps my peace will return. I must find out."

I nodded at her, but I truly believed the old woman's attitude toward Harmony was the real cause of her disquiet. Many years ago, a man who held the position of bishop in the Mennonite Church had caused a lot of disruption in the town. Ida was one of the women who had prayed Harmony would never see that kind of confusion again. Ida believed strongly that Harmony existed as a special place of refuge from the rest of the world. Although I felt the same thing, to Ida it was more than a feeling. It was absolute reality. I was certain the new retirement village was no threat to the residents here, but obviously she had some concern that it might be. I could only hope that tonight's meeting would quell her fears.

I held the door open for her, and we leaned into each other as we fought the wind. I got her into the car, and we headed toward town. The main streets were snowy but passable. The wind actually helped by pushing the snow into drifts on the side of the road. The real problem was blowing snow that made visibility very poor. I wondered if the weather might affect other citizens trying to make it to the meeting. By the time we pulled up to the building Eric had acquired, it was clear that Harmony residents were out in force.

I started to park on the other side of the street, but a man I didn't know came running out of the building, pulling on his coat. He motioned at me to wait and jumped inside a truck parked near the front door. He backed out into the middle of Main Street and waved me into his parking place. After turning off my engine, I looked in my rearview mirror and saw him pull into the spot where I'd started to park. I chuckled to myself at the thought of anyone in Wichita doing something like that. Battling over parking spaces, especially in the winter, seemed to bring out the killer instinct in people. Frankly, I'd rather walk a block in a blizzard than fight with someone over something so trivial. But today, with Ida in the car, the man's kindness wasn't trivial at all. It was a true act of kindness.

I told Ida to wait for me to come around and help her out, but by the time I reached her, the same man who had given up his parking space was already assisting her from the car and guiding her through the blustery wind toward the front door of the building. When we got inside, I caught him by the arm.

"Thank you so much," I said, a little out of breath from fighting the wind. "That was so thoughtful."

"You're welcome. Usually I wouldn't park so close to the door. I was already in town doing business and just got back to my truck." I gauged him to be in his forties or fifties. Graying brown hair, dark green eyes, and an engaging smile. His warm and easy manner made me feel immediately comfortable in his presence.

I held out my hand. "I'm Gracie Temple."

He took my hand and shook it firmly. "Temple. Any relation to Benjamin Temple?"

I nodded. "He was my uncle. He left me his house when he passed away."

He let go of my hand. "I'm Bill Eberly. I own a farm between here and Sunrise. I knew your uncle. We were friends when we were younger. Unfortunately, we didn't see much of each other for many years before he died. Ben kind of kept to himself."

"Yes, he did." I couldn't tell if Bill knew the reason my uncle had been afraid to encourage close friendships or if he was just being nice. Whatever the truth, it would have to wait. Eric had taken his place behind a podium set up at the front of the room, and people were beginning to find their seats. I excused myself to Bill and escorted Ida to a row near the podium so she could hear. As I got closer, I was able to see Eric more clearly. His face was pale, almost devoid of color, and his usual friendly smile was missing. I waved at him, but he seemed to look right through me.

Ida tugged at my sleeve after we sat down. "Is this the man you are working with?"

I nodded.

"This man does not look happy. I wonder why."

All I could do was shrug. It wasn't hard to figure out that Rand was probably involved in some way. I felt sorry for Eric. Having to deal with Rand was a lot for anyone to handle, let alone someone as young and easygoing as Eric.

Slowly the noise and discussions ceased, and the crowd waited for the information they'd come for. I looked around the packed room. John Keystone was here, as were the Crandalls and the Scheidler brothers. I saw Ruth, who smiled at me from across the room. Joe Loudermilk from the hardware store was in deep conversation with Paul Bruner. Gabriel and Sarah Ketterling stood in the back against the wall. I waved at Sarah, who lifted her slender fingers in acknowledgment. I wanted to visit their store so I could see how things were coming along, but I guess it would have to wait until tomorrow. I couldn't ask them to open up tonight, especially with the weather turning bad. I was really looking forward to renewing my lessons in wood-block printing. I gazed across the aisle and saw Abel. I nodded to him and he smiled at me. Emily hadn't come with him. I assumed she was at home taking care of the baby—unless they'd found the mother.

The door in the back of the room opened and closed. I glanced back to see Grant walk in. He'd mentioned coming to the meeting when I was in Wichita, but with the weather I'd figured he'd probably changed his mind. I tried to catch his eye but couldn't. He stood against the back wall looking uncomfortable and out of place in his dark gray suit and long black coat.

Once again the door opened. A few people in the back groaned. The frigid wind cut through the room like an icy knife. It was Sam. For some reason, I turned my head away, afraid he'd see me. My reaction didn't make any sense, but I couldn't chase away the feeling that there was a barrier standing between us that had never been there before. It made me uncomfortable.

Eric pounded on the podium with a small gavel even though it wasn't really necessary. All eyes were on him as the room fell deathly quiet. Just before he spoke, Sam slid into the seat next to me. He stared straight ahead toward the front of the room and didn't acknowledge my presence.

"Ladies and gentlemen," Eric began. "I want to thank you for coming out today." He stared down from his place behind the podium. A few people around us looked at each other. The atmosphere in the room, which had been charged with excitement when we first came in, was so quiet I could hear the people around me breathing. It was easy to see that Eric was under some kind of stress. A light buzz of whispered conversation began to build.

Eric cleared his throat and glanced around the room. Finally he opened his mouth. "I–I'm sorry to report that I don't have good news for you."

The noise in the room increased, and Eric banged the gavel again. "Please, if you could keep it down. I need to explain the situation. I'm still hopeful we can work something out." The hum of voices stopped, but not before a man's voice was heard clearly above the din.

"Told you we couldn't trust no city slicker."

Eric's eyebrows knit together in a frown. "I'm afraid the problem isn't with me. As many of you know, Rand McAllister promised to sell me his land for a fair price. Unfortunately, today he increased what he was asking to an amount I simply can't agree to. I've spent the better part of a day trying to reason with him, but to no avail." He glanced at his watch. "We were supposed to meet an hour ago to try to come to some kind of final understanding, but he didn't show up. I don't know where he is."

"So there's still hope you two might be able to work this out?" Mary's voice cut through the crowd.

Eric shrugged, his face etched with apprehension. "Honestly, I don't think so. Rand's last offer was way above anything I could possibly match. The fact that he didn't bother to show up to meet with me indicates he has no intention of being reasonable."

A few irate shouts exploded from the gathered residents. Joe Loudermilk loudly called out, "Rand McAllister would sell his mother for a few bucks. He couldn't care less about this town."

A man in the front row stood up. I recognized my pastor, Marcus Jensen from Harmony Church. "I know several of you felt this venture would help to undergird your businesses, but it seems to me we were all doing okay before this proposal came along." He turned and smiled at the crowd behind him. "I mean, don't get me wrong, I think it would be great to welcome a few new people into our community. But do we really need to get this upset if it doesn't pan out?"

Paul Bruner from the leather and feed store jumped to his feet. "Small towns are dyin' all over the state, Pastor. Are we makin' it? Yeah, I guess so. But some months we just barely get by." He pointed his finger at Eric. "This man came here and started tellin' us we could do better for our families and our town. I don't want to move away from here just so my kids can have some of the things other kids have. But if that's what I have to do, I may just pack us all up and go to Council Grove or Topeka."

"I'm sorry, Paul," Eric said. "I thought this deal was done. I guess I should have waited until all the papers were signed before I shot off my big mouth. But Rand seemed so set on this venture, it never occurred to me that he would back out."

One by one, three other men shot to their feet. But a hush fell over the room as Ida slowly stood up. The sight of this elderly Mennonite woman clothed in black seemed to quiet even the most outspoken citizens. The men sat down, deferring to one of Harmony's most respected residents.

"I am not used to talking to large groups," she said, her voice strong but quaking with age. "However,

I love this town, and I would like to ask permission to speak." She turned and looked over the crowd. "Is there anyone here who would be offended if I addressed this assembly?"

No one voiced an objection. Several people offered their encouragement.

"Thank you." She turned back to Eric. "Mister Beck, I have no reason to believe your plan was anything more than a good business proposition. One that many of our citizens felt would be a help to our town. I do not fault you for this." She turned back toward the crowd behind her. I held on to her arm as she teetered a little. "That being said, I have had misgivings about this venture since I first heard word of it. You see, many of you were content with your lives until the idea of gaining more money and possessions was held in front of you. I realize that some of you may be experiencing hard times. But in my whole life, I have never seen anyone in Harmony go without assistance when they were in need. Neighbors have helped neighbors as long as I can remember. And the church has reached out whenever someone could not make it on their own. Perhaps we are not what the world would call wealthy in goods or in monetary treasures, but in truth we are very rich, ja?" She smiled. "There are not many towns that have what we have." She looked at Eric. "Now this man comes and our town is in turmoil. There is division. Our sights are set not on what we have, but what we do not have."

Once again she faced the crowd. The room was eerily quiet. "Harmony is an exceptional place. I implore all of you to remember what makes us this way. It is not money, and it is not possessions. It is a sense of community. It is the feeling of family. It is love. Above all, it is God's blessing, ja?" She shook her head. "If this new development is built, then I will pray God's blessings on it. If it is not, then I will pray God's blessing on our town anyway. It is not this proposal I am afraid of. It is the darkness in our souls. The Good Book asks what good there will be if a man gains the world but loses his soul in the process. This is my fear. That Harmony's soul is at risk." She fastened her eyes on Eric. "That is all I have to say, Mr. Beck. I am sure you are a good man who truly believes he is doing what is best for our town. I disagree with respect, and I thank you for giving me time to speak." She grasped my shoulder and slowly sat down.

There was silence for several seconds, and then someone in the back began to clap. Soon many in the room joined in. A glance around told me that not everyone agreed with Ida's sentiments. Mason Schuler, who owned a local dairy farm, stood up.

"First of all, I want to say that I appreciate what Mrs. Turnbauer just said. There's a lot of truth in it. But she can't speak for all of us. I love Harmony as much as anyone else, but I have two teenagers who want to go to college. My desire to see more money come into this town has nothing to do with wanting to be rich or with buying a bunch of stuff. Bonnie and I honestly want to offer our kids the chance to make something more of their lives."

A few other residents asked to be heard. Each one basically said the same thing—that Harmony needed the influx of money. That losing the retirement village would hurt the town and its citizens.

Eric listened patiently to each person but didn't

address their questions until the last person sat down. Then he stepped closer to the podium and stared out at the crowd. His first few words were so soft several people shouted for him to speak up. I was struck by the hurt on his face and couldn't help but remember when I first met with him and Grant about the project. He was so excited about building a place where people could spend their retirement away from the big city but were close enough to necessary services. Council Grove had a hospital and Sunrise had an emergency clinic. Although Sunrise was ten miles from downtown Harmony, from Rand's place, it was only six. As Eric learned more about Harmony and began to realize that his development could also help the town, his enthusiasm only grew. Now he stood in front of the people he thought he would be helping without a clue whether he could deliver on the promises he'd made. I felt sorry for him, but I had to admit that I was a little concerned about my own future as well. If this project fell through, hopefully Grant would be able to send other work my way. I'd been counting on this job to see me through the winter. I had a little money saved up, but paying for electricity and heat in my uncle's old house wouldn't leave me with much to live on.

Eric stepped away from the podium and got closer to the crowd so they could hear him more clearly. He wiped a thin sheen of sweat from his forehead and stared at me. I smiled in an attempt to encourage him. Out of the corner of my eye, I saw Sam watching me. It was my turn to ignore him.

"Look, I know some of you are disappointed that I don't have better news tonight," Eric said loudly. "You have my promise that I'll try to keep this deal alive. I'll find Rand and attempt to talk some sense into him. If there is any way to save the project, I'll do it. We might as well dismiss now. After I speak to Rand, I'll schedule another meeting."

Mary spoke up again. "If Rand doesn't want to sell his land, can't you find another location to build this place of yours? There's lots of acreage out here. I can't believe there aren't folks willing to sell for the right price."

"That's a good idea," Eric acknowledged, "and we did talk to several landowners in the area. Rand was the only one who had what we needed and was willing to sell."

"So let me get this straight," she said. "If you can find something close to the size and location of Rand's farm, you'll continue with the project?"

Eric considered her question for a moment. "It's possible. Just remember that I have several investors. The final decision isn't up to me. It's up to them. It would have to be a pretty good plot of land. Trust me, it's not that easy to find."

Mary sat down. The crowd murmured among themselves, but no one else addressed Eric. He dismissed the group and hurried off the platform, stopping at the end of the row where I sat. He motioned to me. I excused myself and scooted past Sam.

"Gracie, Grant and I would like to talk to you. Can you meet us in the restaurant for dinner?"

I started to explain to him that I had to drive Ida home first, but I felt a hand on my shoulder. It was Sam.

"You go ahead," he said. "I'll take Ida home."

I looked past him at Ida. "Is that all right with you, Ida?"

"Ja, ja. You go to Mary's," she said. "But don't stay in town too long. If it keeps snowing, you might have a problem getting home."

"We won't keep her too long, I promise," Eric said, smiling at Ida. "And if it gets too bad, I'll drive her. My truck has four-wheel drive."

Ida pointed at him. "I will trust you to take care of her, young man. She is precious to me."

I leaned over and kissed her on the cheek. "I'll be fine. You go home and get warm."

She nodded and Sam took her arm, guiding her toward the back of the room. Several people stopped them on their way, wanting to tell Ida how much her comments meant to them. By the time I got my coat and purse, Ida and Sam had left the building. Sam had basically ignored me. Self-pity simmered inside me. He'd told me everything was okay. That he loved me. But his actions tonight sure didn't show it. Just then Eric touched my arm.

"Are you ready?" he asked.

I nodded and followed him toward the door. Before I could reach it, someone grabbed me. I turned to find Ruth staring at me oddly.

"Gracie, I'm sorry to bother you, but I need to speak to you for just a minute. It's important."

"Well, I was on my way to a meeting," I said hesitantly.

"We'll see you at the restaurant," Eric said. "You go ahead."

Ruth took his comment to heart and immediately pulled me to a corner of the room that was empty. In several other areas, residents had formed small groups and were deep in discussion. I looked for Abel, but he was already gone. I'd really wanted to ask him about the baby.

"First of all, I'm so glad you're back," Ruth said. "I missed you so much." She gave me a quick hug, but I could tell her heart wasn't in it.

"What's wrong, Ruth? I can tell you're upset."

"Oh Gracie," she said, her round, red face even more flushed than usual. "People are talking. I mean, I know it's not true, but I just think you should know. Not that it matters what people think, but talking behind someone's back, well, I mean. . ."

"Ruth," I said sharply. "What in the world are you talking about? Spit it out."

She took a deep breath. "It's about that baby someone left on the church's doorstep."

"What did you hear?" I felt my heart sink.

She reached for my hand. "The story is circulating that the baby is yours, Gracie. Everyone's talking about it. Well, almost everyone. I told Esther Crenshaw to shut her trap, and so did Cora and Amos."

"And where did Esther hear it?"

"I have no idea. Esther spreads gossip like wildfire, but she won't tell where the spark started. I guess she thinks it makes her look innocent of spreading her nasty rumors."

I glanced around the room. Sure enough, quite a few of the people who hadn't left were looking my way. Why hadn't I noticed it before?

"Look, Ruth, there's no truth to—"

"Don't you dare deny this stupid lie to *me*, Gracie Temple. I wouldn't believe it if that baby crawled up here, grabbed your leg, and called you Mama. You would never desert your child. We may not have known each other for long, but I know you well enough to be sure of that. You're one of the most honest, thoughtful, and good-hearted people I've ever met."

Her sentiments touched my heart, and I hugged her tightly. "Thank you," I whispered. "At least you and Abel believe in me."

"Abel? What does he have to do with this?"

"He got a letter from someone claiming the baby was mine. He had to ask me if it was true."

Ruth crossed her arms and frowned at me. "You've only been in town less than a day. Someone's already written a letter accusing you of something awful, and Esther has hold of this little nugget of poison." She shook her head. "Something doesn't seem right here. I mean, even Esther can't spread a story that fast." She patted my arm. "You need to be on the lookout. It's like someone is out to get you, Gracie."

I tried to smile at her. "I'm sure it's just Esther and some of her silly friends trying to stir up something interesting in Harmony."

Ruth chuckled. "Seems to me Harmony's already pretty interesting, even without your illegitimate baby."

"Shhhh," I hissed, looking past her. "Don't ever say that."

"Oh. Sorry." Ruth reached over and squeezed my arm. "You'd better get going. It's starting to snow pretty hard. You call me if you need to talk, okay? In the meantime, I'm going to threaten Esther within an inch of her miserable life. If anyone can get her to shut up, it's me. That woman's afraid of me for some reason." She grinned. "Might be because I told her once that if she didn't keep her gossipy comments to herself, I was going to tell Marvin Upshaw that Esther's brown curls aren't really hers." She covered her hand with her mouth, reminding me of a little girl with a secret. "Esther wears a wig, you know. She doesn't think anyone suspects. I think everyone in town knows her hair isn't real. But as long as Esther doesn't know we know. . ."

"You have some control over her?" I finished. I grinned at her. "You're pretty crafty, you know that?"

Ruth giggled. "Let's just keep that between us, okay?"

"You've got a deal."

I left Ruth and made my way to the front door, looking straight ahead. If people were talking about me, I didn't want to know it. I stepped outside to find thick, fat snowflakes filling the sky. In the dark, lit by streetlamps and carried about by the wind, their sparkling dance seemed almost magical. I stood for a moment in the cold, letting the flakes drift down on my face and coat. There's something so special about snow. As I let it fall on me, I felt a sense of peace in the hushed quiet of a winter's night. It was as if God was caressing me with His love.

"Beautiful, isn't it?"

I turned to find Marcus Jensen standing next to me. "It reminds me of the scripture that talks about Jesus washing us as white as snow." He smiled. "Snow covers up the ugly things. It has a way of making everything seem clean."

I nodded. "I feel the same way."

He pointed toward the diner. "Are you going to Mary's, or were you planning to stay here for a while?"

I involuntarily shivered from the cold. "No. I

think I've had enough. I'll be satisfied to sit in the restaurant, drink a hot cup of coffee, and watch the snow where it's a little warmer."

He laughed and held out his arm. I took it, and he guided me across the street. Right before we reached the steps to the diner, he stopped.

"Gracie, I'm your pastor. If you ever need someone to talk to. . ."

I peered at him through the flakes that drifted between us. "I know that, Pastor. I don't think I. . ." My stomach did a flip-flop. "Pastor, if you heard a rumor about that baby dropped off at Abel's church. . ."

He chuckled and patted my shoulder. "Gracie, I am talking about that, but probably not for the reason you think. I know that baby isn't yours. I'm just concerned about you. About having to face these kinds of silly stories."

"How did you hear about it?"

He shook his head and sighed. "You know that Esther Crenshaw is one of my parishioners. Much to my chagrin."

"Well, you could certainly give her a message from me."

"I've probably given her your message already. Although I suspect it was presented in a more charitable fashion than what you might be prone to employ."

Even though I was upset, I smiled at the kindly pastor. "I have no doubt about that."

"Let's get inside and warm up. But my offer holds. Come see me anytime. I mean that."

"Thank you. I know you do."

As we entered the restaurant, I seriously considered taking Pastor Jensen up on his offer. Between this ridiculous baby rumor and the way Sam had reacted to it, I definitely needed someone to talk to.

"Gracie, over here!"

I spotted Eric and Grant sitting at a table near the back of the room. Probably hiding. I pushed my way through the crowded restaurant. It looked like most of the town had decided to eat at Mary's after the meeting. I could hear angry discussions as I passed tables and booths packed with concerned Harmony residents.

I was almost to the table when I spotted Pat Taylor sitting alone only a few feet from where Eric and Grant sat. I must not have hidden my shock well, because he tipped his hat at me and grinned. Why was he here? Had he been in the meeting? It seemed he was popping up all over the place. Feeling unsettled, I nodded his way and kept going. Funny to see him alone at a table that could easily seat four people. Every other table was full, with family and friends eating together. Either no one was brave enough to approach him—or if they had, he'd sent them packing. Nice man.

"We already ordered," Grant said apologetically when I reached them. "Sorry, but I'm starved, and it looks like it's going to take awhile to serve everyone."

I shook my head, slid my coat off, and sat down. "Don't worry about it. Honestly, I'm not hungry anyway."

"Quite a town you've moved to, Gracie," Grant said with a hint of sarcasm. "The physical description you gave me is accurate, but I thought you said this place was peaceful."

"I thought it was, too. Frankly, ever since I hit the

edge of town, everything's been topsy-turvy. I have no idea why."

"I hope we can still work this thing out," he said. "I do have a couple of other jobs I can send your way, but to be honest, I can't pay much for them."

"I understand."

Grant had never had a robust complexion, but tonight, under the lights in the restaurant, he looked pasty and haggard. I knew he was worried about losing the work this venture promised, as well as the additional future work Eric had alluded to. The investment group behind the project had their fingers in many other pies. For both our sakes, as well as the town's, I hoped Eric would find a way to keep the deal with Rand.

I noticed Grant staring past me. I turned to see Cora and Amos Crandall walk in the door with Drew. As they waited for a table, I couldn't help but compare Drew to Grant's son, Jared. Drew's happy nature was controlled and appropriate. Amos and Cora treated him with kindness but applied gentle correction when it was needed. Actually, their attitude toward Drew was one of normalcy. Not that they didn't allow him to be himself, but they also expected him to display proper behavior. They didn't give him a pass because of his disability. Jared, Grant's son with Down syndrome, was much less disciplined, often running through the office, grabbing people, and running off with items from their desks. He reminded me of a playful puppy. Grant seemed uncomfortable correcting him—almost as if he was embarrassed by his son.

"So what should I do now?"

Eric's plaintive question forced me to refocus my

attention on the situation at hand. Problem was, I had no answer for him, and Grant just stared at him blankly.

"Coffee?" I hadn't seen Mary come up behind me.

"Oh yes, please," I answered. "Right now a cup of your coffee is exactly what I need."

"Are you okay? You look stressed." She poured coffee into the cup that sat next to my silverware.

All I could do was shake my head. "You have no idea."

"Sorry to hear it," Mary said. "I guess everyone's skating on the edge a bit." She patted my shoulder. "Don't let it get to you. Everything will work out. It always does."

"From your mouth to God's ear," Eric said under his breath.

"Your food will be out shortly, Mr. Beck," Mary said with a smile.

"Please, call me Eric." He pointed toward Grant. "And this is Grant Hampton."

"Nice to meet you, Grant," she said. "Someone told me you're Gracie's boss. Is that right?"

Grant nodded. "For now anyway."

Mary's eyebrows shot up, but she didn't ask him what he meant. She turned her attention back to me. "What are you hungry for, Gracie? We're backed up some, but I'll push you to the front of the line so you can eat with your friends."

My appetite was almost nonexistent even though I hadn't finished the sandwich I'd made at home, but I ordered a bowl of chili.

"She's very pretty," Grant said after Mary walked away.

I nodded. "Yes, she is."

"By the way, where is Sam?" Grant asked. "I thought I'd get the chance to meet him tonight."

My voice caught. "He—he took my friend Ida home so I could come here. I'm sure you'll meet him later."

I tried to sound nonchalant, but Grant knew me well enough to know something was wrong. He stared at me for a moment but let it go. I was grateful. The last thing I wanted to do right now was talk about my love life. "So why did you two ask me to meet with you?" I glanced toward the big windows at the front of the restaurant. If anything, the snow had thickened. "I need to get going soon. If it snows much more, my little car won't stand a chance."

"We thought since you know the residents better than we do, you could help us navigate this situation," Eric said. He leaned in and lowered his voice. "I truly don't believe Rand is going to come around. I didn't want to say that at the meeting, but it isn't just the money. For some odd reason, he's taken a real dislike to me." He sighed and shook his head. "I don't think I'm a snob, but Rand has convinced himself that I think I'm better than he is. There were signs of his attitude early on in our relationship, but I convinced myself it was my imagination. I mean, I don't see myself as better than anyone else. I try to treat everyone with respect." His blue eyes sought mine for reassurance.

"You're not the least bit stuck-up," I said, trying to match his quiet tone. "From what I've heard, Rand is convinced everyone is out to get him."

"I hope you're right. I'd feel terrible if I'd done

something to make him feel uncomfortable."

"Oh, come on," Grant said, shaking his head. "The man's obviously a fruitcake. This isn't your fault."

Eric's eyes swept the room. The cold expressions tossed his way were everywhere. He sighed again. "Anyway, I want to save this project if at all possible. I'm going to scan the property maps again. Look for another location as close to Harmony as I can find. I may need your help with that, Gracie."

"I'll be glad to do anything I can."

"I want you to keep working on the advertising campaign we started," Grant said to me. "I'll make sure you get paid for your time, no matter what happens."

Eric clapped Grant on the back. "And I'll make sure you get paid for your work so far—even if this project is scrapped. Even if I have to pay you out of my own pocket." His expression turned serious. "I have no intention of allowing people who trusted me to come out of this with a loss of any kind. I intend to find a way to follow through with the development—if it's humanly possible."

His earnestness touched me. I hoped his good intentions would be enough. Weariness began to overtake me just as Mary made it to the table with our food. Across the room, I noticed Hannah and her friend Leah taking orders.

"Mary, do you need help? I used to wait tables on the weekends while I was in school. I'd be happy to put on an apron and do what I can."

She set the bowl of chili in front of me and slid Grant and Eric's plates to them. Then she leaned down and studied my face. "I appreciate your offer more than you know. But I'm going to say no. The girls and I are on top of it. You look so tired, Gracie. I think you could use some rest."

"I'm sorry," Eric said. "I should have realized you were tired. Let's eat and head out of here. Maybe I shouldn't have asked you to meet with us tonight."

I shook my head. "It's fine. I was concerned about you, and I wanted a chance to see Grant."

"The snow's really getting deep," Mary interjected. "You all need to get on the road." She frowned at Grant and Eric. "Hope you two are staying in town."

"I've got a hotel room in Council Grove," Grant said. "Think I'll leave before it gets any worse." He smiled at Mary. "Can I get a box for my hamburger and fries? I'd like to take it with me."

"Here." Mary held her hand out for his plate. "I'll wrap it up in tinfoil first and then put it in a box. That way you've got a fighting chance of keeping it warm."

"Thanks, Mary," he said, holding out his plate.

"What about you?" Mary's question was directed at Eric.

"I'm at the same hotel," he said. "But I'm going to eat here. My truck has four-wheel drive and does great on snow."

"Well, my Bug doesn't have four-wheel drive, and when it sees a flake of snow it immediately drives straight for the nearest ditch." I quickly slurped down a couple of spoonfuls of chili and reached for my coat.

Eric frowned and took hold of my arm. "Listen, Gracie. I don't think you should take a chance with your small car tonight. Why don't we both finish our dinners, and then I'll take you home on my way to the hotel? You can pick up your car later."

I started to say no. If I could count on Sam to drive me back to get my car when the storm moved out, I would have said yes immediately. Eric noticed my hesitation.

"I'll come back by in the morning when it's light and drive you back into town. I can easily pull your car to your place if necessary. I've got a strong bumper and solid chains in the back bed. My cousin has a small car, too. I'm always pulling him out of snowdrifts."

I decided to take him up on his offer. He seemed eager to help, and to be honest, I hate driving on snow and ice. Without giving it further thought, I agreed.

"Great," he said with a smile. "Now let's enjoy the rest of our meal."

A few minutes later, Mary returned with Grant's food. He thanked her, put a big tip on the table, and left. I watched as he made his way through the restaurant. He walked slowly past the Crandalls, his eyes locked on Drew. By the way his shoulders slumped, I knew he was discouraged. It wasn't just because of the business deal he stood to lose. He and Evie must be having a tough time with Jared. It seemed to go in waves. I felt bad for them both.

"So this is the town you gave up your job for?" Eric said, interrupting my thoughts.

"Believe it or not. Of course, when I left, things weren't all stirred up like this."

"I guess you have me to thank for that."

Eric ran his hand through his thick dark hair. I was struck once again by his boy-next-door looks. A slightly turned-up nose and steely blue eyes that made women turn their heads when he walked by. But Eric seemed totally oblivious to how good-looking he was.

"Don't be silly. This deal is good for everyone. If I'd thought for a moment it would hurt Harmony, I would have said something. I still believe in this project."

He grew silent and his forehead creased.

"What are you thinking?" I asked. I immediately regretted my words. An old boyfriend told me once that men hate to be asked what they're thinking. "Most of the time we aren't thinking anything," he'd told me. "So quit asking." We broke up not long after that.

"I can't help but think about your friend—the older woman who spoke at the meeting."

"Ida? Oh, goodness. I'm certain you noticed the way she dresses. She's Old Order Mennonite. They don't like change. I wouldn't worry too much about her. Most everyone else disagreed with her."

As I said the words, I felt disloyal to Ida, but I truthfully felt her allegiance to the "old ways" meant she would never be supportive of anything that could disrupt the status quo in Harmony.

"I don't know," he said. "Quite a few people seemed to respect her opinion." He stopped eating and seemed to scrutinize me for several seconds. "You know, I'm not so sure she's wrong, Gracie."

I put my spoon down. "What do you mean? You're not rethinking this project, are you?"

"No. Not really. It's just that I understand the idea of protecting things that are important to you. I wouldn't want our development to harm this little town in any way. You really do have a special place here."

"But that's just the point, isn't it? We need some money coming into the community to keep Harmony going. Your development is just right. Not too big so as to change the complexion of the town, but big enough to undergird many of our businesspeople." I found myself speaking with more passion than I thought I had. Several of the speakers at the meeting had made sense. And the same was true in my situation. Without the work from this project, I was in a heap of trouble.

Eric shrugged, but I saw the first spark of hope in his face since the meeting. "I pray you're right. All I can do is keep going forward. First thing tomorrow I'm going to try to find Rand. If I can save the deal with him, I'll do it. If I can't, then we need to look for new property."

"You said at the meeting that Rand's was the only property that would work for your project."

He polished off the last bite of his cheeseburger before answering me. "That's right. But I'll look again. And now that the word is out that we could lose the development, maybe someone else will be willing to sell." He scanned the room until he saw Mary and waved his hand, trying to get her attention. "I think we need to get going. Even my truck has its limits. Let's get you home. I'm tired, and I'm afraid the forty miles in front of me will be slow going. It hasn't stopped snowing since we got here."

I scooped up the last spoonful of chili while he and Mary settled the bill. I tried to offer to pay for my own meal, but he wouldn't hear of it.

"I asked you to have dinner with me," he said, his sky blue eyes twinkling. "Besides, just having you to talk to is worth a hundred bowls of chili."

Mary laughed. "Now that is a compliment, Gracie. Especially when it's *my* chili."

I smiled at both of them. "Now on that, I have to agree. It was delicious, Mary. Thank you."

"You're welcome. And don't forget to call me about that dinner. How about Monday night? It's pretty slow here Mondays. I can close early."

"Sounds great as long as we're not both snowed in."

She glanced out the window at the thick, fast-falling flakes. "Boy, you've got that right." She took Eric's money and started to rummage around in her apron pockets for change.

"Hey, just keep it," Eric said. "Best cheeseburger I've had in a long time. It was worth much more than you charged me."

Mary flashed Eric a coquettish grin that lit up her heart-shaped face. Even in the harsh, yellowish hue of the restaurant lighting, I was struck by her looks. Her long black hair glowed, and her dark eyes with their long, thick lashes sparkled. I felt washed out next to her. Her perfect, pale complexion was free of the freckles sprinkled across my nose. Most of the time I tried to hide them with makeup, but by the end of a long day, like today, they seemed to emerge from under their temporary camouflage. Some people in Harmony probably wondered why Sam ended his relationship with Mary to start one with me. A sudden flash of insecurity exploded inside me, and Mary's chili seemed heavy and indigestible.

"I said, are you ready?" Eric's voice caught my attention. Mary had already walked away, but I was still staring at her.

"Sorry. I guess I really am tired. Yes, I'm ready to go."

I pulled on my coat and followed him to the door. Several customers stopped eating to watch us leave. I knew most of them, but some were strangers. I had no idea if their stares were for Eric or for the low-life baby deserter. Either way, they irritated me. By the time we made it to the front porch, my blood was boiling.

"You okay?" Eric asked.

I nodded. "I love Harmony, but one negative aspect of living in a small town is that everyone knows your business—or they think they do, anyway. It's really starting to bug me."

"Sorry if I've added to your stress."

I turned to look at him. He seemed so concerned for me it stirred something deep inside. I needed Sam, but he wasn't here. I was suddenly grateful Eric had come to Harmony.

"No. I'm glad you're here. I just wish I could come up with a solution for you."

"That's not your job, Gracie. Please don't worry about it." He pointed across the street to his huge black truck. "Let's get you home before you turn into a very lovely popsicle."

He held out his arm and I took it. The street was icy, and Eric kept me upright more than once when my feet almost slipped out from underneath me. As we approached his truck, I realized for the first time that it was a Hummer. I'd seen them, but I'd never known anyone who had one. Eric held the passenger side door open for me and helped me climb up into the seat. It was made easier by a metal step that gave me a head start. Then he closed the door and went around to the driver's side door. When he got inside I said, "Wow. This is a Hummer. I've never been inside one before."

He started the engine and the heat came on almost immediately. "Your seat heats up, too. If you get too hot, let me know."

"Again, wow." I couldn't help but compare Eric's Hummer to Sam's old broken-down truck.

"Don't be too impressed," Eric said. "It's not brand new. I bought it from a guy in Kansas City who'd lost his job and had no way to pay his mortgage. I think I paid more for it than it's worth. I just had a new alarm installed, and now sometimes the engine won't start. Most of the time I can fix it by wiggling a few wires around." He grinned. "Real high-tech stuff."

"Well, I still think it's nice." We weren't even out of town yet, and I was already warm and toasty. Eric's heater was much better than the one in Sam's old truck.

We were silent the rest of the way home except for my occasional directions. I assumed Eric was thinking about his project. My thoughts centered around Sam. I had an internal battle going between my selfish side and the other part of me that loved him no matter what. But I had to wonder if it was enough. Would I be debating our relationship if I felt certain we were meant to be together? I was hurt by his request to spend a few days alone. I wanted to understand, but in truth, it just felt like rejection. I suddenly realized that Eric was turning onto the unpaved road that led to my house. Of course, now it was buried under so much snow I was amazed he found it. Especially since there were ditches on both sides.

"How in the world did you locate my driveway?" I asked. "Is there some kind of special Hummer radar that sees under snow?"

He laughed. "No. The snow dips down on both sides of your driveway. I assume those are ditches. It's not that complicated."

"Boy, you're good. Sorry I wasn't watching."

He stopped the car and put it into park. "It might also have something to do with the super-duper headlights this thing has. Of course, any small animals caught in their beam are now permanently blind."

"So when I see bunnies and squirrels running into each other, I'll have you to thank?"

He grinned widely. "Yes ma'am. Happy to serve."

"Well, thanks again. I'm definitely glad I didn't have to take my little car out in this. Not only would I have probably ended up in a ditch—the snow would have buried me in seconds. I might have been missing until next spring."

Eric shook his head. "I doubt that. You're the kind of girl someone would look for right away. You'd be missed."

I felt my face flush, and it wasn't because of the heated seat. "Um, thank you." My hand fumbled for the door handle.

"Let me help you up your porch steps," Eric said, turning off the engine and jumping out of the truck. He came around to my side and opened the door. "I would hate for anyone to find your frozen body during spring thaw."

I laughed and thanked him, holding on to his arm while we tramped through the snow. Once we reached the door, I fumbled around in my purse until my fingers closed over my keys. "I'd ask you to come in," I said as I unlocked the door, "but I know you need to get to Council Grove."

"You're right. Maybe some other time. I'll be back in the morning, and we'll fetch your car." He turned to leave but stopped halfway down the stairs and looked back at me. "Thanks, Gracie. For everything. Most of all for just being there."

The light from my living room bathed his face in a soft glow. The sincerity in his handsome features made me catch my breath. "You're very welcome. I'll see you tomorrow."

I watched as he followed the path we'd made through the snow all the way back to his truck. Then I closed the door and leaned against it. Was I having feelings for Eric? Was I comparing him to Sam? Emotions tumbled around inside me like numbers in a bingo basket, and I couldn't hold back a sob. I wanted to go back in time somehow—grab Sam and hold on to him as hard as I could. But after the way he'd ignored me tonight, I was beginning to wonder if he had already slipped away.

Six

I'd hung up my coat and put a kettle on for tea when a knock on the front door startled me. Who in the world would be stopping by on a night like this? As I hurried toward the insistent pounding, hope sprang up in my heart that Sam had come to apologize. To talk out our situation. I flung the door open expectantly. Eric stood there looking cold, wet, and extremely embarrassed.

"I'm so sorry," he said, shaking his head. "I can't get my stupid truck started. Can I come in for a while? I'll try it again in a little bit."

I held the door open. "Of course. Get in here before you freeze to death. Have you been out there all this time?"

When he came inside, I could see him trembling. "Yes. I really didn't want to bother you."

"Oh, for crying out loud, Eric," I scolded. "I think it would have bothered me more to find your corpse in my front yard."

In spite of his obvious discomfort, he laughed. "Stupid Hummer. I had my eye on a Jeep. I should have bought it instead."

I helped him off with his overcoat. "Take off your

boots and set them on the small rug in front of the door."

He leaned over and pulled off his boots. His socks were soaked. He frowned. "Seems as if I have defective boots as well as a defective vehicle."

"I think you'd better remove those socks, too. I'll get you a dry pair that will make your feet feel better."

"That would be quite an accomplishment since I can't feel them at all." As he slowly pulled off his socks, he reached out a hand and placed it on my shoulder for balance. His toes were bright red.

"Oh, wow. Come over here and sit on the couch. I'll get a fire going." My uncle's unused fireplace had originally been covered by a bookcase. Sam had shown it to me when he was working on the heat and electricity. He'd cleaned it out so I could use it. Benjamin had relied on a cast-iron stove to heat the living room, but with the new gas heating system, I'd had it removed. I guided Eric to the couch and covered him with one of Mama Essie's quilts. Then I took some logs out of the wooden bin Sam had made for me, placed them in the holder, added some kindling, and lit one of the long matches kept on top of the mantel. "While the fire gets going, I'll make you something hot to drink." I smiled at him. "Are you a coffee, tea, or cocoa kind of guy?"

He chuckled. "Hot cocoa in front of a fire sounds like a slice of heaven. Are you sure you want to go to all that trouble?"

"I'm sure. You stay cozy. I'll be back in a few minutes." Before I left the room, I moved his coat, socks, and boots near the fire to dry.

As I prepared our cocoa, my emotions swung back

and forth between being glad Eric was here—and being uneasy Eric was here. We were just acquaintances through work—nothing more. Why did I feel guilty? I stirred the powdered cocoa into the bottom of a pan along with the sugar and a little milk, making a paste. Since my electricity was still a little iffy, Sam had told me to wait on a microwave. However, I had to admit that I'd grown to enjoy my hot chocolate prepared the old-fashioned way. I even liked popcorn popped in a pan on the stove better than the microwave stuff.

I added the rest of the milk and stood next to the pan, stirring it so it wouldn't burn. What if Sam drove by and saw Eric's truck here? What would he think? Had Ida looked out her window and seen Eric's giant Hummer next to my house? Would she think we were up to something? I shook my head. Why was I worried? Wouldn't my real friends know better? I couldn't hold back a harsh laugh. Sure, just like they knew I'd never drop off my baby on the church steps.

The milk started to bubble, so I removed it from the burner and turned off the heat. As I poured the hot chocolate into two cups, I made up my mind. Sam and Ida—in fact, the entire town of Harmony—would just have to think whatever they wanted. I couldn't control them. And I couldn't live my life worrying about what they thought or didn't think.

I found some marshmallows in the pantry, plopped them into the cups, and carried them out to the living room. Eric appeared to be comfy on the couch. Snickle sat on his lap, looking as happy as that spoiled cat could possibly look.

"Oh Eric. I'm so sorry." I glared at my furry

feline friend. "You get down off of there, Snickle, or I'll put you in your carrier."

"No, please," Eric pleaded. "He's a great cat. I think we're bonding."

"Are you sure?"

"I'm certain. He's purring, and if I could purr, I'd join him." He frowned at me. "What did you call him? Did you say 'Snickle'?"

"Yes. It's short for Snicklefritz. It's my father's pet name for me. I decided to give it to the cat as a way to discourage my dad from using it for his daughter. Especially in public."

Eric grinned. "Snicklefritz. I like it."

I held one of the cups up in the air. "If you want this hot chocolate, you will promise right this minute that you will never call me that."

He laughed and put one hand over his heart. "I give you my word, I will never, ever call you Snicklefritz. Even under pain of torture."

"Well, I'm not sure just who would want to torture you to find out my nickname, but I'll accept your promise anyway."

I put his cup on the table in front of him and sat down in the rocking chair. "I must say, you look pretty comfortable."

He sighed. "I am. This has been a very stressful day. Dealing with Rand, the meeting, the truck not starting. This is the first moment of peace I've had."

"I'm sorry everything has turned out so badly. I wish I could do something to help you."

"Thanks, but you're doing that right now." He took a sip from his cup. "Wow. That's delicious. My grandmother used to make cocoa that tasted like this.

Now she makes the instant stuff just like everyone else."

I smiled. "If I had a microwave, I'd probably be doing the same thing. But I really do think this is better."

Eric put his cup down and his expression grew serious. "Gracie, do you mind if I ask you a personal question?"

"Go ahead. My life is an open book."

"I know it's none of my business, but I noticed you and Sam at the meeting. Things seemed, I don't know. . ."

"Strained?" I finished for him.

"Well, yes. Is everything okay? My altercation with Rand. . . It doesn't have anything to do with what's going on between you two, does it?"

"No, Eric. It has nothing to do with it." The fire crackling in the fireplace, the snow falling outside, and a nice hot cup of hot chocolate helped to lower my defenses. I really liked Eric and felt I could trust him. I slowly began to tell him about the baby, the accusatory note, and Sam's reaction. By the time I finished, his features were locked in a deep frown.

"I don't want to interfere in your life," he said gently, "but I have to say I find Sam's reaction strange. I mean, what does this poor baby have to do with you? Surely he believed you when you told him the child wasn't yours."

I was silent for a moment. Finally I said, "Yes. He believed me."

"Then I don't understand. . ."

As the truth tumbled out, I wanted to stop it. On one hand, telling Eric about Sam's mother didn't feel right. Sam would be furious if he knew I'd betrayed his confidence. Yet on the other hand, the pent-up emotions inside me seemed to have a life of their own. I couldn't seem to quit talking. When I finally finished, Eric was silent. "I'm sorry. Maybe I shouldn't have told you about this. I didn't mean to dump my problems on you."

He rubbed Snickle under the chin. The silly cat acted as if he'd never been given an ounce of attention before. "I'm glad you confided in me," Eric said finally. "It's just that. . ." He cleared his throat before speaking again. "I was engaged about a year ago. She was the woman I thought I was meant to be with, you know. My soul mate. Then about two weeks before the wedding, I found out she was adopted and that her birth mother had died of AIDS. Thankfully Michelle didn't contract it." He shook his head. "Her brother actually told me. Michelle didn't. I asked her why she'd never told me. I didn't care about her past. The thing that bothered me was that she didn't trust me. For some weird reason she thought if I knew about her mother, I would think less of her or something."

"But that's ridiculous."

"Of course it is. She was the one with the hang-up about it, not me."

"So what happened?"

"We broke up." His voice trembled slightly. Obviously it was still a very painful subject. "And it had nothing to do with her mother. It had to do with her lack of confidence in me. I mean, how can two people share a life together if they don't trust each other? What about all those situations that come along in life when trust is the only thing that gets you through? How could we make it past those moments?"

I tried to blink away the tears that spilled down my cheeks. Eric was right. Sam hadn't trusted me, not with the truth about his mother and not when he first read the note about the baby. I'd promised Sweetie that he and I could make it through this. But now I wasn't so sure. Even though Sam had assured me he loved me, instead of talking to me about his feelings, he'd tuned me out. How could two people build a life with each other if they couldn't honestly discuss their problems?

Eric sat up straighter and put down his cup. "Oh Gracie. I'm so sorry. I wasn't talking about you and Sam. I'm sure you have a much stronger relationship than Michelle and I had. You two will be fine. I certainly didn't mean to make you cry."

"It's not you. Really. You only said the same things I've been thinking." I stood to my feet. "More cocoa?"

"No. Thank you." Eric moved Snickle, who didn't seem happy about it. Then he pushed back the blanket and got up. "I think I'd better try to get out of here before it gets any worse out there. It will be a long drive back to Council Grove. I hope the highway is open."

"But what if your truck doesn't start?"

"Like I said, this has happened before. The engine almost always turns over after it sits for a while." He shook his head. "I can't believe I shut it off in the first place. I know better." He gave me a sideways smile. "I guess I had you on my mind and forgot everything else."

He grabbed his socks and had started to pull them on when my grandfather clock began to chime.

Eleven o'clock. With the roads so bad, he probably wouldn't get to his hotel until after one or two in the morning.

"Listen, Eric," I said. "Why don't you just sleep on the couch? The idea of you getting stuck in the snow worries me. I'm not as concerned about the highway being closed as I am about the road that leads to the highway. It's several miles of dirt road, and it's probably impassable. You shouldn't try it. Even in your monster machine."

He stopped pulling on his sock and straightened up. "Look, Gracie, as much as I appreciate the offer, I can't do that. It wouldn't look right. The last thing you need is to add another problem between you and Sam. If he knew I spent the night here. . ."

I held my hands up. "I'm getting a little tired of worrying about who might believe what about me. We're not doing anything wrong. It isn't safe for you to leave. I want you to stay. Please."

Eric shook his head. "No. I appreciate what you're trying to do, but I can't do it. I just can't."

I watched silently while he finished putting on his socks and shoes and then pulled on his coat. He walked over and put his hands on my shoulders. His crystal blue eyes gazed into mine. His looks reminded me of drawings of Prince Charming in the storybooks I'd loved as a child. Almost perfect features, from his thick dark hair to his strong chin, full lips, and long dark lashes.

"I'm so glad we're friends now," he said softly. "And I won't allow anything to ruin that relationship. I have to leave. Not just for our friendship, but for you and Sam. Do you understand?"

I nodded but didn't say anything. I didn't trust my voice.

He zipped up his coat without complaint, but I knew it couldn't be completely dry. Going outside in a wet coat wouldn't feel good. I was grateful his truck was so warm.

When he reached the door, I jumped up and followed him. "If the truck starts and you don't get stuck somewhere, will you at least call me when you reach your hotel? I want to know you're safe."

He stopped with his hand on the doorknob and hesitated. "Yes. I'll call you. I promise."

"Do you have my phone number?"

"Grant has it, right? I can get it from him."

"All right." I reached out and put my hand on his arm. "Eric, be careful, okay?"

"I will. Don't worry." He took a deep breath and flipped up the hood on his coat. Then he opened the door, stepped outside, and pulled the door behind him without looking at me. I stood on the other side and leaned my head against the thick, rough wood. I couldn't deny that Eric had sparked strong emotions inside me. How could I love Sam if I had feelings for Eric? I stood there trying to sort out my thoughts while Eric tried starting his Hummer. After several attempts, the engine finally roared to life. I listened as he backed out of my driveway, turned onto the road, and drove away.

I finally picked up our dishes and took them into the kitchen. Usually Snickle followed me everywhere I went, but instead he stayed curled up on the couch. Probably hoping Eric would return. For just a moment I agreed with him, but I quickly dismissed the thought. I loved Sam. I knew that. Now that I was alone, my head and heart were in agreement. Surely tomorrow, in the light of day, everything would be the way it was supposed to be. Eric as my friend and business acquaintance—and Sam as my boyfriend. We had problems, but we would work them out. Still, Eric and Michelle's failure to escape the kind of situation Sam and I faced made me a little uneasy. Before long, exhaustion quickly took over, and all I really wanted to do was put this day behind me. I pushed thoughts of Eric and Sam out of my head.

After cleaning up the kitchen, I trudged upstairs, changed my clothes, and crawled into bed. The space heater hummed in the quiet room, creating an almost hypnotic sound. I'd almost fallen asleep when a loud noise made me sit upright. There it was again. Now what? I got out of bed and hurried down the stairs, Snickle right behind me.

When I got to the door, I turned on the new porch light Sam had installed and peeked through the window. Eric stood there, his arms wrapped around himself. I quickly pulled the door open.

"G–G–Gracie," he said through chattering lips, "I slid off the road about a mile from here. I—I didn't know where else to go."

I reached out and pulled him inside. "Oh Eric. There are other places closer than mine. Why would you walk all the way here?" He shivered so badly I was afraid he'd fall down, so I led him over to the couch.

He shook his head. "Wh–where could I go? Everyone here hates me. I didn't want to ask for help from someone I didn't know. I walked past Sam's house, but I was afraid he'd find out I'd been at your place. I—I didn't want to cause any more trouble between the two of you." He laughed shakily. "And I really thought your place was much closer. If I'd realized how far it actually is, I'd have taken my chances with Sam."

I knelt down and pulled off his shoes and socks. The dry ones he'd worn earlier were still on the arm of the couch. I put them back on his feet. "That's ridiculous. It's dangerously cold out there."

"I know. You don't need to berate me. I've already bawled myself out." He smiled at me as I pulled off his coat. "You know, we just did this. I guess I should have listened to you and stayed in the first place."

I shook my head. "You think?"

"Are you mad? Maybe I shouldn't have come back."

I handed him the quilt. "Yes, I'm mad at you, but only because you could have really gotten hurt. Ever hear of frostbite?"

He grinned at me while I tucked the quilt around him for the second time. "So you're not mad at me for inconveniencing you; you're mad because you care about me?"

I started to answer him when he reached up and put his hand behind my head, pulling me close to him. As he kissed me, a voice in my head yelled at me to stop him—to walk away. But I didn't. After a few seconds I pushed away from him and took a few steps back. "Please, Eric. Don't do that. Not now."

He sat up straighter, still keeping the quilt wrapped tightly around him. I could see he was still shaking, so I grabbed a few more logs and put them on the fire, which had died down to glowing embers.

"Not now?" he repeated softly. "Does that mean there might be a chance in the future?"

As I turned to face him, I realized for the first time that along with my sweats I wore an old, thin T-shirt—with nothing on underneath. I instantly felt exposed and embarrassed. The only thing handy was a blue shawl draped over the back of the rocking chair. I quickly wrapped myself in it. "No, I don't think so. I love Sam, and I intend to see if we can work things out. With God's help, I believe we can. Anyway, I'm going to try as hard as possible to make that happen."

I pulled the rocking chair closer to the couch so I could see him clearly. The look on his face told me I'd hurt him. "Look, Eric. I'm sorry. If Sam wasn't in my life, I'd definitely be interested. I like you. I like you a lot. You're a good man. Any woman would be blessed to have you in her life—but not me. Not now."

He ran his hand through his hair, gazed into the fire, and sighed. "You don't need to be sorry about anything. It's my fault. I know you have strong feelings for Sam." He turned back to look at me, his eyes searching mine. "I apologize. It's just that. . .well, if you were free. . ."

"But I'm not. Not right now. Look," I said, getting to my feet, "let's get you situated for the night. We'll find your truck tomorrow and figure out a way to get it out of the snow. Tonight I want you to stay here, get warm, and stay warm. I don't want any fingers or toes falling off in my living room."

He gazed at me for a moment with the firelight flickering on his face. His expression made it hard for me to breathe. I was definitely attracted to this man, and the immature, fleshly part of me wanted to find out where this relationship could lead. But that still, small voice that spoke to me from the core of my being told me that Sam was the man for me. I knew better than to ignore it.

"You're right," Eric said finally. "Leaving body parts lying around your house is definitely not my intention." He started to get up, but I came over and gently pushed him back down. "I don't want you to leave this couch unless you have to. What do you need?"

He sighed and sank back down. "My insides are freezing. I thought maybe you'd let me make some hot tea or something."

"Or some hot chocolate?" I said with a smile.

He chuckled. "You're reading my mind."

"You stay here. I'll be right back."

"Um. . .Gracie. . ."

I raised my eyebrows. "What is it?"

Even in the low light I could tell he was embarrassed. "It's these pants. They're. . .well. . .I waded through the snow."

Realization dawned on me. "They're wet."

He nodded. "Well, frozen anyway. But I think they're defrosting."

I laughed. "I have some clean sweats downstairs. I'll get them."

Eric's forehead furrowed. "I don't think. . .I mean, you're so tiny. I doubt. . ."

"Don't worry. They're an old pair that used to belong to my dad. I kept stealing them because they're so comfortable. He finally gave them to me. He's larger than you are. They'll fit perfectly."

He sighed with obvious relief. "Thank you. I'm really cold."

"Follow me. You need to get out of those wet things. I'll bring you a clean sweatshirt, too."

I showed him the bathroom, ran down the stairs, and got the sweats and one of the extra-large sweatshirts I liked to sleep in. I found another one and pulled it over my T-shirt, leaving the shawl on top of the clothes basket. When I got upstairs, I knocked on the bathroom door and handed the clothes to him when he stuck his hand out.

While he changed, I made more hot chocolate. My fingers shook as I poured the milk. I'd kissed Eric. Should I tell Sam, or should I keep quiet? We weren't actually engaged, nor had we promised not to date other people. Somehow it was just assumed. But was that fair? I banged the cups down on the counter when I realized I was arguing with myself. I felt tired, confused, and guilty. Tomorrow would be soon enough to sort this all out. I couldn't think straight tonight. I heard Eric leave the bathroom and go back into the living room. I hoped the couch would be comfortable. There were two more bedrooms upstairs. One that had belonged to my uncle and another one that was my father's when he was a boy. I had no intention of offering either one to Eric. I couldn't possibly sleep with him in an adjoining room. Even putting him up on the couch bordered on being inappropriate. Unfortunately, there wasn't any other choice. Eric's truck was out of the picture, and my car was still in town. Not that my Bug had a chance of making it through the huge snowdrifts the wind had created. The only other mode of transportation within a reasonable distance was Zebediah. I was pretty sure he wouldn't take kindly to being hauled out into the middle of a snowstorm. Of course, Eric probably wouldn't be too thrilled either to be stuck on the backside of an old horse in weather like this. Even though our situation wasn't funny, the image that popped into my mind made me giggle.

I stared out the window toward the trees where I'd seen the light the night before. It felt more like a month ago. I'd been so upset. Now the whole thing seemed almost unimportant.

I waited until the cocoa was ready and took it to Eric. I was a little disappointed to find out that he looked better in my sweats and sweatshirt than I did.

"Didn't you make yourself some?" he asked after taking a sip.

"No. I really don't need any more sugar tonight. However, I definitely need some sleep. If you have everything you need, I think I'll head to bed."

"I'm fine, Gracie," he said, smiling. "I'm warm, comfortable, and exhausted. I'm sure I'll sleep like a baby." His gaze swung around the room. "This is quite a house. Sure has a lot of character."

"If by character you mean it's old and needs a lot of work, you're right. It's been in my family a long time."

"I can tell. It must be difficult for a woman alone. Being responsible for a house like this, I mean."

"Yes, it is." I started to mention that Sam did most of the work, but I choked the words back. It suddenly occurred to me that if something happened to Sam and me, I would have to face taking care of the house and property by myself. The thought shook me. "Well, think I'll get myself upstairs. You know where the kitchen is if you're hungry or thirsty." I pointed to the wood bin. "If the fire gets low again, just toss a couple of logs on it. You should be fine."

As if to emphasize my words, a big gust of wind shook the house. I glanced out the window to see the snow being driven almost sideways.

"Thanks, Gracie," Eric said, yawning. "If I sleep too long in the morning, will you wake me up? I'll need to find someone to pull my truck out of the ditch."

"Sure. With all the farmers around here, we shouldn't have too much trouble locating someone with a tractor." Sam had a tractor, but I had no intention of asking him for help.

"That's great. Good night."

"Good night, Eric." I checked the bathroom and found Eric's wet clothes lying on the edge of the tub. I grabbed some hangers and hung them up. If they weren't dry in the morning, I'd toss them in the dryer downstairs. Hopefully that wouldn't trip the breaker. Sam's warning about not putting a lot of stress on the electricity flicked through my thoughts. Trapped in a blizzard without electricity wasn't on my list of things I wanted to experience.

I went upstairs, crawled into bed once again, and lay there staring up at the ceiling. Eventually I fell asleep, the winter wind pounding the house with its fury.

I dreamed I was lost in the woods. Every time I thought I'd found my way out, snow covered my path. I could hear Sam calling my name, but I couldn't respond. For some reason no sound would come out of my mouth. I wanted him to find me—to rescue me. His voice got stronger and louder. I knew he was close. If only I could call out loud enough. . .

"Gracie? Gracie, are you awake?"

I opened my eyes. Daylight. I sat up and found Eric standing over me.

"I'm sorry to wake you," he said. "But the power's out. It's probably my fault. I put my clothes in the dryer downstairs and poof. Everything went off. I flipped all the breaker switches, but nothing happened. I thought you'd want to know."

I ran my hand through my messy bed hair and tried to focus. "No, you did the right thing. If you'll give me a minute, I'll come down. Maybe I can get it going."

He nodded and left the room. Stupid dryer. I should have told him not to use it while my space heater was on, but it hadn't occurred to me he'd take it upon himself to dry his clothes. Probably trying to save me the trouble. I certainly couldn't be upset with him.

I closed the bedroom door and changed into jeans and a sweater. Then I checked the heater. Sure enough, it wasn't working. The upstairs would be an icebox before long. I hurried downstairs and found Eric sitting at the kitchen table, still wearing my clothes.

"I made coffee. I see you do it the old-fashioned way." My aluminum coffeepot sat on one of the burners. Good thing the stove was gas. An oil lamp burned on the table. The sun was up, but the clouds and snow kept much light from filtering in.

"Thanks. I'll take a look at the breaker box, and then I'll make us some breakfast." I grabbed a flashlight from under the sink and headed downstairs. Eric had removed his clothes from the inside of the dryer. They lay on the top. I felt them. They were still pretty damp. We'd have to dry them in front of the fire. I had no intention of restarting the dryer if I got the electricity back on.

I shone the light from the flashlight against the far wall. The door to the breaker box was still open. I checked all the breakers. They seemed to be okay. Sam had taped a list of the different switches and what they were for on the wall next to the box. Not all of the switches had actually been installed yet, though. There were only three. I flipped them all. Nothing. I waited a few minutes and tried again. Still nothing. With a sigh I gave up, grabbed Eric's clothes and some hangers, and tramped back up the stairs.

As I approached the first floor, I heard voices. With a sinking feeling I jogged up the rest of the way and entered the living room.

Eric held my front door open, and Sam stood on the porch, looking daggers at him.

SEVEN

The three of us stared at each other for what seemed like an eternity. In truth, it couldn't have been more than a few seconds. I suppose the correct reaction would have been for me to begin explaining the situation to Sam as quickly as I could. But that isn't what happened. For some reason, the absurdity of our circumstances struck me as incredibly funny, and I began to laugh. Not laugh as in "tee-hee," a ladylike giggle. I mean full-scale, stomach-holding, tears-down-the-cheeks guffawing. I tried to stop, but I couldn't. Sam and Eric both looked at me like I'd lost my mind. And I wondered it myself. Needless to say, neither one of them appeared to find the situation the least bit humorous.

"Sam, it's not what you think," Eric said, keeping a wary eye on me. I'd sunk into the couch, trying hard to control myself. I'd moved past the maniacal cackling that had kicked off this odd episode, and I'd started making little explosive noises created by laughter combined with weird hiccups that forced their way past my tightly locked lips.

"I think it's exactly what I think," Sam snarled. "Where's your truck? And where's Grace's car?"

Eric quickly explained the entire thing, from dinner at Mary's to the reason he'd stayed the night. He specifically detailed exactly where he'd slept—on the couch. As he talked, Sam's frown only deepened. Finally he held his hand up in front of Eric's face.

"Okay, that's it. Get your clothes. I'll take you to your truck. If it won't start, we'll figure out what to do from there." He pointed at me. "You stay here. I'll be back." With that, he turned and walked back to his truck.

Eric looked at me, his eyes wide. "Are you okay?"

His question sent me into another spasm of giggles. I tried to say something but couldn't. Finally I nodded enthusiastically. It was the best I could do. Eric seemed to be evaluating me, probably trying to gauge the level of my nervous breakdown. Then he quietly left the room to change into his clothes and face the angry man who awaited him outside.

While he was in the bathroom, I began to get some control back and tried to figure out why I'd acted so crazy. Yesterday I had two men interested in me. Today, even Snickle had deserted me. He peeked out from underneath a chair, his eyes as big as Eric's had been. For some reason, knowing I'd scared him with my behavior finally snapped me out of it. It took some coaxing, but I finally got him to come out. I was petting him when Eric came back into the room.

"Are you sure you're okay?" he asked.

"I really am," I said sheepishly. "I don't know what came over me. I'm so sorry. You must think I'm deranged."

He smiled tentatively. "Maybe a little."

"It's really not the least bit funny. I think it's all

the pressure of the last couple of days. I guess I just reached the end of my patience with everything. Sam included."

Eric slid his damp coat on. He would be uncomfortable for a while, and I felt bad for him. "Listen, Gracie," he said, wincing slightly, "this is completely inappropriate, I know. But if things between you and Sam don't work out. . ."

"To be honest, Eric, right now, I can't think that far ahead. My ridiculous reaction just proves I need some time to myself. When the roads are passable, I might drive home to Nebraska and stay with my folks for a while. I don't seem to be accomplishing anything here."

He frowned. "But you'll come back, right?"

"I don't know. Maybe. Maybe not." I looked around the room. "I'd need to sell this place so I'd have something to live on for a while. I guess I can find someone in Harmony who'd be interested. . . ."

Eric put his hand on the doorknob. "Before you try to sell this house, let me know first, okay? I might be able to help you."

"Okay. I will. Promise. Now you'd better get out there. I don't think either one of us wants Sam to come back."

"That's an understatement." He gave me a rather sickly smile. "And if no one ever hears from me again, will you please tell my family what happened?"

"I think you're safe. Sam would have to get rid of both of us."

He chuckled and opened the door. But before he stepped out onto the front porch, he paused and looked back at me. "Thanks, Gracie. I know this sounds ridiculous, but I had a really good time last night. And it was because I spent it with you."

After the door closed, I sat on the couch for a while, thinking. It seemed pretty clear that Sam and I were finished. If he hadn't trusted me before, there was no hope he'd believe the truth now. My mind kept wandering back to the first time I'd come to Harmony. Sam and I had developed feelings for each other so quickly. In retrospect, our relationship must have been built on emotion—not day-in, day-out reality. Neither one of us was perfect, and we obviously didn't have the kind of bond that can overcome challenges. Unfortunately, life is full of challenges. My previous hysterical response turned to tears of frustration. Eventually I cried myself to sleep. I awoke to the sound of a male voice. I let loose with a small scream before I realized it was Sam.

"H–how did you get in?" I gently pushed Snickle off my lap and sat up.

"The door was unlocked."

I tried to pat my hair into place, wondering why I should even care what I looked like. Sam had obviously come to tell me we were through.

"What happened to Eric?" I shivered from the cold and wrapped the quilt around me. The fire in the fireplace was low, and the house was freezing.

"I took him to his truck and pulled him out of the ditch. He's on his way to Council Grove."

"Good. I'm glad he's okay. You didn't. . . I mean, he's not. . ."

"Did I beat him up? Is he injured?" Sam shook his head. "No. He's fine."

"Good. Thank you." I stared up at him. "Nothing

happened, you know. Everything was absolutely innocent. I know you don't believe that, but I want to say it anyway, just because it's true." I gave him a moment to respond. When he didn't, I pointed my finger at him. "Why don't you just say what you have to say? I already know what's coming. Let's just get it over with, okay?"

Sam brushed back the bangs that hung down over his stormy gray eyes. Then he sat down in the chair across from me. Snickle promptly jumped off my lap and went to his. Disloyal cat.

"Okay. Here goes." He began stroking Snickle, not looking at me. "I've been a stupid fool. I should have told you about my mother from the beginning. But you need to understand that I never set out to lie to you. Sweetie and I have been telling people my mother is dead for a long time. Not because we wanted to deceive anyone, really. Just because it saves a lot of questions and pain. Honestly, it never occurred to me to tell you. I guess because I thought I'd dealt with it and it wasn't important to me anymore." He laughed harshly. "I seem to have been wrong about that." He finally swung his gaze back to me. "When you showed me that note, I don't know, it brought it all back. The abandonment. The confusion. The hurt. It had nothing to do with you, Gracie. You thought I was afraid you'd done the same thing my mother had—abandoned her child. But that's not it. It has to do with finally facing how angry I've been at my mom for not trying to find another way. I know she thought she was doing the best thing for me, and I'm grateful to Sweetie for the life she's given me. But I loved my mother. I believe we could have found a way to deal with her problems together."

"I'm sorry, Sam. You've always acted as if losing your mother didn't bother you that much anymore. But of course, I didn't know the whole story."

He shrugged. "Hey, I'm as surprised by my response as you are. Even more. I thought it was all behind me, too."

"So where does this leave you and me?"

"You mean how do I feel about finding you and Eric here? Knowing he spent the night and seeing him in your clothes?"

I started to explain, but he stopped me.

"I don't want to hear it, Gracie. Eric tried to tell me the whole story again in the car. I told him to be quiet or I'd kick him out and leave him stranded in the snow."

"So we can't talk about it? Are we finished? It's over? I mean, we're over?" Even though I'd already suspected it, the reality hit me with a finality that made my heart feel as if it would break.

Sam rose from his chair and came over to where I sat sobbing. He reached for my hands and held them. "No, Grace. That's not what I meant. I mean you don't need to explain last night. I know nothing happened. Eric got stuck here, and you gave him a place to stay. That's it." He let go of one of my hands and pushed back the hair from my face. "You silly girl," he said, a tear escaping his eye, "when you started laughing like that, I realized two things. How much stress I've put you under, and how ridiculous it was to think you and Eric were. . .involved." He took my face in his hands. "I know you, Grace. I know your heart. I was stupid to ever let anything come between us. And you have my word it will never happen again. Never. If you can forgive me for the mistakes I've made, then. . ."

Before he could finish, I kissed him. Then I cried a little. And then I kissed him again.

"I take it that means I'm forgiven," he said with a crooked smile.

I laid my head on his chest and cried until I couldn't cry anymore. Except this time it was from relief.

"Why don't you get cleaned up?" he said softly. "I'm going to see if I can get your electricity back on. Then we'll attempt to get your car back here."

I sat up, still sniffling. "I doubt we'll even be able to find it."

"It's stopped snowing, and everyone's trying to dig out. But if we decide to let the car sit for a while, I'll take you wherever you need to go, okay?"

"Okay." I got up and started toward the bathroom.

"Grace?" Sam called out.

I turned around and found him standing near the couch, still smiling at me. "I love you."

"I love you, too," I choked out. Then I fled to the bathroom before another round of tears began. When I closed the door, the room was pretty dark. I raised the window shade. Sure enough, the snow had come to an end. The world was covered in glistening white. The beauty outside my window certainly wasn't evident inside my bathroom. I looked in the mirror and was horrified to find a disheveled woman with a runny red nose, pink eyes, and hair that looked like it hadn't been brushed anytime during the current century. Besides the way I looked, my behavior over the last few hours had left me feeling drained. I'd gotten nervous giggles before—most people have. But launching into bizarre and uncontrolled hilarity was a new experience. Funny, though. I felt better now. Not just because Sam and I were okay, but because I felt released from the tension that had held me in its grip since I'd come back to Harmony.

I closed my eyes and prayed quietly. "Lord, I don't know if You sent the laughter—or the tears. But I feel better. Allowing myself to worry so much isn't much of a testament to my faith in You. I'm sorry. I truly believe You led me to this place, so I intend to trust You to complete what You started. I'll do a better job of casting my care—if You'll help me. Show me what You want me to see through everything that's happened. I know You love Harmony and the people who live here. Let Your perfect will be done. And use me to bring that about. Thank You."

I took a deep breath and shook myself. Like Sweetie said, God doesn't send the storm, but without faith in Him and in His goodness, I would certainly end up tossed around. . .and wet.

After attempting to fix my makeup and hair, I finally felt presentable enough to face Sam. As I left the bathroom, the light suddenly flickered on. I opened the door to the stairs and yelled, "The lights are back!"

"Great!" Sam hollered. "Let me work on this switch just a few more minutes. I want to make sure the connection is tight."

"Okay." I decided to run upstairs and change my clothes. When I came downstairs he was standing in the kitchen, drinking a glass of milk.

"Say, I'm starving," he said. "You have anything here to eat?"

"Well, like I told you, I'm not a great cook, but I can rustle up some bacon and eggs."

"Sounds wonderful. If you'll do that, I'll make the coffee."

"It's a deal."

The chilly kitchen warmed up quickly, and before long we were eating. We talked about the snow and how Buddy had jumped around in it as if it had been sent just for him to play in.

"He's not that tall," Sam said, chuckling. "He almost disappeared."

Sam told me that Sweetie had gone out first thing in the morning to clear the driveway as if the storm had been a personal attack on her. By the time we finished, I felt like things were almost back to normal between Sam and me. I knew we needed to talk more about what had happened, but I wasn't quite ready to do that yet, and it appeared that Sam felt the same way. Right now, laughing and talking together felt good. Like medicine to my bruised soul.

Finally we decided it was time to brave the outdoors. Sam's truck started right away. I wanted to make a comment about the old vehicle being more dependable than Eric's Hummer, but I kept my mouth shut. The less said about Eric the better. At least his huge truck had made some deep tracks we could use to get out of the driveway. Once we got to Faith Street, I realized the road was in pretty good condition.

"This isn't so bad," I remarked.

"I stuck a plow on the tractor and went up and down between my house and Ida's," Sam said. "See the snow piled up on the side of the road? That was on the street before I moved it."

"Shouldn't we check on Ida before we go into town? I'd like to know she's all right."

"Already did that. Brought some wood in for her fire and fed Zebediah. Shoveled most of the snow out of his stable and fired up the old woodstove in there so he'd be warm."

"Wow. You have been busy. What time did you get up this morning?"

He shook his head. "Way too early. I'm tired. But at least I'm not hungry now."

I smiled. "Well, if you're happy eating breakfast all day, I'd be glad to cook for you anytime."

He grinned. "Hey, I'll just keep Sweetie nearby. That way there's no pressure on you."

"You're a funny, funny man."

"I know."

I scooted up closer to him, and not just for warmth. We turned onto Main Street. That road was pretty snow packed. We bounced and slid, almost getting stuck several times. Finally we pulled into Harmony. The town sat silently, no one outside. However, several cars were parked on the street. Most of them still covered with snow. I saw Gabe and Sarah's buggy in front of their store.

"Gabe and Sarah are in town?"

"Doesn't look like they went anywhere. Probably stayed the night in the shop rather than try to get home in the storm."

"I'd like to check on them."

Sam nodded. "You go ahead. I'm going to see if I can dig your car out."

I glanced over to see my poor little Bug almost completely covered. I balled up my fist and lightly punched Sam on the arm. "Slug Bug."

He shook his head and laughed. "Boy, I'm going to be sorry I told you about that game, aren't I?"

"You betcha."

I got out of the truck and waded through the snow toward the candle shop. Gabe and Sarah's horse had been unhooked from the buggy. He'd probably been moved to a nearby stable, out of the cold and snow. When I opened the front door, a wonderful aroma greeted me. Sarah sat in a chair near the front counter. She smiled when she saw me. "Gracie! I'm so happy you're home."

I hugged her. "Me, too. Did you get stuck here last night?"

She grabbed my hand. "Yes. The snow was too much for Molasses."

I laughed. "Your horse's name is Molasses?"

She winked at me and lowered her voice to a whisper. "Papa says she's as slow as molasses but just as sweet. Sometimes I think he worries more about that horse than he does me."

"I doubt that's true. By the way, where is he?"

"Where is who?" a deep voice bellowed from behind me. I turned around to find Gabe standing in the doorway that separates the store from the workroom. "Is that Gracie Temple? It's been so long, I almost forgot what you looked like."

My relationship with Sarah's father had improved greatly since we first met, but I had no plans to hug him. Something like that could set us back to where we started. I was really glad to see him, though.

"Well, you weren't missing much. I saw you at the meeting, but maybe you didn't see me. I sat in the front."

Gabe walked over to the counter next to Sarah and put the candle he held in his hand on the glass top. "I guess I did spot you sitting next to Ida Turnbauer." His frown made it clear something bothered him.

"Did you hear what she had to say?"

He nodded, and the lines in his face deepened. "Yes, I did."

Sarah and I glanced at each other. She rolled her eyes.

"You didn't agree with her?" I asked.

"Oh, I agreed with her. I just don't think it was proper for her to speak."

Even though I like Gabe, I could feel my blood pressure ratchet up a notch. "Because she's a woman?"

He raised his eyebrows and stared at me with amusement. "No, not because she's a woman, although I do believe a man should speak in a situation like that if one is available. But Ida is a widow. She has no man to intercede for her."

I wanted to go off on a mini tangent and let him know that the only time a man would ever talk for me would happen after I completely lost the power of speech, but I reined myself in. "So you're not upset because she's a woman. So what are you upset about?"

"I don't think Mennonites should get involved in disputes that have to do with the governing of a town. It isn't our place."

"But this isn't about governing anything. It's about building something that will benefit the town."

He raised his eyebrows again. "And how will this wonderful new development benefit me?"

I swung my hand around the room. "People will come here to buy candles. To buy Sarah's stationery and note cards. You'll make money."

He crossed his arms over his chest. "Money. That's what it always comes down to, isn't it. Man's greedy desire for money."

I sighed. Gabe and I had been over this ground many times before. Unfortunately, neither one of us intended to budge.

"Money is the root of all—," he started.

I shook my finger at him. "Not money. The *love* of money. You know that, Gabe. We've been over and over this. Sometimes I think you—"

"Stop that right now," Sarah said sharply. "You two do this every time you get together. If I didn't know how much you liked each other. . ."

"Now who said I liked this skinny little red-headed girl?" Gabe growled, shooting me his fiercest expression.

"You did, Papa," Sarah said softly. "You said Gracie reminded you of your sister, Abigail. You said—"

"That's enough," Gabe barked. His expression softened as he gazed at his beautiful daughter. "I see I can't say anything to you in confidence ever again. You love to tell all my secrets."

"How you feel about Gracie isn't any secret." She fastened her large, dark-chocolate brown eyes on me. "And I know you like Papa. Isn't that right, Gracie?"

"I'm sure I have no idea what you're talking about," I quipped, grinning at Gabe.

He shook his head and held up the candle he'd brought with him into the room. "Now that my daughter has restored peace between us, I'd like to show you one of my newest creations."

I moved over to where he stood behind the

counter and examined the soft buttercream-colored candle he referred to. "This isn't your hay candle, I hope. I heard it smelled like—"

"It would be advantageous for you to stop right there," he said. "This town. You make one small mistake and you never hear the end of it."

Sarah laughed. It was a light, airy sound that made me feel good. "Oh my. It took us a week to get the smell out. I had no idea a little candle could stink that badly."

"Well, I think I can safely say this candle won't cause the same reaction." He held it up near my nose. "What do you think of this?"

I breathed deeply. "Why, it's honeysuckle. Oh Gabe. It's perfect. Beautiful."

"Is it good enough for you to forget all about the hay-scented candle?"

"Actually, yes. And I intended to get quite a bit of traction out of that."

"I'm sure you did." Gabe rolled the candle around in his hands for several seconds before putting it down. He cleared his throat. "You said you love the smell of honeysuckle. That you would miss it in the winter."

"Yes, I did. You didn't. I mean you didn't. . ."

"Make this candle for you?" Sarah finished gently. "Yes. Yes, he did. And he named the scent Honeysuckle Grace."

"You did that for me?" My words came out in a whisper as I forced back tears. This man had been so harsh and unyielding when I'd first met him. He kept Sarah with him at all times, never allowing her out of his sight. And he had no love or trust for any human being. But over the past several months, he'd changed. And now he'd made me a candle. It was too much, and tears coursed down my cheeks.

Gabe looked horrified. "My goodness, girl. It's just a candle."

Sarah came around from the other side of the counter and put her arms around me. "Gracie, is something wrong?"

I clung to her. "It's just. . .it's just that things have been so messed up since I got back. I almost forgot how much this town means to me." I looked past Sarah's shoulder at her father. "How much everyone here means to me."

At that moment the shop's front door opened, and Sam came inside to find me bawling. "For crying out loud, it's only been a few minutes. What happened?"

I tried to explain but couldn't get the words out. Sarah patiently tried to tell him my tears were about the candle, but Sam only looked more confused. He shook his head. "I don't know. Earlier today she was laughing like a maniac. Then she bawled like a baby. Now she's at it again. I guess I just don't understand women at all."

"This is why men must band together," Gabe said with a sigh. "We need to have rational people around us."

I let go of Sarah. "You two stop it," I said sharply. "I just thought the candle was a sweet gesture. Since I got back, I haven't had too many *sweet* moments."

Sam came over and put his arm around me. "I guess that's true. I'll tell you what. From here on out I will shower you with sweet moments. Would that make you feel better?"

"I can't promise anything"—I sniffed—"but it's a good start."

"Can I change the subject now, or are you going to start blubbering again?" Gabe asked. "I have something I want to talk to Sam about."

I shrugged. "Depends on what you say."

Gabe looked at me carefully. "I'm not sure the odds are good enough. . . ."

I pushed Sam away. "Honestly, change the subject, I don't care." I grabbed Sarah's arm. "I want to see what you've been doing since I left. Will you show me?"

Sarah nodded enthusiastically. "I have a worktable set up in back. Come with me."

I followed her to the back room, leaving Sam and Gabe to their conversation. The room behind the curtain was warm and cozy. A fire burned in a big potbellied stove that sat in the middle of the space. A long workbench sat against one wall where candles cooled in their various molds. The aromas were intoxicating. Homemade curtains covered the windows, the fabric decorated with small flowers and finished with lace. Sarah's touch was evident. She led me to a corner of the room where a wooden table had been set up for her wood-block printing projects. Several blocks lined the back of the table. Two rollers sat next to them as well as a couple of small paint trays. Sarah reached across the table to some shelves that had been attached to the wall. "Papa made these cubbies for me so I could stack my paper and cards here." She pointed to one section. "This is all my blank paper and card stock. And over here," she said, moving her finger to the right, "is all my finished work." She motioned to me to follow her over to another table a few feet away.

"And this is where everything dries. I wanted to show you three new patterns I've designed." She pointed to a lovely sheet of stationery with a flowering vine that crept up one side. "It's a passion flower," she said softly. "I've only seen it in pictures, but it's really beautiful, isn't it?"

The dark blue color of the flowers intermingled with the green vines. The design was set against a cream-colored paper. The effect was striking. "It's beautiful, Sarah. I love it."

She smiled and pointed me to the next row of drying paper. "And I'm certain you know what this is." The light yellow paper was edged with honeysuckle.

"I'm sure I don't have to tell you how much I like this," I said. "You won't keep much of it in the store."

We looked at the third design, which was a combination of deep red and purple flowers against a dark blue background. The paper itself was light blue. Sarah had outlined the flowers in a way that made them seem three-dimensional. "This must have taken hours to design and print," I said. "It's absolutely incredible. Put me down for the first order."

She laughed. "I already have twelve orders. Papa brought several people back here so he could show them my work."

I hugged her arm. "That's wonderful. I'm really not surprised, though."

Sarah pointed toward a small table with two chairs. "Why don't we sit down for a minute? I'd like to talk to you if you don't mind."

"Of course I don't mind. You're my friend."

Sarah sat across from me, folding her long blue dress under her. Her dark hair matched the black apron over her dress. White ribbons on the sides of her prayer covering touched her smooth, unblemished skin. Her natural beauty had no need of makeup. I envied her in this respect. Although I didn't use much makeup myself, I was certainly too insecure to go out in public au naturel.

"This is where Papa and I have our lunch," she said. "Sometimes we go to Mary's, but Papa doesn't like to spend money in restaurants."

That sounded like Gabe. "Where did you and your father sleep last night?" I looked around the room. There didn't seem to be any place to bed down.

"Oh, Papa brought the blankets in from the carriage. We always carry some in the winter. And John Keystone brought us a couple of cots he keeps in his shop. When he first moved here, he actually lived in the back of his store for a while. Now he has a nice little house outside of town. Papa and I were quite comfortable." She flushed at the mention of John's name.

"I saw John briefly when I got into town. He seemed to be doing well."

She cast her eyes down and wouldn't look at me. "Oh? I'm pleased to hear that."

I didn't say anything. Sarah had never confided in me about their relationship. Not directly anyway.

She raised her head and looked toward the door to the shop. "I—I wonder if I could talk to you, Gracie. About something. . .personal." She swung her large, doelike eyes back to me. "I haven't really had any friends for such a long time. Papa has kept me away from everyone except the people in our small church group for the past several years. He's afraid I'll leave him—like my mother did." She reached up to wipe away a tear that slid down her cheek. "I could never cause my father that kind of pain. I know how much it hurt him. I wonder if being abandoned by the person you love isn't the worst thing that can happen to a person." She let out a deep sigh. "You know, I've wondered for many years if she left because of me. Perhaps I was too much trouble. It hurts me to think that might be the reason." She gave me a sad smile. "I realize I don't know much about the world. I'm sure there are things much worse that people must bear."

I reached over and put my hand on hers. "There may be," I acknowledged. "But losing a parent is right there at the top." I squeezed her hand. "Your mother left because she was unhappy with herself, Sarah. Not with you. Perhaps not even with Gabe. She may have gone away with another man, but there was something wrong inside her. A healthy person doesn't walk away from their family. You should never, ever blame yourself for her choices."

"It's hard not to. In all these years, I've never heard a word from her. If she cared about me, I would think she would contact me, don't you?"

I didn't know how to answer the beautiful Mennonite girl so full of grace, dignity, kindness, and pain. I thought carefully. At that moment, the idea of having about ten minutes alone in a room with her so-called mother for some real "come to Jesus" justice sounded very appealing. But that probably wouldn't set well with someone like Sarah who believed in peaceful solutions. "I have no idea why you haven't heard from her. But wondering about things you can't control or situations you have no direct knowledge of is useless."

I smiled at her. "There is one thing I do know. Missing out on being with you should be the greatest regret of her life. You're a wonderful person. Any mother would be proud to have you for a daughter."

Another tear coursed down her face. "Oh thank you, Gracie. You're so kind. And such a dear friend." She hesitated and looked toward the door again. "I'm so torn. I need some advice, and you're the only person I feel safe enough to confide in."

I knew where this was going, and to be honest, I wanted to get up and run away. Instead I gave her a smile of encouragement.

"There's a. . .situation," she said, almost whispering. "And I'm afraid Papa will be very upset if I tell him about it." She shook her head. "He was so angry for so many years. I'm afraid. Afraid if I'm honest with him, life will go back to the way it was before. When he had nothing to do with others, and I had to stay inside all the time." She stared deeply into my eyes. "I can't cause him more pain, Gracie. Yet I can't continue to deceive him either. I don't know what to do." She took a deep breath. "You see, I am in love. I am in love with John Keystone."

From behind us came a strangled sound—more of a groan, really. Sarah's face turned deathly white. I turned around to find Gabe standing in the doorway, his expression one of incredible rage.

EIGHT

No one moved for several seconds. Then Sarah stood up. "Papa. . . ," she whispered. She swayed suddenly, and I jumped up to catch her before she fell. I lowered her gently to the floor and put her head on my lap. Gabe seemed rooted to his spot by the door.

As I called Sarah's name and stroked her cheek, Sam came into the room. He had to gently push Gabe out of the way. "What in the world?" he said when he spotted Sarah and me. "Is she okay?" he asked as he hurried to my side. "Is she sick?"

I shook my head at him. "No. She's not sick. She's afraid."

Sam raised his eyebrows in surprise. "Afraid. Afraid of what?"

I met Gabe's fixed glare. "Of her father. This poor girl is afraid of her father."

Sam stared at Gabe, too. "Gabe. I don't understand. What's going on?"

Gabe looked back and forth between the two of us. "What's going on is that I allowed my daughter to come in contact with the world," he snapped. "I see I have made a terrible mistake."

I pulled Sam down to the floor and transferred

the unconscious girl to his arms. Then I rose to my feet and approached her furious father. "Listen to me, Gabriel Ketterling. Sarah is terrified of hurting you. She loves you more than anything in the world. She certainly didn't set out to cause you pain. Please don't turn this into something that will create even more destruction." I tried to take his arm, but he pulled away from me.

"What part did you have in this?" he railed at me. "Did you encourage her to chase after that. . .that ungodly man?"

"Gabe," I said as soothingly as I could. "Sarah just now told me about her feelings for John. You heard her."

"So you had no idea this betrayal was going on behind my back?"

"Betrayal? What are you talking about? Sarah didn't betray you. This isn't about you. It's about her—and John."

He took one step closer to me and peered directly into my face. "I asked you a question, Grace Temple. Did you know about this?"

I looked back at Sam, who still held Sarah. She had begun to moan and blink her eyes. There was no way out. I had to tell the truth. I turned to meet Gabe's eyes with mine. "I suspected it, Gabe."

He took a couple of steps away from the door. "I want you to leave. Now. You and your boyfriend. And you're not to ever come around here again. Ever. And let me make this very clear so you understand me." His whole demeanor was menacing. "You are never to see my daughter again. I mean it."

"Papa. Papa, please. . ." Sarah's plaintive wail shook me. She struggled to get to her feet with Sam holding her tightly. "This is all my fault. Gracie had nothing to do with it. Please don't take it out on her."

"Take your hands off her," Gabe shouted at Sam. "And follow your girlfriend out of my shop. And out of my life." He rushed over to Sarah and pulled her out of Sam's arms. She almost tripped and fell, but Gabe caught her and guided her over to the table, helping her back into her chair. Sarah seemed helpless against her father's control over her.

Sam stood next to me. "Let's talk about this," he said to the enraged man. "You're being irrational. We're your friends. You're important to us. And Sarah is an adult. She has the right to make her own choices."

Gabe let go of Sarah and advanced toward us. For a moment I was afraid he intended to hit Sam, but Sam held his ground and refused to be intimidated. I prayed there wouldn't be a fight. Gabe's anger showed no sign of the passivity his faith embraced. Would physical violence be next? He stopped about two feet away from us, his face twisted with contempt.

"I don't need your advice on anything. My daughter and I are not your business. Not anymore. And we were never friends. Friends don't bring pollution into your life." He focused his attention on me. "If you'd been my friend, you would have told me about John Keystone. You wouldn't have allowed that. . .that disgusting heathen to put his hands on my daughter!"

His last few words were screamed at us. Sam took my arm and began to pull me out of the room. At first my concern for Sarah made me fight him, but I could see that Gabe was coming unglued. Sobbing, Sarah waved at us to go. I decided to leave for her benefit, but not before I made sure of one last thing.

I pointed my finger at Gabe. "I want you to know that I will be checking up on Sarah whether you like it or not. If you lay one hand on her, so help me. . ."

With that, Sam pulled me from the room. We got our coats and made our way out the front door. I couldn't help but notice the Honeysuckle Grace candle still sitting on the counter. Emotion hit me like a punch in the gut as we stepped outside and closed the door behind us. The snow that covered Harmony sparkled like millions of little diamonds. But the hurt in my heart dulled the beauty before me. I'd lost my friend. No, I'd just lost two friends.

"We've got to warn John," I said to Sam. "He needs to know what's coming."

He shook his head in disgust. "Great. All we need is for him to go tearing in there to save Sarah." He put his arm around me. "Are you okay?"

"Yes, I'm fine. I'm just worried about Sarah. And Gabe, too."

He sighed. "You want to tell me what happened? I mean, I realize your suspicions about John and Sarah turned out to be correct. But what set Gabe off?"

"Sarah told me she loves John. She'd never told anyone before. Wanted someone to confide in. Wonderful result, huh? The first time she shares her heart, Gabe goes crazy and bans her from ever talking to anyone again."

"He didn't actually tell her she couldn't talk to anyone."

I stamped my foot in frustration. "I know that. I'm just trying to make a point."

He hugged me. "I know. Sorry. Let's see if John is in his store."

We hurried as quickly as we could through the snow to John's, but the windows were dark, the door locked. "He must have made it home," Sam said. "Good thing. It would be best if he stayed out of town until Gabe calms down."

"Calms down? I don't think that's going to happen anytime soon. Let's check Mary's. If he's not there, we need to call him."

"I agree. How about a hot cup of coffee? I'll use Mary's phone."

We walked across the snow-covered street to the restaurant. Sure enough, it was open. I wondered if Mary had spent the night in town, too. When we stepped inside, it was obvious several Harmony residents hadn't made it home. Many of them were wearing the same clothes they'd had on the night before. The Crandalls sat together at a table against the back wall. Cora waved and smiled as I approached their table.

"Have you all been here the whole night?" I asked.

Amos nodded. "Our place is too far away, and our car is too old to make it through that much snow. So Mary put us up. Some of us slept in booths, and the rest of us slept on the floor. Ruth and Carol gave us blankets to keep us warm."

Cora laughed. "Ruth's beautiful quilts were certainly more comfortable than Paul and Carol's horse blankets. But we were all warm and overly fed."

As if on cue, Mary came out of the back room with plates of food in her hands. She dropped them off at a nearby table, laughing and joking with the people who sat there. She turned and spotted us. "Hey, you guys back already? This is getting to be a habit."

"Just couldn't stay away, Mary," I said. "I see you have some captive customers."

"Tried to get them to leave, but they kept whining about the snow and the bad roads." She grinned. "Bunch of big babies."

Her comment brought laughter from the assembled "babies."

"You two hungry?"

"Thanks," Sam said, "but we already ate. Maybe we could give you a hand."

"I appreciate the offer, but I've got lots of help taking orders and getting food to the tables." As if on cue, Ruth came out of the kitchen carrying some trays, along with Pastor Jensen and his wife, Wynonna.

"I see what you mean. But if there's anything else I can do. . ."

"Not unless you can cook."

"Unfortunately, it's not one of my strong points. But if Hector can tell me what he needs, I'm more than willing to try."

Mary picked up some dirty plates from one of the tables and cocked her head toward the kitchen. "Follow me. If you can flip pancakes and make toast, it would be a big help."

"I'm going to round up some of the men and see what we can do about getting Main Street cleared," Sam said.

"And maybe you could make that call?"

Sam understood I was talking about John and nodded.

"I'll take care of it." His grim expression made it clear he didn't look forward to telling John about the dramatic scene we'd witnessed between Gabe and Sarah.

Mary looked at us oddly but thankfully didn't ask any questions.

"And while you big men are working to clear the streets, be careful not to run over my car, okay?"

Sam hugged me. "I'll try, but it's so small we might not be able to see it."

He tried to give me a quick kiss, but I pushed away from him. "Sorry, bub. No more of that until I know my Slug Bug is safe."

"I'll do my best, but when a guy can't get a kiss, it throws everything off. Not sure what will happen now."

I gave him a quick shove. "Get out of here. I've got to flip pancakes. That's real work."

Sam grinned at me and waved good-bye. I waved back and followed Mary to the kitchen. I'd never been in the back room and was surprised to see how big it was. A large grill took up most of one wall. Hector was busy pushing a large pile of bacon around with a spatula. Several eggs crackled on the hot grill. He greeted me quickly, but it was obvious his concentration was on the work at hand. On the other side of the kitchen, rows of shelves held all kinds of pots and pans. Nearby, a huge refrigerator hummed away, and a large dishwasher whirred softly as it cleaned the dirty dishes. I noticed a door near the refrigerator and asked Mary where it led.

She put her tray on the counter. "Follow me," she said. She swung the door open to reveal a walk-in freezer full of different kinds of frozen foods. "A lot of what we keep in here is meat. Some folks like to buy a side of beef because it's cheaper, but they don't have anyplace to put it. I let them store it in my freezer as long as I have the room." She pointed to some large chest freezers in the back.

"Wow. I had no idea so much went on back here. You could feed a small army from this place."

She closed the door. "Harmony isn't a big town, and there's not a lot to do. Eating out is special to folks. You'd be surprised how many people come through here in a week."

"I guess I would."

She handed me an apron slung over a nearby chair. "I need you to put this on. And you either need to put your hair in a net or pin it back."

"I've got a scrunchie in my purse. What if I put my hair in a ponytail?"

"That'll work. And you'll have to wash your hands thoroughly." She pointed to a dispenser on the wall. "Hot water. Use lots of soap, and dry thoroughly. Then put on gloves." She pointed to a box of plastic gloves. "You've got to put on fresh gloves if you touch anything new or if the gloves get dirty. And rewash your hands every time."

"Boy, lots of things to remember."

"It's not that bad. We just work hard to keep everyone healthy."

Hector pushed some plates onto a counter next to the grill. "Order up," he said.

"You get ready, and then Hector will tell you everything you need to know. And thanks, Gracie. I appreciate your help."

She grabbed the new plates and left the kitchen. I found my scrunchie, pulled my hair back, thoroughly washed my hands, and put on my gloves. I spent the next two hours following Hector's orders. I flipped pancakes, made toast, held out the plates for him to fill with hot, steaming food, and listened to Hector's stories about growing up in Mexico. The minutes flew by, and I had a wonderful time. I could hardly believe it when Mary told me Sam was looking for me.

"We're all caught up, Gracie. Thanks," she said, smiling. "How'd she do, Hector?"

He laughed and pointed his spatula at Mary. "You should hire this little gal full-time. She did a great job, and she didn't get bored by my stories. *Ella es muy buena trabajadora.*"

"He says you're a very good worker. Seems you've made another fan," Mary said as she held out her hand for my apron. "I guess we'll just have to add Hector to your list of conquests."

There was a tone in her voice that took me by surprise. I looked carefully at her but couldn't detect anything unfriendly in her face. I decided she must be joking and shrugged it off.

I thanked Hector and left the kitchen. The main room had emptied to only a few people. Sam stood near the kitchen door.

"Where'd everyone go?" I asked him.

"We were able to clear enough of Main Street so folks had a chance to get home. 'Course the side streets are still bad, but almost everyone decided to chance it. A few of the guys followed behind some of the cars just to make sure everyone made it home safely."

I looked out the window to see the street definitely looking better. The cleared area was just a little bigger than one lane. "What if two great big vehicles meet each other going opposite directions?"

"Then someone better turn around. Leave it to you to find the fly in the ointment."

"How in the world did you guys accomplish all this?"

He shrugged. "Besides a few of us who have our own snowplows, Joe has a couple of small plows, and Paul keeps one in the storage shed behind his store. It's not in great shape, but it does the job. Boy, it's a lot of work, though." He rubbed the side of his face. "I'm really tired. Do you think we could sit here a bit and grab a sandwich before we head home?"

I had to admit that all that cooking had made me a bit weary as well. And all that food had stirred up my appetite even though we'd had a fairly substantial breakfast. We sat down at a nearby table. I glanced around to see if we were in earshot of anyone else. "What did John say when you called him?"

Sam shook his head. "I couldn't reach him. The phone just rang and rang. Either he's not home or the storm has caused some trouble on the lines."

"Oh Sam. What if he comes to town not knowing what's happened?"

"There's nothing I can do about it, Grace. We'll try him again from my house. Maybe we'll get through."

Just then Mary came out of the kitchen. "I thought you two were leaving."

Sam explained his need for food, and before long we were eating. Sam had a hot roast beef sandwich, but I had a stack of pancakes. Watching those light, puffy rounds of dough brown and sizzle on the grill had given me a real desire for a stack of my own. I wasn't disappointed.

"This is your second breakfast," Sam noted.

"What's for dinner? Cereal?"

I waved my fork at him. "Maybe. What business is it of yours, bub?"

"Absolutely none," he replied with his mouth full of roast beef. "Your dietary dilemma is your own."

"Oh thanks."

Mary walked over to the table with a frown on her face. "Have you heard the weather report?" she asked.

We both shook our heads. She aimed the remote control in her hand toward the small TV mounted on the wall near the counter. A man from the Weather Channel had a big map behind him with a large white and pink mass displayed in the middle of the country. And Kansas was in its path. A few minutes into the broadcast, the weariness in Sam's face turned to concern and he stopped eating. When the forecast was over, Mary lowered the volume.

"Looks like we're in for another round," she said.

"Worse than this one," Sam said. "I'm afraid the work we did on the streets will only last a few more hours before it's completely covered up."

"What do we do?" I asked.

"You all get out of here as soon as possible," Mary said. "I don't mind being an impromptu boardinghouse for one night, but I'm not looking to do it again."

"We need to get the word out," I told them. "What about all the people without TVs? How will they know what's coming?"

Mary smiled. "That's nice of you to think of them, but this isn't our first big storm. The Mennonite people take care of each other. A warning will be passed around faster than you can imagine."

I wanted to feel reassured by her words, but I didn't. "Sam, at least call Abel. Okay?"

"Sure. Can I use the phone again, Mary?" he asked.

"You can use the phone whenever you want. You don't have to ask." She took off toward the kitchen.

Sam went to make the call while I thought about being snowed in at home. With the electricity being so unreliable, was it a good idea? I didn't need to worry. When Sam came back, he told me he'd reached Abel, and sure enough, as Mary had said, the news was already being spread throughout the Mennonite community that a big snow was coming. He assured Sam that everyone would be fine.

"Now that we've taken care of that," Sam said, pulling on his coat, "let's get out of here. I'll take you to your house to get Snickle and some clothes, but you're coming home with me. I don't want to worry about you alone in that old house, not sure if you have electricity. There's some wood for the fire, but not enough to last out a long period if it comes to that."

I breathed a sigh of relief. "Thanks. I was hoping you'd offer."

"I've already called Sweetie to tell her you're coming. She's thrilled." He shook his head. "She comes off like a tough old bird, but she's more tender than most people think. And she loves you, Grace. Very much."

"I know she does, and I love her, too."

He held out my coat. I quickly took a couple more bites of my pancakes then stuck my arms in my coat sleeves and grabbed my purse. Before we left, Sam checked with the few remaining customers, making sure they had a way home or a place to go. When he was satisfied everyone was okay, we left the restaurant.

Sure enough, my Volkswagen was uncovered from its snowy tomb. "Can I drive it home?" I asked. "I really don't want to leave it here."

"Okay. I'll follow behind you."

As I walked toward my car, I noticed Gabe's buggy was gone. "So Gabe and Sarah got out okay," I said. "Did you see them go?"

"Yeah, I sure did. Gabe didn't acknowledge me, and Sarah looked absolutely miserable."

"Can we drive past John's on the way home and tell him what's going on?"

Sam shook his head. "That storm could hit anytime. We just can't. Not now. As soon as it's possible, I'll try to get over to his place."

I didn't like not being able to talk to John about Gabe and Sarah, but it didn't seem like there was much choice. I tried to open my car door but couldn't get the key to turn. Sam fetched some deicer out of his truck and sprayed it into the lock. A few seconds later, I was able to open my door, and soon we were on our way.

Even though Sam and the men had made the main road better, it certainly wasn't ideal. I slipped and slid so much, it felt as if my little car had skate blades instead of tires. I got stuck twice. One time I was able to get myself out; the second time Sam had to help me.

Finally we made it to my house. It didn't take long to pack a few things, but it took a little longer to catch Snickle and put him back in his carrier. Sam and I chased him around the house for at least fifteen minutes before Sam finally trapped him in the bathroom.

As he carried Snickle out, the very offended feline hissed to let us know he wasn't happy to be imprisoned again.

"I hope he doesn't drive Sweetie up the wall," I told Sam as he deposited my cat in his carrier. "Being trapped for a day or two with your aunt when she's unhappy isn't a pleasant prospect."

Sam chuckled as he snapped the carrier door shut. "Around my house, that's pretty much life as usual." He handed the carrier to me while Snickle yowled with unhappiness. "Although I must admit, she's trying to change. Now when she begins to lose her temper or say something nasty about someone, she'll usually catch herself and stop." He grunted. "Makes for some rather quiet moments while she searches for something positive to say. Sometimes she just gives up, goes out on the back porch for a while, and stomps around. 'Course even though the porch is enclosed, it still gets pretty cold out there, so she doesn't stay long."

"Hey, she's trying. That's the most important thing. I respect that."

"You know what? I do, too. I'm proud of her."

"Have you told her?"

He snorted. "No, because then she gets upset and tells me I'm imagining things."

I laughed.

Sam checked around the house to make sure everything that should be off was off and everything that should be on was on, and we left. I felt bad leaving my home once again, but the idea of being snowed in alone, without heat, made me feel even worse.

I watched my house grow smaller in the rearview

window as I drove away. Even though I was excited to be staying once again in Sam's big, beautiful house, I'd grown to love my simpler home with its history and old-fashioned character. I forced myself to focus on the next few days. Maybe the storm wouldn't be as bad as predicted. Maybe I'd be able to go home tomorrow. That prospect made me feel a little better. After some more slipping and sliding, we finally made it to Sam's place. I could see the road up ahead, past the big red house, and wondered just where Eric had gotten stuck. Neither Sam nor I had mentioned him since *the incident*. Of course, Eric would be back to Harmony sooner or later to work on his real estate deal, so at some point, Sam would have to face him. Hopefully things would be peaceful between them.

Sam got out of his truck and came over to my car. He took Snickle out of the backseat and grabbed my suitcase while I got the extra tote bag full of Snickle's "supplies." I giggled when I realized that his "box" would most probably end up on the back porch. Maybe the next time Sweetie got upset, her bout of bad temper would be cut even shorter. Even though I cleaned his box out every day, a litter box doesn't always remind one of springtime flowers.

As we walked through the snow up to the front porch, Sweetie waited to greet us. She grabbed me before I crossed over the threshold.

"I knowed you two would get everything sorted out," she whispered in my ear.

I gave her a quick hug. "Thanks for talking to me about his situation," I said softly. "It really helped."

She glanced toward Sam, who was already to the kitchen door. "Let's keep our little discussion between us, okay? I'm not sure how he'd take my comin' to you like that."

I didn't answer her, but I felt uncomfortable keeping secrets from Sam. At some point, I'd have to find a way to tell him about Sweetie's visit. But for now, it was enough for us to be back together. That little bit of information could wait for a while.

As Sweetie closed the door behind us and I followed Sam to the kitchen, I wondered if Sweetie's ecstasy at finding out Sam and I were back on track had caused her some kind of temporary blindness. She hadn't said a thing about Snickle. When we all reached the kitchen, though, her vision cleared.

"You brought that cat over here?" she shrieked. "Why can't that thing stay in Gracie's house? Put out some food and water. He'll be fine."

Sam leaned up against the table, Snickle's carrier at his feet. "And if the electricity goes out? Cats may be adaptive, but they're not part of the polar bear family. Wouldn't you feel bad if we'd left him there and Gracie went home to find a frozen Snickle?"

He said it tongue in cheek, but Sweetie didn't find it very funny. "Sounds like some kinda dessert," she mumbled. "Frozen Snickle."

I had to bite my lip to keep from laughing.

Sam shot his aunt an amused look. "Why don't you go unpack?" he said to me. "I want to check the weather report and see if there's an update."

"Does it matter which bedroom I take?" I directed my question to Sweetie, who grinned like the cat who ate the canary, the Snickle controversy seemingly behind her.

"Well, let's see. I could set up a cot in the basement.

'Course it gets a little cold down there." She rubbed her chin like she was thinking. "I don't know."

"You're very funny," I said, smiling at her antics. "Think I'll take the purple room." Sweetie knew how much I loved it. I grabbed my suitcase and hurried up the stairs to the most gorgeous room I'd ever slept in. Purple violets on the wallpaper accented a beautiful lavender and gold oriental rug. Intricately carved oak furniture with a Victorian design completed the room perfectly. It was cozy, spacious, and absolutely stunning.

When I swung the door open, I found a fire burning in the fireplace and an extra quilt lying at the foot of the four-poster bed. I pulled it out and ran my hand over it. Sweetie's Christmas quilt. She'd shown it to me once when I was here for dinner. Her mother had made it for her when Sweetie was a young girl. Unfortunately, Sweetie's mother died before she could give it to her. In fact, the Christmas after her mother's death, Sweetie's father had given her the quilt. It was almost as if her mother had reached down from heaven and given her daughter a special Christmas gift. The beautiful reds and greens were so bright, the quilt looked like it had been made yesterday. In the middle was a Christmas wreath. It was the most beautiful quilt I'd ever seen.

I folded it back up. Putting the quilt on the bed was Sweetie's way of telling me she'd planned for me to stay in this room all along. I took my clothes out of the suitcase and placed them in the drawers of the huge dresser that sat against one wall. Then I unpacked my toiletries in the bathroom down the hall. I spent a few minutes enjoying the room before I headed back downstairs.

I could hear the TV in the den, so I knew Sam was watching the weather. I started to join him, but the cold outside seemed to have seeped into my bones. A hot cup of raspberry tea called my name. I'd just reached the door of the kitchen when I saw Sweetie bent over, talking to herself. I started to say something when I realized she wasn't alone. At her feet lay the much-hated Snicklefritz. He was on his back, purring to beat the band while Sweetie stroked his stomach and talked baby talk to him. I almost laughed out loud, but I held it in. No sense in embarrassing Sweetie and setting this love fest back several months.

I crept down the hall and then turned back toward the kitchen, this time stepping loudly and even emitting a couple of coughs. By the time I reached the doorway, Sweetie stood near the stove. Snickle sat nearby, staring at her with an expression that clearly demonstrated his displeasure at being suddenly deserted.

"Hope Snickle isn't bothering you," I said. "I guess Sam let him out of his carrier."

Sweetie shrugged. "Is that mangy cat in here? Had no idea it was already loose." She waved a large spoon at me. "You'd best keep that big rat catcher outta my hair. That's all I gotta say." With that she went back to stirring whatever she had on the stove.

"Okay, I'll try. Any chance for a cup of tea?"

"Sure. You want raspberry?"

"Sounds wonderful. I'm going to check on Sam, and I'll be back in a few minutes. Do you want me to take Snickle with me?"

"Nah, that's okay. Silly cat would probably just run back in here. He loves to irritate me."

"Okay. Thanks, Sweetie. I'm really sorry to cause so much trouble."

She turned to look at me, and her expression softened. "Shoot, Gracie. You ain't no trouble a'tall. I'm glad you're here." She gave Snickle a dirty look. "Me and this cat will find a way to get used to each other. Some way. Don't you worry none about it."

I gave her a smile and went to find Sam. Sure enough, he had parked himself in front of the TV in the home's large study. Wooden bookshelves lined the walls, and a beautifully carved fireplace mantel held the only pictures I'd ever seen from Sam's childhood. Several of Hannah's paintings hung on the walls. Although this room was decorated in a heavier style than the other rooms in the house, it was still one of my favorites. Sam sat behind a huge mahogany desk, watching a flat-screen TV mounted on a nearby wall. I barely got out "What's going on?" before he shushed me.

The forecaster was pointing right at Kansas. "This system is likely to dump another ten to twelve inches on an area already reeling from a recent storm. And it could get even worse, folks. Should the system stall over northeast Kansas, some areas could see record amounts of snowfall. Unfortunately, it isn't just the amount of snow that's a concern with this storm. It's the strong winds and the possible subzero temperatures. Blizzard conditions could exist over a large part of the state. To call this storm dangerous is an understatement."

Sam picked up the remote control and turned the sound down. "Good thing you're here. This is starting to look pretty bad." His taut expression told me he was worried.

"Sam, that forecaster said something about temperatures below zero. Could that affect your trees?"

"When they're dormant, they can stand pretty cold temps, but if we hit several days below zero, we could be in trouble."

"Isn't there anything you can do?"

He nodded slowly. "We can put out smudge pots and light our burn barrels, but I don't know if it will do any good. I can only raise the ground temperature a few degrees. Hopefully it will be enough to protect the roots of the trees."

"And if you can't get it warm enough?" I was suddenly hit with a wave of apprehension. The tone in his voice was one I hadn't heard before.

"It means we lose our trees, and we'll have no crop next year."

The idea of something like that happening had never occurred to me. "Well, I'm going to pray that God will protect your trees. Psalm 91 says, 'He will call upon me, and I will answer him; I will be with him in trouble, I will deliver him and honor him.' " I smiled at Sam. "I believe that."

He stared down at the floor for a moment before raising his head to return my smile. "Guess I need to put my faith to work, huh? I have to admit that owning a farm can make a person start thinking everything depends on however the weather decides to turn. Thanks for reminding me who is really in charge."

"You're welcome." The grim weather forecast made me think of Ida, all alone in her old house. "Sam, what about Ida? We should have checked on her before we came here."

He clicked the TV off. "You're right. I didn't realize it was going to be quite this bad. I'm going to head over there now before the storm hits."

"I'll go with you."

He shook his head. "I'd rather you stay here. If she decides she'd like to come with me, I'll need room in the front seat for her and her things."

"But you could put her stuff in the truck bed."

"Can't you feel that wind? It's already blowing pretty good out there. I don't want to take the time to tie anything down, and I doubt lightweight items would stay in the truck very long."

Sure enough, a blast of air shook the house. The storm was moving in quickly. "All right. But don't take too long. I swear, if you're not back in thirty minutes, I'm coming after you."

Sam rose from his chair. "That little Slug Bug of yours wouldn't last a minute in a big wind. You'd be blown away just like Dorothy and her house." He pointed his finger at me. "You stay put. And I mean it."

I followed him to the coat closet in the hall. He quickly kissed me and left.

"Where in blazes is that boy goin'?" Sweetie asked as she came out of the kitchen. "Don't he know how bad it's fixin' to get out there?"

I explained our concerns about Ida.

"Oh my. I shoulda thought about her myself, but I thought Sam just stopped by there yesterday."

"Well, he did, but now it looks like the storm may be worse than we originally thought. He's going to try to bring her here."

She nodded. "That's a good idea. This house is built to last. Not so sure about her little place, although

Sam has done a good job of keepin' things tight and weatherproof." She wiped her hands on the apron she wore on top of her overalls. "Your tea is ready. Why don't you come in and keep me company? I'm makin' a roasted chicken for dinner."

I'd just sat down at the kitchen table with my cup of tea when the phone rang. Sweetie was cutting potatoes, so I grabbed it for her.

Before I could say hello, a frantic male voice blasted through the receiver. "Sweetie? Sweetie, is that you?"

"No, this is Gracie. Sweetie's busy. What—"

"Gracie. Gracie, this is John Keystone. I need your help."

"John, I thought your phone might be out."

"It was. It's only been up a few minutes, and I'm not sure how long the connection will hold. Gracie, I need to talk to Sam. Right now."

"John, he's gone to check on Ida. He's not here. What's wrong?"

There were several seconds of silence on his end of the phone. I could hear his heavy breathing. Finally, when he spoke, his voice was shaky with emotion. "Look, Gracie, I know about what happened between Gabe and Sarah."

"We tried to call you right away, John, but—"

"That's not important now," he said, cutting me off. "Gabe is at my place. Sarah's missing."

I felt my body turn cold. "What do you mean, missing?"

"She and Gabe had an argument, and Sarah took off in the buggy. Gabe thought she might have come here and had a neighbor drive him over. Gracie, we need help looking for Sarah. Sam was the first person I called."

"Oh John. The storm's moving in really fast. If Sarah is caught in it. . ."

"I know," he said, his voice tinged with desperation. "That's why we don't have a moment to lose."

I thought for a moment. "Do you have any idea where she might have gone?"

"No. Gabe thinks she could be on her way to your place or to town. I'm hopeful we'll find her on the road. But if not. . ."

"I'll call Sam and tell him to hurry home. He should be back by the time you get here."

"Could you also call some other people and ask for help? The more folks looking for her the better."

"Of course. I'll start calling as soon as we hang up."

"Okay, Gracie. Thanks, and—"

As a major gust of wind hit the house, I lost the phone connection. I called John's name several times, but the line was dead. I clicked the receiver, hoping the problem was on John's end. No such luck. I put the receiver down and explained the situation to Sweetie.

"Oh my lands," she said. "That little girl don't stand a chance in one of them rickety buggies. Not in this wind. And when the snow starts. . ." As if on cue, the scene outside the kitchen windows turned white. The snow was so thick and the wind so strong that it created an instant whiteout.

I began to feel panic rise inside me. "Sweetie, what are we going to do? I can't contact anyone else for help, and I can't call Sam."

She popped her chicken in the oven, took off her old apron, and came over to the table. "Well, I may not be the spiritual one in this family, but I believe we should pray, don't you?"

"I think that's a great idea." Sweetie being the one to initiate prayer was something new, but I was grateful. We certainly needed God's protection working for Sarah. We joined hands and thanked Him that His angels had charge over her. We also asked that she would be found quickly. When we finished, I felt a calm assurance drift over me.

After our prayer, I got up and went to the front door. At this point, I had two choices. Either I could wait for Sam to come back, or I could get in my car and go after him. But when I opened the door and looked outside, I knew my car didn't stand a chance. This wasn't a snowstorm; this was a bona fide blizzard. I watched the snow shriek and swoop past the house, carried by wild winds. I couldn't even see the road. Visibility was almost nothing. I'd put my trust in God to deliver Sarah, but thinking about her out there, alone in this storm, brought tears to my eyes.

I'd just decided to go back into the kitchen when I heard the sound of a motor. Through the blanket of blowing snow, Sam's truck became visible. He pulled up as close as he could to the house. His door opened and he got out, fighting against the wind, almost falling down twice, until he reached the porch. It took the both of us to get the outer door open and then hold it so the wind wouldn't break it off its hinges.

"Where's Ida?" I asked as soon as he got inside and closed the door behind us.

"Snug as a bug in a rug," he said. "She doesn't want to leave. She's nice and warm, has plenty of food, and wants to be near Zebediah."

"What about Zeb? Will he be all right?"

Sam nodded and started to take off his coat. "I closed him inside the stable and started a small fire in the stove. As soon as things die down some, I'll go back and check on both of them again."

I grabbed him before he could completely remove his coat. "Better leave it on. Something awful has happened." I quickly filled him in on John's frantic call. As I talked, Sam's expression grew more ominous.

"It's awful out there, Grace. Sarah is in real danger. We need more people than just Gabe, John, and me out there searching for her. Have you checked the phone again? Maybe it's working."

Sweetie walked out into the hallway. "It's still deader than a doornail, son. Sorry."

Sam stared at both of us for a minute. I could almost hear the gears grinding in his head. "You said John and Gabe are on their way over here?"

"Yes. Knowing Sarah is in danger seemed to pull them together. John sounded so frightened. And I'm sure Gabe is beside himself."

Sam sighed deeply and shook his head. "All I can do is wait for them and hope they find her on the road coming here. If they do. . ."

The sound of a vehicle pulling into the driveway stopped Sam from finishing his thought. He flung the door open. John's SUV had pulled up next to Sam's truck. The driver's side door opened and John got out. He shut the door behind him with great difficulty and made his way to the front porch. Sam held the door open and struggled to close it once John was inside.

"Did you get anyone else to help us?" were the first words out of his mouth.

"The phone lines are down," Sam said. "There's just me. I take it you didn't find her on your way over here."

John's look of panic made my insides churn. "No. No sign of her." He stared wide-eyed at Sam. "What are we going to do?"

Sam buttoned up his coat and hurried to the closet to find his wool hat. He pulled it down over his ears. "We're going to go look for her. Let's take your car. It's much sturdier than my truck. We'll figure out which way to go when we get in the car."

I pushed my way past him and opened the closet door. "I'm coming with you."

"No," Sam said forcefully. "I want you to stay here. The phone might come back on. You can start calling for help."

I finished pulling on my coat and put the hood up. "Sweetie knows how to use the phone. You have no idea what you're going to find out there or how much help you'll need. I'm strong."

Sam started to say something else, but Sweetie spoke up from behind us. "You listen to that girl, son. She can help. I'll man the phones. If the line comes up, I'll start callin' everyone in this here county. Now you all get a-goin'."

I could tell Sam wanted to argue, but I had no intention of letting him leave without me. Sarah was my friend, and I was determined to find her.

Without another word, the three of us fought our way back to the SUV where Gabe waited for us. Sam held on tightly to my arm. The force of the wind almost knocked me down several times. But it wasn't just the wind. The snow hit my face like tiny needles, making it impossible to keep my eyes open. By the time I climbed into the car, I felt exhausted.

Once everyone was inside, Sam asked, "Where would she have gone, Gabe? If she didn't go to John's or Ida's or my house, what places are left?"

Sam and I sat in the backseat with John and Gabe in the front. I couldn't see Gabe's face, but the snap of his head told me something had occurred to him.

"She told me once that she always feels safe and calm when she's in church," he said. "Maybe she'd go there."

"In this storm?" I asked incredulously. "Surely she knows Abel wouldn't be there. The church wouldn't be open."

"But it wasn't snowing when she left. We had no idea a blizzard was on its way."

John put the SUV into gear and started down the driveway. "Actually, that could be good news. If she made it to town, someone would have seen her and taken her in. Let's hope that's what happened."

We drove slowly down Faith Street. Even though the SUV was massive, it rocked back and forth when hit by strong gusts of wind.

"Watch out the windows," John said loudly. "If you see anything that doesn't look right, whatever it is, yell. I'll stop and we'll check it out."

It was almost impossible to even make out where the road was supposed to be, let alone a buggy. But we all kept our eyes peeled as John drove slowly. Finally we reached Main Street. The only way I could tell was by the street sign, which flapped violently in the wind. John turned carefully. I prayed silently that God would let us see the buggy, that it wouldn't be totally covered by snow. We'd gone about a quarter of a mile when I thought I saw something odd several yards from the road. At first I wasn't certain. It looked like a small hill covered with snow. But then a gust of wind blew past it and uncovered something round. A wheel!

"Stop! Stop!" I hollered. "Over there. I think it's the buggy!"

John put the SUV in park. "Where?" he shouted. "I don't see—"

"Yes!" Gabe yelled. "Over there."

We all got out of the car and fought our way through the blowing snow. Sam held on to me, but once again I struggled to stay upright. I put my hand up to shield my eyes, but it didn't help. Finally we reached the buggy.

Gabe was yelling something, but I couldn't hear him over the wind. We started trying to clear the snow off the buggy, which lay on its side. Was Sarah still inside? Was she alive?

All four of us pushed the snow away, but Sarah wasn't there. During a lull in the wind, I heard Sam say something about the horse.

Gabe checked the harness. "It's been undone," he shouted over the howling wind. "Sarah must have let her loose."

I knew that horses usually try to find their way home when they get away from their owners. So at least Sarah had the presence of mind to unhook Molasses. But what happened after that?

Gabe began digging through the snow like a madman. If Sarah was anywhere near. . . I pulled on Sam's arm. "There!" I shouted. About thirty or forty yards from us, something lay in the snow. It was almost completely covered, but there was a strip of black showing through. Sam grabbed Gabe and John and pointed. Then he motioned for me to stay where I was. This time I didn't argue. I tried to watch the men, but every time the wind blew, I had to put my head down and wait for it to stop. The next time I looked up, I saw John lift something out of the snow and start back toward me. Sarah! As they got closer, I could see her still, white face. Tears streamed down my cheeks. Was she alive? Were we too late? Sam grabbed me and pulled me to the SUV. The wind, which had died down long enough for me to see Sarah in the snow, suddenly regained strength. If Sam hadn't taken my arm, I would have fallen backward.

John gently laid Sarah's body in the backseat. Then he scooted in, putting her head on his lap. Gabe ran around to the other side and got in. Sam pushed me toward the passenger door and helped me into the front seat. Then he got behind the wheel. I turned around in my seat, wanting to see if Sarah was breathing. Thankfully I could see her chest rise and fall—slowly.

"It's going to be almost impossible to get her to Sunrise," Sam said to the two worried men. "The storm is getting worse. Where do you want me to go?"

"Drive back to your house," John said in a controlled voice that belied the distraught look on his face.

"Wait a minute," Gabe barked. "I'm her father. I'll decide what we do."

"Gabe," John said in a no-nonsense tone, "you've forgotten I'm a doctor. We don't need to go to Sunrise.

I can help her." He stared at Gabe intensely. "I know you disapprove of Sarah and me. And I know you probably blame me for this, but we have to put our differences aside now. Sarah needs us. Both of us. I'm going to ask you to trust me. I know that sounds crazy with everything that's happened, but I know what I'm doing. I'm actually an excellent doctor. And whether you believe this or not, I love your daughter. Very much."

Both men kept their eyes locked on each other for what seemed like minutes. I could feel the thick emotion between them. Finally Gabe broke the staring contest.

"All right. But when Sarah is well. . ."

"When Sarah is well, we'll talk. I promise."

Gabe fell silent, and John apparently took it as a sign of his agreement.

"There's a blanket in the back of the car. I want you to lean over the seat and get it." Gabe did as John asked without hesitation.

Sam, who'd been struggling to turn the SUV around on the slick, snow-packed road, finally got us going in the right direction. I watched carefully, trying to help him navigate in zero visibility. I could hear John giving Gabe instructions in the backseat to elevate Sarah's legs. When I turned around to check on them, Sarah was fully covered by a thick, heavy blanket. John had his hand on her wrist while he looked at his wristwatch. He kept saying Sarah's name, trying to get her to wake up.

Suddenly I felt the SUV slip, and we went into a spin. It happened so fast, all I could do was grab the handgrip over the door with one hand and put my other hand on the dashboard. Thankfully Sam didn't panic and brought the large vehicle under control.

"Sorry," he said. "I'm doing the best I can."

"It's fine, Sam," John said soothingly. "You're doing great, and so is Sarah. Just getting her into a warm car is helping to bring up her temperature. Gracie?"

I cranked my head around again, still shaken by the unexpected slide. "Yes?"

"When we get to Sam's, we need to take Sarah into bed as soon as possible. I need you and Sweetie to get these clothes off her. She needs something warm and dry. Can you do that?"

"Yes."

"Maybe I should take off her shoes now and rub her feet," Gabe said.

John shook his head. "No. That's one of the worst things you can do. If the tissue is damaged, rubbing it will make it worse. We need to get her warm—outside and inside. Gracie, is there a room with a fireplace?"

"Yes. She can stay in my room."

"Okay. Thanks."

"Is there anything we can do for her now?" her father asked. I could hear the apprehension in his voice.

"We're doing everything possible," John said. "Her respiration is good. I think she'll be fine. I just can't tell about frostbite until I can get a better look at her."

"John?" Sarah's voice was so soft at first I almost mistook it for the sound of the wind rushing past the car. "Are you really here?"

I turned around again. Man, I was going to have the mother of all neck aches by the time we got back to Sam's. Sarah's eyes were open. They looked almost black against her pale skin. "What happened?" she asked weakly.

"You went out in the buggy," John said, gently stroking her face. "That was a foolish thing to do, Sarah. You could have been seriously hurt."

"I–I'm sorry. It's just that Papa. . .Papa said I couldn't see you anymore. I'm so sorry. Papa will be so mad."

"Sarah, I'm here," Gabe said. "And I'm not mad. I'm just grateful. Grateful you're alive."

Sarah raised her head to find her father holding her feet, tears on his face. "Papa. Why. . .why are you here? Oh my. Please forgive me. It was wrong of me to leave in anger. I just wanted time to think. I had no idea the storm would come up so quickly."

"There is nothing to forgive, daughter. I'm so thankful to the Lord that He kept you safe. I shouldn't have been so harsh with you. This is all my fault."

"No," she replied in a weak voice. "I made the decision. I took the buggy. No one else is to blame."

"Okay," John said. "Let's not worry about whose fault this is right now. Let's just be grateful we found you. I want you to be quiet and rest. We'll be at Sam's soon, and we'll get you warmed up and feeling like yourself again."

"I would love some hot tea. I'm so cold."

"I'm sure we can find you some tea. Now rest."

She closed her eyes again. Within seconds her breathing deepened. Although she was still abnormally pale, at least she'd started to lose the corpselike pallor she'd had when we found her.

It took us forty-five minutes to make a trip that should have taken ten, but we finally made it back to the house. Sweetie held the door open as we struggled to get up the steps.

"Land sakes alive," she said when she saw Sarah. "You found her. Is the child all right?"

"We need to warm her up, Sweetie," I said when we got inside. "We're taking her to the purple room. Can you stoke the fire in there? And make her some hot tea?"

"You bet."

I led John up the stairs with Sarah in his arms. Gabe followed behind us. Sweetie added some logs to the fireplace while John carried Sarah to the bed.

"You two go downstairs while I get these wet things off her," I told them. "I'll call you when she's situated."

They nodded and left the room. Sarah helped me remove the heavy, wet garments. Sweetie, who had the fire blazing, took them from me.

"I'll get this stuff washed and dried," she said.

I got a heavy flannel nightgown from the dresser drawer and helped Sarah into it. Throughout the entire process, she didn't say a word. I removed the quilt on top of the bed that had gotten wet from melting snow and unfolded Sweetie's beautiful Christmas quilt. Before long, I had Sarah under the covers, dry and warm. I got a towel from the bathroom and undid her braids. Then I dried her hair and brushed it out. With her long black hair, pale skin, and dark eyes, she reminded me of a picture in one of my books as a child. She was the spitting image of Snow White. As I finished brushing her hair, she grabbed my hand. Her grip was weak and her fingers were still cold.

"Thank you," she said in her small voice. "I'm so

grateful for everything you're doing for me. I'm so sorry to have caused all this trouble."

I put my hand over hers. "It's no trouble, Sarah. This is what friends do." I noticed she flinched when I touched her skin. "Does your hand hurt?"

She nodded and her eyes filled with tears. "They both sting. And my feet." She wiped a tear that snaked down her cheek. "I hope Molasses made it back to her stable. I had to release her. I couldn't get the buggy right side up. I hoped she would find her way back and alert Papa there was a problem."

"I'm sure she's fine. But Sarah, why didn't you stay in the buggy? Why were you in that field?"

"I thought I could make it to your house," she whispered. "But I got so turned around. When the wind blew, I couldn't see anything. I'm still not sure how you found me."

"God led us to you. I'm convinced of it. There's no other explanation."

Another tear ran down her cheek. "He is too good to me. I don't deserve. . ."

"I don't believe God loves us because we deserve it. I think He loves us because that's just who He is. I find comfort knowing His love isn't based on my goodness. . .or lack of it."

She brushed a strand of dark hair that fell across her face. "You're right, Gracie." She gave me a quick smile. "Your name fits you. You seem to really understand the grace of God. Sometimes I have a hard time comprehending how God can love me so much no matter what I do."

I wanted to explain to Sarah that having a father who'd spent so many years being bitter toward people and God would certainly make it difficult for her to grasp the concept of unconditional love and forgiveness, but I held my tongue.

"Do you think Papa will ever forgive me?" The plaintive tone of her voice tore at my heart.

"Sarah, believe me, your father isn't thinking about anything except how much he loves you and how badly he needed to find you."

"But after his relief lifts. . ." She grabbed my arm, wincing at the pain in her fingers. "How did he treat John? Did they have words? What—"

"Whoa. They were both too worried about you to be upset with each other. You might be surprised. Maybe this situation will bring them together."

The sound of angry, raised voices took the wind out of my hopeful declaration. "You stay in bed," I told Sarah, whose eyes had grown large with fear. "Let me see what's going on. I'll be right back."

I closed the door gently behind me and hurried down the stairs. I followed the sound of shouting to the kitchen. Sweetie was near the stove, holding a pot of coffee, her mouth hanging open. Sam stood between Gabe and John, one hand on each man's chest.

"If your relationship with my daughter is as innocent as you make it out to be," Gabe said loudly, his face red with anger, "why did you hide in the shadows? Why did you skulk around behind my back?"

"Because your daughter asked me to keep my feelings for her secret. She was afraid to tell you. Afraid of your reaction. You caused us to sneak around. I hated it. I told Sarah more than once that we should tell you the truth, but her fear of you—"

"Fear? What are you talking about? My daughter is not afraid of me!"

John opened his mouth to lob back what promised to be another accusation, but I shouted at them to shut up. They turned to look at me, their faces masks of resentment.

"What are you doing?" I said crossly. "Sarah can hear you yelling at each other, and she doesn't need that right now."

Gabe pointed a finger at John. "If he'd stayed away from her, she wouldn't be suffering now. She'd be safe at home where she belongs."

"What are you talking about?" John's fierce scowl signaled their argument was far from over. "It's the way you reacted when you found out about us that drove her to run away. This entire situation is your fault."

Gabe took a menacing step toward John, and Sam quickly pushed him back. "Stop it," he said sharply. "Grace is right. Sarah doesn't need to listen to you two go at each other. Sarah made the decision to jump in that buggy. She's an adult." He glared at Gabe. "That's something you don't seem to get." His voice softened slightly. "I know you've been hurt, Gabe. But Sarah isn't your ex-wife. And John isn't the man she took off with. These are two good people who fell in love. That's all."

Gabe's face blanched. "I know that. Sarah isn't anything like Greta. She loves God. Greta only loved what she thought the world could give her."

"Then why do you treat Sarah the way you do?" I asked. "Why don't you give her a chance to prove she is capable of making good decisions?"

Gabe stepped away from Sam and dropped into

one of the chairs at the kitchen table. "I do trust her, but she can't have a relationship with someone outside our church. It would be an unequal yoking. I don't want her to make a choice that will only hurt her in the end. Sarah's faith is everything to her." He fastened his eyes on John. "If you really knew my daughter, you'd know that. If she betrays her faith, she will be miserable. It will haunt her the rest of her life."

"I would never ask her to give up her faith," John said forcefully. "Why would you think that? I realize it's part of who she is."

"Not part," Gabe replied. "Everything. If she married you, she would be turning her back on scripture. It is a commandment not to be unequally yoked."

John slid into a chair next to Gabe. "Look, I may not go to church, but I do believe in God. Anyway, I think I do. I'll go to church with her. Maybe her faith will rub off on me. But it has to be real. I can't pretend to believe the way she does. It would not only dishonor her; it would dishonor God."

I sat down across from the two of them. "You're both good and decent men," I said tentatively. "I hope you can at least see that about each other. And if Sarah and John should take their relationship further, I pray you can have peace with it, Gabe. Going back to the way things were—locking Sarah away—not allowing her to have a life. That's not the right way to do things."

"I know that now," he said. "Even if I wanted to, Sarah wouldn't allow it. She showed me that clearly today." He covered his face with his hands. "I'm so afraid for her," he said brokenly. "Making this decision will bring her so much pain, and I can't stop it."

"I think you can't stand the thought of losing her." John's comment seemed to hit home.

"You're right," Gabe said, taking his hands from his face. "I'm afraid to be alone, but I'd do it for Sarah, gladly, if I thought she would be happy. But believe me, marrying outside her faith won't do that. It will destroy her."

"Papa!" Sarah's voice was so faint we almost didn't hear her. She stood in the doorway, holding on to the frame for support. Her long black hair cascaded past her shoulders and fell across her chest. In my white nightgown, the contrast was startling. Even though she was still abnormally pale, she had never looked more beautiful. I heard John's sharp intake of breath.

"Daughter, what are you doing out of bed?" Gabe rose to his feet and started toward her, but Sarah held up her hand for him to stop. "Papa, I must say something. Then I will go back to bed." She gazed at John, who seemed almost transfixed by her presence. There was no mistaking the naked emotion in her face. It was obvious she loved him. That's why her next words took me by surprise.

"I'm sorry, John, but my father is right. There's no future for us. It's best that we end things. Besides, our relationship was never that serious. You never even kissed me." With that, she turned and started to leave the kitchen. I noticed that she faltered, obviously still weak and unsteady.

I jumped up to assist her. "You all stay here," I ordered the three men. "I'll help Sarah back to bed."

I slid my arm around her tiny waist while she leaned against me. A few times as we climbed the stairs, I worried she would fall. Finally I got her back into bed. Although she tried valiantly to look calm and resolute, I could feel her body tremble as I pulled the covers over her. Before she turned her head away from me, I saw the stark pain on her face.

"You love him very much, don't you?"

No answer.

"Sarah, you can talk to me. Really. I won't repeat anything you tell me."

Her small body began to heave with sobs. I sat down on the bed next to her and opened my arms. She sat up and wrapped her slender arms around my neck. I could feel her tears falling on my skin.

"Oh Gracie. I do. I love him more than I can bear."

"Then why? Why would you say what you did? Surely this can be worked out."

She shook her head. "No. No, it can't." She let go of my neck and put her head back on the pillow, tears running down the sides of her face. "You heard Papa. He is afraid to be alone." She reached for my hand, and I gave it to her. Her grip was surprisingly strong. "My father raised me after Mother left. It was so hard for him, Gracie. I know he was devastated by her betrayal. He loved her so. But he kept going for me." Sarah stared at the ceiling, her expression resolute. "What if John and I wanted to marry? I would have to leave home. I will not do that to my father."

I started to protest, to tell her that she couldn't spend the rest of her life taking care of Gabe, but she put her fingers up to my mouth, softly touching my lips.

"Hush, dear friend. I know what you would say. I know the Bible talks about leaving our mothers and fathers and cleaving to our husbands. But I cannot leave him. Not yet. Not until I know he'll be okay. Right or wrong, I know it's what I must do." She smiled sadly. "Maybe the day will come when things change. I don't know. But I can't build happiness on my father's pain. It's impossible." Her eyes searched mine. "Do you understand—even a little?"

I had to bite my lip to keep the words I wanted to say inside. Sarah deserved a life. Her mother's abandonment had hurt her, too. Her father certainly wasn't the only victim. Yet as I gazed into her face, I knew she spoke the truth. Sarah didn't have it in her to hurt Gabe. With her gentle spirit and loving nature, to do so would rip her to shreds. "I understand, Sarah. I'll support you, whatever you decide." I squeezed her hand and saw her wince. "Are your hands still sore?"

She nodded. "And my feet. They are very painful. I didn't want to say anything."

I stood up. "I need to check with John. He should know."

A look of terror washed over her features. "Please, Gracie. Don't let him come here. Not now. I—"

"Nonsense." John's sharp retort startled me. I turned to find him standing in the doorway, frowning at us. "I'm still the doctor here. No matter what else, I intend to take care of your physical needs, Sarah." He came into the room, Gabe close on his heels. Before approaching the bed where Sarah lay, he stopped and looked at her, almost expressionless. "I've talked to your father. I want you to know that I agree with you. Whatever we thought we had is over. I see now that it was never meant to be. I was fooling myself to think that someone like you could love me. And it was wrong to put you in a position where you would have to choose between your religion or me. You can't give up your beliefs, and I can't manufacture beliefs I simply don't have. So I guess that makes our choice clear. Now I want to look at your hands and feet. As your doctor. Is that all right with you?"

Sarah was so still her nod was almost imperceptible. Her dark eyes looked huge in her delicate face, and I could only imagine her emotions as John approached her. He sat on the side of her bed and took her hands in his, turning them over and asking questions. Her response was either "Yes" or "No" to each inquiry. John moved to the end of the bed and uncovered her feet, asking her the same questions. Finally he stood up.

"Everything is fine. The tingling and pain are actually signs the skin is recovering. When you get her home, Gabe, just let her rest, and make sure she has plenty of fluids. She'll recover completely."

"Thank you, John. For everything." Gabe walked over to John and held out his hand. John took it and covered it with his other one.

"The one thing I ask of you," John said in a husky voice, "is that you don't pull back from your friends again. It isn't right. For you or for Sarah. Please don't let my selfishness cause you to cut yourself off from us again."

Gabe's eyes widened, and he placed his other hand over John's. "I promise. I don't want that for either one of us. I'm sorry for the way I acted. I was just so hurt. . .and afraid."

"I know exactly how that feels. But this town, and these people. . .well, they changed me. I want you and Sarah to be happy here, too."

"You have my word."

I couldn't stop the tears that filled my eyes. I glanced over at Sam, who stood in the doorway watching. He had to wipe his own eyes. But my joy at seeing these two men find reconciliation was marred by the pain I knew Sarah and John felt. Were they doing the right thing? I couldn't be sure, but one thing Gabe said made sense. Sarah did love God. How could she become involved with a man who didn't? I watched as Sarah smiled, seeing her father and John make peace, yet the sadness in her eyes caught at my heart.

Sweetie's shrill voice suddenly disrupted the quiet atmosphere. I looked over at Sam. "What's she yelling about?"

He shrugged. "Hold on. I'll check." He stuck his head out the door and called loudly to his aunt.

I heard her clomping up the stairs. "I said, there's someone outside. Looks like Dan and Dale Scheidler."

"I'm surprised they got through," Gabe said. He looked toward his daughter. "Will you be all right for a few minutes?"

"I'm fine, Papa. Go ahead." The men followed Sweetie down the stairs.

I picked up the teapot on the tray by Sarah's bed. "I'm going to get you more tea. This is lukewarm. I'll be right back."

"Thank you," Sarah said. "But to be honest, I'm tired. I think I'd like to sleep for a while if it's okay."

I wasn't certain whether she wanted to be alone because she was sleepy or if she just needed some time to cry, but either way, I understood. "Okay. I'll come back and check on you in an hour or so." I patted her shoulder. "You get some rest."

She nodded and turned away from me, her long dark hair in stark contrast to the white bedspread covering her. Once again she reminded me of Snow White. I couldn't help but wonder if this beautiful princess would ever experience love's first kiss. I left the room and closed the door quietly behind me.

As I came down the stairs, I heard the sound of excited voices. Dale and Dan had just entered the foyer when I heard Dan exclaim, "We were trying to clear some of the roads when we found something."

As I joined the group gathered around the two brothers, Sam said, "You found something? What are you talking about?"

"We found a body, Sam," Dale said in a somber voice. "It's Rand McAllister. Dead as a doornail."

NINE

What do you mean dead?" Sweetie's nonsensical question only echoed the shock I felt at Dale's stunning announcement.

The brothers stared at her like she was demented. "Dead, Sweetie," Dale said. "Can't put it any other way. He's frozen stiff as a board." He fixed his gaze on John. "Glad to find you here, John. Heard you used to be a doctor. Can you take him off our hands?"

John's mouth dropped open. "Take him off your hands? And just what would you like me to do with him?"

Dale shrugged. "Have no idea, but he can't stay with us."

"We need to call the police," I said. "Or the sheriff. Or someone."

"Good idea," Sam said, "except the phones don't work, and I doubt they could get here anyway."

"The phones in town were okay earlier," Dan said. "When we get back, we'll call the sheriff. It may take awhile though. It's mighty slow going. It could be a few hours before we can contact anyone."

"And we can't guarantee the phones will be working by the time we get there," Dale interjected. He looked at his brother. "Doesn't Joe Loudermilk still have that old CB radio he plays with in his back room?"

Dan shrugged. "I have no idea, but if the phones are out, we could ask him about it."

"But Joe's probably at home," I said. "How will you get into his store?"

The brothers both frowned at me. "We just take the key off the hook by the door."

Living in Harmony took some getting used to. Obviously I hadn't completely retrained my thinking from the way things are done in the big city. "Sorry. Guess I hadn't thought it out."

The brothers nodded at me simultaneously. For a second, I was reminded of Tweedledum and Tweedledee from *Through the Looking Glass*. I shook my head. Second time today I'd compared someone who lived in Harmony with a fictional character. Somehow it just seemed appropriate.

"Well, if you men could help us get Rand off the roof of the tractor cab—"

"He's on the roof?" I asked, aghast. "Why is he on the roof?"

There was the look again. "Just where would you have put him?" Dale asked while Dan nodded briskly. "Guess we could have dragged him along behind us, but it didn't seem. . .well. . .respectful. Thank goodness we had some rope with us. We just strapped him up there and drove to the closest farm." The brothers looked at each other. "Seemed like the polite way of handling the situation."

"Polite? Tying someone on the roof of a tractor?" I was obviously out of my league, so I just gave up.

"Now what?" My question was directed to Sam, but Sweetie answered.

"Just put him in the barn," she ordered. "On the big wood table in the middle. And for cryin' out loud, cover him up with a horse blanket or somethin'."

The brothers nodded together again. "Good idea," Dan said. "He'll stay nice and cold out there until someone comes for him."

"What about his family?" I said. "Someone needs to let them know."

Once again the brothers shook their heads at the same time. "Too far from here. Rand's place is halfway to Sunrise. It may be some time before we can get word to them."

"We'll help you take care of Rand," Gabe said. "Let us grab our coats and meet you outside."

Sweetie trotted quickly toward the front door, probably wanting to see Rand McAllister hog-tied to the top of a tractor cab. I, on the other hand, didn't need that image in my mind. I turned the other way. Sam followed me to the kitchen.

"Guess I'll go with them." His expression made it clear he wasn't enthusiastic about the proposition. But there really wasn't much choice. Moving frozen dead bodies was definitely men's work. At that moment, I was thoroughly grateful to be female. He returned my smile with a sickly one of his own and left the room to help the men take care of their macabre business.

As I fixed myself a cup of hot tea, I wondered how Rand got caught outside in the middle of a storm. Sam had told me more than once that snowstorms could be brutal in this part of the country. Surely Rand knew that. Maybe his car broke down, and he tried to go somewhere for help, just like Sarah. I felt bad for him and for his family. He'd been a very unpleasant man, but anytime someone dies tragically, it's a sad event.

I sipped my tea while Sweetie spent her time checking her chicken and rolling out dough for biscuits. She didn't share what she'd seen when she rushed out to see Rand's body, and I didn't ask. Actually, we didn't talk much at all about anything. It had been an extremely stressful day. I was exhausted, mentally and physically. Sweetie must have felt it as well. For her to spend thirty minutes in silence was something that didn't happen very often.

Finally Sam, John, and Gabe came back into the house. Their expressions were grim.

I stood up when they entered the kitchen. "Is. . .is everything. . .um, taken care of?"

Sam and John sat down in the chairs at the kitchen table while Gabe leaned up against the wall near the door.

"Well, he's in the barn," Sam said. "It doesn't feel quite. . .proper. But I can't think of anything else we could possibly do. Hopefully Dale and Dan will be able to contact the sheriff." He shrugged. "I have no idea how long it'll be until he's picked up."

"John, did you, um, look at him? Did he die of exposure?"

John shook his head. "It's impossible to be certain without a thorough examination, but it's a very good possibility. One thing I can tell you for certain, though. He's been dead awhile." He gestured toward the window. "This storm didn't do it. My guess is he got drunk and lost his way. Wandered off and passed out. He probably never woke up."

"So he was already dead by the time this storm hit?" I asked.

"I'm just guessing, but I think it's the reason he didn't show up for his meeting with Eric Thursday night."

I frowned. "I know Rand hasn't lived in Harmony as long as the rest of you, but he's been here through several winters, right?"

The men nodded in unison.

"You're wondering how he could get caught out in a storm like this." Gabe said it matter-of-factly. "I think John's right. He must have been three sheets to the wind. That's the only way he'd be wandering around outside in the winter. He knew better."

"I hope you're right," Sam said. "I'd hate to think his wife and daughter got stranded somewhere, and he was out looking for them."

I couldn't hold back a gasp. "Oh Sam. Surely not."

He rubbed his hand over his face. "Let's not worry about it yet. My guess is that John and Gabe have it right. Man, I sure wish the phones were working so we could check on them, though."

Great. One more thing to think about. I'm a snow nut. Love it. But even I have my limits. This blizzard had exceeded them. First Sarah got stranded; now Rand was found dead. Jessica's sad face floated through my mind. I said a silent prayer for her protection as well as her mother's.

"Don't start worryin' about that girl," Sweetie said, breaking her silence. "Her mama's too smart to let her run around outside in nasty weather." She pointed her spatula at us. "Look, I know I get cranky and say things I shouldn't about people, and I know it's wrong to speak ill of the dead, but what no one is sayin' here is that Rand McAllister didn't have the sense God gave a duck. Makin' bad choices was par for the course with that man. Seems to me his last bad choice was. . ." Sweetie stared at us for a moment. "Well. . .his last bad choice. It's an awful tragedy, but now it's our job to help take care of his family. Isn't that what the Good Book says to do? What was that scripture about takin' care of widows and orphans?"

"James 1:27," Gabe said. " 'Pure religion and undefiled before God and the Father is this, To visit the fatherless and widows in their affliction, and to keep himself unspotted from the world.' "

"That's it," Sweetie announced triumphantly. "Boy, I used to think religion was just a bunch of rules and regulations. When I read that scripture, I saw God in a whole new way."

"Wait a minute," John said. "You people believe in more than just helping widows and orphans. I thought you loved your religion."

"We love God," I said gently. "Religion is a set of beliefs, but it isn't necessarily a relationship with God. Jesus had some pretty harsh things to say about the religious leaders of His day."

"God is love," Sam said. "Religion can actually push love out while it tries to enforce rules and restrictions on people." He looked down at Buddy, who was curled up at his feet. Snickle leaned up against his old friend. Both snoozed away, oblivious to life's trials. "It's kind of like having a pet. I can try to train him through rules and punishment. Or I can love him. Develop a relationship of trust.

Buddy would do anything I asked him to do because he trusts me so much. It would never occur to him that I would lead him in a direction that would hurt him. It's kind of like that with God. He wants us to obey Him because we love Him and trust Him so much. Not because we're trying to follow a set of regulations." He sneaked a quick look at us, and his face flushed pink. "That's probably an overly simple explanation. . . ."

"It's a perfect explanation," Gabe said. "Take it from someone who's been doing it the wrong way." His gaze drifted toward the hallway stairs. "I've spent too much time trying to teach Sarah the rules. Not enough time showing her God's love." He smiled at John. "I still don't believe you and Sarah should be together, son. But I like you very much. I hope we can be good friends."

"That would make me very happy," John said. He shook his head. "You people are something else. I've spent a little time around religious people, and it made me want to run away. But there's something different about Harmony. About most of the people. I would hate to leave here."

"Why, there ain't no way you're gonna get outta here, John Keystone," Sweetie said. "You're a part of us now. Besides, we're still hopin' you'll take up doctorin' again. Sure could use you around here. Shoot. We can get all the meat we want in Sunrise."

He chuckled. "I don't know whether to be touched or offended, Sweetie. I think you just told me my business is inconsequential."

Everyone laughed. Watching John and Gabe together seemed to be a miracle happening right in front of me. I'd been afraid finding out about Sarah and John might send Gabe back to his former temperament. Thankfully it hadn't. If John hadn't backed off, perhaps things would be different. But at least for now, there was peace. And that was good enough for tonight.

While the rest of us got cleaned up for dinner, Gabe slipped away to tell Sarah about Rand McAllister. I hated that she would be faced with another unpleasant situation, but when Gabe came downstairs, he assured us that she had taken the news as well as could be expected.

Sweetie served us a delicious meal. Sam told us that Dan and Dale planned to come back in the morning. The men would be helping others dig us out from the almost two feet of snow that had been dumped on us. The snowfall totals were bad enough, but the winds had created monster snowdrifts that had trapped people in their homes and on their farms. Sam promised me Ida's would be the first place they'd check.

"I guess we'll know in the morning if the Scheidler brothers got through to the sheriff," I said.

He nodded while chewing a big bite of roasted potatoes and gravy. "Not sure how long it will be before he can get here after he gets the news. Council Grove got hit just as bad as we did."

I swallowed hard. "You—you mean we might have to keep Rand in the barn indefinitely?"

He raised his eyebrows. "I don't like it either. But we might as well get used to the idea. He's not going anywhere for a while."

"I wonder if this will change things in regard to

that retirement community," John said. "With Rand dead, I guess Thelma could sell their farm to Eric and his investors."

I almost dropped my fork. "Wow. I'd almost completely forgotten about that with everything that's been happening." I sighed. "I sure don't look forward to watching everyone get all riled up again."

"Me neither," Sweetie said as she passed around her hot rolls for a second round. "Never seen people snipin' at each other like they were at that town meetin'. And I ain't interested in seein' it again. Wish that Eric Beck had never come to this town. Ain't brought nothin' but trouble."

"That's not fair," I retorted. "Eric wanted to do something to help Harmony. Rand is the one who caused all the trouble. Besides, you forget that working on that project was supposed to be my bread and butter. Without the work, I don't know if I can stay here."

"Don't say that," Sweetie snapped. "I told you we'd take care of you. You ain't got nothin' to worry about. I could feed this whole town, let alone a little, skinny girl."

"Sweetie, you're a doll," I said. "But you're forgetting things like utilities." Sam started to say something, but I quickly stopped him. "Before you tell me you'll cover my utilities, let me make it clear that I would never accept that. Besides, I also have student loans that have to be repaid. The truth is, unless I can get some fairly steady freelance work, I won't have a choice. I'll have to move back to Wichita."

Sweetie snorted. "It ain't gonna happen, and that's all I want to hear about that now. For land's sakes, been enough drama around here to last a lifetime. Let's not stir up any more worries tonight. How about a game of checkers after we eat?"

"You all go ahead," I said. "I'm going to take some dinner up to Sarah and see if she feels like coming downstairs."

"Don't be silly, Gracie," Gabe said. "I'll take care of my daughter."

I shook my head at him. "I think you'd better relax this evening and get to bed early. Sounds like you guys will be working pretty hard the next few days. Besides, Sarah's my closest female friend here. I like taking care of her."

"Come on, Gabe," John said good-naturedly. "Or maybe you're afraid I'll beat you at checkers."

Gabe laughed. "You know something funny? Games were frowned upon when I was a boy. Competition and all that. But a neighbor taught my brother and me how to play checkers. We made our own board and hid it in the barn. We made pieces out of our dad's metal washers. And we got pretty good." He looked over at me. "Tell Sarah I'll check on her later if she doesn't feel like joining us."

"I will." I got up from the table and took an extra plate from the cupboard. Then I filled it with servings of Sweetie's fine food.

Sam offered to help Sweetie clean up, but she shooed everyone out of the kitchen. "Won't take me more than a few minutes to straighten this mess up. Then I'll come in and play a round of checkers with whoever's ahead." She grinned at the assembled men. "Ain't no one alive able to best me at checkers. You all are on notice."

Sam grinned. "You might think she's kidding, but I assure you she's not."

"Well, let's do the best we can until she comes after us," John said.

The men kept teasing each other good-naturedly as Sam got the checkerboard and checkers out of the cupboard and set them up on a card table in the living room. I took Sarah's plate upstairs while Sweetie followed me with a fresh pot of tea and a tray. When we walked into the bedroom, Sarah sat up in bed. She looked much better. There was some color in her cheeks, and her eyes didn't look as tired as they had earlier.

"Oh my, you didn't have to bring dinner to me. I could have come to the kitchen," she said. Although her voice was a little stronger, it was clear she would need more time to recover completely.

"Pshaw," Sweetie sputtered. "You take it easy until you get all your strength back. Gracie and I don't mind waitin' on you some. Kinda reminds me of the time I tended to my pa. It ain't work when you're helpin' someone you care about."

Sweetie didn't talk much about the time she took care of her father after he was severely injured in a farming accident. It had to have been very difficult. I could see her swipe at her eyes with the back of her hand after she set the teapot down. She was an enigma. Just when I thought I had her figured out, she went a different direction. Maybe her determination to follow the Lord more closely was beginning to show. No matter what it was, my affection for her grew every day.

She carried the tray over to the bed, pulling out metal legs that fit over Sarah's lap. She motioned for me to put her plate down on the top. "I gotta get back downstairs and clean up the kitchen," she said to Sarah after she poured her a fresh cup of tea and grabbed the old pot. "I'll check on you later. If you're hungry enough, I'll bring you a piece of my peach pie."

Sarah smiled at her. "I don't know if I can eat everything you just brought, but if I can't eat pie now, I'd love a piece later." She shook her head. "I wish you'd teach me how to cook the way you do. I'm so awful at it."

If Sweetie liked Sarah before, her comment garnered her undying favor. There was nothing you could say to Sweetie that went straight to her heart faster than praising her culinary skills. Of course with Sweetie, that wasn't hard. She had a natural gift for cooking, thus the extra ten pounds I'd taken home to Wichita. Obviously I needed to practice restraint from here on out or there might be talk of little brothers and sisters to go with the imaginary baby I'd already given birth to.

"When you get to feelin' better, why don't you and Gracie come over once a week, and I'll teach you both to cook?"

"Hey, how did I get pulled into this?"

She pointed her finger at me. "I heard you tell Sam you can't cook. I ain't havin' my nephew saddled with some gal who can't keep him strong and fed right." She turned and walked out of the room mumbling something I couldn't hear. Sarah and I both giggled after she left.

"Looks like while you're teaching me how to do wood-block printing, Sweetie will be teaching us both how to cook."

Sarah took a bite of the roast chicken on her plate. "Oh my," she said after she put her fork down. "If I could learn to cook like this, maybe Papa wouldn't be so skinny."

I sat down next to her on the bed. "John's on the thin side, too, you know."

She didn't respond, just took another bite of food.

I reached over and took her hand. "Look, I know what you said earlier, and I won't keep bugging you. But don't shut that door completely, okay? God can do miraculous things."

She smiled sadly and stared at the food on her plate. "I know you're right, but unless John finds the Lord, there's no way we can ever be together. I never should have allowed these feelings to start. I knew better. I honestly can't explain how it happened. It took me by surprise. His warmth and. . .kindness. . .touched me." When she looked at me, her eyes were shiny with tears. "I know Papa loves me, but no one has ever listened to me like John does. It's as if everything I say is important. I really opened up to him and expressed feelings I didn't even know I had." Her eyebrows knit together in a frown. "Does this make any sense? Am I babbling?"

I squeezed her hand gently. "No, you're not babbling. I understand completely. I hadn't really thought about it before, but Sam makes me feel the same way."

"Well, as you said, I will put this in God's hands. But for now, I know we must keep our distance. It will be difficult. . . ."

"You know what? John knows this is what you want. He'll respect that and make it as easy as possible." I wanted to add that John's motive was his great love for the quiet Mennonite girl, but saying it wouldn't help anything. "Now let's see if we can get the rest of Sweetie's delicious dinner down. How do your hands and feet feel now?"

Sarah's eyes widened. "I hadn't thought about it, but they don't sting anymore. They feel perfectly normal."

"That's great. I predict you'll start getting back to your old self before long."

She nodded and took a bite of potatoes. "When will Papa and I be able to go home?"

I explained about the roads and the conditions. I also told her that the men would be leaving in the morning to help clear some of the snow away. "You might as well plan on staying here for a couple of days."

"Oh my. That means we'll have to spend the Sabbath here."

I chuckled. "Don't look so alarmed. We actually worship God on Sundays, too. I promise we won't do anything weird like build an altar and sacrifice one of Sam's animals."

Sarah's worried expression disappeared as she laughed. "I'm sorry. Of course you're right. It's just that Papa and I have worshipped with other Old Order believers since I was a child. That is, until last spring when we began to go to Bethel." She sighed. "I love it there. It's not that I didn't care for our other brothers and sisters; it's just that there is so much fellowship and joy now in our services. I can hardly wait to get to church every Sunday. Those are my only two group worship experiences."

"Besides you, your father, and Ida, who else in Harmony belongs to the Old Order?"

"Of course you knew that your uncle Benjamin used to be part of us."

I nodded.

"There are three other families. There is a large farm on Faith Road about two miles north of you. The Voglers have three children. Then there are two bachelor brothers, the Beckenbauers, who live a mile out of town to the south of us." Her brow furrowed and a troubled look crossed her delicate features. "The only other person is Abigail Bradley, who lives not far from Papa and me."

"I know the large farm you mentioned on Faith Road. I've seen the children outside playing, but I've never met them. I don't believe I've ever met the other people you mentioned."

"You wouldn't. They don't come into town much. They're fairly self-sufficient. We used to take turns having services in the homes of the Beckenbauer brothers and the Voglers. We still meet during the week for Bible study, and they respect our decision to attend Bethel on Sundays. In fact, the Voglers talk about joining us someday. It's possible the brothers will come one day as well. They're rather quiet and keep to themselves."

"And this Abigail woman?"

A shadow fell across Sarah's face. "We don't see her anymore. She's a very strange person. I think she prefers to stay away from other people. One of the Beckenbauer brothers checks on her from time to time."

Sarah yawned and handed me her tray. "I'm sorry, Gracie. I'm still rather weary. Do you mind if we talk more tomorrow?"

I wondered at the way she cut off any further

questions about Abigail Bradley. What was that about? But I knew Sarah was telling the truth about being tired. I could see it in her face.

"How about that peach pie?"

She gave me a tired smile. "Let's try that tomorrow, okay? I'm stuffed." She yawned again. "Please tell Sweetie how much I enjoyed everything, will you?"

I told her I'd take care of it and watched as she scooted down in the bed and pulled up her covers. "I'm sure your father will want to say good night. I'll send him up."

She nodded, but her eyes were already closing. I carried the tray out of the room and down the stairs. The men were intent on their game, and I could hear Sweetie rattling dishes in the kitchen.

"Gabe, Sarah's calling it a night. She's waiting for you to tuck her in."

He slapped down a checker and said, "Perfect timing. That's the game!"

Sam shook his head and tossed me a quick smile. "He's beat us every game so far. John and I don't stand a chance."

Gabe stood to his feet. "You two go ahead and play each other until I get back. At least that way one of you should win."

"Now just hold on there." Sweetie came into the room, wiping her hands on her overalls. "I think I can keep that from happenin'."

I winked at her. "You put these men in their places while I load Sarah's dishes in the dishwasher. Then we'll both show them how to really play checkers."

"You got a deal," she said. "Come on, boys, set 'em up again."

I carried the tray into the kitchen while Gabe went upstairs to check on Sarah. John followed me. "How's she feeling?"

"Much better. Her hands and feet have stopped tingling. She's still a little tired, though."

"Good." He looked relieved. "She'll be just fine. Thanks for taking such good care of her."

"No problem."

He left the room without saying anything else. Maybe he really would be able to keep his distance from Sarah. They both seemed committed to breaking the bonds of their relationship, but I had my doubts. When they looked at each other, their strong feelings were evident and the haunted expression in their eyes identical. While I rinsed Sarah's dishes and put them in the dishwasher, I prayed for them both.

The rest of the evening was spent playing games and having fun. It was as if the storm had never happened, outside or inside the hearts of those gathered together. And also as if there wasn't a dead body out in the barn.

We all headed to bed around ten o'clock, after a round of peach pie and ice cream had been served. Thankfully the big house had plenty of room for everyone. I slept in the bedroom next to Sarah's with the connecting door open enough so I could hear her if she cried out in the night. Either she slept very soundly or I did, because I woke up to sunlight streaming in the windows. I got dressed, checked on Sarah, who was still sleeping, and went downstairs. Sweetie was in the kitchen, sitting at the table. It was evident breakfast had already been served. The smell of bacon hung in the air.

"They're already gone," she told me before I could ask. "Don't know what time they'll get back tonight. Sam said to tell you he would make sure Ida was okay and would also find out if Thelma and Jessica heard yet about Rand."

I grabbed a cup from the cupboard and poured myself some coffee. The rich, hot liquid chased away the remnants of sleepiness that tried to hold on to me like an uncomfortable, heavy coat.

"Did Sam take his truck?"

"Nah. That old thing just ain't reliable enough with this much snow. Dan drove his tractor with the snowplow, and Dale brought their SUV. Guess they're roundin' up other farmers with tractors and plows. We have a tractor, but it's not heavy enough. With all of them workin' together, they should make some good headway today."

"I wonder if anyone's been able to reach Sheriff Taylor."

"Nope. According to the brothers, phones are out all over town, and Joe's old CB is busted. But believe me, first chance that nasty old sheriff gets, he'll show up."

I thought about what waited for him out in the barn and shuddered.

"You cold, honey?" Sweetie sputtered. "You sit down, and I'll rustle you up some breakfast."

"I'm not cold. And I'm not very hungry. I'm still full of your peach pie."

She laughed. "Peach pie can do that, all right. How about some oatmeal?"

"Perfect. That would hit the spot."

Sweetie nodded and set about making round two of breakfast. I should have offered to help, but for some reason my energy was zapped. Not sure why. Maybe it was all the excitement from the day before.

"What's the latest on the cold snap the forecasters have been predicting?"

Sweetie whirled around, a large spoon in her hand. "Land sakes, I'm plumb worried about it. Last I heard it could be comin' today or tomorrow. Not sure how long it will last. If the temperatures hit below zero and stay that way too long, we could lose our trees."

"Sam said something about burn barrels?"

She nodded. "Yep, we got 'em all over the orchards, but with all this snow keepin' the ground even colder. . . I just don't know, Gracie girl. It ain't lookin' good. If the clouds come back in, things will warm up a bit. If not, there's no tellin' what will happen."

I told her about praying for God's protection and quoted the scripture in Psalm 91 that I'd mentioned to Sam.

"My, that's a good one," Sweetie said. "It brings peace to my soul." She stirred the pot a couple of times. Then she took it off the burner. "You know, my papa believed everything that happened in this world was God's will. That we just take whatever comes and thank Him for it." She shook her head. "Wished I knowed God then the way I know Him now. I woulda showed my papa that we gotta have faith in God's Word to chase the devil away. That we ain't supposed to be ignorant of his devices. Maybe my papa and I coulda fought that ole snaggletoothed liar, and Daddy woulda been here today." Her eyes met mine. "Can you imagine thinkin' the devil's dirty deeds are God's will?" She dabbed at her eyes with her apron. "My daddy jes' didn't know no better. I think about that quite a bit, you know. Wonderin' if I coulda made things turn out different."

I reached for her hand. "Sweetie, I'm sure God doesn't want you blaming yourself or your father for his death. I'm not a Bible scholar or anything, but I've figured out one thing. Even if the devil gets one over on us in this life, he still loses. Your father is living in God's glorious heaven, waiting for his beautiful daughter to join him. No regrets. Just joyous anticipation."

Sweetie threw her head back and laughed. "My goodness, girl. Your middle name Pollyanna or somethin'?"

"No, but isn't it cool that no matter what happens, when we know God, we always have hope?"

She ambled back to the stove to check on her oatmeal. "I guess it is. Like the Good Book says, nothin' is impossible with Him." She tended to the stove a minute then said something I didn't hear at first.

"What? Did you say something?" I asked.

"Yes," she said a little louder. "I sure was worried you and Sam weren't going to work things out, but God made a way." She turned around and stared at me as if she wanted to say something. I waited, but she didn't open her mouth. Just kept watching me.

"I believe He did. Don't you?"

She folded her arms across her chest and rocked back and forth on her heels a few times. "I don't want to cause you no undo concern, Gracie girl. I hope everything is fine and dandy. It's just that I know my nephew pretty well. To be perfectly honest, I don't think he's settled in his mind about his mama yet." She rubbed her arms as if she felt cold. "I mean, think about it. The way he reacted to that story about the baby. Well, it showed he still had lotsa bad feelin's about the past. I mean, to treat you the way he did. Then suddenly everything's all right? Like nothin' ever happened?" She shook her head. "It just don't make sense to me. Through all these years, I've watched Sam stuff his real feelin's in a place down deep inside himself. In fact, he's spent a lot of his life doin' that." She stared at me, her expression guarded. "Just be careful, Gracie," she cautioned. "Make sure he's got all that sad stuff out and dealt with. If you don't, it could hurt you and him both." With that she turned her attention back to her oatmeal.

Her warning struck deep. The same thought had crossed my mind more than once. That Sam had changed too quickly after my emotional upheaval. Maybe Sweetie was right. Maybe it was a bad sign. My mother had the same kind of personality. She would always pick herself up after an emotional hurt and act like everything was okay. She'd done that after she was diagnosed with cancer, but one day her fear and anger boiled over, taking all of us by surprise. She began acting like a different person, yelling at my father and me, treating us as if everything we did irritated her. The change was so abrupt and so obvious that we knew immediately something was wrong. After some tears, venting, and counseling, she finally started to express her fear and frustration.

I learned a huge lesson from her. That to exercise our faith and walk in it, we must first deal honestly with our emotions. God can only help us when we admit we need it. Once my mom got hold of this important truth, she began to trust God for her complete healing. And she received it. She finished chemo with a positive attitude. I was thinking about her when a knock on the door almost made me spill my coffee.

"Now who in tarnation could that be?" Sweetie declared. "Shouldn't be nobody out 'cept our men, and they're gone." She frowned at me. "Can you get that? I gotta stir this oatmeal."

I hopped up from the table and hurried to the door. When I saw who waited on the porch, my mouth dropped open in surprise. Standing there as if there weren't six-foot snowdrifts surrounding us stood Sheriff Pat Taylor, his arms crossed, his feet spread apart, and his face screwed up into a fierce scowl.

"I hear you got another dead body to contend with, young lady. You wanna show me just where you stored this one?"

Ten

After changing my clothes and checking on Sarah, I led Sheriff Taylor to the barn, where Rand McAllister was laid out on a large wooden table used to hold feed for Ranger and Tonto, Sam's horses. The feed had been moved to accommodate the very deceased Mr. McAllister.

Thankfully he was covered with a blanket. I turned my head as the sheriff pulled up one edge to get a look at the dead man.

"Still pretty frozen," he grumbled. "Dang fool thing to do—wanderin' around outside in this weather." He paused a moment. "Any idea what he was doin' out there?"

I quickly looked his way and saw that he'd recovered Rand's face. "I have no idea, Sheriff. I didn't really know him. Sam and a couple other men found him in the snow not far from here."

"Near here, huh? Figures."

"What does that mean?" I asked hotly. "Look, the last couple of days have been very stressful for everyone. Now a cold front is moving in, and I'm worried about Sam's trees. He could lose them. I don't feel like sparring with you about Rand McAllister."

The surprised sheriff rocked back on his heels, his eyes wide. "Now just a minute, young lady. It might do you some good to speak a little more respectfully to me. After all, I am the sheriff in these parts."

"Yes, you are. And you certainly let everyone know it. You've been throwing your weight around ever since I got to Harmony. Even before that, now that I think about it. Why did you stop me on the highway the other day? There's nothing wrong with my tail-light. Surely you have something better to do than detain innocent people and make up stories. Now we have this body. I mean, a man has died, and all you can do is attempt to blame me somehow."

I felt like a balloon that suddenly ran out of air. Deflated, dejected, and dumb. Of course, I'm pretty sure a balloon can't feel dumb—or anything else for that matter. I would have slapped my hand over my mouth if it wouldn't have looked too dramatic. We stood there and glared at each other for a while. To my chagrin, Taylor began to look somewhat amused. I, on the other hand, was not. Finally I decided to break our stalemate while trying to retain a shred of my shattered dignity. "I'm sorry. I've been under a lot of stress. I shouldn't have yelled at you."

He kept staring at me strangely. Then he reached for his handcuffs.

"Whoa! I don't think you can arrest someone for losing their temper," I sputtered. "This is America."

"I'm not arresting you, Miss Temple. I'm getting my handkerchief." With that he put his hand in his pocket, ignoring the nearby handcuffs hooked on his belt.

"I—I don't need a handkerchief. I. . ." With a

start I realized that tears were dripping down my face. Oh brother. Another emotional meltdown. This was getting ridiculous. Taylor walked over and held out his handkerchief. I took it and wiped my face. The thought crossed my mind of blowing my nose and handing it back, but I'd already given the grouchy lawman more than enough reason to shoot me and call it self-defense. Putting a snotty hankie in his hand might be the last straw. With my face dry and my leaky eyes under control, I gave him back his only slightly used handkerchief. "Sorry," I said again.

He grunted.

I wasn't sure how to interpret that, not being fluent in grunts, so I just nodded. "So what now? Are you going to, uh. . ."

"Take Rand off your hands?"

I nodded again. At that moment nonverbal responses seemed safer. I couldn't risk going off again. Next he might actually pull out those handcuffs on purpose.

"So you're sure McAllister got caught out in the snow," he said. "No foul play or anything?"

I sighed with exasperation. "Look, Sheriff. Just because I used to have a dead body on my property, and just because I figured out who killed him. . . Well, that doesn't make me Jessica Fletcher. I assume Rand McAllister got caught out in the snowstorm and died of exposure. The same thing almost happened to my friend Sarah."

He frowned at me. "Who's Jessica Fletcher?"

I opened my mouth to respond but closed it before actual words came out. There wasn't anything I could say that wouldn't sound condescending and make the sheriff grab his handcuffs—or his gun.

He crossed his arms and examined me much the way a hawk might look at a field mouse running for its life. "Did you look at the body?"

I shook my head. "As much fun as that sounds, I'm not big on viewing corpses. But John Keystone helped bring him in here. I'm sure he checked him over."

The lawman's eyes widened. "So you think the butcher's opinion of the deceased's condition oughta be good enough to determine COD?"

I flashed him a grin. "I do watch *CSI*, Sheriff. John Keystone used to be a doctor. I'm sure if he'd seen anything that made him suspicious in terms of *cause of death*, he would have said something."

"Good show. Wait a minute. The butcher used to be a doctor? Now that's just plumb funny."

"Not really. And how is it you've watched *CSI* but you have no idea what *Murder, She Wrote* is?"

His bemused expression switched to one of confusion. "Someone wrote you about a murder? Who was it?"

By this point my limbs were beginning to freeze, and I was becoming convinced the sheriff was playing mind games with me. Besides, I'd begun to feel rather outmatched. "Is there anything else I can do for you?" I asked, hoping the answer would be "no."

He shuffled back and forth on his feet. "Yep, little lady. You can tell your doctor/butcher friend to give me a call. And you can help me move Mr. McAllister to my truck."

Wow, this really wasn't *CSI*. Those guys would have crime scene technicians all over this place before the coroner moved the body. But I was standing in the middle of Harmony, Kansas. I guess here we just throw 'em in a truck and forget it.

"In case you're wondering," he said, as if reading my mind, "I can't get anyone out here. Not the coroner's office or an ambulance. I'd just leave him where he is until the roads clear up, but since the butcher thinks this death is natural, I might as well take him off your hands." He took a deep breath like he was getting ready to jump in a lake for a swim. "Now if you'll just grab his feet. . ."

I held up both hands. "Hold on there. I have no intention of starting my day by grabbing a dead body and flinging it around. Call me a wimp, but there are just some things that will now and forever stay out of my repertoire of life experiences."

"I could force you to help me at gunpoint."

"Funny. But I have another idea." I pointed to a wheelbarrow behind us. "Let's try that first."

"Hard to get a wheelbarrow through all the snow."

"Good point. But if you'll drive your truck up to the barn door, we won't have to worry about it."

He considered my idea for a moment. Thankfully the scenario seemed to work for him. "Bring the wheelbarrow. I'll slide him in and then get my truck. You think you can at least roll him up to the door?"

Although I couldn't think of anything else I would rather *not* do, I was smart enough to realize I was getting off easy. So I just nodded, since the words "I'd love to push a frozen dead body in a wheelbarrow like some kind of macabre game at a church picnic" didn't seem appropriate.

Taylor got the wheelbarrow and brought it over

to the table. I turned my head as he put the body in it, but the thump I heard as the transfer was made would probably stay lodged in my memory for the rest of my life.

"Okay," he said in his deep, raspy voice. "I'll get the truck, and I'll honk when I'm ready."

"Fine."

There was a prolonged silence. Then I heard, "Miss Temple?"

"Yes?"

The sheriff cleared his throat. "Do you have some kind of plan to push the wheelbarrow without looking at it?"

"No."

"Okay. So. . ."

I reluctantly swung my head around. Great. Frozen bodies don't fit perfectly in a wheelbarrow. This was going to be a delicate balancing act. "Hey, maybe you could. . ." But I was talking to Taylor's backside. He left through the barn door without looking back. Obviously I was alone. Well, not completely alone. But alone enough.

I took a deep breath and grabbed the handles of the wheelbarrow, trying to completely avoid Rand's boots that stuck out from under the blanket. I noticed his blue socks showing through the holes in the bottom of his boots. Odd that he would wear lightweight boots like these outside—especially in the snow. It seemed to line up with John's assessment that Rand had gotten smashed and accidentally ended up outside. As I carefully navigated the barrow toward the barn door, trying desperately to keep the body balanced so it wouldn't slide off, the thought occurred to me that Rand might not be wearing socks after all. The idea made me a little nauseated. I could have checked out my theory, but let's just say that being right isn't always the most important thing.

We finally made it to the door. I waited while the sheriff backed his truck up next to us. I'd begun to notice that everyone and their brother owned trucks in Harmony. At first I wondered if it was just a country thing, but now I realized that trucks could make it through snow, high water, and the kind of rough terrain that cars like my Slug Bug couldn't. Although I had no intention of getting a truck, the idea of trading in my beloved Volkswagen for something more appropriate was noodling around in my head. What good is having a car you can't drive?

I turned my head once again as the sheriff loaded poor Rand up into the back of his truck. Kind of an undignified way to be transported to wherever he was going.

I heard the door on the truck bed slam shut. "Guess that's it," Taylor said. "You folks gonna be all right here?"

Did this tough character care about us or was he just being nosy? "Um, we'll be fine. Sure would like to get our phone service back, though."

The sheriff rubbed his stubbly chin. "Anyone I can call for you?" I thought about my parents, but they were used to big snows since they lived in Nebraska. Not hearing from me for a couple of days wouldn't worry them. "Sam and the other guys should be contacting everyone I'm concerned about. But thanks anyway."

"And who are these folks?"

"My friend Ida Turnbauer and of course Thelma and Jessica McAllister."

He nodded. "I ran into your boyfriend on my way here. He and his friends had already been to Mrs. Turnbauer's and were on their way to the McAllisters'. I guess you can quit worryin' about them."

"So that's how you found out about Rand."

He nodded.

"Then you were already on your way to Harmony? With the roads in such awful condition?" I shook my head. "Why? Surely you had enough going on in your own town."

He shrugged. "Had my reasons." He left me standing there as he got in his truck and slowly began driving back to the road. Even though his vehicle was heavy, it slipped on the ice several times.

I stood there and watched him go. Why would he come to Harmony if he didn't know about Rand? What was it here that interested him so much? I remembered Sam's stories about Taylor hanging around and asking questions not long after he took office. Between his bad attitude toward Harmony, his unusual interest in its citizens, his stopping me on the highway into town for no reason, and the fact that right after a major blizzard his first action was to head here—something wasn't right. A blast of bitter wind convinced me I needed to get indoors. Sweetie was waiting for me. She'd probably been keeping watch over the entire procedure.

"That old sheriff take Rand with him?" she asked as I came up the stairs.

"Yeah. He's gone."

She held the door open. I gladly left the cold

behind and entered the house. It felt like walking into a warm hug.

"Goodness, honey. You go sit by the fire. I'll bring you a nice cup of hot cocoa."

At that moment a cup of hot chocolate sounded like the most fantastic thing in the world. I headed for the living room, ready to curl up in front of the fire and let the warmth seep into my chilled bones. When I got there, I was pleasantly surprised to find Sarah on the couch, a comforter tucked around her.

"Hey, you're downstairs. I take it you're feeling better?"

"Yes, I am, thanks to you and Sweetie. I know I'm supposed to take it easy, but I just couldn't stay upstairs anymore. I'm lonely."

"Boredom. A sure sign of recovery. I remember when I was sick as a child and had to stay home from school. As soon as I told my mother I was bored, she knew the worst was over."

Sarah giggled. "I guess that's exactly where I am. So I must be getting better."

"I'm glad."

She pulled her legs up and pointed to the other end of the couch. "Sit with me for a while, will you? I want to talk to you."

I scooted into the area left open and tucked my legs under me so I could face her. "Sure. Anything you want to talk about, I'm here for you."

"I know that, Gracie. The last time I had a close friend was before my mother left. Having you in my life means more than you could possibly know."

I reached over and patted her knee. "And you're the best friend I have in Harmony. I miss our teaching sessions. When you're better, let's start them again. I've been working on a couple of things I'd like you to look at."

She laughed lightly. "Oh Gracie. You really don't need me to teach you any more about wood-block printing. The process is easy, and you've got a knack for it."

I shook my head. "Well, my 'knack' isn't anything close to your wonderful talent, Sarah. That's something I'll never learn, but I'd like to at least watch you work. I truly enjoy it."

She pushed her long dark hair back behind her ear. "I would love to spend more time with you, too. Surely by next week the roads will be clear, and we can all get back to normal."

"I hope so. Right now, though, I'm concerned about the weather forecast. They're calling for temperatures around zero. Sam's worried about his fruit trees."

Sarah frowned. "I hadn't heard that. But he has smudge pots, right? Hopefully that will help."

"He has them, along with the burn barrels already in the orchards. I have no idea how they work, but yes, he intends to use them if necessary."

"I will pray for him," she said earnestly. And I knew she meant it.

At that moment, Sweetie came into the room carrying a tray with two bowls of oatmeal and two cups of hot chocolate topped off with big dollops of whipped cream.

"You two need somethin' to warm you up. Oatmeal with cinnamon and sugar along with some good old hot chocolate oughta do it."

"Sounds perfect, Sweetie," I said. "But you didn't need to bring us breakfast. We could have gone into the kitchen."

"Nah," she retorted. "It's nice and warm in here. You two just relax in front of the fire."

"Oh my," Sarah said. "I love oatmeal, and you make the most wonderful cocoa, Sweetie. I could almost swear it has medicine in it. Every time I drink it, I feel stronger."

Sweetie's weathered face broke into a huge grin. "I ain't never had no one compare my hot chocolate to medicine, but I guess if it makes you feel better, it's all right with me!"

I laughed. "As long as it doesn't *taste* like medicine, it's okay with me, too."

"Sweetie, why don't you sit with us for a while?" Sarah urged.

"Why, thank you, honey. How 'bout later? I got some cookin' to do. Them boys is gonna be hungry when they get back. I wanna be prepared."

"Can we help?" I asked.

She waved her hand at me. "You two sit and have some girl talk. I work better alone."

"Okay, but don't forget. You promised you'd teach us both to cook."

"I won't forget. If you ever intend to hook my nephew, you gotta learn to fix his favorite foods."

I giggled. "Hook him? You make him sound like a fish."

Sarah laughed and almost spilled her hot chocolate. A couple of drops splashed on her blanket.

"Well, men are kinda like fish sometimes. You gotta have the right bait on your hook."

For some reason, the picture of a fish with Sam's face wiggling at the end of a fishing line popped into my mind. I had to set my cup down so I wouldn't suffer the same fate as Sarah. I picked up the bowl of oatmeal Sweetie had put on the table in front of me and took a bite. It was the best I'd ever tasted.

Sweetie flushed. "Now it ain't funny at all. The way to a man's heart is through his gullet. And that's just the truth."

I wanted to ask her why, if she was such an expert on men, she was still single. But I knew some about Sweetie's difficult past and the reason she was still alone. "You're right," I said, straight-faced. "When can we start the lessons?"

"Let's get past the weekend, girls. Next week we'll start. I'll have you two cookin' like old pros in no time."

"Thank you," Sarah said with a big smile. "I can hardly wait. We'll have so much fun."

I wasn't so sure learning anything from Sweetie, who could be caustic and difficult to get along with even on a good day, was really going to be "fun," but I voiced my agreement anyway.

Sweetie left the room with a spring in her step, buoyed by the prospect of whipping Sarah and me into shape.

"Oh Gracie. This is so exciting," Sarah said.

"Will your father approve?"

"Yes. Papa and John have made up. I don't believe Papa is upset anymore. Of course my silly stunt probably frightened him so much that he will spoil me for a while." She sighed. "I'm really sorry I scared him."

"We were all frightened. Especially your father. . . and John."

Sarah stared down into her cup, her expression so sad it touched my heart. "John really does love me, you know," she said softly. "And I love him, too."

"I know that. And I understand why you both made the decision to break off the relationship. You're worried about your father."

She nodded slowly. "Yes, my father. But not just my earthly father. I did it for my heavenly Father, too."

"Because of that scripture about not being unequally yoked?"

"Yes."

"What if John became a Christian after the two of you married?"

"There are no guarantees of that," she said. "What if he didn't? How could we have a good marriage if we don't share the most important thing there is? The most important aspect of my life?"

I knew that would be her response. I agreed with her stand, but I felt sorry for them—two really good people who truly loved each other. In my mind's eye, I could still see John lifting Sarah from the snow, although the expression on his face was something I never wanted to see again. Fear and intense love are powerful companions, but they certainly aren't friends. I thought about the scripture that says perfect love casts out fear. The only way to have perfect love is to have the perfect One in your life. And John didn't have Him.

"I know you're right," I said. "But I also know you're both hurting. You're trying to protect your father and obey God, and John is trying to protect you." I sighed. "I guess I'm just one of those people who believes in happy endings."

"But life is not a fairy tale, Gracie," Sarah replied. "Sometimes the endings aren't the ones we envisioned. However, if God is in them, we can find joy and blessing. He doesn't want us to be unhappy. He wants us to have joy. Leading us away from things that will hurt us is His way of directing us to the abundant life He has for us. He's the Good Shepherd, you know."

"You're a very wise woman, you know that?"

"Sometimes. When I'm not getting lost in a snowstorm."

At first I thought she was serious, but then I noticed her mouth quiver. We both laughed at the same time. It was great to see her on the road to recovery from her ordeal, but I sensed the pain over her broken relationship with John was still strong. Hopefully she would begin to heal, but right now I felt she needed to think about something else. I started to change the subject and bring up our scheduled cooking lessons when we heard a loud sound from outside, like the roar of an engine. Sweetie heard it, too. She came hurrying out of the kitchen, drying her hands on her apron.

"Are they back so soon? I figgered they'd be gone most of the day."

I got up and followed her to the front door. When Sweetie swung it open, I saw her expression instantly change. I peeked around her to see Eric standing on the porch.

"What in blue blazes do you want?" Sweetie said, her tone not the least bit welcoming.

Eric looked taken aback. "I—I came to see if everything was all right here. I went to Gracie's, but no one was there."

I stepped in front of Sweetie, who stood her ground, not giving me much room to maneuver. "I'm here, Eric." I shot Sweetie a sideways glance of disapproval. Reluctantly, she moved back. "Come on in." I pushed the door open and Eric came inside, although hesitantly. Sweetie's fixed glare obviously made him nervous.

"Seems that big fancy truck of yours can stay on the road when you want it to," Sweetie said sarcastically.

His eyes widened as he looked to me for help.

"Excuse me a minute, will you, Eric?" I grabbed Sweetie's arm and pulled her down the hall and into the kitchen. "What are you doing?" I whispered once we were out of Eric's line of vision.

"That man almost ruined things between you and Sam," she hissed. "He's a snake in the grass for sure."

"Sweetie, Eric didn't do anything wrong. At all. Sam misread the entire situation. You know that. Why are you acting like this? You're embarrassing me."

"I don't trust him as far as I can pick him up and toss him." She spoke a little too loudly for my comfort.

"You don't trust anyone. You barely trust me."

"Now that's just not true, Gracie. I trust you completely."

I grabbed her hand. "Then prove it. Eric is a very nice man. He risked coming here today through the snow just to make sure we're all right. And you treat him like he's an escaped criminal." The pitch in my voice had risen close to a tone only dogs could hear. In fact, Buddy got up from his favorite spot under the table to see what was going on. Snickle followed him. Seeing them scrutinize me like I was some kind of interesting phenomenon made me want to laugh.

But I needed to make sure Sweetie backed off of her unreasonable attitude, so I kept my cool.

She looked into my eyes for a moment; then she dropped her head. "Okay, Gracie. You say he's a good guy, so I'll believe you. I won't pick on him no more."

I would have asked her to apologize to Eric, but that would have been pushing my luck. I left the kitchen and hurried back to the front door.

"I'm sorry," I said to Eric. "Sweetie gets things in her head sometimes. It's hard to reason with her, but I think everything will be okay."

"Man, I was worried about Sam. I had no idea I'd be facing his aunt's wrath as well."

I smiled at him. "Sam's not mad at you. In fact, no one is mad at you. Come on in."

He followed me down the hall to the living room. Sarah was gone. Her blanket had been folded and was draped over the arm of the couch.

"I heard about Rand McAllister. I can hardly believe it," Eric said, his eyes darting toward the kitchen.

"That was fast. Who told you?"

"Dale Scheidler. He was clearing off the intersection at Faith and Main." He shook his head slowly. "At least I know now why he wasn't returning my calls."

I motioned toward the couch. "Sit down. How about some coffee?"

"I'd love it. Thank you."

"How do you take it?"

"With a little cream if you have some."

I grinned. "You're in Sweetie Goodrich's house. There isn't a food created she doesn't have. Anyway, I've never found it."

I heard him chuckle as I left the room. In the kitchen, I found Sweetie chopping vegetables with a little too much zeal. Even though she'd apologized, I could tell she was still bothered by Eric's presence in her house.

I got a cup from the cabinet and poured coffee into it. Then I got the cream from the refrigerator and mixed it into the cup. Sweetie didn't utter one word. It was almost worse than having her go off on a tangent. I set the cup on the counter and eyeballed her. "Sweetie, you have to trust God. If Sam and I are meant to be together, there is no man on the face of the planet who will be able to break us up. If you don't trust me, can you at least trust Him?"

When she turned around, I was shocked to see she'd been crying. Sweetie didn't cry very often. She usually yelled when she was upset.

"More than anything in this world, I want to see my boy happy," she said. "I'd give everything I own for that. And I know he will have that with you." She wiped a tear from her eye. "He's had so much pain in his life, and I've done all I can to make it better. But I know what he needs now can't come from me." She paused for a moment and cleared her throat. "It's time for me to become less important in his life. He needs—he needs someone to love. Someone to share his life." She focused her gaze on me. "He needs you, Gracie. And the idea that something could go wrong—that he might be hurt again. . . Well, I just can't bear to think about it."

I took her hand. "Like I said, if Sam and I are meant to be together, it will happen. You and I both need to believe that."

She shook her head. "But sometimes things don't seem to work out right. What about Gabe and his wife? I bet he thought they'd be together forever, and she walked out on her husband and daughter without so much as a fare-thee-well and spit in your face."

I was trying to figure out what a "fare-thee-well and spit in your face" was when I heard Sarah's voice coming from behind me. "Oh no."

I turned to find her dressed in her dark blue frock, her hair back up and covered by her matching prayer cap. Although she was beautiful no matter what she wore, I missed seeing her hair down.

"My mother wasn't dedicated to God, Sweetie," she said. "That's the difference between Gracie and Mama." She came into the kitchen and sat down at the table. There was still a shadow of weariness in her face. "She was raised in the Old Order ways, but she followed them because she had to. She married my father because he was the only boy close to her age that she liked at all." Sarah clasped her hands together and stared at them. "You see, she never really gave her heart to the Lord—or to our faith. So when she met the man she left with, all she could see was a new and different life. In her mind, a better life." She raised her head and smiled sweetly. "But Gracie has chosen her faith. She has chosen her God. And that is the difference. We cannot serve God because our parents do—or even because we think it is the right thing. Our commitment needs to come from our hearts—not just our minds." A frown creased her smooth forehead. "Am I saying this clearly? Do you understand?"

Sweetie nodded. "I think I do. I was readin' somethin' 'bout that the other day. Jesus asked Peter if he knew who He was, and Peter said Jesus was the Son of God. Then Jesus said somethin' that I had to read a few times before I got it. He spoke about flesh and blood not tellin' Peter who He was. But that his knowin' the truth about Jesus came straight from God." She frowned. "What Jesus said then was kinda amazin'. He said that the gates of hell couldn't come against that. I finally figgered out He was talkin' about the devil not bein' able to take away what we get straight from heaven." She looked at Sarah questioningly. "Is that what you mean?"

Sarah smiled at her. "That's exactly what I mean. Peter knew about Jesus because God revealed it to him. Not because someone else told him. I believe we all must have that moment when we choose to believe of our own free will." A sad countenance came over her. "My mother never made that choice. When she did finally choose, she chose the wrong thing."

"Sarah, in all these years have you or Gabe ever heard from your mom?"

"A few years ago a letter came. I will never forget my father's expression when he looked at the return address. He stared at it for the longest time. Then he threw it away without reading it or mentioning it again." She shrugged her thin shoulders. "He never said, but I think it might have been from my mother."

"You never asked him?" I said.

"No. I felt it would cause him pain. And to be honest, I feel more committed to caring about the parent who stayed with me—who raised me—than the one who walked away."

"I understand if Gabe just tossed out that letter," Sweetie said. "I kept things from my father the last year of his life because I didn't want him to worry. After his accident, he was so sick it was all I could do to keep him alive. Worryin' about things he couldn't fix. . .well, it just seemed wrong. Your papa didn't want your mama to cause you any more hurt. That's why he didn't open that letter."

Sarah nodded. "And I guess it isn't just the parents who protect their children. Sometimes the children protect the parents. And they may never know it."

Like Sarah was protecting Gabe from his fear of being alone. I had to wonder what Gabe would think if he knew the truth. "I'd better get this coffee to Eric before it gets cold," I said. "Sarah, would you like to meet him?"

"That would be nice."

I carried Eric's cup into the living room. He'd probably begun to wonder what was taking so long. "Eric Beck, this is Sarah Ketterling, Gabe Ketterling's daughter."

Eric stood to his feet. "Nice to meet you, Miss Ketterling. I visited with your father at your store in downtown Harmony. Unfortunately, he wasn't too enthusiastic about my project."

Sarah nodded at him and sat down in a chair across from the couch. Eric sat down as well.

"I hope he wasn't rude, Mr. Beck. My father is rather opinionated on most subjects."

Eric smiled. "No, he wasn't rude. He was just suspicious. And please, call me Eric."

"I would be happy to, but you must call me Sarah."

"Thank you." Eric finally had a chance to sip his coffee. I hoped it was still hot.

"Eric, can you tell me what will happen to your

project now? Now that Rand McAllister is. . .deceased?"

"I honestly don't know. I'm actually in a rather difficult situation. Time is ticking away on this deal, but I can't run over and talk to Thelma right away. It wouldn't be respectful. I'm not sure just what I'll do."

"Perhaps Pastor Mueller could intercede for you," Sarah said. "I'm certain he will be spending time with Thelma and Jessica as they deal with their loss. Maybe you could speak to him, and he could broach the subject?"

Eric's face brightened. "That's a wonderful idea. Thank you, Sarah."

"I tend to wonder if Thelma will be ready to move for a while," I said to Eric. "I mean, her husband dies, and she's going to sell her home right away? I don't know. That might be a lot of upheaval for someone dealing with grief."

"I know," Eric said. "But the problem is that unless we move quickly, this deal will fold. The investors are looking at some property in northwest Kansas. Lakefront property. Of course, that would be the most desirable choice."

"Well, maybe they should just buy it and forget about Harmony," I said.

"They're thinking seriously about it. It's much more expensive than Rand's property, but a better site overall."

I frowned at him. "Why don't they just buy some of the property around Trouble Lake? The lake is large, and except for my place and Sam's, the area hasn't been developed."

Eric smiled and picked up his coffee cup. "We looked at that first, but your place and Sam's are the only privately owned land around the lake. The rest of it is owned by the county, and they're not selling." He took a sip of coffee and put the cup down. It had to be cold by now.

"Let me warm that up for you," I said, rising to my feet. "What about you, Sarah? Can I get you anything?"

She shook her head. "No, thank you. I'm fine."

As I walked away, I heard Sarah say, "But if you could buy affordable land on Trouble Lake, your investors would probably decide to build here?"

"Absolutely. This area is still their first choice."

When I got to the kitchen, Sweetie wasn't there, but the door to the basement was open. She kept an extensive pantry downstairs. I'd found most folks who live in the country have big pantries. When you don't have a grocery store nearby, you have to stock up for situations just like the blizzard we'd just gone through. Anytime a big storm was predicted for Wichita, the stores ran out of bread and milk almost immediately. I always found that funny. How much bread and milk can anyone use at one time? Well, in Harmony, most women made their own bread and there were enough milk cows around to make sure everyone had all they wanted. Those weren't the items folks around here stocked up on.

The coffeemaker was still on, so I poured Eric a fresh cup of coffee, added cream, and headed back to the living room. As I entered the room, Eric was telling Sarah about growing up in Mound City, Kansas.

"I've never been to Mound City," I said as I set Eric's cup down on the table in front of him, "but I had a friend in Wichita who grew up there. She had such fond memories of her childhood. Sounds like a nice place."

"It is. I miss it. My folks still live there." He flashed me a grin. "Go, Hawks!"

"You played sports?" Sarah asked.

"Baseball. Nothing like playing for a high school team in a small town. Everyone comes to the games."

"I grew up in a small town in Nebraska," I said as I sat down, "and you're right. The games were the most exciting thing going. People brought their grills and cooked hot dogs and hamburgers before the game. We certainly never went hungry."

Eric laughed. "I know exactly what you mean."

"It sounds wonderful," Sarah said.

I'd heard that a lot of Mennonite children weren't allowed to play sports as children. Gabe had mentioned as much. Not wanting to make the conversation uncomfortable for Sarah, I changed the subject back to something I'd heard before I went into the kitchen. "Eric, did I hear you say something about your investors having an interest in lakefront property?"

"Well, sure. Anytime you can build a property near a lake, it adds to the value. Especially if you can offer swimming, boating, and fishing."

"How much land do you need?"

"As much as we can get, with most of the property next to the water," he said. "I'd want to give a majority of the condos a view of the water with easy access to the shore."

"I was just thinking that since originally my land was used for farming and I'm not doing that, maybe I could sell off part of it to help the town."

"You're very generous. I wish it was the answer,

but there's just not enough acreage. Rand's place is a little over forty acres, and yours is what. . .around thirty?"

I nodded.

"Excuse me," Sarah said softly. "I don't understand something. Even though Gracie's land is smaller, wouldn't your. . .investors. . .rather build a smaller community instead of giving up altogether?"

"The problem is that right now they're thinking about bailing out of the project completely since it seems our original plans won't work. And it isn't just the size of the land. Rand's place was just off a paved country road that connects to the highway. To reach Gracie's, you have to travel quite a distance on a dirt road. It's just not as attractive to older residents. My recent experiences in the snow show the importance of well-developed and well-maintained roads."

"So even if you could buy my place and Sam's, you still couldn't move the development here?" I asked.

"Well, I'd have to get the county to pave the road. I suppose if they were agreeable, we might be very interested." He smiled at me. "If the investors could be talked into looking at the possibility, there's a chance they'd be willing to offer you a great deal of money. Lakefront property is hard to come by. I'm sure they'd pay a lot more for your land than they would have for Rand's." He hesitated for a moment and then frowned at us. "But your property is much closer to downtown Harmony than Rand's. How would the residents feel about having the retirement community so close to town? The last thing I want to do is bring division to Harmony. This is a very special place." He shook his head. "On the other hand, having the development closer would definitely make shopping in Harmony more attractive to our residents."

The prospect of making Harmony stronger appealed to me. If Eric's project would really help the town, I'd actually be willing to move. But of course Sam and Sweetie would never sell their home or their orchards. This place was in their blood. And I couldn't stand to see the big red house destroyed. I pushed the idea out of my head. I'd just started to ask Sarah and Eric if they wanted more coffee when I heard the front door open.

I excused myself and hurried to see who it was. Sam stood in the hallway with the door still ajar. He was staring at Eric's Hummer parked in the driveway.

"What's he doing here?" he asked when he saw me.

"Well, hello to you, too."

"Sorry. Just wasn't expecting to find Eric here. I figured he'd hole up in Council Grove until the highways were in better shape."

I peered outside. Gabe and John had gotten out of the truck and were coming up the stairs.

"He came to help," I whispered. "You be nice. He was worried about all of us."

Sam glared at me but didn't pursue it.

"I thought you'd be gone all day. Why are you home so early?"

"We weren't the only ones out clearing the roads. Lots of men are working to make things passable. I decided the best place for me was back here. I have a lot of work to do before the freeze sets in."

"I guess you've been through this before?"

"Yeah, several times. And I've lost trees. I don't want to lose any more if I can help it."

With his mind on his orchards, at least he wasn't concentrated on Eric—or so I thought. When we walked into the living room, something in his expression must have alarmed Eric, who looked concerned when he spotted Sam. Sam still hadn't shared everything he'd said to Eric when he drove him to his truck the morning after the storm—just that he'd threatened to kick him out if he tried to explain the awkward situation. If anything else had transpired, both Sam and Eric were keeping it to themselves. I had the distinct feeling it would be best to let it stay that way.

"Gracie says you drove through the snow to make sure everyone here was okay," Sam said. He hesitated a moment while I prayed he wouldn't say something I might regret. "Thanks." Although he more or less mumbled it, I was relieved. Eric appeared to feel the same way.

"You're welcome," he said. "I heard on the news that temperatures are supposed to keep dropping. They interviewed a farmer near Garden City who was worried about his orchards. It made me wonder if you needed some help."

Sam sat down on the couch and stretched his legs. I could tell he was tired. "That's exactly why we came home early. I've got to clean out my barrels and set out some smudge pots. John and Gabe plan to help. I could use you, too, if you're interested."

"That's why I'm here."

At that moment John and Gabe both came into the room. John noticed Sarah up and dressed. The weariness in his face disappeared, and he broke into a wide smile. He opened his mouth to say something but suddenly stopped. Sarah lit up when she saw him, too, but when she observed his hesitancy, she immediately broke her gaze from his and focused it on her father. Gabe didn't seem to notice.

"Why, Sarah," Gabe said, "you must be feeling better."

She offered her father a small smile, but the color that had flushed her cheeks moments before faded. "I am, Papa. Gracie and Sweetie have been such wonderful nurses."

He walked over to where his daughter sat and grabbed her hand. "Thank you, Gracie," he said to me. "I'll have to thank Sweetie, too."

"Well, you can do that in my kitchen." Sweetie stood in the doorway, her apron speckled with flour and other ingredients from this evening's dinner preparations. "You all need some good food inside you before you tackle the orchards. Alls I got right now is some sandwiches, but I'm cookin' up the best pot roast you ever ate for dinner later on. Now everyone get on in here, and let's have a little lunch before you go outside."

As if obeying orders, we all followed her to the kitchen. I went last and was able to see the exchange of glances between John and Sarah. I also caught a warning glare Sam sent to Eric. I shook my head. Two situations with different kinds of emotions bubbling below the surface. Before the weekend was over, I wondered if one or both of them would boil over.

Eleven

Sweetie's idea of "a little lunch" wouldn't meet that definition by anyone's standards. Thick slabs of turkey on homemade bread topped with pepper bacon and thick mayonnaise was accompanied by creamy red potato salad. And of course, pie. In Sweetie's kitchen, pie was served like a condiment. You have coffee, you have pie. You have lunch—pie. Dinner—pie. Before bed—pie. I was waiting to come down to breakfast to find a thick slice of peach pie and whipped cream instead of the usual bacon, eggs, and pancakes. I ate half a sandwich, a couple of bites of potato salad, and said no to pie.

During lunch I told Sam and the others that the sheriff had stopped by to pick up our unwelcome guest.

"Seems kind of odd," Sam said. "But I guess if the coroner can't get here, there isn't much choice."

I shrugged. "He died of exposure. Nothing nefarious about that."

"Nef-fairy. . .what?" Sweetie frowned at me.

"Nefarious. Shady."

"Well then, why don't you just say shady?" she retorted. "Ain't no reason to use fancy-schmancy words when plain old proper English will work just as good."

I looked sideways at Sarah, who wouldn't meet my gaze. Her short bout of coughing was nothing more than an excuse to cover a case of the giggles. I fought to keep my composure. "You're right, Sweetie. Sorry."

John's raised eyebrow told me he also found Sweetie's admonition to use "plain old proper English" humorous. There wasn't a phrase Sweetie couldn't fracture, and she was incredibly fluent in colorful expressions.

"So just what are we doing this afternoon?" I asked Sam, trying to change the subject before Sarah embarrassed herself.

"*We* aren't doing anything. The men are going out to the orchards. *You* are staying here."

"Nonsense." I felt my temper flare. "I can work just as hard as you can."

"I know that, Gracie," Sam said patiently, "but Sarah is still recuperating. I think you should stay here with her."

"I'm fine, Sam," Sarah said with a smile. "Gracie doesn't need to watch me. Besides, Sweetie will be here."

"Only reason I won't be out there helpin' in my orchards is 'cause I need to keep an eye on what's in the oven," Sweetie snapped. "Don't you go tellin' any womenfolk where they belong, boy."

"I'm not trying to tell the 'womenfolk' anything," Sam said with a sigh. "I'm just pointing out that someone needs to stay with Sarah." He paused. "And watch the food, it seems. Sweetie, you and Gracie work it out between you. Whichever one of you wants to help, get bundled up. It's cold and getting colder. You're liable to be looking at frostbite before we're done."

"I—I didn't bring any gloves, and I'm afraid these pants aren't very thick," Eric said.

"No problem," Sam said. "I've got the proper clothes you can borrow—if you still want to help. If you don't, I totally understand." Maybe no one else noticed the touch of sarcasm in his tone, but I did. I scowled at him when Eric wasn't looking. I knew what he was up to. He was hoping Eric would give up and leave.

"Thanks, Sam," Eric said. "I'll take you up on that."

I smiled at Eric. Good for him. Sam wouldn't discourage him so easily. It was obvious Eric really wanted to help. Hopefully today would start to change things between Eric and Sam. I had no idea how long the young real estate developer would actually be hanging around Harmony. It depended on what happened with his quest for land. But however much longer it was, it would be helpful if the two men could bury the hatchet and find a way to get along.

After a brief argument with Sweetie about who would go and who would stay, I won. Or maybe I lost. The jury's still out on that. The winning point was struck when I pointed out that if I stayed to watch her food, I couldn't guarantee anything. Fear that her pot roast might not survive—and that any gravy from said pot roast might have more lumps than a prizefighter's head—sealed the deal. She would stay to watch Sarah and the food, and I would work in the orchards.

I changed into my heaviest jeans and the thickest sweater I'd brought with me. Double socks and my boots seemed to pass inspection with Sam, but he made me wear one of Sweetie's knit caps and a jacket that was so bulky I was reminded of the little boy in the movie *The Christmas Story* who complained that after his mother bundled him up against the cold, he lost the ability to "put my arms down." Feeling like a big, stuffed snowman, I clomped down the stairs and joined the men. We drove both trucks over to the orchards.

The first order of business was to dump the snow out of the burn barrels that were situated at various locations throughout the trees. This was difficult since the snow had blown up next to them, almost cementing them to the ground. Sam worked with me while directing John, Gabe, and Eric to follow our lead. I marveled at how well John and Gabe worked together. It was as if there had never been any tension between them. They seemed to really like each other. Maybe in the end, that was enough of a victory. Still, I couldn't help but hope that one day Gabe, Sarah, and John would be a real family.

"Hey, pay attention," Sam barked at me. I realized I'd been staring into a barrel Sam was trying to loosen while I did nothing to help him.

"Sorry, just thinking about Sarah and John." We were far enough away from the others that they couldn't hear us, so I didn't try to keep my voice down.

"You're wasting your time worrying about it." Sam grunted as he tried to wiggle the barrel loose. "Sarah isn't going to leave her faith. And I sure don't see John throwing in with their Old Order beliefs."

"You know, the gap between people like Abel and Emily and Mennonites like Gabe and Sarah seems to be closing rapidly. Ida has a phone now. And almost every Conservative Mennonite in Harmony has electricity. I think the old ideas about some of the modern conveniences are changing. I read something the other day that said there really aren't many true Old Order sects left."

Sam finally freed the barrel. He and I turned it upside down to shake out the snow. "I've lived in Harmony almost my entire life," he said after we set it back down. "And one thing I've learned: Just like with all people everywhere, you can't put titles on the folks in this town." He stopped for a minute and stared toward Gabe and John. "They all live by what they think is best for them and their families. Most don't have television, but some do. Most have cars, but some don't. Most have electricity, but a very few, like Ida and Gabe, don't. And everyone respects individual choices. You might be right. Someday soon, some unimportant differences might fade. But the faith of the people here will remain. Gabe doesn't care whether John has electricity. But he does care that John knows God, and that won't change. Ever."

He was right. Gabe and Sarah had made the decision to put God first. Sarah's feelings for John had been pushed to second place. . .well, third place actually. Behind her heavenly Father and her earthly father.

A surprised shout rang out from Eric. Sam and I turned to see him backing up from a barrel that was lying on its side. He'd started to set it right side up when he jumped back, tripped, and almost fell. Gabe's laughter brought us running. One look inside the barrel explained Eric's reaction. A mother raccoon looked up from a nest she'd made in the barrel. Several baby raccoons snuggled up next to her. The mother's bared teeth made it clear no one would be removing her and her family without a fight.

"Let's carefully move the barrel near the barn," Sam said with a grin. "They'll be warmer there. We've got plenty of other barrels."

Gabe, Eric, and I watched John and Sam pick up the barrel and carry it as gently as possible so as not to disturb the new family.

"I almost stuck my hand in there," Eric said, his voice quivering. I couldn't be sure if it was from fear or the cold.

"Good thing you didn't, son," Gabe said. "Raccoons are cute, but they can be vicious. Especially when they're protecting their young."

Eric's expression testified to the fact that Gabe's words brought no reassurance.

Gabe and I kept our eyes on Eric as he carefully approached the next barrel. He gingerly peeked over the edge before attempting to clean it out. Gabe grinned at me, but neither one of us said anything. I appreciated Eric's willingness to help out and had no desire to ridicule him—even though it was pretty funny.

The five of us worked for several hours. Sam and John pushed the snow out of the orchards the best they could so the barrels and pots could warm the ground as much as possible. Sam drove his tractor with the plow on the front while John shoveled snow by hand and dumped it in piles outside the tree line. Finally they began bringing out bunches of kindling wood, which we placed inside the large metal containers. As the weather forecasters had predicted, the temperature continued to plummet. My hands and feet were almost numb, but I didn't complain. None of the men mentioned the cold, so I didn't either. A couple of times I came close, but I felt protective of Sam's trees and determined to save them. After the barrels were ready, the men began dragging the smudge pots out of the barn. Black metal, with a long pipe that stuck out of the top, they were positioned in various spots around the orchard. Then the men put logs soaked in oil in the bottoms of the pots, added more fuel, and lit them. The flame shot out of the top flue and burned so hot it was almost invisible. After that they began lighting the kindling in the barrels.

"Go on back to the house," Sam shouted to me as I stood back to watch. "You've done all you can do. We'll finish up."

I wanted to argue, but I was really beginning to worry about my extremities. Besides, I could let Sweetie know they would be coming in soon, so she could have dinner ready. It was already dark, although I had no idea what time it actually was. I trudged back to the house, praying my feet would get some feeling back. Worry about Sam's trees filled my mind. What if the orchard was lost? What would Sam and Sweetie do?

As I neared the house, I caught myself. What was I doing? Even though I felt as if I would freeze to the spot if I didn't keep moving, I stopped.

"Father," I said out loud, "You said that without faith it is impossible to please You. You also said we're not to be anxious about anything, but with thanksgiving to send our requests to You. So I'm doing that now. I thank You for giving Sam this incredible home and these magnificent trees. I'm asking You to protect them, and I believe You will. Thank You for loving us so much and for caring about every part of our lives. Amen." I felt better and realized my feet had begun to tingle. I guess they weren't going to fall off after all.

When I reached the house, Sweetie stood by the door that led to the screened-in back porch. " 'Bout time someone came in. It's after seven o'clock. You people been out there for hours and hours." She held the door open and frowned at me. "Where's the rest of 'em?"

The fires from the barrels and pots lit up the encroaching darkness, so my answer seemed unnecessary, but I explained anyway. "The men are starting the fires. Sam told me to come in."

"Can you feel your feet?" she asked.

"Kind of."

"Come on over here and sit down. We'll get you warmed up while I get dinner on the table. Those men are gonna be ready to chow down when they get back."

I gladly entered the warm kitchen. Sarah sat at the table drinking something hot. I didn't even care what it was; I just pointed at it and plopped down in the nearest chair. She poured me a cup of what turned out to be coffee. I pulled off my gloves and wrapped my frozen fingers around the cup. It felt so good my whole body shivered.

Sweetie knelt down next to me and pulled off my shoes and socks. Then she went to the sink and poured some water in a tub. "Let your feet dangle in this for a while," she said, carrying it over and putting it down in front of me. "I'll go get you some nice warm socks."

Grateful for her help, I stuck my toes in the water. Immediately it felt as if thousands of little needles pierced my skin. I instinctively pulled my feet out.

"Put 'em back in," Sweetie said gruffly. "I know it stings, but that water is just room temperature. It won't hurt you."

Gingerly I lowered my tingling digits back into the tub. Slowly the rest of each foot followed. It didn't feel quite so bad this time.

"Are the men almost finished?" Sarah asked after Sweetie left the room.

"Yes. It was a lot of work. I hope it does the trick."

"It's usually pretty effective, I guess. The past few winters have been rather mild, so it's been awhile since I've seen it done."

"Between our work and our prayers, I'm expecting good results. I'd hate to think I almost sacrificed my toes for nothing."

She smiled. "I would, too."

I drank the last of the coffee in my cup. "This might be the best coffee I've ever tasted."

"That's because you're cold and tired." She reached for my cup and went to the coffeemaker to pour me another cup.

"Oh thank you. I think I'm beginning to feel human again."

Sweetie came into the room carrying a thick pair of clean socks and a towel, which was thrown over her shoulder. She knelt down and removed my feet from the water. She dried them carefully and pulled a sock over each one. Her actions reminded me of Jesus washing the feet of His disciples. I almost pulled away, embarrassed to have someone do something so personal for me, but I felt a still, small voice tell me not to. As I stared down at Sweetie, who was focused on caring for me, I didn't realize I was weeping until a tear fell from my face and onto my lap. I wiped my face, but not before Sweetie noticed.

"Well, for cryin' out loud, girl. Whatcha bawlin' about? I ain't hurtin' you, am I?"

I shook my head and smiled through my tears. "No. You're not hurting me. I guess I'm just a little tired."

She grunted and gave me a worried look. "After I get you warmed up, I want you to take it easy. That's hard work out there. Shoulda left it for the men."

"Actually, I would have enjoyed it if we hadn't been out there for such a serious reason and it wasn't so cold. It feels good to work hard." I told the women about the barrel with the raccoons and Eric's reaction to it. They both laughed along with me.

"How many times have you and Sam had to do this, Sweetie?" Sarah asked.

After getting the new warm socks on my feet, Sweetie picked up the tub and towel and stood up. She paused a moment and squinted like she was trying to see something far away. "Let's see. Altogether I'd say we've been hit five or six times with temperatures below zero. Some was real serious." She smiled and bobbed her head up and down. "But every time the good Lord was faithful and answered our prayers. I know He'll do it this time, too."

Sarah sighed. "You have such faith. I wish I had more. I worry too much about things."

I wiggled my now-warm feet around, trying to make sure the circulation was back. "You worry about people, Sarah. Not things. There's a difference."

Sweetie dumped the water from the tub into the sink, splashing some of it on her apron. "Worry is worry, girls. Faith is faith." She turned around, leaned against the sink, and stared at us, her features wrinkled in thought. "I been wonderin' a lot about this faith stuff." She shook her head. "I started worryin' about it until I realized I was worryin' about not worryin'!" She let loose a raucous laugh. "Now don't that just take the cake?"

Then her expression turned somber. "You know, I'm right grateful to God for all He done for me. Sendin' Sam into my life. Helpin' me to have this wonderful place to live and all. And most of all, lovin' a rough old broad like me. All He asks me to do is to trust Him and to cast my care on Him. I been figgerin' that since He's done so much for me, it's a pretty little thing He's askin' me back. I'm gonna try harder to do just that. I really am." With that she turned around and went back to rinsing out her tub and sink.

Sarah and I just looked at each other. Sweetie Goodrich surprised me almost every day with her homespun wisdom. She had a way of talking about herself and convicting me right down in the bottom of my heart without knowing she'd done it. Seemed like lately she'd been full of little sermonettes. The time she'd spent studying God's Word was starting to show.

"Sweetie, I think you're a pretty smart woman, you know that?" Sarah's tone was soft but sincere. "And I truly believe you're right. It *is* a pretty little thing to ask. I think we'll all quit worrying about the orchards and believe they'll be just fine. How about that?"

I could only nod at her. The concern over Sam's trees lifted, and I had a knowing down deep inside me that we would pass through this trial and come out victorious. A peace came into the room—and with it, a loud rumble from my stomach. "When is dinner ready, Sweetie?" I asked. "I'm starving!"

Just then the front door opened, and we heard the men clomping down the hall.

"It's ready right now," she said. "I've been keepin' things warm for you all."

I started to get up so I could help her, but she stopped me. "You stay right there, young lady. You're plumb tuckered out. I got this well in hand."

Sam stuck his head in the kitchen. "We're gonna clean up a bit; then we're ready to eat." He sniffed the air. "Wow, that smells amazing. I could eat my dinner and everyone else's."

Sweetie jabbed a big spoon at him. "You ain't eatin' anyone's food but your own. You ain't never starved for nothin' in my kitchen and you never will!"

Sam laughed and left the room. Within a matter of minutes, Sweetie had the table loaded with enough food to feel a small army. Even though I wasn't allowed to do anything, she did let Sarah help set the table and carry over some delicious-looking dishes. The aroma from Sweetie's roast beef along with huge browned potatoes, onions, and carrots made my mouth water. A broccoli and cheese casserole sat next to a big bowl of homemade applesauce. And big fluffy rolls came out of the oven, browned and slathered with butter. It didn't take long for the men to file in. Sam said grace and we began filling our plates. No one spoke for a while. I could tell the men were even more exhausted and hungry than I was. Sam shoved his food down faster than anyone. Then he stood up and looked at his watch.

"It's almost nine," he said. "I'm taking the first watch. John, you volunteered for the second. Eric, you have the third, and Gabe, you offered to take the fourth. Am I remembering that right?"

"What are you talking about?" I asked. "Aren't you through?"

Sam's smile only emphasized the weariness in his eyes. "Can't leave those fires burning without someone watching them. Along with the cold, we need to be concerned about the wind. If any of those pots blow over, it could start a fire and cause us some real damage. Also, we need to make sure the fires don't go out. Someone has to be on guard almost constantly." He shook his head. "I'd feel better if we had more than one person at a time, but we're all too tired to pull that off. As long as we're careful, we can take turns."

"I can take a shift," I said.

Sarah and Sweetie both jumped in at the same time to offer their services. I could tell Sam was starting to say no, but I stopped him before he could get any further. "Look, Sam. You've spent time clearing the streets and now this. Except for tonight, I've been sitting around doing nothing. I admit I was a little tired before we ate, but I'm fine now. For crying out loud, all I have to do is watch the barrels and the pots, right? If there's anything wrong, I'll come and get you." Again he started to say something, but I held my hand up. "Listen, if you guys get a couple hours of shut-eye, you'll have a better chance of staying awake out there. You sit around for long in the cab of a warm truck, as tired as you are now, you won't last more than fifteen minutes. Why don't you let me take the first watch? You all get some rest, and someone can relieve me in two hours. Okay?"

It was clear he wanted to argue with me, but it wasn't any use. My logic was too sound. Truthfully, I was still a little bit tired, but at least I wasn't sleepy. I knew I could stay awake. Sam and the other guys were fighting to keep their eyes open. After some hesitation, he shrugged.

"All right. I have to admit that your way makes more sense." He dug the keys to his truck out of his pocket and handed them to me. "Just drive up near the orchards. Park and watch for a while. About every fifteen minutes, drive all the way around. You're looking for fires that have gone out or pots that have blown over. If you see anything that concerns you, come and get me. Don't try to deal with it yourself."

I threw him a mock salute. "Yes sir. I understand."

He smiled at me and then turned his attention to his aunt and Sarah. "Sweetie, I think you need to stay here. You're cooking for a houseful of people." She began to protest, but he interrupted her. "Let me finish. These are your orchards. Whatever you say goes. If you want to take a shift, that's up to you."

"Well, thank you for that. I was startin' to wonder if you thought I was just some weak-willed woman." She thought for a minute. "Why don't I take the shift after Gracie? While she's gone, I'll put some breakfast casseroles together. That way in the mornin' alls I gotta do is pop 'em in the oven. That'll give you guys four hours of sleep."

"That sounds wonderful. But if either of you run

into trouble, you hightail it back here and wake me up. Better yet, where are our walkie-talkies?"

"They're right here." Sweetie got up and went over to a drawer next to her sink. She pulled it open and removed two black instruments.

"So that's how you guys keep in touch when you're working outside?" Eric asked. "I noticed my cell phone is worthless out here."

Sam nodded. "Cell phone service is spotty at best. These work great." He turned his attention back to me. "I'll keep one with me. If you need help, you call me." He looked around at everyone seated at the table. "When your shift is over, you give your walkie-talkie to the next person."

He handed the walkie-talkie to me, and I got up from the table. "I'd like to change my clothes first. I won't take long."

"You go get ready," Sweetie said. "I'll make you a thermos of coffee to take with you. Should help to keep you alert. In fact, I'll keep the pot on all night. If any of you want to take the thermos with you, just wash it out and fill it. Pass it to the next one."

Everyone around the table expressed their thanks, but Sarah looked troubled. "What about me? Can't I take a shift?"

"Daughter, we're still concerned about you," Gabe said. "You need to rest. Why don't you help Sweetie?" Seeing her crestfallen expression, he smiled. "Tell you what, if you want, you can come with me. That way I know I can stay awake. Besides, you haven't driven a truck like Sam's before."

She bristled at his comment. "I *have* driven a truck, Papa. I drove Uncle Matthew's truck when we went to visit. And I can drive our tractor."

Gabe tried to hide his quick grin. "Uncle Matthew's truck is an automatic. And you drive the tractor in one gear, Sarah. You can't do that with Sam's truck. I don't want you to get stranded outside in this weather—again."

Sarah still looked somewhat disappointed, so he added, "I'll tell you what, with Sam's permission, while we're keeping an eye on things, perhaps I could give you a driving lesson." He looked at Sam for agreement.

"I think that's a great idea," Sam said. "Please feel free."

Sarah's face lit up, and she clapped her hands together. I noticed that color had come back into her cheeks. I was relieved to see her looking more and more like her old self.

I excused myself and ran upstairs. I had to change my jeans. The bottoms were still damp from the snow. After getting myself ready as quickly as I could, I said good-bye to everyone and headed for the orchards, Sweetie's thermos beside me. A drive around the outer rim revealed everything was okay. I parked the truck and poured some steaming coffee into the cup on top of the thermos. I tried to sip it, but it was too hot, so I let it cool for a couple of minutes.

I was wishing I'd brought Buddy with me for company when I spotted something that looked odd. A smudge pot appeared to be missing. Although I couldn't memorize every position of every pot and barrel, I was certain I'd seen it at a particular location my first time around. But now there was only a dark space where the pot had been. Had it fallen over?

Sam not only had warned all of us earlier about a fire starting from a tipped pot but also had mentioned that kerosene was deadly to the trees. The wind didn't seem that strong at the moment, though.

Where could it be? It seemed silly to call Sam until I knew something was actually wrong, so I left the truck running and jogged into the orchard to get a closer look. When I reached the spot where the pot was supposed to be, I found nothing. I started to chalk it up to my own confusion, when I looked down and saw a bare spot where heat from the pot had melted the snow that still remained on the ground. So how could a large metal pot completely disappear? It didn't make sense. I'd just turned to go back to the truck and call Sam when a sharp pain exploded on the side of my head, and everything around me turned dark.

TWELVE

I lay on my bed in the purple bedroom, but for some reason it was really, really cold. I noticed a fire blazing in the fireplace. I tried to get closer to it, but it grew too big, pushing past the fire screen as if it were trying to reach me. Instead of drawing nearer, I found myself pushing away. The heat was intense. Sam began to call my name.

"Gracie, are you all right? We need to get you out of here. Come on, let's get you up."

I started to tell him I was trying to get away from the fire, when I remembered where I really was. In the orchard, lying in the snow.

"Come on, young lady. Can you stand up?"

Now why was Sam calling me "young lady"? I stared up at the figure that stood over me. "Sam? Is that you?"

"No, it's not Sam. It's Sheriff Taylor."

As my vision cleared, I realized it really was the sheriff who stared at me, not Sam at all. "Wh–what happened?"

He grabbed my arms and pulled me to my feet. The orchard spun around me. "You got hit on the head," he said gruffly. I realized with a start that the orchard was on fire.

"The trees are burning," I gasped.

"Yes, I know. Can you drive back and get some help?"

I nodded. The action caused pain to shoot through my temples. The feeling was all too familiar. A good strong helmet might have to be added to my clothing list if this kept up. "Th–there's a walkie-talkie in the truck. I can call Sam."

"Do it, and then go back to the house. Alert everyone about the fire. I'm going to do what I can until they get here." He peered into my face. "Do you understand what I'm saying?"

I rubbed my head. "Yes, I understand what you're saying. My head hurts, but my brain is intact."

I staggered toward the truck while the sheriff went the other way. What was he doing here? As I reached the truck, I turned around to watch him. Could he have started the fire? And if so, would he try to do more damage after I left? In my fuzzy mind, the only thing to do was to get Sam and the other men out here as quickly as possible. I flung the door to Sam's truck open.

It wasn't running, even though I was certain I'd left it that way. A quick search revealed no walkie-talkie and no keys in the ignition. I slammed the door shut and had decided to run to the house, even though I felt unsteady on my feet, when I spotted the sheriff's truck parked a few yards away. I hurried over to it, opened the driver's door, and saw the keys in the ignition.

The sheriff had disappeared into the trees, so I jumped in, started the truck, and drove as quickly as I could toward the house. As I neared Sam's, I couldn't help but wonder if Pat Taylor was the one who attacked me. I looked around the truck cab, trying to see if there was anything he could have used as a weapon. Nothing fit the bill.

I steered with one hand and popped open the glove compartment with the other. I had to turn on the interior light to see what was inside. I pulled out registration papers and a manual for the truck, along with a small personal phone book and a receipt for new tires. As I tried to shove the papers back where they'd come from, something fell out and dropped to the floor. Shoot. I couldn't reach it and drive with any kind of safety, so I waited until I pulled up in front of the house, quickly picking up what had fallen out and holding it under the light. It was a picture of a woman and a small child. A boy.

Frankly, it startled me. It hadn't occurred to me that Pat Taylor had a family. I put the picture back in the glove compartment. Then I jumped out of the truck and ran inside the house, hollering at the top of my lungs. It didn't take long for everyone to come running. When I announced the fire in the orchards, the men began grabbing their coats, hats, and gloves from the closet, and their boots from the front hall where Sweetie had put them on a towel to dry. As they all rushed to get to the orchards, I quickly told Sam what had happened.

"Someone hit you?" he asked, stunned.

"Yes, I have no idea who did it. Sheriff Taylor found me."

"Sheriff Taylor?" Sam and Sweetie echoed his name at the same time.

"What in blue blazes is he doin' here?" Sweetie's

tone had raised itself several notches.

Sam grabbed my shoulder. "Grace, could he have done it?"

I shook my head. Ouch. "Maybe. He acted like he was trying to help me. Honestly, I just don't know."

Sam looked troubled, but we didn't have enough time to talk about it any more. The men raced for the door. John stopped and looked at me before he followed them.

"Sit down. Take some aspirin. Don't exert yourself. I'll check you when I return." He sighed. "You know the drill since we've been through this before."

I smiled weakly. "Yeah. But I think this will do it for a while. I've been told I'm hardheaded, but I really need to stop testing that out."

"You've got that right," John said. And with that they were gone.

"Land sakes, Gracie. Get in there and sit down." Sweetie took my hand and led me into the living room. Sarah followed behind us. She wore my flannel nightgown and her hair was down. She looked like an angel. I sat down on the couch and pulled off my boots. Sweetie held her hand out for them.

"Better put them on the towel," I said, "or that snow will melt all over the place."

"I will, but I guess that system didn't work so well. Someone's boots left a trail of water and dirt all down the hallway. I'm gonna clean that mess up and get you some aspirin."

"Some hot tea would be nice, too," I said, shivering involuntarily.

"Gracie, you need to change clothes," Sarah said. "You're wet."

I'd forgotten I'd been lying in the snow. I jumped up from the couch before I made a mess of it.

"You stay there. I'll get you something. Do you have another nightgown like this one?"

"Yes, it's in the drawer in my. . .I mean, your room."

"Why don't you go strip off those clothes in the bathroom, and I'll bring it to you. Along with some fresh underwear and socks."

I agreed and walked slowly to the bathroom, still feeling a little dizzy. Man, I was running through socks—and heads—like nobody's business. Once in the bathroom, I stared at myself carefully in the mirror. I looked like I'd been "rode hard and hung up wet," another one of Sweetie's colorful colloquialisms. I had no idea what it meant, but if anyone ever fit the description, it was me. Maybe the first time I'd hit my head it had been my own fault. But not this time. Someone had deliberately attacked me and then set the orchard on fire.

The orchard! I'd been thinking about myself so much, I'd almost forgotten about it.

I stripped off my clothes, which were now soaked. Then I dried off with a towel that I wrapped around my body. My hair was a tangled mess and smelled of smoke. Thankfully there was a brush on the counter. I brushed my hair out the best I could and waited for Sarah. When she knocked on the door, I reached out and took the clothes she held out to me. The warm flannel nightgown felt good on my skin.

There's something about flannel nightgowns that makes me feel safe. They remind me of the gowns my grandmother used to make for me. Beautiful, soft colors with ribbons sewn into the neckline. Although it was impossible to buy a nightgown as nice as my grandmother's, I still loved them. I felt like a child when I wore them. And I was. A child of my heavenly Father. I prayed quietly for the men, asking God to help them. Then I prayed that Sam's trees would survive the fire. I hung my wet clothes over the shower curtain rod and opened the door.

"What's going on in the orchard?" I asked Sarah, who stood waiting on the other side.

"I don't know. Sweetie's on the back porch."

I grabbed her hand and we hurried to the porch. The windows of the enclosed room faced the orchards. Sweetie stood at the window near the outside door. Sarah and I joined her. Although I could see the fire from the barrels and the smudge pots, I could only see one tree ablaze. I sighed with relief.

"I was afraid the entire orchard would be lost," I said. "But it doesn't look so bad."

Sweetie shook her head. "No, it doesn't. Even if we lose a few trees, we'll be all right. As long as the cold snap doesn't do the rest of them in."

"Wow, growing fruit is a lot tougher than I realized."

Sweetie snorted. "It sure ain't for sissies, I can tell you that."

I reached over and took her hand. "You're certainly not a sissy, Sweetie Goodrich. In fact, you're one of the strongest people I've ever met. I hope I can be even half the woman you are."

She didn't respond, but I didn't care. I'd grown used to her inability to accept praise or personal gestures, so it surprised me when she suddenly put her arms around me and gave me a big hug.

"Thank you, Gracie. That means more to me than I could ever say." She released me and went back to staring outside.

I still felt a little shaky and was in need of that aspirin she'd promised me, but I knew she wanted to keep an eye on her trees. I excused myself and went into the kitchen. There on the table was the bottle of aspirin sitting next to a glass of water. She hadn't forgotten. Tea steeped on the stove. I took about four pills and poured myself a cup of hot raspberry tea. I took it into the living room and settled down on the couch, covering myself with the same quilt I'd used for Sarah. Although I didn't mean to, after sipping about half a cup of tea, I promptly fell asleep.

"Gracie? Are you all right?"

Sam's voice again. I woke with a start. Was I back in the orchard? No. This time it really was Sam, and I was still on the couch. His face was streaked with soot, but he looked happy.

"What happened? Are the trees okay?"

He sat down next to me. "Only a couple burned. The rest are fine." He shook his head. "You may not believe this, but the sheriff actually saved most of them. He shoveled snow around the bottoms of the trees. When the fire reached the snow, it burned out." He leaned closer to me. "That fire was deliberately set." He kept his voice low and his eyes darted around to see if anyone was within hearing range. "Someone poured kerosene around about ten of my trees and sprinkled more on the ground so the fire would spread. Thanks to the sheriff's quick actions, the plan didn't succeed."

"But who—"

"I have no idea," he said, interrupting me. "But I don't believe it was Sheriff Taylor." He sighed and shook his head. "For the life of me, I can't think of anyone who would want to burn down my orchards. Someone must really have it out for me."

"That doesn't make sense."

He shrugged. "Not to me either. There aren't any more buried bodies you haven't told me about, are there?"

"No, no buried bodies. No murderers trying to keep me from discovering their crime." I pulled myself up to a sitting position and frowned at him. "Are you sure someone actually set the fires, Sam? Is there any way the smudge pot could have blown over and rolled near the trees? Maybe the kerosene just escaped on the ground."

He shook his head. "I thought the same thing at first, and to be honest, if the trees had burned more, I would have come to that conclusion. I found the missing pot near the base of one of the trees. But the trail of kerosene was way beyond the path of a rolling smudge pot. Besides, two things make that theory even more unlikely."

"What do you mean?"

"Well, I'm not convinced it's windy enough to blow over those pots in the first place. And someone smacked you on the head. Someone who didn't want you to catch them. You're sure you didn't fall over your own clumsy feet this time, right?"

"Hey, my feet aren't clumsy. And no, I'm sure of it. I was standing perfectly still."

He nodded. "I checked all around the area where

the sheriff found you, just in case a large branch had broken off and fallen on you. But there wasn't anything like that."

"Man, Harmony may be a small town, but it's always interesting."

Sam chuckled and ran his fingers down the side of my face. "I need you to stay here. John wants to check you out. Again. I think he also wants to tell you that frequent hits on the head can have a lasting effect. You really need to stop it. I can't have the woman I love forgetting my name."

"That will never happen, Seymour," I said with a smirk. "Now get out of here. You need to sleep. Who's taking the next watch?"

"If I tell you, you won't believe it."

"I have no idea."

"Sheriff Taylor. He said he's well rested and pointed out that he has a gun. I took that two ways. Number one is that he is fully capable of watching the orchards and protecting himself. And number two is. . ."

"Never argue with a man who has a gun?"

"You got it." He kissed me, and then he rose slowly to his feet. I could see how tired he was. "I'll get John. Then I'll see you in a few hours."

"Not if I see you first."

"Look, I don't want you out of Sweetie's sight while I'm gone. Do you understand me?"

I rubbed my head. "Why?"

"Because I'm not sure what's going on here, and I want you to be safe. Promise me."

I held up my hand. "I solemnly swear to stay near Sweetie at all times. Like she'd let me get away from her anyway."

He leaned down and kissed me again. "I happen to love you. Do you know that?"

"I believe I do."

He left, and I closed my eyes. I'd almost drifted off to sleep again when John came in.

"We've really got to stop meeting like this," he said with a smile. "I told you I was just a general practitioner. You seem to have confused me with a neurologist."

I grinned at him. "Actually, I'm just waiting for the day you quit practicing and become a real doctor."

He sat down next to me on the couch. "I can tell your sense of humor is still operational. Now let's see if anything else has held together." He felt my head and then looked into my eyes. "You have a bump. Surprisingly it's not too far from your previous bump." He sighed deeply. "The next time could you go for the other side of your head? This one is about used up."

"Sure. The next time a crazy arsonist approaches me, I will immediately offer the other side of my head to him. No problem."

"Are you having a lot of pain?"

"No. In fact, it hurts less this time."

"I think you're just getting used to it." He frowned at me. "Well, Gracie, everything looks okay. But now I really want you to drive to Sunrise when the roads clear and get yourself checked out. I mean it. Will you do it, or do I have to forcibly deliver you myself?"

I knew he was serious. And quite honestly, I was beginning to wonder how many times one person could get knocked in the noggin before it caused complications. "You have my word. I will get myself to Sunrise and ask them to check me out for drain bramage."

"Funny. I'm going to follow up and make sure you do. Now get some rest."

"Yes sir."

He started to rise, but I grabbed his arm. "John, don't you think this whole thing is a little weird? Why would anyone want to burn Sam's orchards?" I lowered my voice so no one else could hear me. "And one other thing. If the sheriff hadn't come along, and if the fire had caught the way whoever started it had wanted it to, what would have happened to me? I was unconscious and pretty close to the kerosene."

John's face paled. "I hadn't thought of that. If you hadn't been found or if you'd been hit harder, you could have been seriously injured."

"Just what was this guy after? Sam's orchards—or me?"

"Well, if it's any consolation, I doubt anyone would have set the trees on fire if you were the target. Wouldn't they have just finished you off and left? Why start a fire?"

"I don't know. And the sheriff showing up when he did. Don't you find that strange?"

He shrugged. "He says he was in the area, trying to make sure everyone was okay, when he saw the flames. Makes sense to me. Doesn't it to you?"

"I guess so. Still, something feels odd about it."

"I don't know what to tell you, Gracie. I'm just glad you're okay."

"Thanks. I think I'll shove down some more aspirin and get some sleep."

"Sounds like a great idea. Good night."

After John left, I got up and went to the kitchen for a glass of water and some more aspirin. After swallowing them, I sat down at the kitchen table for a while. The house was dark and silent. I took the time to pray for wisdom. I couldn't help but remember something Ida had said. About having a bad feeling—a stirring in her spirit telling her that something was wrong. I had that same feeling now, and I had no idea why.

THIRTEEN

Though I speak with the tongues of men and of angels, and have not charity, I am become as sounding brass, or a tinkling cymbal. And though I have the gift of prophecy, and understand all mysteries, and all knowledge; and though I have all faith, so that I could remove mountains, and have not charity, I am nothing. And though I bestow all my goods to feed the poor, and though I give my body to be burned, and have not charity, it profiteth me nothing. Charity suffereth long, and is kind; charity envieth not; charity vaunteth not itself, is not puffed up, doth not behave itself unseemly, seeketh not her own, is not easily provoked, thinketh no evil; rejoiceth not in iniquity, but rejoiceth in the truth; beareth all things, believeth all things, hopeth all things, endureth all things. Charity never faileth.' "

With that, Gabe closed the Bible and put it on the kitchen table. Instead of sitting down in his chair, he remained standing, his eyes cast downward. After several seconds, he looked up at us. "I haven't always lived by these scriptures. I guess I don't really need to tell you people that. You've seen the worst side of me. Bitterness and anger ruled my life." He hesitated a moment and then cleared his throat. "I hope you will all forgive me. I've realized that Paul's admonition to forget the past and press on toward the future must also be my goal. And it starts with love." He smiled at us, but his mouth quivered slightly. This was clearly an emotional moment for him. "I know that none of us can completely trust human beings. We're fragile, and from time to time we all fail. But we can always trust God, and His way is the way of love. To leave behind anger, to trust, to hope, and to keep no record of wrongs. I'm afraid I had quite a lengthy ledger of the wrongs that I thought had been done to me. And to be honest, I've realized that when others do things that hurt you, they are the ones who should be pitied. I just want to tell all of you, my dear, dear friends, that I am letting go of the past today and intend to press on—with my friends and my God." He sat down.

John slowly stood to his feet. "First of all, thank you for allowing me to sit in this morning. I—I know I don't really belong in this group, not being a Christian and all, but would it be all right if I said something?"

"Of course," Gabe said. "This is just an informal gathering of friends."

I glanced around the table at the rest of our group. Sweetie, Eric, Sam, Gabe, Sarah, John, and me. An eclectic group to be sure, but everyone seemed to be enjoying our makeshift Sunday service.

"I came to Harmony on a quest to find my father," John continued, "and I certainly accomplished that. Unfortunately, as most of you know, my quest turned up harsh truths that were difficult for me to accept. Like Gabe, I held resentment and anger, not only toward my father, but toward the world in general. That anger was directed at some of you. So I'm also asking for forgiveness, and like Gabe, I'm determined to leave the past where it belongs. In the past." He ran his hand through his thick black hair. "I have to admit that I've been thinking about what happens next. My first reaction was to leave Harmony. I thought it would be best for me—and for Sarah and Gabe. But if it's okay with them, I'd like to stay. I feel at home here, and I've never felt that way before. In fact, I think it might be time to turn my meat shop into something different—like a doctor's office."

I heard Sweetie's sharp intake of breath. Having a doctor in Harmony was a dream come true for all of us.

"But here's the thing," he said, his dark eyes full of concern. "I can't make that decision alone. Those scriptures Gabe read made it clear. If my living here would be hard for you, Gabe, or for you, Sarah, I'll leave. No argument, no hard feelings. If staying causes either one of you pain, well, I just won't do it." He watched Gabe closely. "So what would you like me to do? It's all up to you."

He sat down slowly, and for quite a while Gabe didn't say anything. The rest of us kept quiet, waiting for his response. I could feel my heart pounding. Surely he wouldn't send John away.

"I appreciate how you feel," Gabe said finally. "And I appreciate your concern for Sarah and me. In many ways it would be easier if you left. But I won't ask you to do that. You see, I've spent years trying to protect Sarah—and myself—from pain. But all I did was make it worse." He reached over and took his daughter's hand. "Sending you away seems wrong." His eyes sought John's. "I believe you're an honorable man, John. I believe you when you say you won't pursue Sarah. Besides, I trust my daughter completely." He broke his gaze away and looked at Sarah. "If I tell you to leave, it will be out of fear. Not faith. And not love." He directed his attention to John again. "I don't want fear to rule me anymore. Do you understand?"

I thought John would look relieved, but he didn't. "I do understand. But since we're being completely honest, I have to say one more thing. And it may cause you to change your mind."

Gabe gave him a tight smile. "You mean that you're still in love with my daughter?"

John's mouth dropped open, but no words came out.

"I know that, son. I'm not stupid. And I know my Sarah loves you, too. If that wasn't true, this decision wouldn't be difficult at all. Your promise would be easy, and I know it isn't. I still want you to stay."

"Thank you," John said quietly. "Then I will do that. And I intend to make you glad I did."

There was silence at the table. I had no idea what to say, and everyone else seemed to be in the same boat I was.

Finally Sweetie broke the quiet. "Well, land sakes, Gabe. There for a while you had me nervous as a long-tailed cat in a room full of rocking chairs. If you'd sent this young man packin', I woulda been right disappointed in you." She flashed him a toothy grin. "You done the right thing here."

"Thank you, Sweetie. Coming from you that means a lot."

"I hate to hurry off," Sam said, "but I need to get

outside. Please continue. Don't end early for my sake."

Gabe let out a long sigh that seemed to come from somewhere deep inside. "Frankly, I'm drained. How about a prayer, and we'll bring this to an end?"

Everyone agreed. We held hands and Gabe led us in prayer. Then before he left, Sam made sure Sweetie and I had Sheriff Taylor's number.

"He's still in the area," Sam said. "He told us to call him if we need anything or if we see someone hanging around who doesn't belong here."

"That would be a mite sight easier if the phones were working," Sweetie said.

"I know that. But until then, if you need something, all you have to do is come out to the orchards and get me."

"Wish we had them walkie-talkies. Did you ever find 'em?"

Sam sighed. "No. Haven't found them or the keys to the truck. Thankfully I have another set of keys. Maybe we'll run across them today since the sun's up. Couldn't see much of anything last night."

Sam left the kitchen to get his coat. Eric had offered a ride home to Gabe and Sarah, and they'd accepted. I hated to see them leave, but they wanted their own clothes and their own beds. Besides, Sarah was worried about Molasses. I prayed the horse had made it home safely. I knew Sarah would blame herself if she didn't.

I got another cup of coffee while everyone got ready to leave. Then I sat back down at the kitchen table to relax a little. When the phone rang, it startled me so much I almost spilled my coffee.

"Glory be, the phone's workin'!" Sweetie screeched. She grabbed it and hollered, "Hello?" so loud, I hoped the person on the other end hadn't lost some of their hearing. "Why, howdy, Pastor," she said. "Glad to hear from someone. Our phone's been out for a couple of days." After listening to his response, she handed the instrument to me. "Pastor wants a word with you, Gracie."

I took the phone from her.

"Gracie? You all doing okay over there?"

"We're fine, Abel. Had some trouble in the orchards last night, but everything is under control now. How about you?"

"Everyone's fine. We're all digging out."

"Same here."

"Listen, Gracie. I need to talk to you, but I don't really want to do it on the phone. Are you planning to come into town anytime soon?"

Uh-oh. What now? Another letter? "I'm not sure. Is something wrong?"

Abel's gentle laugh drifted through the receiver. "No. Nothing's wrong. The baby's mother came to see me this morning. I want to talk to you about it, but as I said, I'd rather do it in person."

I was thrilled to hear the news but unsure how soon we'd be able to make it to town. I told Abel I'd have to speak to Sam and get back to him.

I hung up the phone, thrilled the mother had been found, but disappointed that Abel wasn't willing to tell me more until I saw him. Just then, Sam came into the kitchen.

"Can I get a thermos of coffee, Sweetie?" he asked his aunt. "It's really cold out there."

She laughed. "I'm way ahead of you, son." She handed him the thermos, already prepared. "And here's an extra cup for John. This should last for a while."

"Thanks." He came over and put his hand on my shoulder. "We'll be out there most of the day, Gracie. You and Sweetie could really help out by watching the weather forecasts. According to the most recent report, this cold spell could break sooner than expected. If it does, I need to know right away."

I nodded. "No problem, but I have a question. When are we going into town again?"

"If the temperature goes up the way they're predicting, we could go tonight. I'd like to take you both to dinner. Sweetie needs a break. She's been cooking for a houseful of people. I'd like to have someone cook for her instead."

"Sounds great. Abel says he knows who the baby's mother is and wants to tell me about it."

"You let me know what the weatherman says. If we can get up another twenty degrees and they tell us we'll stay above zero for a while, we'll put out the fires and go to town, okay?"

"Sounds good."

"Sounds real good to me, too," Sweetie said. "I love cookin', the Lord knows I do, but I gotta admit that I'm tuckered out. I ain't as young as I used to be, you know."

"Well," Sam drawled, "none of us are, Sweetie."

"Are you sassin' me, boy?"

"No ma'am." He turned his face and winked at me. "I would never sass you."

Sweetie took after him with a hand towel, ready to snap it on his backside, but he quickly kissed me on the cheek and sidestepped his aunt. Laughing, he bade us both good-bye and hurried out of the kitchen before his aunt regrouped.

Sweetie came over and sat down next to me. She was quiet until she heard the front door close. "Gracie girl, I'm worried."

"About what happened in the orchard?"

She nodded. "Sam hasn't said much to me because he doesn't want me to stew about it, but I know somethin's wrong. I got a gut feelin' there's more goin' on than meets the eye. I want you to tell me what really happened out there."

As I began telling her the events of the night before, her face wrinkled up in a frown. The longer I talked, the more worried she looked.

"And that sorry excuse for a sheriff just *happened* to show up when he did?" She snorted. "That's plumb ridiculous. There's somethin' wrong with that man. I been feelin' it ever since I first met him. There's deep, dark water runnin' under the surface of his pond."

"But Sweetie, he saved the trees, and he probably saved me. If the fire had spread and someone hadn't found me. . ."

"Don't you even go there," she said, shaking her head with vigor. "Ain't nothin' bad gonna happen to you. I pray much too hard for you, Gracie Temple."

I squeezed her arm. "Thank you. I seem to need all the prayer I can get."

"Has it occurred to you that the sheriff only pretended to save you so he could cover up his tracks? I mean, maybe he wasn't countin' on anyone findin' out what he was up to. Maybe when you showed up, he had no choice but to play the hero."

I could only stare at her. "But why not just run away? Why slug me?"

She shrugged. "Maybe he couldn't get away

without you seein' his face."

"Maybe," I said slowly. "But what about my keys and the walkie-talkie?"

"I been ponderin' that," she said in a conspiratorial whisper. "Maybe he didn't actually want you to get back to the house for help. Maybe he thought if it took you longer, the trees could burn faster. You fooled him by takin' his truck. Then he had no choice but to put the trees out." She frowned. "If that's true, then he ain't done, 'cause he ain't accomplished what he set out to do."

I considered her words. They made a twisted kind of sense. "I don't know, Sweetie. All we can do is pray for God's protection and keep our eyes peeled. But I'm still not convinced about the sheriff. He acted really concerned about me—and about the orchards."

"Well, here's somethin' else, Gracie. Somethin' I forgot to tell you. It didn't seem all that important until now, but while you was gone, I saw Taylor at your place, snoopin' around. In fact, one night he was out there after dark with a flashlight."

My head snapped up. "A flashlight? You didn't tell Sam about it?"

She shook her head. "Nah. He gets aggravated at me sometimes when I complain about folks. I'd already been tellin' him that snoopy sheriff was hangin' around too much. I knew he'd think I was hallucinatin' or somethin'. I was gonna tell you, but with everything going on, it slipped plumb outta my head." She frowned at me. "Is it important?"

I told her about seeing someone in the woods behind my house the first night I came back.

"See what I mean? I'm tellin' you, Gracie.

There's somethin' goin' on with that man. Somethin'. . .nefa-fairy-us."

Even though our conversation was serious, I couldn't hold back a smile. "I thought you said *nefarious* was a fancy-schmancy word."

She grunted. "Well, it certainly fits in this situation." She got up and went to the coffeemaker, grabbed the carafe, and carried it back to the table. "All I know is we need to do what Sam said. Keep our eyes open for anything suspicious." She filled our cups with fresh coffee. "I swear, I wish things would settle down for a while. The past few days have been real confusin'." She carried the carafe back and placed it on the warmer. "I can't shake this strange feelin' in my gut," she said when she came back to the table. "I think that old lion, the devil, is roamin' around, and we need to make sure we got our armor on good and tight."

Her declaration sent a shiver down my spine. I was just getting ready to respond when Sarah came into the kitchen.

"We're getting ready to leave," she said. "I wanted to thank you both so much for everything. There's no way I could ever repay you for your kindnesses to me or my father, but I would love it if you'd come by the shop next week after we open and pick out something you'd like."

Sweetie rose from her chair and gave Sarah a hug. "That's real nice of you, Sarah, but you don't owe us nothin'. We're all family, and lookin' out for each other is just what we do."

She smiled at us. "I know that, but I still would like to bless you in my small way."

"Thank you," I said. "I appreciate it. Hopefully all the businesses will be ready to open this week. We're going to try to go to town tonight if the temperatures keep rising."

"Papa said the forecaster predicted several days of below-zero weather. Has that changed?"

I nodded. "This morning they said the severe cold could break as early as today."

Sarah beamed. "God is answering our prayers, isn't He? This is wonderful news. I will continue to pray until the trees are safe."

"Please do," I said. "Where's your father? I wanted to say good-bye to him."

"I'm right here." Gabe's bass voice rang out loud and clear. "I'm sure Sarah has thanked all of you for your incredible help in finding her and nursing her to health, but I also want to express my gratitude. You've made both of us feel welcome. I won't ever forget it."

I went over and hugged Sarah. Then I held my hand out to Gabe. I wanted to hug him as well but wasn't sure if it would offend him. I shouldn't have worried. He disregarded my hand and wrapped me up in a big bear hug. I found my nose buried in the scratchy material of his thick wool coat. It felt wonderful.

"Well, I guess we need to get going," he said when he let me go.

Eric came up behind him. "Whenever you two are ready, we can head out. I've already been outside. The truck started." He grinned at me. "And I have no intention of turning off the engine until I get to my hotel."

"That's probably a good idea," I said, smiling.

"When you go back to Wichita, you might look into trading that thing in for something more reliable."

"You've got that right," he said, shaking his head. "Believe me, I've learned my lesson." He smiled at Sweetie. "Thank you so much for your hospitality—and your magnificent food." He patted his stomach. "I'm going to avoid the scale for a few days. The hotel food should help me lose whatever I put on here. You're an incredible cook, Sweetie."

"Young man, I ain't usually wrong about people, but it seems I've been a mite unfair to you. I ain't sayin' I trust you completely. And I ain't sayin' I'm not still a little peeved with you, but you jumped in to help us when we needed it, and I'm mighty grateful. You're welcome back here anytime."

Sweetie's little speech took all of us by surprise, including Eric. "Well. . .well, thank you. I don't know what to say. That means a lot to me."

Sweetie nodded at him. "Now you all get out of here and get home." She pointed at Eric. "I'd be obliged if you'd give us a call when you get to your hotel. Let us know everyone made it back safe."

"I'll do that," Eric promised.

I followed them to the front door, grabbing Eric's arm before he could leave. I pulled him back a bit, letting Sarah and Gabe go ahead. "I wanted to thank you, too," I said. "And to apologize for the way you were treated. Sam and Sweetie were out of line. I'm glad everything's okay now."

"I wouldn't say it's okay," he said quietly. "Sweetie may have come around, but Sam still doesn't trust me."

"I'm sorry. I know he appreciates your help."

Eric's deep blue eyes peered into mine. "You know

what Gabe said this morning about John still having feelings for Sarah?"

"Yes."

"Sam shouldn't trust me. If I thought I had a chance with you, I wouldn't hesitate to tell you how much I care about you. How deeply I'm attracted to you."

I shook my head at him and took a step back.

"Don't worry, Gracie. Like John, I'm a man of honor. I have no intention of acting on my feelings. I know how much you love Sam. You're safe. I just thought you should know." With that he walked out the door.

I stood and stared at the closed door, my heart beating so hard I could feel it. At the beginning of this strange weekend, I'd forecast that hidden emotions would come to the surface. Well, they certainly had. But I'd been looking in the wrong direction, never dreaming my prediction would come back to haunt me.

FOURTEEN

Sweetie and I spent the afternoon cleaning up after our guests—doing all the dishes, washing sheets, towels, and blankets. The entire time we kept one ear open to the weather forecasts. The temperature climbed into the thirties by late afternoon, and the announcer finally declared that although at first they'd expected it to stay below zero for several days, things had changed. It would stay bitterly cold, but the temperatures were predicted to stay well above zero. Sweetie and I thanked the Lord together for answering our prayers. When Sam came in around three o'clock, we told him the good news.

"Hallelujah." He sighed with relief. "Except for the two trees that burned, they all seem okay. Of course, we can't be sure until spring, but all in all, I'm very optimistic."

"So what now?" I asked.

"Now we put out the fires, and I tell John to go home. I'll put the smudge pots away tomorrow."

Sweetie crooked her finger toward him. "Does this mean we get to go out tonight? I could use me one of Mary's great steaks." The eagerness in her face made Sam smile.

"I think that sounds like a great idea."

"How do you know Mary will be open?" I asked. "You two act like she lives there."

Sweetie laughed. "Maybe that's because she does. Mary's got an apartment over the restaurant. Cute little place. I saw it once when Sam and her was seein' each other."

"I guess that explains why she didn't seem worried about getting home the other night after our first round of snow. I never really thought about it."

"It's also one of the reasons she's always open," Sam said. "Besides the fact that she enjoys having people around her. I think she's pretty lonely when the restaurant is closed." He shook his head. "Twenty-nine years old, and her life revolves around that place."

I felt a wave of pity for Mary. She seemed so self-confident and comfortable with people. Goes to show we just don't know what's really hiding below the surface. "She asked if I could come by and have dinner with her tomorrow night. Do you think my Bug will be able to make it back and forth?"

Sam shrugged. "I guess we'll get a better idea of road conditions tonight. I expect some of the snow has melted, but it's likely to refreeze later. Let's leave early, okay? That way we can get back before it gets too slick."

"Hey, you're the one who has somethin' to do," Sweetie reminded him. "We're ready to go whenever you are."

"Why don't you see if John wants to come?" I said. "He deserves a night out. On you."

Sam grinned. "You're right about that. I'll ask him."

After he left to put out the fires, Sweetie and I

finished up our work. About an hour later, Sam came stomping in the door, trying to shake the snow off his boots.

"Hey there," he said when he saw me on my way upstairs with an armload of clean towels and sheets to put in the linen closet. "Give me about thirty minutes to wash up, and we'll take off."

"What about John?"

"What about me?" John had come in the door without my hearing him.

"What about going to dinner with us?"

He looked down at his clothes. "I appreciate the offer, but I'm a mess."

"I've got clothes you can borrow," Sam said. "We'd really like you to come."

John grinned at him. "I'm already wearing your clothes."

"The clothes you had on when you came here are clean," I interjected. "If that makes any difference."

"Well, it just might at that," he replied. "I would like to rinse off some, though."

"No problem," Sam said. "You can use the downstairs bathroom. I'll use the one upstairs."

Something suddenly struck me. "Wait a minute. I've been so excited about the trees being okay, I just realized we've forgotten something. We can't go to town. What about the orchards? Whoever started the fire last night might come back."

"I already thought of that," Sam said. "Sheriff Taylor came by while John and I were outside. He offered to keep an eye on things while we're gone."

"But what if he's the arsonist? We could be making a big mistake."

Sam frowned. "What? Sheriff Taylor had nothing to do with that. You've got him all wrong, Grace. He's trying to help us. He saved the trees—and you. Why are you so suspicious of him?"

I told him what Sweetie had said about Sheriff Taylor snooping around my house late at night.

He frowned at me. "So what? He's the sheriff. He could have been investigating something. I'm sorry, but a sheriff outside with a flashlight sounds perfectly normal."

"Then why didn't he come and tell me why he was out there?"

"I have no idea. But I think you're being paranoid."

"Can I interrupt here?" John said. "I think Gracie has a point. We really don't know much about Sheriff Taylor. I mean, he might be a good guy and all, but why take chances? You guys go to town, and let me stay here. I'll keep an eye on things until you get back."

"No way," Sam said. "You've got to be exhausted. We'll just go another night."

"Don't be goofy," John said. "I saw some leftover meat loaf in Sweetie's fridge. I'd love nothing more than to sit in a quiet house, eat a meat loaf sandwich, and spend some time with Buddy and Snickle. To be perfectly honest, tonight I'd really like some time to myself. I love you guys, but I live alone. I'm not used to this many people around all the time. It kind of wears me out."

I started to object, but John stopped me. "Please. I'm with you, Gracie. Someone needs to watch this place until we know who started that fire. You all may be stuck at home for a while. Let this be my gift to you. Let me be your tree sitter for tonight. Besides, there will be lots of other times to go out to dinner. It's not like you don't know where to find me."

"It's up to you, Sam," I said. "These towels and bedsheets are heavier than they look. Why don't you two duke it out? I'll be back in a minute."

I continued up the stairs, put the towels and sheets away, and was headed back down when Sam came bounding up the stairs.

"So what's the verdict?" I asked.

"Get spruced up, good lookin'. We're going out."

"John talked you into it?"

"Yeah, I think he really wants to stay here. We need to get away, and he wants to be by himself for a while." He chuckled. "Besides, I think he's serious about Sweetie's meat loaf. I know how he feels. It's great."

I had to agree. Sweetie had a way with meat loaf. I wasn't sure what she put in it, but it was better than my mother's. Even better than my grandmother's. "Okay. I'm going to call Abel and tell him we'll be at Mary's tonight. Maybe he can meet us there."

"That's the real reason you want to go to town. Admit it. You want to know the identity of the baby's mother." He reached over and tweaked my nose.

"Hey, don't do that!" I gave him a lighthearted slap on the hand. "It's not just because I'm nosy, although I have to admit I'm really curious." I sighed. "As much as I love this house, I would like to see some different walls for a few hours."

He grabbed my hand and kissed it. "And so you shall. The next walls you see will be a weird shade of blue and decorated with grease splatters." He offered me a goofy bow. "Only the best for you, my dear."

"Stand up straight, you big dork," I said, laughing. "You really do need a night out, don't you? And by the way, those walls are cerulean blue. And they're not the least bit weird."

He got to his feet. "It's a little bright for me. I guess I like my blues a little more subtle."

I kissed his cheek. "Because you have no imagination, my friend. Now get your shower. Trust me, you need it."

He grinned and put his hand over his heart. "You have wounded me to the depths of my soul. I shall take my stinky body to the showers, posthaste."

"Not posthaste enough. Now get out of here."

He bowed again and headed down the hall to the bathroom. My heart felt lighter than it had for a while. Even though we still had no idea who'd tried to destroy the orchards and given me a second bump on the head, Sam was obviously so relieved that his fruit trees were safe, his spirits were flying high.

I changed clothes and waited downstairs while Sam got ready. John made it to the kitchen first with his own clean clothes on. "Wow. Feels good to wear my own stuff. Not that I don't like Sam's wardrobe, but I'd started to feel like a homeless waif who had to rely on the kindness of others."

"And how do you know how a homeless waif feels?" I asked innocently.

"Okay. You got me. I'm just guessing about that. But now I'm about to beg for my dinner, so I'm right back where I started."

"You ain't gotta beg for nothin'," Sweetie said, walking into the room. John and I both did a double take. Sweetie's ever-present overalls had disappeared.

Instead she wore a pair of nice black slacks and a cream-colored sweater with beadwork on the bodice. And her ratty tennis shoes were replaced with black pumps. Her dark gray hair was still in a bun, but it was neatly wrapped and accentuated with a decorative, beaded comb. Although Sweetie abhorred makeup, I could detect a slight bit of blush, mascara, and lipstick.

"Wow. You look great, Sweetie," I said.

John nodded his agreement.

"Well, for cryin' out loud," she barked. "You know I been goin' to Abel's church. Did you think I was wearin' my coveralls there every Sunday?"

"No. . .I guess not," I agreed. "I've never seen you right after church. I don't know what I thought."

"Goodness gracious, Gracie. I'm not some hick from the sticks, you know."

John and I exchanged quick glances. He turned away and stared out the window.

"Now about the food you thought you had to beg for," she said, opening up the refrigerator. "I heard you wanted a meat loaf sandwich, is that right?"

John had recovered enough to turn and face her. "Yes ma'am," he said with a smile. "I've had your meat loaf sandwich on my mind all day."

"How 'bout some of my homemade potato salad and a big piece of peach pie to go with that?"

I could almost feel John's contentment rise and fill the room. "That sounds perfect."

"Everyone about ready?" Not only was Sam clean; he looked incredibly handsome in a black sweater and blue jeans. The sweater highlighted his blond hair and gray eyes. I almost gulped when I saw him, but forced it back. I'd have felt like a cartoon character. Next my tongue would be rolling out of my mouth and my eyes would pop way out of my head. None of those options seemed particularly attractive.

"Let me finish gettin' this young man somethin' to eat," Sweetie admonished. "Then we can get goin'."

"Hey, you look beautiful," Sam said to me, his eyes sweeping over me with appreciation.

"Funny, I was going to tell you the same thing."

He laughed easily. "And Sweetie, you look gorgeous, too. Maybe we're all too good-looking for Mary's Kitchen."

John snorted. "Guess it's a good thing I'm not going with you guys. I hate to lower the beauty bar."

"Thank you," I said sweetly. "We really appreciate that."

He stuck his tongue out at me but quit paying attention to the rest of us when Sweetie put his plate in front of him. Sweetie's meat loaf had taken over his brain, and further communication would fall on deaf ears.

"I'm going outside to warm up the truck," Sam said. "You two ladies join me when you're done here."

"Won't be more than a minute," Sweetie said while cutting John a piece of pie big enough for two people.

"As soon as I eat, I'll take a tour of the orchards, Sam," John said with his mouth half full.

"That's great," Sam replied. "But remember what I said. Once every hour is plenty. You can see almost everything from the back porch. I don't expect any trouble tonight. Not with you here and the sheriff circling around."

The expression on John's face agreed with my feelings. Watching Sheriff Taylor might be the most important part of John's vigilance. But neither of us said anything.

Sam left to start the truck, while Sweetie made sure John was set up with enough food to feed a small army. While she fussed with him, the phone rang and I picked it up. It was Eric letting us know that everyone had made it home safely. I thanked him and hung up. I still felt uncomfortable with what he'd said to me as he was leaving. I hoped it wouldn't hurt our working relationship should he find a way to complete the project.

We got our coats and went outside. Fitting the three of us in the front seat was pretty snug, but the arrangement actually offered additional protection against the cold. Maybe the temperature was climbing, but you couldn't prove it by me. It was still chilly enough to make me wonder if staying home and having a meat loaf sandwich hadn't been the wiser choice.

The roads were in much better shape than I'd imagined, thanks to Sam and the other men who'd worked so hard to clear away the snow. As Sam had predicted, some of the snow had melted. As the temperature rose, the roads would get even better, although it would be a long time until the snow was gone.

As we drove past the spot where we'd found Sarah, I shuddered involuntarily. I couldn't help but wonder what would have happened if we hadn't found her when we did. Gabe and Sarah's buggy was gone, but I had no idea who had moved it or where it was. Hopefully it was back at their house. I forced myself to push the thoughts of Sarah from my mind. Tonight was supposed to be a fun break from the tension of the past few days. My mind needed a vacation just as much or more than my body.

Although we had to drive slowly, we made it to downtown Harmony just fine. These streets looked as if they'd received very careful attention. There were quite a few cars parked near Mary's. I recognized many of them. They belonged to members of Bethel who'd stopped in for dinner before church began at seven. We parked next to Abel's car.

"He's here," I said.

"I'm sure happy to know that poor little baby is back with its mama," Sweetie said. "I hope things go good for her. Wonder if there's somethin' I can do to help."

"I thought you said someone who left their baby wasn't much of a mother," I said. "Now you want to help her? That's a big change. What happened?"

Sweetie sighed and looked at Sam. "I figgered out that I was just mad at my sister for leavin' Sam. I don't know this baby's mama or why she thought she had to walk away." She looked at me and smiled. "I'm far from perfect, Gracie. But at least I'm aware of it. I asked God to help me change 'cause I know I can't change myself. And you know what? He's doin' it. I'll start to say somethin' that I wouldn't have thought about twice a few months ago, and suddenly the Holy Spirit reminds me that my words ain't right. That I'm gettin' ready to say somethin' I shouldn't. It might take me a bit longer than most to clean up my act 'cause I been so mean-minded for so long, but God don't give up on us—ever."

"Good for you, Sweetie," I said, hugging her. "I'm

proud of you. Very proud of you." I looked over at Sam, but he seemed preoccupied.

"You both stay in the truck until I get you," he ordered. "There's still some snow and ice near the steps, and I don't want you slipping and falling."

He climbed out and came around to the passenger door. First he escorted Sweetie up to the front door of the restaurant and then came back to get me.

"You need to say something encouraging to your aunt," I said quietly as he helped me out of the truck. "She's trying so hard to change."

"Humph," he grunted. "She's said stuff like this before. Let's see how long her newfound personality lasts. Just a couple of days ago she ripped some TV commentator to shreds because she didn't agree with his politics."

"Wow. That's a really negative attitude. How about cutting her a little slack, Mister Self-Righteous?"

He grunted. "Okay, I get the point. You're right." We walked up the steps to where Sweetie waited for us.

"Man, I can hardly wait to rip into one of Mary's rib eye steaks. Hector does somethin' to 'em that makes 'em so juicy, you think you're drinkin' meat instead of eatin' it."

As we entered the restaurant, I tried to get the concept of liquid meat out of my mind. Mary spotted us when we came in.

"Hey, I've been wondering about all of you. How are you guys?"

Before Sam or I had a chance to open our mouths, Sweetie launched into a diatribe of our experiences over the last few days. By the time we sat down, Mary had been thoroughly briefed. The only things Sweetie didn't reveal were my bump on the head and our suspicion that the fire that started in the orchard was arson. I was pleased she hadn't spilled out all our business.

"I'm glad the trees are okay," she said, "but what about Sarah?"

"She's fine," I said, "but we sure were worried at first."

"She's such a sweet person," Mary said with a frown. "I hate the idea of her being out in that blizzard by herself."

"Thank God He led us right to her," Sweetie said. "It was a miracle if you ask me."

Mary nodded. "Sounds like it." She took her notepad out of her pocket. "What can I get for you all?"

We placed our drink orders, but I asked Mary to give us more time to decide what we wanted to eat. She left our table and I glanced around the room, looking for Abel. I spotted him across the room sitting with Emily and Hannah. I hadn't seen either one of them since I got back to town. I excused myself and headed for their table. Abel saw me coming and waved me over.

"Gracie," he said with a big smile, "I'm so glad to see you. I heard about the fire in Sam and Sweetie's orchard. Glad everything's okay."

"Who told you about that?" I asked, surprised.

Emily grabbed my hand and squeezed it. "It was Sheriff Taylor," she said. "We ran into him here at lunch. We don't usually eat out twice in one day like this, but the road to our house is still pretty bad. Abel decided we should hang around town today so we wouldn't run into any problems getting back for tonight's service."

Abel chuckled. "I was as surprised as anyone when he came up to our table to talk to us. I was giving Mary my order when he interrupted and told us about the fire. He seemed very concerned about all of you. Said he intends to keep a watchful eye on Sam's place."

"For a minute, I wondered if we were under arrest," Hannah said, giggling. "He doesn't like Mennonites, you know."

"Hannah!" Emily said. "Don't tell tales. As far as I know, he's never specifically said he doesn't like *us*."

"My wife's right. I don't think it's just Mennonites the man finds so repulsive. I think he feels the same about all faiths. He's an equal opportunity heathen." Abel's eyes twinkled and he winked at me.

"Abel! My goodness. Calling a law enforcement official a heathen," Emily said with a sigh. "I'm glad we're going to church tonight so you can repent." Even though she sounded serious, I noticed the sides of her mouth curve up.

"When can we get together to paint?" Hannah asked. Even though I'd only been gone a few months, I could see the gorgeous blond-haired, blue-eyed girl maturing right before my eyes. Not only did she possess God-given talent; she'd been blessed with a delicate, almost angelic beauty.

"If the weather holds, we'll get together this week sometime. How's that?"

Her face lit up. "That would be wonderful. I've missed you, Gracie."

I leaned over and kissed her on the cheek. "I've missed you, too, Hannah."

"Add me to the list," Emily said with a smile.

"Why don't you come to dinner one night during the week? You and Hannah could paint afterward."

"I'd love it. Can I call you tomorrow to set it up?"

She squeezed my arm. "That would be wonderful."

Abel stood to his feet. "If you both will excuse Gracie and me for a moment, I'd like to talk to her privately."

"You're always talking privately to people," Hannah said. Her bottom lip stuck out slightly.

Abel raised one eyebrow and stared at his daughter through narrowed eyes. "You're right, Hannah. It comes with the territory. I'm a pastor. Maybe you weren't aware of that."

She blushed. "I know, I know. But I'd like to have a secret once in a while."

"Tell you what," I said. "When we get together, I'll tell you a secret about me. As long as you promise to keep it to yourself."

"Oh Gracie," she breathed. "I promise."

I winked at Emily, who smiled at me. I had no idea what secret I could share with the teenager, so I'd have to do some thinking first. I said good-bye to the women and followed Abel to an empty table.

"I'm almost glad Hannah mentioned secrets, because this will have to be a secret between us for now. The mother's identity won't stay quiet for long since people will see her with the baby, but it's up to her to decide how to tell people."

"I understand, but boy, Sweetie and Sam are really going to be disappointed."

He chuckled. "Emily respects my position, but she's tried once or twice to get me to reveal the truth."

"You mean Emily doesn't even know?"

"No. A pastor isn't any different than a priest or a psychiatrist when it comes to protecting the privacy of our parishioners. The only person I have permission to tell is you."

"I don't understand."

Abel leaned in closer to me. "I told her about the letter and how it had upset you. She felt you should know, and she asked me to apologize to you. Not only for being accused of something you didn't do, but also for running away from you the night she brought me the baby. She saw you fall down but was too afraid to go back and check on you. She feels bad about it."

"Please tell her I'm fine. There aren't any hard feelings. And the letter certainly wasn't her fault." I scooted my chair nearer to him. "I don't suppose the letter writer has also confessed?"

He shook his head. "Sorry. I still have no idea who wrote it. What about you?"

"Not a clue."

"I'm still hoping we'll find out one of these days. I keep talking about the seriousness of gossip and false accusations in my sermons, hoping the culprit will confess. But so far no one has said anything." He laughed softly. "I think my congregation is getting a little nervous. I was told that the ladies' Bible study had a real revival last week. They were crying and repenting and carrying on so loudly our outreach committee left their meeting to find out what was wrong."

I giggled at the picture that popped into my mind.

"Now to the reason I asked to see you."

His tone turned solemn, and I suddenly felt apprehensive. Was the mother someone I knew? Would I be shocked?

"Not only is the mother almost a child herself, only seventeen, but this past week has been a terrible time for this family. You see, her father just passed away."

I shook my head, puzzled by his comment. I had no way of knowing who had recently died in Abel's church. I started to tell him that when the realization exploded in my mind. "Oh my goodness. Do you mean. . . ?"

"Yes. The baby belongs to Jessica McAllister."

"Oh Abel. That poor girl. She just lost her father. How awful."

"Yes, it is awful," he agreed. "But there's more to it than you know."

"What do you mean?"

"Well, let's just say that Jessica brought the baby to me for protection. Rand McAllister was a very abusive father. She feared for the child and for herself. When Rand found out about the baby, he was furious. Thelma and Jessica had kept her pregnancy a secret right up until a few weeks before the baby's birth. Rand threatened to kill his daughter and her child unless she figured out a way to get rid of it. He told them he had no intention of supporting Jessica's illegitimate child." Abel winced. "Of course, he didn't use the word *illegitimate*."

"Boy, he really was an awful man. So after he was found dead, Jessica came to claim the little girl?"

He nodded. "That's right. And the look on her face when she saw that baby." He dabbed at his eyes with a handkerchief he took from his pocket. "Well, let's just say that I'm not the least bit worried about the baby getting all the love she needs. And Thelma is just as crazy about her. They named her Trinity, by the way."

"Oh my. That's lovely."

"Yes, it is."

"I hesitate to say this, but from what you've told me, it almost sounds like Rand's death was a blessing in some ways."

He studied the surface of the table for a moment before replying. "The death of any man who doesn't know God is a tragedy beyond description," he said. His voice broke. "Believe me, I stay up some nights thinking about people like him. People I couldn't get through to. I wonder if I'd done something different—or better—maybe they would have found the Lord."

I started to say something, but he shook his head. "I know those thoughts are wrong. The Holy Spirit convicts every person, and in the end, it is their decision. But thoughts like these are part of the territory when you're a minister." He cleared his throat. "But back to your comment. As far as Thelma and Jessica, yes. Their lives will be much better now that Rand is gone."

"That's a sad commentary on anyone's life," I said.

"It certainly is."

"Will they be okay? Financially, that is?"

Abel smiled. "You know better than to ask that."

I returned the smile. "You're right. Sorry. The church will step in and take care of them."

"That's what we're called to do. And we love doing His work."

A thought popped into my mind. "Will they sell their property to Eric now?"

Abel frowned. "Strange about that."

"What do you mean?"

"Thelma has no idea what Rand was thinking in trying to sell his land to Mr. Beck. Rand had mortgaged the place to the hilt. Of course, he didn't spend the money on his family. He used it for drinking and gambling. I guess he was a regular at a casino near Topeka. All Thelma can surmise is that Rand figured he could pay off his first mortgage and get another loan on the house so he could throw that money away as well."

"And then he got greedy and decided he wanted to not only pay off his loan but make a little more from Eric and his investors."

Abel shrugged. "That's about the only thing that makes sense. I think he kept the fact that he didn't have a clear title from Mr. Beck."

"So if Thelma sells her place to Eric, will she make any money?"

"Not much after paying off the mortgage. But it doesn't really matter since she never wanted to leave her home in the first place. Thelma feels as strongly about Harmony as most of us do. She wants to stay here—in her own home."

"So what now?" I felt overwhelming compassion for Thelma and her daughter. Rand had certainly left them an unhappy legacy.

"That's an interesting question. Seems when Thelma started calling family this afternoon to tell them about Rand's death, she found out Rand has a life insurance policy. It was taken out on him when he worked for the family business back in Iowa. After Rand left to come to Harmony, Thelma's brother kept it going because he was concerned about Thelma and

Jessica. With Rand's drinking, he figured there was a good chance he'd die early, and the brother wanted his sister and niece to be protected. It's enough money to pay off the mortgage and get the farm back on its feet."

"Oh Abel. That's wonderful news. I can hardly believe it."

"God is already providing," he said with a wide smile. "And the church will make sure those fields are taken care of the way they should be. Thelma will have enough money to live comfortably on her land as long as she wants."

I didn't say anything for a moment, and Abel noticed the pensive look on my face.

"What's wrong?" he asked.

"Nothing. It's just that. . ."

"That Rand's death has actually benefited his family?"

I nodded.

Abel put his hand on my arm and patted it. "Rand chose to use the gift of life God gave him to be selfish and cruel to the people he should have cherished. His life could have been completely different. We can do a lot of things to help others, but we can't make their choices, Gracie. Even God Himself won't override our will."

I nodded my agreement. There wasn't much else to say. It was a sad ending for a sad man.

"I won't keep you any longer," Abel said. "I'm sure after the past few days, you're looking forward to enjoying some time relaxing with Sweetie and Sam." He patted his round stomach. "And eating Mary's food." He beamed. "I recommend the sauerbraten. It's delicious."

I laughed. "Is there anything Hector can't cook?"

"He is a marvel, isn't he? Please keep him and his family in your prayers. His wife, Carmen, is pregnant and has been having some problems. Her doctor has ordered bed rest for the last three months of her pregnancy. That means she has to leave her teaching job at the school in Sunrise. With three other children, things are already tight. Hector has no idea how they'll make it."

"I'm sure folks here will pitch in and help."

"Of course. Several of the town's women have volunteered to help Carmen around the house and with the children. But that's as much as Hector will allow us to do. He won't accept financial assistance. He believes supporting his family is his responsibility."

"I respect that, but all of us need help sometimes."

Abel sighed. "I agree. But I have to respect his wishes."

"I'll definitely keep him and his family in my prayers."

"I know you will." He rose to his feet. "I think I see Mary with my sauerbraten. Now I must enjoy my dinner—but without showing too much enthusiasm."

I stood up, too. "I don't understand."

He leaned over and whispered in my ear. "Because if my wife suspects I enjoy Hector's sauerbraten more than hers, I'll never hear the end of it." He stepped back with a big grin on his face. "You be sure and call us so we can set up a time for dinner. And bring Sam with you."

I kissed the big man on the cheek. "I can hardly wait. And thanks, Abel, for telling me about the baby. Please thank Jessica for me, too."

"I will. God bless you, Gracie."

I watched him go back to his table. Emily and Hannah waved at me. What a great family. And what wonderful friends they had become. I could hardly believe that when I first came to Harmony, I'd been so negative toward Abel and his religion. Just proves it's impossible to judge justly through preconceived opinions and prejudices.

When I got back to our table, Sam and Sweetie looked at me expectantly. "Well," Sweetie said, "who's the mother?"

I sat down. "I can't tell you."

"What?" Sweetie screeched loudly enough to be heard by dogs in the next county. Several patrons turned and looked our way. I noticed the Crandalls sitting in a booth across the room. They smiled at me, and I raised my hand in greeting.

"Hush," I scolded. "The mother has asked Abel to keep her identity secret—for now. You'll know the truth soon."

Sweetie wasn't happy about being kept out of the loop, but she grudgingly accepted my promise that she wouldn't have to wait long for the information she wanted. "Why did Abel tell you who the mama is?" she asked in a subdued voice.

"Because of that awful letter. The mother felt bad about it and asked Abel to apologize to me."

"Well, it wasn't her fault," Sam said. "But that's very thoughtful." He shook his head. "When the truth comes out, I hope the person who wrote that letter feels like the judgmental gossip they are."

"Most critical, judgmental people are too busy thinking about everyone else to look at themselves. I think that's why God commanded us not to judge people. We can't see into another person's heart, and we have no idea what we're talking about."

"Besides that, we got that huge two-by-four stuck in our eyeballs," Sweetie added.

I chuckled. "You've got it right, Sweetie."

Sam winked at me.

"Here you go," Mary said, stepping up to our table with a tray of drinks. She put a coffee pitcher and two cups down in front of me and Sweetie. Then she handed a huge glass of Mountain Dew to Sam. "I don't know how you can drink caffeine this late in the day. It would keep me up all night."

"Sweetie and I can drink coffee almost up to bed-time, and it doesn't bother us," I said.

She grinned. "I wasn't talking to you." She looked at Sam. "I never understood how you can drink that stuff any time of the day and never have a problem."

He smacked his lips and took a big gulp. "Best drink on the face of the earth," he said with a sigh. "Hardly ever go through a day without it."

"That's the truth," Sweetie said. "I cart that stuff back from Sunrise by the caseload."

"You guys decide what you want?" Mary asked.

"Abel recommended the sauerbraten," I said. "Think I'll go with that."

"You won't be sorry. It's fabulous." Mary scribbled my order on her pad. "It comes with potato pancakes and sauerkraut—is that okay?"

"Sounds great."

"And what about you two?"

"Bring me the biggest, juiciest rib eye you got," Sweetie said. "I've got a real hankerin' for steak tonight."

Mary wrote down her order, not asking about side dishes because she already knew what Sweetie wanted. "Sam?"

"Put me down for the second biggest, juiciest rib eye in the place," he said. "After all that work in the orchards, I've got the same hankerin'."

"You got it," Mary said. As with Sweetie, she didn't ask about sides. "Hey Gracie, you still coming here tomorrow night? The roads should be pretty good by then."

"Sure. It sounds great. What time?"

"I'll close up around seven. It might take me another thirty minutes to get everyone out of here. Will that work for you?"

"Perfect. I'll be here. I look forward to it."

She left to take an order at a nearby table. I recognized Bill Eberly, the kind man who had moved his car for Ida and me the day of the meeting. I held my hand up and smiled at him. He waved back. I noticed he sat alone at his table. "Sam, do you know Bill Eberly?" I asked when Bill turned his attention to Mary.

"Sure. Nice man. He and your uncle got along really well. He and his wife moved here about ten years ago with their two kids. A boy and a girl. They're both in college now. One's in California and the other is somewhere back east. Edith passed away almost four years ago. Cancer, if I remember right."

"So he lives all alone?"

Sam nodded.

"He's about Joyce Bechtold's age, isn't he?"

"Yep, they're about the same age," Sweetie said. "But it won't do you no good to try to fix them two up.

Bill ain't been interested in any woman since Edith passed. He's a one-woman man, I guess. And anyways, Joyce is gone."

"What do you mean she's gone?" Joyce had been in love with my uncle for many years before he died. Although I was certain he'd felt the same way about her, he'd never acknowledged it. Before I left town the last time, Joyce and I had spent several hours painting the last birdhouses, feeders, and rocking chairs my uncle had crafted before his death. Working together had been a joy, and we'd begun developing a real friendship.

"Her sister died, and Joyce moved to Dodge City to take care of her nieces and nephew," Sam said. "She left about a month ago."

"I wonder why she didn't tell me." I couldn't help feeling a little hurt. Maybe we weren't as close as I thought.

"To be honest," Sam said, "I'm not sure her brother-in-law needs her that much. I think Joyce just wanted to get away. Harmony reminded her of your uncle. She needs time to heal. Maybe she'll come back someday."

I sighed. "Well, I hope so. We still had some birdhouses left to paint."

"She finished 'em," Sweetie said. "I shoulda told you, but with everything goin' on I just forgot. They're all stacked up in the basement. She told me to tell you to do whatever you want with them."

"Don't take it personally," Sam said kindly. "Joyce didn't leave you; she left her painful memories. She thinks the world of you."

"Well, I'll miss her. Guess I'll have to come up

with someone else for Bill."

Sweetie snorted. "You don't listen much, do you? I told you he ain't looking for nobody."

I smiled at her. "Everyone's looking for someone, Sweetie."

Sam laughed. "You're incorrigible, you know that?"

"Why, thank you so much," I replied. "I resemble that remark."

Sweetie and Sam started talking about what work needed to be done on the farm during the upcoming week. I'd certainly learned the hard way that farmwork continues even when the trees aren't blooming. My attention began to drift when Cora, Amos, and Drew Crandall approached our table.

"I'm so sorry to interrupt," Cora said in her sweet, high-pitched voice.

"Not at all," I said, happy for a reprieve from farm duties. "How are you guys?"

"We're doing very well," Amos said. "Thanks to Sam and the other men who cleared the roads near our house."

"We didn't get to every street," Sam said. "Wish we could have done more."

"Well, you made it possible for us to get home and to church tonight," Cora said. "We want to thank you."

"You're very welcome," Sam said with a smile.

"We're really looking forward to spending some time with Mr. Hampton tomorrow," Cora said.

"Grant?" I said. "I don't understand. I figured he was on his way back to Wichita."

"He called us yesterday and asked if he could talk to us about Drew. He has a special son like ours." Cora put her arm around Drew, who gave his mother a big smile. "I told him we are far from perfect, but we would be happy to help him in any way we can. He's staying a few more days so we can spend some time together."

I was touched that Grant had seen something helpful in this wonderful couple. "I know you'll be able to give him some needed advice," I said. "He really does need it."

"I hope we can be of assistance," Amos said. "We intend to do our best." He tipped his hat. "You folks have a nice dinner. It's time for us to head over to the church."

We said good-bye, and I watched them as they left. "What wonderful people. Isn't it odd that with all the organizations and social workers in Wichita, it took a Conservative Mennonite couple in Harmony, Kansas, to give Grant the support he's been looking for?"

"Maybe Grant needed to see someone like Drew," Sam said. "Probably gave him hope."

"You must be right."

Just then Mary arrived with our food. We spent the next hour talking, laughing, and stuffing ourselves. It was just the break I needed. On the way home, I told Sam that if the roads were clear enough, I felt I could drive home. "Besides, I really want to check on Ida."

"Remember what I said about the roads being slick tonight," he said. "Why don't you stay one more night and go home in the morning?"

The possibility of icy roads, along with my growing sleepiness, made me easy to convince, so I agreed.

Sam smiled. "Good. Besides, when you leave, Buddy will have to start sleeping with me again. And he seems to prefer you."

"He does like curling up next to me. Snickle used

to do that, but he hasn't been sleeping on my bed since I got here. I'm not sure where he goes at night."

Sam's truck suddenly hit an icy patch, but he was able to regain control. Just as he had predicted, the moisture on the roads was refreezing.

"I'm not so sure about you driving alone to Mary's tomorrow night," Sam said. "If it's like this. . ."

"Tell you what. If it seems bad, I'll call you. Or maybe Mary can put me up for the night. I'm not a hero when it comes to icy roads. Trust me."

He hesitated.

"Look, Sam. I really want to do this. Mary and I need to get the past behind us for good. I promise I won't put myself in a bad situation."

"For crying out loud, Sam," Sweetie said. "Gracie's not a dummy. She'll be fine."

He sighed. "Well, with two opinionated females against me, I guess I don't have much choice."

When we pulled onto Faith Road, we could see John's truck still in the driveway, but behind it was Sheriff Taylor's patrol car.

"What's he doin' here?" Sweetie grumbled.

"He said he'd be keeping an eye on things," Sam said with a frown. "I still don't see why you two have such a problem with him. We should be thanking him, not criticizing him."

Sweetie mumbled something under her breath that even I couldn't understand, and I sat right next to her. Since I was positioned between her and Sam, he probably didn't hear her either. Probably for the best.

When we pulled up to the house, Sheriff Taylor came walking around the side of the house with John.

"I hope nothing else has happened," I said.

Sam didn't respond, but he turned off the truck engine and jumped out, jogging over to where the two men stood. Sam almost always opened the truck door for me and Sweetie, so I knew he was concerned. We got out and joined the three men.

"Is something wrong?" I asked.

"Everything's fine," Sam said. "Sheriff Taylor drove by and didn't recognize John's truck. He wanted to make sure John wasn't trying to burn down our orchards."

John grinned. "I was getting a little concerned about coming up with bail money."

Sam laughed. "I wouldn't worry about it. As long as your crime isn't too costly, you can count on me."

"So how are the roads into town?" John asked. "I was thinking about going to the store before I head home."

Sam shook his head. "They were pretty good going in, but they're refreezing. I'd wait if I were you." He cocked his head toward me. "Of course, Miss Demolition Derby here is planning a late-night private dinner with Mary tomorrow night."

"Might be best if you don't do that," Sheriff Taylor said gruffly. "Sounds like you'd do better to stay where you are."

I wanted to thank him for his advice and inform him that I didn't need him to tell me where I could go or what I could do, but I just smiled and nodded. "I'm going inside," I said. "It's too cold out here for me."

"I'm with you," Sweetie said.

We left for the house, the three men still deep in conversation. Once inside, Sweetie pulled her coat off and almost threw it into the closet. "I still don't trust that man, Gracie." Her harsh tone echoed her suspicions toward the lawman. "I mean, why is he showin' up here all the time? What about the rest of the county? I'm tellin' you, somethin' is wrong here. Real, real wrong."

I had to agree with her. A county sheriff shouldn't be hanging around one of the smallest towns in the state with as much frequency as Taylor. It didn't make sense.

"I don't understand it either. I still think we need to keep an eye on him."

"Both eyes would be better," she grumbled. "Well, I'm gonna head to bed a little early. I'm plumb tuckered out. 'Sides, there's a show I don't want to miss. Hope I can stay awake through the whole thing."

Almost every night Sweetie turned on the small TV set in her room before she went to sleep. And almost every night she fell asleep with it on. She appeared to use it as a sleeping aid. Didn't speak much for whatever she watched, but it seemed to work for her. I said good night and went into the living room. The fire in the fireplace was getting low, so I added a few more logs. Knowing that this was my last night in the beautiful house made me a little sad. I hadn't been on the couch long before Sam came in the front door and called out my name.

"I'm in here," I said.

A few seconds later, he stuck his head around the corner. "There you are. I sent John home. Things seem to be quiet. I'll get up a couple times during the night to look around outside, though. Sheriff Taylor told me to call him if anything happens." He came over and plopped down next to me on the couch.

"Where will Sheriff Taylor be?"

"He's headed back to Council Grove, but he said he'd check in sometime tomorrow."

I wanted to say that the orchards might actually be safe with him gone, but I decided to keep my comment to myself since Sam seemed to trust the sheriff.

"Hey, I want to talk to you about something," Sam said, drawing his words out with hesitation.

"Sure. As long as this isn't the 'It's not you—it's me' speech."

He laughed nervously. "Well, in a way. . ."

My heart almost leapt from my throat. "What are you saying?"

He put his arm around me and pulled me up close to him. "Relax. This isn't *that*; it's something else."

I leaned against his chest. "Okay, hit me. What's going on?"

He took a deep breath and released it slowly. I could hear the air leave his chest, followed by the beating of his heart. "I've been doing a lot of thinking. About the way I reacted when you showed me that note. I realized that I've never really forgiven my mother for leaving me. I thought I had. I thought putting it out of my mind was forgiveness. But it wasn't. Now don't get me wrong. When we forgive someone, eventually we need to quit thinking about it. Dwelling on it. But if we just refuse to think about it, well, it just isn't forgiveness." He ran his hand over my hair. "And that's why I acted so badly with you. It brought back those painful memories. Waiting at that church for my mother. Wondering where she was. Finally realizing she wasn't coming back. The looks of pity on the faces of the people at the church when they realized

I'd been abandoned." At this, he choked up.

I sat up and grabbed his hand. "What happened to you was awful, Sam. No child should ever go through something like that."

He quickly wiped his eyes. "No, you're right. But I know in my heart that my mother thought she was protecting me. Giving me a better life. Her drug habit cost us both plenty. Many times we didn't have food. Sometimes we had nowhere to live. We slept out on the street or crashed at some other druggie's house. A few months before she left me, things seemed to have turned around. She had a job, and we lived in a decent apartment. But right before she took me to that church, I could tell she was using again. It was the way she acted. Her mannerisms and our lack of money." He paused for a moment and gazed into the fire. When he started speaking again, his voice was so low it was hard to hear him. "I know that's why she decided to send me to live with Sweetie. She didn't want to put me through that again."

"But you didn't know that at the time?"

He shook his head. "No. I began to realize it as the years went by." He shrugged. "Even though I started to understand her decision, I held on tight to my anger. It took my reaction to the note to finally make it clear to me that I've got to forgive my mother if I have any hope of having a normal life." He squeezed my hand and looked deeply into my eyes. His own gray eyes were shiny with tears. "Or to have a good future with you." He smiled crookedly. "That's why I said that our problems weren't you. They were me." He leaned over and kissed me.

When he pulled back, he reached for my other

hand. "I've decided to forgive my mother, Grace. Completely. And to let go of the past so we can have the kind of life together I know is within our grasp. And I also want to ask you to forgive me for treating you the way I did. I hope you understand why I acted so badly."

It was difficult to answer him with a catch in my throat and tears in my eyes, but I have to believe that the long kiss I gave him said what words couldn't begin to express.

FIFTEEN

After a breakfast of Sweetie's homemade waffles with bacon crumbled into the batter, I felt fortified enough to drive home. I was sad having to say good-bye, but I actually looked forward to some time at home. Snickle's low rumbling from inside his carrier made it abundantly clear that all the going back and forth between cities and houses was beginning to fray his kitty nerves. I tried to reassure him, but watching for slick spots didn't allow me to focus much of my attention on my irritated feline friend. Sam had been right about the roads freezing overnight. If the trip to my house hadn't been a short one, I might have turned back.

All in all, though, I didn't have much pity for Snickle. Last night, during a midnight trip to the bathroom, I heard Sweetie's TV still playing loud enough to make it difficult for me to go back to sleep. I sneaked quietly into her room, expecting her to be sound asleep—which she was. But what I didn't expect was to find Snickle contentedly curled up next to her. This solved the question of where he'd been at night. I turned off the TV, petted him, and whispered, "Fraud," to Sweetie even though she was out like a light.

By the time I got home, I'd decided to take Sam's advice about driving after dark. Even though he'd offered to come and get me, I didn't want him out on icy roads either. I called Mary to see if I could stay the night if the conditions were treacherous. She reassured me that her foldout couch was at my disposal. Feeling better about my plans, I set about doing some housework, unpacking, and washing my laundry. But instead of even trying to use the dryer, I hung everything up on the clothesline I'd put up in the basement. I could hardly wait for the day when the electrical setup in the house was more dependable. As I pinned my clothes on the line, I thought about Ida, who did this all the time. Maybe having certain conveniences spoils people when they have to go without them, but not having them in the first place keeps you from ever missing them. Perhaps it was that way for Ida, Sarah, and Gabe.

After I felt caught up, I drove slowly over to Ida's to check on her.

"Ach, Gracie," she said when she opened the door. "You and Sam are too worried about me. I am used to this kind of weather, you know. I grew up where winters were much harsher than they are in Kansas."

I entered the door she held open. "I know, but with the phones out, we wanted to make sure."

She clucked her tongue at me. "I did not even realize the phone was inoperable."

I went over and picked up the receiver, happy to hear a hum. "Well, it's working now. And you have my word. We'll quit bothering you so much."

"My dear, I love knowing you and Sam care so much for me. You may drop in anytime. You are always welcome."

I stayed for a little while to visit, telling her about Sarah, the fire in the orchard, and lastly about Rand McAllister.

"Ach, no," she said sadly. "Poor Thelma and Jessica. How will they get by?"

Although I didn't tell her that Jessica was the abandoned baby's mother, I did share the news about the insurance policy.

She clapped her hands together. "God is so good, ja? He goes before us and provides for situations we don't even know are coming."

I also left out my hit on the head because I knew she'd worry. But passing the fire off as an accident didn't get past her sharp mind.

"How could a fire start like that, Gracie?" she asked with a frown. "I know about burn barrels and smudge pots. Although the pots can blow over, it is rare. It did not seem windy enough that night to cause such a problem."

I shrugged and tried to look innocent. "I don't know much about this kind of thing, Ida."

She searched my face for a moment. The thought crossed my mind that I wouldn't want to play poker with the astute Mennonite woman. I'd lose. But there was little chance she'd be caught dead playing poker anyway. A mental picture of Ida with a cigar hanging out of her mouth, saying, "I'll call your five and raise you ten," flashed in my mind, and I smiled. For some reason the gesture seemed to reassure her, and she changed the subject.

"So how does Rand's death affect the sale of his land to Mr. Beck?"

"It doesn't. Thelma wants to stay in Harmony.

She never wanted to sell the land in the first place."

Ida breathed a deep sigh. "Good. So maybe the development will go somewhere else?"

"Unless he finds other property." I had no intention of telling her I'd asked Eric if he was interested in part of my land. Being so close to her place, I was certain she'd be horrified.

Suddenly she grabbed my arm. "Listen to me, child. There is still something that disturbs my peace. Even this news does not calm it. You must promise that you will be very careful the next few days. I feel. . .I don't know. . .as if you might be in some kind of danger."

I could see the sincerity in her face. "Okay, Ida. I will. I promise." Although I still believed Ida's overdeveloped sense of protection toward Harmony was the cause of her disquiet, her warning made me even more committed to staying off the roads after dark tonight. My assurance seemed to bring her a little comfort, and we visited for another hour. Then I left, promising to come back soon. The temperature had risen some, and the drive home was better than the drive there. Snow, melting some from the large piles pushed up against the sides of the road, had turned into wet, sloppy mud. Not a good sign since it was definitely supposed to drop down below freezing tonight.

I puttered around the house until six thirty then took off for Mary's, bringing a change of clothes and some pajamas. When I got to the restaurant, Mary was shooing out the last of her customers, including the ever-present Harold.

"Thanks for coming, guys," she said to one family who'd just paid for their meals. "Sorry to rush you out, but I've got plans tonight."

"'Bout time you had something to do besides boss me around," Harold interjected as he waited next in line.

Mary laughed. "Someone's gotta do it, Harold. And it's my pleasure. Now you get out of here. Why don't you go visit Esther Crenshaw? I saw her making goo-goo eyes at you in church last week."

Harold's florid face lost some of its color. "Esther Crenshaw? That woman's a menace. All she does is gossip. And those wigs of hers." He shook his head. "No thank you." A smile lit up his face. "But I might stop by that pretty Kay Curless's place."

Mary's mouth dropped open. "Why, you old rascal. Have you been seeing Kay?"

Harold blushed. "We got together to play cards last week. I asked her to come to dinner with me Thursday night. We'll be here around six."

Mary came around the counter and gave him a hug. "I'll have the best seat in the house waiting for you two. I'm so happy to hear this news. Kay is a lovely woman."

With that, Harold said good night, stopping first to ask me how Sam was doing. I assured him that the fruit trees were fine without going into details. After the door closed behind him, Mary rushed over and locked it. She'd already turned the OPEN sign to CLOSED. But now she pulled down all the shades.

"That should do it," she said with satisfaction. "I rarely close early, but almost every time I do, people keep coming—trying the door and hollering for me. For some reason when I pull down the blinds, they take it more seriously."

"Out of sight, out of mind?"

She chuckled. "Maybe so." She waved toward a table in the back that had been specially set. "Have a seat. I have our dinner warming in the oven."

"Is Hector gone?" If he was still here, I wanted to say hello. I'd grown to like the friendly man who'd taken me so graciously under his wing after the first storm though he'd been under so much pressure.

"Yep. I told him to take off after he cooked the last order. Nice chance for him to spend a night with his family."

I sat down at the table, which had been covered with a beautiful white linen tablecloth and set with flowered china. "Pretty fancy for just us gals," I quipped.

"We deserve the best, don't we?" Mary disappeared into the kitchen while I waited. I'd been a little nervous about this dinner, but her easy manner and extra effort put me at ease. I had high hopes we could be good friends. Not an easy thing to do with a background like ours. The silence in the restaurant felt strange. Usually this place bustled with chatter and laughter. Drifting through the overwhelming quiet, I was certain I heard low voices. A conversation. But Mary said no one else was here. Who could it be? I got up to check out the kitchen when Mary suddenly pushed the door open and came toward me with two large plates of food.

"I thought I heard you talking to someone," I said. "Is there anyone else here?"

She laughed. "Just me talking to myself. I do that from time to time. Sorry."

"Wow. Thought I heard two different voices.

Must be the strain of the last few days."

Mary placed the plates on the table and pulled out my chair. "Sit back down. Hopefully dinner will help to take some of that stress away."

I sat down and checked out my plate. "This looks incredible. What is it?"

"Chicken paprikash with spaetzle. It's a family recipe. My mom was famous all around M–Marion for this dish. The secret is the paprika. It can't be just any old paprika. I get mine shipped from a special store that orders their spices from Europe."

"Marion? Is that where you're from? My friend Allison grew up in Marion. Did you know the Cunninghams?"

Mary cleared her throat and stared blankly at me. "No. . .no, I don't think so. But we moved away when I was eleven. I don't remember many people." She picked up the glasses on the table. "I made raspberry tea, but if you'd rather have coffee, I've got a pot on."

"I adore raspberry tea. Maybe I'll have a cup of coffee after dinner if it's okay."

"Sure. I'll get the tea and rolls and be right back."

"Mary, you shouldn't have gone to all this trouble. This wonderful food and the raspberry tea. How did you pull it off after working all day?"

"I've been looking forward to this for quite some time, Gracie. It was a pleasure to cook this dinner for you." She smiled and headed back toward the kitchen.

For a moment she'd seemed uncomfortable. Was it my question about Marion? And I couldn't believe she hadn't known the Cunninghams. Mr.

Cunningham was the principal of the elementary school. Had been for thirty years. But maybe she'd just forgotten. Still, it seemed odd. Just then she came back into the room.

"Here we go. Fresh iced tea and rolls hot from the oven. Hope you enjoy everything. Although I can cook pretty good main dishes, desserts are not my specialty. I bought a cake from Menlo's. They make a carrot cake to die for."

"Yummy. I can hardly wait."

Mary sat down across from me and picked up her fork. Then she set it down. "Oh. I guess we should say grace. Why don't you do it?"

I bowed my head and thanked God for the food. Then I prayed blessings over Mary and her restaurant, also asking God to bless our friendship and help it to grow into something that honored Him. When I raised my head, I found Mary frowning at me, the same funny look on her face she'd had earlier. I wanted to ask her if something was bothering her, but I didn't want to come off as nosy or paranoid. Again I blamed it on the strain of the last several days.

I'd started to take a bite of my paprikash when Mary stopped me.

"Here," she said. "Put some extra paprika on it. It really brings out the flavor."

As I took the bottle from her, I noticed a ring she always wore. I'd never looked at it up close. At first I didn't recognize it, but suddenly I remembered where I'd seen the exact same ring before.

"That ring," I said slowly. "It's a high school ring. From Mound City." I raised my eyes to meet hers, which had grown wide. For several moments there was silence between us. Finally I said, "Mary, what's going on? You don't know Mr. Cunningham who was the principal of the school when you lived in Marion. And you act like you don't know Eric Beck, who went to school in Mound City at the same time you did. The school was too small for you two not to have known each other."

My mind began acting like a minicomputer, processing comments and different incidents, bringing them together. One dot connected to another until the picture that was left seemed extraordinarily ugly and unthinkable. Unfortunately, the conclusions couldn't be denied. Why hadn't I seen it? The truth had been right in front of me the whole time. "But you do know Eric, don't you? You. . .you and Eric. . . What have you been up to?" I set my fork down. "I don't understand, Mary. Obviously you two are working together to accomplish something. But what?"

Mary's face was blank, devoid of emotion, but there was something in her eyes. Was it fear?

I took the linen napkin off my lap and put it on the table and stood. "I don't think this dinner is a good idea. Unless you want to tell me why you and Eric have kept your relationship secret, I don't think we have anything to talk about. Some really strange things have been happening in Harmony, and they started not long after Eric arrived. I don't think it will take a lot of effort to trace most of them, maybe all of them, back to one or both of you. Maybe Sheriff Taylor would be interested in putting the pieces together."

Mary opened her mouth to say something, but

no words came out. Her eyes darted quickly to a spot behind me.

"Sit down, Gracie. Unfortunately, you won't be going anywhere."

I turned around to find Eric Beck standing at the kitchen door, a gun in his hand. And it was pointed directly at me.

Sixteen

"I told you to take off that stupid ring."

Eric's scolding seemed to vanquish whatever spark of willpower remained in Mary's body. Her shoulders slumped and her eyes became lifeless. "I—I couldn't get it off. I've put on weight since high school, and I didn't want to ruin it." Tears filled her almost expressionless face. "Please, Eric. You don't have to hurt Gracie."

Eric pulled up a chair from a nearby table and sat next to me, his gun still leveled at my chest. "Actually, I really do have to hurt her." Gone was the kindness I'd thought I'd seen in him. It had been replaced by a cold hardness that sent chills throughout my body. He glared at Mary. "Thanks to your incompetence, it's our only way out."

Although I had no desire to anger him, for some odd reason I felt the urge to keep him talking. "If you're going to shoot me anyway, why don't you explain what's going on?" I said. "I get that you and Mary have been trying to acquire land in Harmony, but why go through all this? Did you ever really want Rand McAllister's property?"

Eric, seemingly pleased to have a chance to spout

off about his plan, some of which I'd already figured out, sat back in his chair and relaxed his grip on the gun. "No, I never wanted Rand's property. Waste of time, piece of dirt. I paid him to pretend I wanted his land, then to back out after everyone in town was pumped about having a new development to help the town.

I shook my head. "But why did you feel you had to go through all this? A quiet retirement community would be a blessing here. Unless that's not what you intended at all."

Eric grinned. I couldn't understand what I'd ever seen in him. There was no warmth or compassion in this man—absolutely nothing appealing.

"Smart girl," he said. "No, there's no retirement community. My investors are looking for a resort that will be close to the new casino being built near the highway."

"Casino? I haven't heard anything about a casino in this area. I doubt the citizens of this county would vote one in."

Eric's laugh was full of contempt. "The hicks who live around here won't have a say. Not when several of their county officials are in the pocket of the group I work for. There are ways to push things through without asking permission, you know."

"A casino near Harmony would ruin the town," I said, stating something I was sure Eric already knew.

He shrugged. "Maybe. Maybe not. It will still bring in revenue."

"And a lot of other influences we don't need here. Harmony is. . .special. Your plan would destroy the very qualities that make this place unique."

He sighed. "Not my problem."

Again something whispered inside me to stall. "So if you didn't really want Rand's property, what did you want?"

Even before he opened his mouth, I knew the answer. I looked at Mary. "You said something once about grandkids fishing and swimming at the retirement community. At the time I thought it was odd, since there's no place like that around here. I should have paid more attention. I thought it was just a slip of the tongue." I swung my gaze back to Eric. "You want my land, don't you?"

He grunted. "Not just yours. Your boyfriend's, too. My investors want lakefront condos for their high rollers." He jabbed his finger at Mary, who'd sat silently since he'd come out of the kitchen. "I told you your stupid slipups would cost us. Good thing she didn't figure it out until now. When it's too late."

Mary's head drooped lower, and she wouldn't look at me.

"So when did you two put this thing together?"

"It's been in the works ever since Mary and I ran into each other at a bar in Topeka. I hadn't seen her since high school. When I told her I needed lakefront property for a new resort near a future casino, she mentioned Harmony—and you and your boyfriend's property. But she told me you wouldn't sell outright. That I'd have to trick one or both of you out of your land. We've been working on this ever since." He slapped the table with the hand that didn't hold the gun. "Your sites are the only spots in the right area that will work. They're perfect."

I shook my head. "But why, Eric? Is this deal really

so important you'd risk everything to put it through?"

"He owes money to the men behind the casino." Mary's first words since Eric sat down were matter-of-fact. "If he doesn't pay them, they'll hurt him. Maybe even kill him." She lifted her head a little higher. "If he doesn't get your land, his life isn't worth a plug nickel."

Anger flashed in Eric's eyes. "Shut up."

Instead of heeding his warning, Mary turned toward me. "The plan was to split you and Sam up. If you left Harmony, Eric would buy your place and the building would begin. He figured that would force Sam to sell his property, too. Trust me, Sam and Sweetie wouldn't be happy living next door to the kind of people the resort would bring in."

"You two started the rumors about the baby, didn't you? And you told Esther the baby was mine. Did you write the note, too?"

"Mary wrote it. I delivered it," Eric said. "I thought it was a great opportunity dropped right into our laps. Too bad it didn't work."

I frowned at Mary. "You knew about Sam's past, didn't you? You figured making him think I'd done the same thing as his mother would destroy our relationship."

She shrugged. "Sam told me once about his mother dropping him off at a church. I could tell it still bothered him."

"But why, Mary? Do you still hate me that much?"

"I did. I don't know; I guess I do." She shrugged. "Eric promised me money—and a new life. I planned to leave Harmony and start over with him." She sighed. "I know you love this town, but I want out. I'm tired of seeing the same people day after day. Having the same conversations over and over. Not everyone wants what you do, Gracie."

"I thought you were happy here. I thought this place meant something to you."

"It does. But just not what it means to you."

I frowned at Eric as a mental picture flashed in my mind. "It was you in the orchard, wasn't it? Sweetie said one pair of boots was still wet after she put them on the rug to dry. They were yours, weren't they?"

His grin made my stomach turn. He was pleased with the evil he'd done. He was proud of the web of deceit he'd woven throughout Harmony.

"I snuck out after everyone went to bed. Sam said something about the wind knocking over the smudge pots. It was a spur-of-the-moment decision. I had no idea what would happen. I planned to set quite a few trees on fire. In retrospect, my actions were ill conceived. The fire probably wouldn't have caused the kind of damage I'd hoped for."

"And hitting me on the head? What was that for?"

He laughed harshly. "I thought you were on the other side of the orchard, but you surprised me by showing up when I wasn't expecting you. I couldn't allow you to find me out there. After you passed out, I took your car keys and your walkie-talkie. I had to stall you long enough for me to get back into the house and act surprised when the fire was discovered." He shrugged. "I wanted to give Sam a reason to sell his property. If his trees were destroyed, that would have done it."

"She could have been killed out there," Mary said. "You said no one would get hurt." Although she still seemed somewhat disconnected, I could see something smoldering in her eyes. Maybe Eric was losing his partner in crime.

Keep stalling. The words were so loud in my mind I almost looked around to see who else was in the room.

Eric waved the gun around wildly. "I told you I didn't *plan* to hurt anyone." He glared at Mary and swung the gun her way. "I guess things change, don't they? If the fire had done its job, I'd be sitting pretty right now. With Gracie dead, everything would have fallen into place. I could buy her place and poor, distraught Sam would gladly hand over his property." He turned his attention back to me, his lips drawn up in a snarl. "I should have finished you off, but I didn't have enough time to come up with a plan to make it look like an accident. If that nosy sheriff hadn't shown up when he did, I could have figured out a way to do it without having to count on that stupid fire." He banged his hand on the table. "Don't look at me like that," he yelled at Mary, who stared at him like she'd never seen him before. "I've only done what I was forced to do. None of this is my fault."

"What really happened to Rand?" I asked, trying to keep my voice calm and steady. Eric was losing it. If he suddenly went completely off the deep end, the results could be tragic. "I knew something was wrong with the story that he'd accidentally wandered outside."

"What is she talking about?" The timbre of Mary's voice climbed a couple of notches. "You said Rand's death was an accident."

"But it wasn't, was it?" I asked Eric. "Did he renege on your deal?"

"Little creep figured out something big was up," Eric sneered. "He thought he could get more money out of me. Threatened to go to the sheriff with what he knew." He let out a long, slow breath. "He tried to extort more money out of me. What happened to him was his own fault."

Mary rose partially to her feet. "You. . .you killed him? You murdered Rand McAllister?"

He laughed harshly. "You're really stupid, you know it? I killed him on Thursday night after I took Gracie home. Then I brought him back here and stuffed him in one of your empty freezers until I got the chance to pick him up and toss him in the snow. You never even knew it." He laughed again and looked at me. "Now you know what I was really doing before I ditched my truck and walked back to your house that night."

Mary's face turned ashen and she looked ill. Her eyes sought mine. "I didn't know, Gracie. I swear I didn't know."

"Shut up, Mary," Eric shouted. "Just shut up." His fierce gaze swung back to me. "I gave you every chance to get out of this alive. If you and your boyfriend had parted ways, I could have bought you out lock, stock, and barrel."

"But I offered you my property once," I said.

"No. You offered me part of it. I need all of it." He chuckled. "My plan was to get you to willingly hand it over. After disposing of Rand, I arranged that supposed breakdown so your boyfriend would find us in a compromising position and break up with you. I figured you'd leave town after that. Like I said, if I got your place, I knew I could drive Sam and his old-maid aunt out." He put his head back and giggled crazily. "I even turned on the charm, hoping you'd decide to leave your hick boyfriend behind and go for me. Then I planned to nicely talk you out of your place."

"Well, it seems that none of your brilliant plans worked. So now what?"

He grinned wildly, his eyes frightening orbs of madness. "Now you have an accident, just like Rand. You know, the roads are slippery. After you leave Mary's, your little car runs off the road and you're fatally injured. Or at least that's what it will look like."

At that moment several things happened at once. Mary shouted, "No!" and stood to her feet. Eric pointed his gun at her, and I heard a gunshot. But instead of seeing Mary take a bullet, I watched a slow stain of blood spread across Eric's chest as he fell to the ground.

Seventeen

Sam reached for another hot muffin. "I feel like a fool," he said. "I should have realized Eric was up to no good." He put the hot muffin on his plate next to the sausage and cheese omelet Jessica had just delivered to the table. "I thought the only thing he had his eye on was you."

I shook my head. "I guess I'm not as irresistible as you thought. Turns out my land was my best asset in Eric's eyes."

"This whole thing is my fault," Grant said. "I should have realized something was wrong with that guy. When Eric first came to me, he said I'd been recommended to him, but he didn't seem to know any of our clients. I should have pressed him, but I didn't. I realize now he only looked me up so he could get to you."

"Mary told him about you, Grant. You had no way of knowing what Eric was up to. And you have nothing to feel bad about. Eric fooled everyone. He and Mary are the only people at fault. They're the ones who chose a path of deceit."

"Well, Eric will have a long time to think about his choices in prison." Sheriff Taylor stuck a mouthful of Hector's banana pancakes in his mouth.

"I sure was wrong about you," Sweetie said to the sheriff. "Here I thought you were a meddlin' busybody, and it turns out you was keepin' an eye on those two rattlesnakes all the time." She cut off a piece of sausage and held it up to her mouth. "But how'd you know they was up to no good?"

Pat swallowed his food and wiped his mouth. "I heard rumors about Eric Beck from several sources—that he was working with a group of very questionable people and that he had his sights set on this area. I didn't know Harmony was the target at first, but after following him around some, his motives became pretty clear. I did some research on him and found his high school records. I saw that Mary Whittenbauer had gone to the same school. I started hanging around here, keeping an eye on both of them. When I heard her act like she'd never met him before, I knew they were in on it together."

"That's why you was near the orchards the night of the fire. You was watchin' Eric," Sweetie said. "You mighta saved Gracie's life."

He shrugged. "I wasn't sure what he was going to do at the time. I figured he wouldn't risk another murder. I was sure wrong about that." He scooped up a big forkful of scrambled eggs. "I did try to protect Sam and Gracie by telling that Mennonite pastor I was watching Sam's place after the fire so Mary would hear me and carry the information back to her partner. I just didn't count on Eric confronting Gracie here. Good thing Sam told me you were having dinner with Mary Monday night," he said to me. "I followed you and snuck into the back." He shook his head. "No one locks their doors in this town. Strangest thing I've ever seen. Glad the back door was open that night, though. I almost waited too long."

"Yeah. Thanks for delaying until the very last second to waltz in and shoot Eric," I said. "Made everything much more exciting."

The sheriff grunted and stuck the eggs in his mouth.

"And by the way, just what were you doing behind my house with a flashlight?" I asked.

He chased the eggs down with a mouthful of coffee. "Just following Eric. He'd been out there earlier in the day. I think he was just sizing up your property, trying to figure out how many trees they'd need to clear out for their resort."

"That explains why he knew just where my driveway was even though it was covered with snow. And he was aware that I own thirty acres. I'd never told him that. Wish I would have put two and two together a little sooner."

"None of those comments caught your attention because you never suspected Eric was up to anything," Sam said. "I was suspicious of him, but not for the right reasons. I was too busy being jealous to realize what was really going on."

"I guess you're right," I said. "But now I can see all the clues I missed. Mary's mention of fishing and swimming and Eric's comment about Rand making money 'free and clear' from the sale of his property. Eric would have known there was a mortgage on that land if he was really going to buy it." I shook my head. "And that stupid story about his supposed ex-girlfriend. He concocted that to make me unsure of our relationship. To make me doubt you." I reached over and took Sam's hand. "I'll never allow anyone to come between us like that again." I laughed lightly. "Of course, the biggest clue I missed wasn't anything natural. It was spiritual."

"What do you mean?" Grant asked.

"When an old Mennonite woman told me she had 'a stirring inside my spirit that tells me something is wrong,' I should have listened. Ida was right all along. Next time something stirs inside her, I will be the first person in line to pay attention."

"Pat, when did you suspect Eric had killed Rand?" Sam asked.

"Right away. I wish I'd seen that comin'. I'd like to have prevented it. In the end, all I could do was get the body to the coroner as quickly as possible so he could back up my suspicions. After he got a chance to look closely at him, he discovered that Rand had been asphyxiated before he was dumped in the snow. I knew Eric was responsible, but I still had no direct evidence." He shook his head. "I'm just sorry things got so serious before I was able to prove his guilt."

I grunted. "No one's as sorry as I am. I think I lost about ten years of my life that night in the restaurant. Thank God you came in when you did. I thought Eric was going to shoot Mary—or me."

"Unfortunately, he almost did."

"So he'll recover completely?" Sam asked.

Pat chuckled. "Yes, but I doubt he'll be able to use that right arm to hold a gun for a long, long time."

"And what about Mary?" Sweetie asked. "Is she goin' to jail?"

"I think she'll get a deal from the prosecutor for turning state's evidence. Whether or not she gets jail time or probation. . . I just don't know. But I don't think she'll be back here anytime soon—if ever. Turning the restaurant over to Hector seems pretty final."

I agreed with him that we'd probably seen the last of Mary, but in an odd way, I felt some pity for her. She'd been stupid and careless, but she almost died in an attempt to save my life. The notion that all this time she'd hated me because of Sam made me sad. Shows what unforgiveness and deception can do. Mary's life would never be the same. Learning a lesson from the tragic results of the last few days forced me to forgive her—and Eric—as quickly as I could. I didn't want the same kind of poison festering inside my soul.

"More coffee?" Jessica's smile was evidence that her life was improving. Her daughter, Trinity, was at home with her grandmother. She'd taken a job working at the restaurant after deciding she didn't want to go back to school. I wasn't certain it was the best decision, but Jessica didn't want to face the boy who had taken advantage of her insecurity and then pushed her away when she became pregnant. At least for now, she had a place to work and a loving environment at home.

Sweetie held up her cup. "I'll take some more. Hector makes a good cup of coffee. Not as good as mine, but it comes pretty close."

"I'm glad you like it," she said. She filled Sweetie's cup and warmed up everyone else's.

"Thank you, Jessica," I said with a smile.

"Actually, it's Jessie," she responded. "I—I decided I want to be called Jessie from now on."

"I like it," I said. "Jessie it is."

She twirled around and headed toward another table. A new name for a new person. It was a good sign.

I gazed around the room. The restaurant was full. Mary's Kitchen would continue but with Hector at the helm. Running the restaurant was the answer to his prayers. Several of the town's women were helping Carmen stay in bed by doing her housework and caring for her children, and now the Ramirezes wouldn't have to worry about paying the bills.

"I'm still worried about that casino," Sweetie said, her mouth full of scrambled eggs. "What's gonna happen with that?"

Pat chuckled. "Let's just say that our county government is going through a thorough housecleaning. Everyone involved with Eric's shady group is being shoved out of office. Several will be prosecuted for taking bribes. I don't think anyone will be talking about a casino in this area for a long, long time."

"Well then, everything turned out all right, didn't it?" She stabbed another sausage and happily stuffed it in her mouth.

"I guess it did," he replied.

The sheriff finished his breakfast and stood to his feet. "Thanks for askin' me to eat with you folks. I enjoyed it. But it's time for me to head back to the office. I've neglected it way too long chasin' after this case."

Sam stood up and held out his hand. "Thanks for everything, Sheriff. I don't know what we would have done without you."

"Happy to help. Y'all take care now."

I grabbed my coat. "Wait a minute, Sheriff. I'll walk out with you."

Sam gave me an odd look, but I smiled and motioned for him to sit down. I had something to talk to Pat about that couldn't wait. He held the door open for me, and I stepped out into a cold but sunny day. The roads had improved greatly, although snow still covered everything else. When we got to his car, the sheriff turned to me.

"Did you walk me out here because you think I'm too old to make it alone, or did you have another agenda? You've thanked me enough for a while."

I leaned against his truck and stared at him. "Well, I have a question, Sheriff. Just when do you intend to tell Sam the truth?"

He eyed me suspiciously. "Tell him the truth about what?"

I wrapped my arms around myself to stave off the cold. "The night I drove your truck from the orchard to the house, I went through your glove compartment. I was looking for evidence because I suspected you were the person who'd knocked me out." I waited for his reaction, but his expression didn't change. "I saw the picture. At first I didn't recognize the people, but the boy seemed so familiar. It kept bothering me. And then a couple of days ago I remembered something you said to me when you pulled my car over on the way to Harmony. You mentioned blood ties. Finally everything clicked."

He stared past me. "And what was it that clicked, Gracie?"

"You're Sam's father."

He didn't say anything, just kept looking at something over my shoulder.

"That's why you started hanging around, asking

questions right after you took office. It's also why you kept such a close eye on us throughout this whole ordeal. You were protecting your son. Actually, I should have figured it out sooner. When you pulled me over on the way to Harmony, probably so you could check me out to see if I was someone you wanted in Sam's life, you made that strange comment about blood ties. You were talking about yours and Sam's."

Finally he met my gaze. I detected a shadow of apprehension in his eyes. "I didn't know about him until two years ago. Bernie found me in Colorado. It wasn't hard. I was the sheriff of a much larger area than this. She was sick. Real sick. She told me about Sam and gave me that picture. Then she told me where he was. Not long after that, I found out Morris County needed a sheriff because theirs had quit. I offered to fill in until a new sheriff was elected. Luckily, I won the election."

"I can't keep this from Sam for long, you know. If he finds out I knew and didn't tell him. . . Well, I can't take that chance. One thing I've learned since coming to Harmony is that secrets don't keep here. Eventually the truth comes out. It would be best if you told him yourself, though. And soon."

He nodded. "I know. But give me a little time, please. I want him to trust me before I tell him who I am."

I patted his arm. "You saved my life, you know. I don't think there's much more you can do to get on his good side."

He grunted. "I'll tell you what. If you'll keep my secret for a while, I'll tell you one. And trust me, you really want to know this."

"Okay. As long as you realize I won't wait too long."

He stuck his hand out. "Agreed."

I shook it. "Okay, so what's the secret?"

"I ran into Sam yesterday in Council Grove. He was coming out of Meyer's Fine Jewelry." He grinned at me. "He had a little black box in his hand and a great big smile on his face."

He tipped his hat and started toward his car. But before he opened the door, he turned around and looked at me. "By the way, you're right," he said. "I was checking you out that day on the road to Harmony. Just so you know, you passed." With that, he got in his car and took off.

I stood there and watched him drive away. I'd meant what I said about secrets. I'd had to tell Sam that Eric had kissed me, and that I'd told him about Sam's mother. It wasn't easy to confess, but I knew if we had a future together, he needed to know. He not only understood; he blamed himself for putting me in a situation where I felt I had no one to talk to. I think I fell in love with him even more at that moment—if it's even possible. I'd keep Pat's secret for a while. I owed them a chance to work it out. I prayed Sam's decision to let go of the pain from his past would allow him to open his heart to his father.

Cora Crandall called out my name, and I waved to the three of them as they went into the restaurant to meet with Grant. I looked across the street to see Molasses hitched to Gabe and Sarah's buggy, waiting to take her owners home. All in all, Harmony was back to normal.

Hopefully things would stay quiet for a while. I'd

learned something important over the last few days. Just because a storm comes, it doesn't necessarily mean you've stepped out of God's will. It just means you have to find the rock God sends to hold you up. I had no doubt I was exactly where I was supposed to be. For a while I'd looked at the storm. From now on, I intended to keep my eyes on the Rock.

I looked up as the sun poked its head from behind the clouds that had covered Harmony for quite some time. Today promised to be a beautiful day. Sam had asked me to dinner at a very nice restaurant in Topeka. He said he had something important to ask me.

I headed into Mary's with a smile on my face. Yes, today certainly promised to be an exceptionally beautiful day.

DISCUSSION QUESTIONS

1. Gracie moved to Harmony because she loved Sam and she loved the town. She believed her life would be peaceful and happy there. But can a place or a person actually give us happiness or peace? Were Gracie's expectations unrealistic? Where does true peace come from?

2. Was Abel's decision to keep the abandoned baby until he could find the mother the right choice, or should he have called the authorities immediately? What would you have done in his place?

3. When Sam read the note claiming the baby belonged to Gracie, why did he react the way he did? Is there anything in your past that might cause you to react unreasonably in a similar situation?

4. What did Sam finally do to break free from his past? Do you need to do this in any area of your life?

5. Why did Gracie have feelings for Eric? Was there something lacking in her relationship with Sam? Or was the problem inside Gracie herself?

6. Should Gracie have been more understanding about Sam's insecurities, or were her feelings understandable?

7. What was it that Eric and his investors offered the citizens of Harmony? Were the residents right to get excited, or should they have been more protective of what they already had?

8. When it looked as if there might be a problem with the development project, people began to turn on each other. What should they have done? What would you have done?

9. Were you surprised to find out who the baby's mother was? Did you have compassion for her, or did you feel angry with her decision?

10. Deceit can cause all kinds of evil. Is deceit always an outright lie? What about choosing not to tell the complete truth? What about lies that protect someone? Was Sweetie right to tell Sam to lie? Was Sam wrong for not telling Gracie the truth sooner? Is it ever right to deceive someone?

About the Author

Nancy Mehl is the author of six novels, one of which, *For Whom the Wedding Bell Tolls*, won the 2009 American Christian Fiction Writers' Book of the Year Award in Mystery. Her Harmony Series takes her a step away from the mystery genre she's used to and into romantic suspense. "This series is a little different for me," she says. "But that element of mystery has followed me to Harmony. I hope mystery readers will find a little something for them in this new venture. It has been so much fun creating the town of Harmony and getting to know the Mennonite people a little better. I hope I've done justice to their wonderful legacy and incredible spirit."

Nancy lives in Kansas with her husband, Norman, their son, Danny, and a Puggle named Watson. She spends her extra time with her volunteer group, Wichita Homebound Outreach.

Nancy's website is www.nancymehl.com and you can find her blog at www.nancymehl.blogspot.com. She loves to hear from her readers.

Be sure to read Book 3 in
the Charles Towne Belles series
from MaryLu Tyndall!

The Raven Saint

Captain Rafe Dubois kidnapped Grace Westcott for the money, but once she invaded his life with her religious piety—and her goodness and kindness—he knew he would never be the same. But falling in love means risking another betrayal.

Available January 2014